About the Author

I have been a writer in my free time since I was in school, and I always considered "The Chronicles of Coverdale" to be one of my greatest works. It has been a joy for me to write, and I am thrilled to be able to share my writings with the public.

The Chronicles of Coverdale

Charles R Fulmer

The Chronicles of Coverdale

Olympia Publishers
London

www.olympiapublishers.com
OLYMPIA PAPERBACK EDITION

Copyright © Charles R Fulmer 2023

The right of Charles R Fulmer to be identified as author of
this work has been asserted in accordance with sections 77 and 78 of
the Copyright, Designs and Patents Act 1988.

All Rights Reserved

No reproduction, copy or transmission of this publication
may be made without written permission.
No paragraph of this publication may be reproduced,
copied or transmitted save with the written permission of the publisher,
or in accordance with the provisions
of the Copyright Act 1956 (as amended).

Any person who commits any unauthorised act in relation to
this publication may be liable to criminal
prosecution and civil claims for damage.

A CIP catalogue record for this title is
available from the British Library.

ISBN: 978-1-80439-652-0

This is a work of fiction.
Names, characters, places and incidents originate from the writer's
imagination. Any resemblance to actual persons, living or dead, is
purely coincidental.

First Published in 2023

Olympia Publishers
Tallis House
2 Tallis Street
London
EC4Y 0AB

Printed in Great Britain

Acknowledgements

I would like to thank my family and friends who have supported me on this journey of writing. Their support and encouragement mean everything to me.

Chapter 1

Welcome to Coverdale!

Timothy was a twenty-nine-year-old man who lived in the village of Coverdale, one of the many villages that make up Coverdale Island, located in the World of Exodus. The man was a smaller build, around five-feet-seven, with brown hair and gray eyes.

Timothy awoke to his alarm at seven a.m. He shut off his alarm before sitting up in his bed and stretching up his arms. He then got out of his bed and grabbed a black three-piece suit before walking into the bathroom to take a shower.

When he walked out, he noticed his young friend, named Heather, sitting on the living room couch, looking at her phone. Heather, who was nineteen years of age, had light-to-medium-toned brown skin, with long silver hair and a black headband, with stunning lilac purple eyes. She was wearing a white satin minidress with white mesh sleeves and neckline, with white tights.

"Good morning, Timothy," she said softly while blushing. She stood up and gave him a loving hug.

"Good morning, Heather. How long have you been awake?"

"A couple hours. I woke up and just couldn't go back to sleep. Would you like some breakfast?"

"Yes, I'm starving. Thank you."

Timothy sat down with Heather, who had cooked a breakfast of sausage, eggs and toast.

"I can't get over how good a cook you are," Timothy commented.

Heather blushed after hearing the compliment.

After having their breakfast, the two of them left the house. As they walked, they noticed it starting to rain. Heather pulled out an umbrella and opened it. She then handed it to Timothy, who then held the umbrella above the two. Heather then wrapped her arms around Timothy's right arm.

When Timothy and Heather entered the store, they were greeted by the owner, named Kelsie. The fifty-one-year-old woman had long white hair and shimmering purple eyes and was dressed in a pink strapped shirt and black slacks.

"Good morning, you two," Kelsie greeted.

"Good morning, ma'am," they both replied.

"So, where would you like me to start?" Timothy questioned.

"Why don't you start with setting up that display for me, please?"

Throughout the day, Timothy and Kelsie worked on stocking the shelves, building some displays, and assisting some of the customers that came in to shop for the day. Heather ran the register. Together they worked an eight-hour day at the market.

At the end of the day, Timothy and Heather got ready to leave the store.

"I'll see you tomorrow, ma'am," Timothy stated.

"Here, please take this," Kelsie told him. She handed him a bag that had a dinner and four cupcakes inside. "That's for a great job you two have done for me. I'm really grateful."

"Thank you," Timothy responded. Kelsie hugged Timothy

and kissed Heather on the cheek. They said their goodbyes and they left the market to go back home.

When Timothy and Heather arrived at their home, Timothy sat down on the couch as Heather took the meal into the kitchen to prepare. Timothy then heard his phone ring. He saw on the screen it was his mother calling. He answered, setting the phone on speaker. "Hello?"

"Hello, dear!"

"Hi, Mom. How's it going?"

"I'm just great, dear. So, how's the job search going? I trust you and Heather found a different job by now?"

"No, Mom, we still work at the market."

His mother started showing some disgust. "Why are you still working there?"

"We really like the job, Mom. The people are great, and the owner's really nice."

"Yeah, but it's not paying you enough!"

"Mom, it's fine. We can pay our bills, and we both have some money saved back for emergencies."

At that moment, Heather stated, "Dinner's ready," and Timothy walked into the kitchen, sitting down at the table across from Heather.

"We're not hurting as bad as you think we are."

"Whatever you say, dear. Oh, I was also wondering, how is Heather?"

"She's doing well. She's been a blessing to me."

"That's good. So, have you asked Heather to be your girlfriend yet?"

Heather, shocked by what his mother said, spat out her drink. It got all over Timothy. Seeing what she did, Heather gasped, placing her hands over her mouth.

"Mom, for crying out loud…"

"Timothy, you're twenty-nine years old! Don't you think it's time to settle down with her?"

"Forgive me," Heather cut in, "but aren't you getting a little pushy about this?"

As they continued talking, Heather grabbed a towel and gave it to Timothy.

"Don't you want him to be happy, Heather?"

"Of course, I do, but… if he wants to have a girlfriend, that's his choice. Besides, no offense to Timothy, but I would rather find someone closer to my own age."

"But think about your future, sweetie."

Timothy became defensive. "Why are you always doing this to us, Mom? You hate my job, you hate my apartment, you hate that I'm single… you're even pressuring Heather! Why can't you just be happy for us like Dad is? He doesn't judge us this way."

His mom's voice became sterner. "I just want you two to have a good life!"

"We *do* have a good life! You should be happy that I've been able to have my own place, a good job and the ability to support myself and Heather. Look, if someone comes along that I fall in love with, so be it. But for right now, I'm happy and thankful with what I have."

"All right then, I'm gonna go. I love you so much, both of you."

"We love you too, Mom. Bye-bye."

"Bye, Son."

Timothy hung up the phone.

"Why does your mother insist on us dating each other?" Heather wondered.

Timothy sighed. "I don't know. It seems no matter what I do, I can't make her happy. I'm really sorry about that."

"You don't have to apologize, Timothy. I know how she is." Heather looked down as she twiddled her fingers. "Talking to her and what you've done for us got me to thinking about the morning that you found me, Timothy... I'll never forget it." Tears began to fall from her eyes.

Timothy wrapped his arms around her. "I'm sorry if I upset you, Heather."

"No, it's okay. It's just... I wish I could forget the pain."

The following day, on Coverdale Island, in a darkened realm was Nuriel, trying to figure out what he was doing wrong in trying to take over Coverdale. Nuriel had short unruly brown hair with red eyes, and wore a brown tunic, scarf and pants that matched the color of his hair.

Tori and Celina approached the distressed man. Tori had shoulder-length silver hair and red eyes and was dressed in a black leather leotard with matching shorts that were very short in length along with striped black stockings. Celina had matching purple eyes and medium-length hair and was wearing a black leotard with bright violet trim with a matching skirt and stockings.

"I'm tired of those brats putting a stop to my plans!" He pounded his right fist on the arm of his throne. "I must find a way to stop them, and Queen Luna of Coverdale will be in my arms forever."

"What do you suggest we do, my lord?" Celina questioned.

Nuriel sighed deeply. "I don't know. It's just... I'm so tired of being in this gloomy castle and this depressing realm. Once I have what I desire, this world will feel a renewed sense of darkness, and I will have Luna next to me."

"Well, whatever you need, just let me know," Tori assured him.

"Thank you, Tori. You're so loyal. I don't know what I would do without you and Celina. Leave me be for now. I'll get back with you soon."

"Very good, my lord."

Tori and Celina walked out of the throne room.

"It pains me to see Nuriel so distressed," Celina commented. "We must find a way to help him."

"I've already figured it out," Tori mentioned.

Tori then smashed a vase over Celina's head. Celina fell to the floor unconscious. At that moment, some of Nuriel's ninjas approached.

"Lock her up in the dungeon," Tori ordered. "Let's get ready."

Nuriel walked out onto his balcony, looking over to the direction of Coverdale, sighing deeply. "I will have you by my side, Queen Luna. We will be as one, where light and darkness shall be united as one."

Then, as Nuriel walked back into the throne room, he heard a bit of commotion coming from behind the doors. He seemed confused.

"What's going on?" Nuriel wondered. As he went to walk towards the doors, suddenly there was an explosion that blew the doors off their hinges. Nuriel was thrown back into his throne from the explosion. The guards standing beside the doors were killed instantly. As Nuriel got back on his feet and pulled out his sword, he saw Tori approaching him.

Nuriel was stunned. "Tori? What is this?"

Tori pointed her sword towards Nuriel. Nuriel saw his ninjas now surrounding him. Nuriel realized that the ninjas were now pledging their allegiance to Tori. The ninjas began to attack, but Nuriel, now with his sword glowing the color of blood, used his sword to strike several ninjas down. However, Nuriel quickly became overwhelmed by the sheer number of ninjas that were attacking him.

At that moment, another woman with medium-length brown hair and red eyes walked behind Nuriel. She pulled her long sword from her holster as she sneaked up to Nuriel, and then suddenly stabbed Nuriel in his side. Nuriel gasped as he felt the sword pierce into his body. He dropped his sword. Nuriel looked over and was stunned to see who had stabbed him. The woman had a darker shade of brown hair and glowing red eyes. She wore a black two-piece bikini with a mesh lining covering the rest of her body.

"Excellent, Fiera," Tori responded.

Tori walked ever closer to Nuriel with a smile on her face.

"Tori… why?"

Fiera then pulled her sword out of Nuriel's side, and Nuriel fell to his knees. Tori placed her hand on Nuriel's chin so that he would face her. "Sorry, Nuriel, but I had to do this. If you were any kind of enemy, you would have already destroyed Coverdale. Once and for all, I will show everyone how it is to be done."

Nuriel fell to the floor, dying from his injuries. Two ninjas removed Nuriel's body.

Then Tori heard her phone ring. She answered it. "Yes… good, keep an eye on her until we get there." Then she told Fiera, "She's been located in Coverdale. Let's get going. We must find that girl."

With that, Tori, Fiera and the ninjas left the castle, making their way to Coverdale.

Chapter 2

The Search for Max

After working a couple hours of overtime, Timothy had finally finished up another day at work one late evening. After saying good night to Kelsie, Timothy and Heather walked out of the building to see that the sun had already set and nighttime was rolling in.

On the way home, while holding a plastic grocery bag, Timothy was looking at the screen on his phone. As he and Heather turned to walk around a corner, he suddenly was knocked off his feet by someone who inadvertently ran into him. They both fell to the sidewalk, with Timothy dropping his groceries. The person had fallen on top of him. Heather was stunned, uncertain as to what to do.

As Timothy sat up, rubbing his head, he noticed the person who had run into him: a taller woman, aged twenty-four, who was now sitting on her knees in front of him, who had longer light violet hair and stunning green eyes. Timothy noticed her skin was a lighter shade of blue and she had a birthmark on the left side her face, but was awestruck by how beautiful the woman was. She was dressed in a very short white dress and black pantyhose. She had a look of shame on her face and was blushing as she looked away from Timothy.

Timothy said to the woman, "Are you okay, ma'am?"

The woman was surprised as she saw Timothy, who was

now standing up, reaching his hand out to her. She spoke hesitantly. "Ye… yeah, I'm fine. Are you okay? You're not hurt, are you?"

"No, I'm fine, thank you. I'm Timothy. Can I ask your name?"

The woman smiled softly. "It's Tamera."

"Tamera? That's a unique name. I like it."

Tamera blushed. "Thank you."

Tamera chuckled, still blushing. Timothy couldn't keep his eyes off the woman, who he noticed was a bit taller than he was.

"Who is this beautiful girl?" Tamera asked.

Heather, hearing what Tamera said, blushed.

"This is my best friend, Heather."

Tamera, without any thought, hugged her tightly. "It's nice to meet you, and I'm sorry for what happened to Timothy."

Heather blushed. "No, it's quite all right. It's nice to meet you too."

"I'm really sorry, Timothy, but I'm in a bit of a hurry." She pulled out a picture of a woman who had shorter blonde hair and gold eyes. "I'm looking for my sister, Max. Have either of you seen her at all?"

Timothy and Heather observed the picture. Max had shoulder-length blonde hair and hazel eyes, and was wearing a white button short-sleeved shirt and a short black form-fitting skirt with nude pantyhose. Heather shook her head negatively, and Timothy replied, "No, I'm sorry, I haven't. Would you like some help?"

"No, that's okay, but thank you. Well, I need to get going. It was nice to meet you both. Take care of yourself."

The woman ran away, heading in the direction Timothy came from. She turned back to see Timothy and Heather walking in the opposite direction. Then Timothy looked back in her direction, and he saw her looking back at him. He then saw her blushing before she ran away.

"Tamera?" Heather said to herself. "Why does that name sound familiar?"

Heather grabbed a magazine out of her handbag, looking through the pages until she found a picture she was looking for. She showed Timothy the picture.

"I thought so. That was one of Queen Luna's guardians. It's kind of strange to see her mingling with us commoners."

Heather then teased, "I think she liked you."

Timothy tried to deny it. "Come on, Heather. What would someone like Tamera want with somebody like me? I'm not in her league."

"How do you know? She looked back at you. If that wasn't a sign, I don't know what would be."

Timothy smirked.

"You like her too, don't you?" asked Heather to Timothy.

"Well, she was quite beautiful."

As Timothy and Heather were walking home, he couldn't get his mind off Tamera. Not only did she seem to be a gentle soul, but he thought she looked so cute when she blushed.

Timothy and Heather arrived at the front of their home when he then happened to notice a woman running around the corner in front of him was heading towards him, who had blonde hair and golden eyes. He was able to see as she ran past him that she had tears in her eyes. Something did not seem right as he watched the woman run around the corner.

"That's strange," he said out loud as he turned to her direction. "I wonder what could be wrong with her." Then he thought about the picture that Tamera showed him earlier. "Hey, that looked like Max!"

"Maybe we should help her to find Tamera," Heather noted.

Then they turned the other way to see two others heading towards him who were dressed up like ninjas. Before Timothy could react, the man forcefully pushed Timothy, and he fell to the ground.

"Watch what you're doing!" said the ninja that pushed him. Heather helped Timothy back on his feet.

"You're quite the pushover today," Heather teased.

The two ninjas reached the corner. They looked both ways at the street.

"Where is she?" asked one of the ninjas.

"Shut up!" the other ninja demanded. He looked to his left and his eyes grew wide. "Come on!" They ran to the left.

Heather was now filled with disbelief. "Am I dreaming, or did I... just see two people dressed as ninjas?"

"Maybe we should follow them. They may be after Max."

Timothy and Heather tried their best to make sure the ninjas did not see them following.

Timothy and Heather watched as the two strangers walked into a local restaurant. They looked around to see if the girl was lurking inside. They noticed a person reading a newspaper. The man pulled down the newspaper to reveal an older man reading.

"Do you mind?" asked the man. He then straightened up his paper to continue reading. The two strangers continued to look around. In the meantime, some of the customers were snickering about the two people looking so peculiar.

"Excuse me," said the owner, who was behind the counter. "Can I help you?"

The two ninjas walked over to the owner.

"We're looking for this girl," said one of the ninjas. "Have you seen her?" The man showed the owner a photo of Max, one like the picture Tamera had.

"No, can't say I have," the owner informed them. "Why are you interested in her?"

"She's a runaway. We are just trying to take her back home."

The owner was not buying the story the ninja told him. "If that's the case, why are you dressed like... ninjas?"

Before the man could answer, a customer walked over to the two men and saw the picture of Max.

"Oh yeah, I've seen her! She just went into the restroom."

The owner placed his hand over his face. The ninja pointed for the other to go to the restroom. Hearing what was said, Max ran out of the restroom. The ninja saw her and quickly chased her until he was able to catch her.

"Let me go!" Max demanded. "What do you want with me?"

"Our new master wants us to bring you to her so he can obtain the Golden Sapphire."

"But I don't have that..."

"Shut up!" said the ninja. "You're coming with us!"

"No!" Max cried out. She managed to break free from their grasp. A ninja went to give chase but unexpectedly got hit by a tray. He then fell to the ground. Max then noticed Timothy.

"Who are you?" she questioned.

"I'm Timothy. Your sister is looking for you."

"Max!" was yelled. They looked to see a woman running towards them.

"Tamera!" Max cried out.

Tamera looked confused. "Timothy? What are you doing here?"

"We... found Max." He pointed to her.

Timothy was still amazed by Tamera's beauty, even with her skin color and birthmark.

Max was stunned. "You know them?"

"Yeah, we kind of ran into each other while I was looking for you."

She then noticed the two men. The one ninja threw a metal star at Timothy. Tamera formed a wall of ice in front of Timothy, and the stars pierced into the ice. Timothy was amazed at what Tamera could do. Max, Tamera and Timothy then turned to see Tori, Fiera and several other ninjas approach.

"Tori?" Tamera was puzzled. "What are you doing?"

"Hello, Tamera. I've come for your sister, Max. She possesses the Golden Sapphire. Give her to me this instant."

Tamera had a confused look on her face. She turned to Max, who looked as baffled as she was. "She doesn't have the Golden Sapphire. It doesn't exist!"

"Don't lie to me!" Tori said angrily. She began to glow. "Surrender her to me now!"

"Not a chance, Tori," Tamera responded as she and her ax began to glow an ice-blue color. Then Tori approached, smiling devilishly as she pulled out her sword. It glowed a dark black color.

"And who are they?" Tori asked.

"My name's Timothy, and this is Heather."

"Well, too bad for you all, for you will become my prisoners as well."

Tori charged at Tamera, swinging her sword. Tamera blocked with her ax. The two began to swing their weapons at each other, both blocking their opponent's moves. Tori spun her body to swing her sword with much force, but again, Tamera was able to block with her ax.

"You've gotten better, Tamera, I'll admit," Tori complimented.

"There's plenty I have learned. I see you haven't changed."

Then Tamera tried throwing icicles at Tori, but Tori used her black magic, forming a large orb in front of her. The orb absorbed the icicles.

At that moment, two ninjas walked up behind Timothy, Max and Heather. Then the ninjas grabbed them, and they struggled to free themselves.

"You're not going anywhere!" the ninja told Timothy.

Max bit the arm of the ninja holding onto her, and the ninja cried out in pain as he let go. Timothy then stepped on the other ninja's foot, and while the ninja was distracted with his pain, Timothy punched the ninja holding Heather, and he fell to the ground.

"You fool!" Fiera yelled in frustration. Fiera then moved towards Timothy and proceeded to punch him, easily knocking Timothy out.

"Timothy!" Tamera cried out.

At that moment, Tori punched Tamera hard in the face, and she fell to the ground. As she tried to get up, Tori pointed her sword at Tamera's face. As Heather had a hold of Timothy, other ninjas grabbed Max.

"Finally, it is done," Tori stated as she walked over to Fiera and Max. "You did well, Fiera." She then said to Max. "You're a coward, Max, not even trying to help your own sister."

"I wanted to help," Max said with her head lowered. "I just figured we didn't stand a chance against you."

At that moment, a magical purple fireball shot one of the ninjas in the chest, and he fell to the ground, dead. Tori and the others looked to see a beautiful woman standing a short distance from them. The woman, who had cat ears and a tail, with hair colored a deep purple, and eyes a different shade of purple approached, wearing a bikini-styled top, short form-fitting shorts and thigh-high stockings, with brighter purple boots. Timothy, Heather and Max ran over to where the woman was.

"Are you okay, Max?" she questioned.

"I am, thank you," Max answered.

"Well, hello, beautiful!" Tamera responded. "I was wondering when you would join us."

"Well," Tori commented. "If it isn't Kirbie, guardian of the Jewel of Coverdale."

"Why do I get the displeasure of seeing you, Tori?" Kirbie asked.

"I have come for Max, who has the Golden Sapphire in her possession. I need her powers to become the ultimate ruler of Coverdale. And I'll stop anyone who gets in my way."

Kirbie had a puzzled look as she looked over to Max, Tamera, Heather and Timothy. Then she said to Tori, "That's just a myth. Max doesn't have that jewel."

"We know for a fact she does and we are going to take it," Tori exclaimed.

Fiera then approached Kirbie with her sword drawn. Kirbie used her magic to form two smaller swords. Both weapons began to glow a color of purple fire.

Kirbie spoke as she prepared to battle, "Nuriel wasn't good enough for you, Fiera?"

"He was weak, and blinded by his love for Queen Luna. But now that we have him out of our way, Tori will become the dominant ruler of this pathetic island."

Then all of a sudden, a medium-sized ship appeared over the

enemies.

"Fiera," Tori told her, "Let them be for now. Let's assemble the army."

Fiera approached Tori, and they went to board the ship, along with the ninjas.

"We'll be back, Fire Girl," Tori warned. "Come soon, the Sapphire will be mine!"

The enemies boarded the ship, and it flew away.

"Aw, jeez," Kirbie said with a frown. "I was hoping to get some more practice."

Kirbie walked over to Tamera, placing her right hand on Tamera's left shoulder. They both started laughing as they hugged.

"Thanks, Kirbie," Tamera stated.

"Anytime, my love. Let's get back home... all of us."

Max lowered her head, irritated.

Kirbie flew Timothy, Heather, Tamera and Max to Coverdale, to Queen Luna's Castle. Upon entering the castle, they were approached by Princess Camille, Queen Luna's biological daughter. Camille, who had pure white angel wings, had longer sky-blue hair and ice-blue eyes and was wearing a red strapless gown, with the ruffled skirt being much shorter in the front than in the back. She had a red rose pinned to her hair on the left side of her head, and also had on fancy black lace stockings that had patterns of roses in them.

Camille hugged Tamera. "I was so worried about you, Tamera. Where did you go?"

"I'm really sorry, Camille. I was... just trying to bring Max from..."

"Max? Did she..."

Then Camille walked over to Max. Camille gave her a tight hug.

"Thank God you're okay, Max," Camille told her.

Max hugged Camille back, but didn't say a word.

"Gee, thank you for your help," Timothy told them. "I guess I got mixed up in something I wasn't prepared for." He then looked at the people standing in front of him. "So, this is Queen Luna's castle? I never thought I would ever be in this place."

"Max, did you bring a boyfriend home?" Camille wondered.

"No, no, he just got caught up in our battle. This is Timothy."

Max ignored Heather's presence for some reason, and this irritated Timothy.

"This is my good friend, Heather. She's been part of my life for a little while now."

"Five years," Heather mentioned. "It's hard to believe it's been that long."

Camille walked over to Timothy and Heather, and they shook hands. "Hello there. I'm Princess Camille. Welcome to Coverdale."

Timothy and Heather bowed. "Thank you, princess," Timothy replied.

Camille then turned to Max. "Why did you leave the castle?"

Max lowered her head. "I was just… I…"

Kirbie was stern. "Max, I thought Luna told you to stay with us."

Max got lippy. "I'm tired of being trapped in this castle all the time!"

Kirbie became angry. She grabbed Max and pinned her up against the wall. "Because of you, my sister was in trouble again! Why are you always doing this to her?"

"Kirbie, let her go, please," said a female voice. Everyone

looked to see Queen Luna approaching them. Luna had very long blonde hair and blue eyes, and was dressed in a short white strapless satin dress that had a blue lace pattern across the top, long white gloves, and nude pantyhose.

Kirbie released her grip from Max. "I'm sorry, my queen. It's just that... Max is always causing problems for Tamera."

"Are you... the Jewel of Coverdale, Queen Luna?" Timothy questioned.

"I am. Camille gave me the nickname," Luna told Timothy, "And for some reason, it spread like wildfire throughout all of Exodus." She walked to the man and she held his hand. "It's a pleasure to meet you. What's your name?"

Timothy bowed. "I am Timothy, your majesty, and this is my precious friend, Heather." He then noticed the four women in front of him. "What I've heard is true: there *is* a lot of beauty in these walls."

Tamera and Kirbie both blushed.

"Thank you, Timothy," Luna responded. "I'm glad you all are safe. I worry so much about you." Then Luna said, "Max, what were you doing out of the castle? You know well that you are forbidden from doing so."

"I'm sorry, Mother. I wanted to..."

"If Tori gets a hold of you, baby, you know she'll kill you."

Max looked down to the ground, saddened. "I know. Again, I'm very sorry."

Luna hugged Max. "I'm sorry, too for being so stern. It's just that... you, Kirbie and Tamera are so precious to me and I don't want to lose any of you."

"Why is Tori so interested in Max?" Timothy questioned.

"Well, apparently she thinks Max holds the Golden Sapphire," Luna explained. "But that's not the case. She just happens to have golden powers, just like Kirbie's is of purple fire, and Tamera is of ice."

"And what does this Golden Sapphire do?" Heather wondered.

Tamera explained, "Legend has it that the Golden Sapphire can magnify a weapon's power exponentially, much more than the jewels everyone currently possesses. It was supposed to be able to do amazing things."

"But such a thing doesn't exist," Luna stated. "At least not that anyone's aware of. We really don't know what it could do if it existed."

"If it did, though," Kirbie commented, "if it was obtained by someone like Tori, the results could be catastrophic."

Tamera followed, "And if Tori is like the other enemies in Exodus, she will destroy anyone and anything to get what she wants."

"Get a hold of Tessa," Luna stated. "Let her know we will need her help."

"Agreed," Camille replied.

Tamera grabbed her phone. After a couple of rings, someone said, "Hello?"

"Tessa? It's Tamera."

"Hi, Tamera, what's going on?"

"We have a problem: Tori is trying to kidnap Max again, and we fear she is going to attack. Would you be able to help?"

"Of course. I'd do anything for you, beautiful. I'll get there as soon as I can."

"Great! I'll see you then."

"Bye, my love."

Tamera hung up the phone.

Tori and Fiera arrived back at Nuriel's castle. Tori was frustrated.

"I am sick and tired of people meddling with our business," Tori said after she slammed her fists on a table. "Queen Luna and the others will suffer for this!"

Fiera approached Tori. "Their skills have definitely improved. They may actually be a credible threat, but it seems like Max has not tapped into the jewel's power."

"It's time we put an end to their shenanigans. We must get the Golden Sapphire before Max can use its power!"

"I am ready to lead the army against them, with your permission, my lord," Fiera mentioned. "I will not fail you, and we will retrieve Max."

"Very well, Fiera. Lead the army against Coverdale. Bring her to me, and kill anyone who gets in your way."

Fiera saluted her and then walked out of the room.

"Come hell or high water, we will get that sapphire!"

Chapter 3

The Battle Against Tori

As the others were talking with each other in the castle, Timothy was admiring the view of the back of the castle. At that moment, Kirbie walked up to him.

"You all right, Timothy?"

"It's so beautiful," Timothy noted.

"Are you talking about the scenery," Kirbie asked, "or about Tamera?"

Timothy blushed as he lowered his head. "Tamera certainly is beautiful. I could say the same thing about you."

Kirbie was caught off-guard by the comment.

"I… thank you, Timothy," Kirbie replied. She blushed as well. "I'm sure Tamera would love to hear that as well."

Kirbie was surprised to hear somebody complement Tamera, something she had never heard from others outside the castle. She then thought about how Tamera acted when she was around Timothy. "She's so in love with him," Kirbie thought to herself. "I can see joy in her eyes I haven't seen in a long time."

Timothy turned to Kirbie. "So, are you all Luna's children?"

Kirbie responded, "Actually, I'm one of Queen Luna's guardians. Camille is actually Luna's only child. She took in Tamera and Max after their parents were killed during the Riverton War. I also lost my parents in the war."

Timothy lowered his head. "Yeah, so many lives were taken

unnecessarily."

Kirbie continued, "I'm so thankful for what she has done for me, Max and Tamera, and Camille has been so amazing. I don't know what I would do without them."

Timothy then asked Kirbie, "So, you were just a child during the war?"

"I was a teenager at the time. Tamera is the oldest at 27. I'm 21, Camille is 23, and Max is eighteen. It's hard to believe our parents have been gone so long."

"I'm sorry to hear that, Kirbie. But I'm glad to see you have all bonded together."

Kirbie's curiosity got the better of her. "So, what do you think of Tamera?"

"Wow, where to begin…"

Kirbie thought he may end up saying something negative when he said that comment, but said nothing, wanting to see what his response was.

"She seems to be an absolute sweetheart. She's so kind and gentle… and I just love it when she blushes. She's just so beautiful inside and out."

Kirbie was blown away by his response.

"Wow… I've never heard anyone talk about Tamera that way. It fills my heart with joy to see someone so in love with her."

Many of the guards were watching the village of Coverdale as Queen Luna, Heather, Max, Camille and Tamera talked to each other in the throne room. They happened to hear a commotion coming from behind the doors to the throne room. As they went to investigate, the doors to the throne room were forced opened, with the guards being killed from the blast, and Tori, along with

Fiera and their ninjas, stormed into the throne room. Tori walked over to Luna.

"Surrender Max to me now!"

Tamera revealed her ax. "Never! You'll have to kill us."

Tori pulled out her sword. "Seize them!"

Many of the ninjas attacked Tamera and Camille as Luna stayed back. Tamera and Camille were trying to hold the ninjas off by striking them with their swords, but they quickly became overwhelmed by the large horde of ninjas around them. Fiera punched Tamera in the face, and she fell to the floor in pain. She then kicked Tamera hard in the face, knocking Tamera out.

"Nice try, Tamera," she stated. She then turned to Max. "Now, tell me where is the Golden Sapphire?"

"I don't have it! It doesn't exist!"

"Take them to the ship!" Tori ordered.

As Timothy and Kirbie headed back into the castle, they saw some of Tori's soldiers. The soldiers ran towards Kirbie, who pulled out her swords and began to attack them.

Kirbie and Timothy then made their way to the throne room, where they saw Tamera coming back to her senses.

"Tamera, what happened?" Timothy questioned.

"It was Tori... where are the others?"

"Tori must have taken them," Kirbie answered. "Let's go."

Kirbie, Tamera and Timothy made their way out of the castle. More ninjas charged at the heroes with all their might. As Timothy and Heather did their best to stay back from the battle, Max and Kirbie were doing whatever they could to hold off the ninjas.

At that moment, there was a loud roaring. Everyone looked to see a full-figured woman, about six-feet-two inches tall, with features like that of a dragon, her hair was colored pink, with green eyes, appeared from out of the forest. She had claws with gold-accented metallic black and red armor covering them, and wore a metallic two-piece bikini the same color as the rest of her armor, along with large red dragon wings.

"Tessa!" Tamera cried out.

Timothy was surprised. "That's Tessa?"

Tessa began fighting off the other ninjas using her claws. Several other soldiers charged, and Tessa put her hands together, throwing a large wall of flames at the soldiers, who turned to dust after being hit by the fire. In the meantime, Kirbie saw Tori and some of her ninjas getting into a ship with Luna, Camille and Max. After finishing off the ninjas, Kirbie flew up in a ship after Tori's ship.

"Tori," said a spirit trooper. "Kirbie is approaching."

"Take her down!" she ordered.

The ship began to fire laser beams at Kirbie, who was trying to dodge the lasers, but one laser ended up hitting one of the ship's wings. The ship crashed to the ground. Timothy saw the ship crash.

"Kirbie needs help!" Timothy cried out.

"Go with Tessa!" Tamera stated. "I'll finish these guys off."

Timothy got onto Tessa's back and she flew into the sky.

"I don't remember you," Tessa commented. "Are you Tamera's boyfriend?"

"No... well, I mean..."

"So, you just met? Well, let me tell you, you won't find a more beautiful person than Tamera. She is truly one of a kind."

Moments later, Timothy and Tessa made their way over to Kirbie, who was walking away from the wreckage, but was holding her arm in pain.

"Are you okay, Kirbie?" Timothy asked.

"I tore up my arm," she told him. They noticed a large wound on Kirbie's forearm. At that moment, several ninjas approached Tessa, Kirbie and Timothy.

"Get behind me, Timothy," Tessa instructed. "I'll handle them."

The ninjas charged, but Tessa was able to strike them down with her claws and fire.

"You're amazing, Tessa," Timothy commented.

"Thank you," she stated.

"Let's get back to the castle," Kirbie replied.

Tessa, Timothy and Kirbie headed back to the castle. Tamera had taken down the other ninjas.

"Well done, beautiful!"

"Same to you, Tessa."

"Where could they have gone?" Timothy wondered.

"I'll bet you anything they are still at Nuriel's castle," Kirbie implied.

"What about Timothy?" Tamera questioned. "He shouldn't be caught up in this."

"I'll stay here in Coverdale and help the citizens clean things up, okay?"

"I'll stay here too," Tessa implied. "You all go get the others."

Timothy walked over to Tamera. "Please bring Heather back to me, sweetie."

Tamera blushed as she said confidently, "I will. That's a promise."

Tamera and Kirbie made their way into the ship. Timothy waved to them and they waved back. Timothy and Tessa watched as the ship flew away before walking back into Coverdale and helping the others to clean up the village.

Tori led Queen Luna, Max and Heather to Tori, who was waiting in the throne room.

"Well done, Fiera," Tori stated proudly. "Put Luna and the girl in the cage, and bring Max to me."

As Fiera placed Luna and Heather in the cage, two ninjas led Max over to Tori.

Celina suddenly opened her eyes. She happened to look over her surroundings and recognized where she was.

"I'm in... the dungeon?" she said softly.

Celina then looked to see two ninjas standing guard in front of the dungeon, facing away from her. She raised her arm, squinting in pain, but still managed to form a large orb the color of blood in her hand. She then threw the orb at the bars the ninjas were standing by. An explosion ensued, and the ninjas were killed. Celina then cautiously walked out of the dungeon.

At that time, the ship arrived at Nuriel's castle. Kirbie and Tamera got off the ship, approaching the castle with caution.

Tori then looked over Max's body in search of the jewel she thought Max possessed.

"All right, Max, where are you hiding the jewel?"

"For the last time, Tori, I don't have it!"

Tori pulled her sword out and pointed the end of it at Max's throat. "I'm getting tired of your mouth! Now give it to me this instant!"

She and Fiera heard a loud commotion coming from the

throne room.

"Find out what's going on," Tori simply stated.

"Yes, my lord." Fiera left the room.

The heroes continued to battle against the servants of Tori. At that moment, Kirbie and Tamera entered the throne room.

Fiera noticed them. "Kirbie."

Kirbie formed her swords in her hands. "Fiera. Where's my family?"

Fiera answered, "You won't live long enough to see them."

Several ninjas then entered the room. Angered, Kirbie charged at Fiera with her swords. The two exchanged quickly, clashing their weapons. Tamera fought the ninjas.

"How could you do this?" Kirbie asked her bitterly.

"I wasn't going to stop until Tori had the Sapphire in her possession," Fiera defended. "She will do anything to get what she desires."

Fiera charged again at Kirbie, and their weapons slammed against each other once again. Kirbie happened to trip up Fiera, and Fiera fell to the floor. Fiera quickly rolled back to her feet, and feeling outmatched, she ran back into the other room where Tori was. In the meantime, Tamera took care of the other ninjas.

When Kirbie and Tamera ran into the room, they saw Tori standing in the middle of the room, looking unfazed. Kirbie approached her, glowing as she formed her swords again.

"So, the guardian has come to stop me," Tori responded as she pulled out her sword. "Give it your best shot, Kirbie!"

Tori charged at Kirbie, swinging her long sword at her, but Kirbie moved out of the way. Tamera fought Fiera.

At that time, a large horde of ninjas made their way into the room. Before they could attack, suddenly there was a large explosion at the doors, killing many of Tori's ninjas. Everyone looked to see Celina approaching, her eyes glowing a blood red. Celina had her long sword revealed, also ready to fight.

Tamera was surprised. "Celina?"

Celina walked in Tori's direction.

"You will die for betraying my lord," Celina simply said.

Tori couldn't comment. She then simply turned and fired an orb at Celina, but Celina used a shield made of blood and the blood absorbed the magic. Celina then fired off a beam of blood at Tori, but Tori rolled out of the way.

"It's nice to see you on our side," Kirbie commented.

"Nuriel and I were always on Luna's side."

"Perhaps, but you have a strange way of showing it."

Fiera focused on Tamera, trying to slice her with her sword, but Tamera would dodge her moves or would block using her ax. Celina continued fighting the soldiers. Kirbie fought against Tori.

Tamera tried striking Fiera with her ax, but Fiera was able to dodge her attacks. Then Fiera blew a large fireball from her mouth at Tamera, but Tamera rolled out of the way of the flames.

Kirbie and Tori continued to battle. Tori used her sword to try slicing Kirbie. She caught Kirbie in the arm. Unfazed, Kirbie then backed away, and then proceeded to throw one of her swords at Tori. The sword revealed a long rope that was attached to it. She managed to catch Tori's side with the sword, and the wound began to bleed.

Tamera charged at Fiera, attacking her with all her might with her ax. Fiera continued to block her moves. Then Fiera smacked Tamera across her face, and she fell to the ground, in much pain. Fiera walked over to Tamera, standing over her, and she raised her arms, ready to strike Tamera with her sword. As Fiera went to swing her arms down, she suddenly stopped and gasped. Tamera was surprised at this reaction.

Tamera, wide-eyed, looked to see Celina had pierced Fiera's chest with her sword, which was glowing with a purplish fire.

"NO!" Tori cried out loud. Kirbie went to strike Tori, but Tori hit Kirbie with a large ball of black magic, and Kirbie flew backwards. In the meantime, Fiera rested her hands over the wound. Then Fiera fell first to her knees before falling to the floor, lifeless. Tori seized the opportunity to run away, making her way out of the castle, along with many other ninjas.

Celina walked over and freed Heather, Max and Luna out of the cage. Everyone watched to see what Celina would do.

"I'll see you later," Celina said. Then Celina simply walked out of the room.

Tamera observed her surroundings. "Where's Tori?"

Everyone then looked around the room but did not see her. "She must have got away," Camille noted. "We'll have to keep our eyes open."

Kirbie got back on her feet and walked over to the group.

"Where's Timothy?" Max questioned sternly.

"He's safe, Max," Kirbie assured her. "He stayed in Coverdale with Tessa to help."

"Well done, everyone," Luna told them. "Now let's get back home."

The group boarded the ship as the prisoners were rounded up by some of Coverdale's soldiers. A short time passed before they arrived at Coverdale to cheers and whistles from the citizens. Max ran over to Timothy. She then jumped into his arms.

"I'm glad to see you!" Max yelled. "Did you miss me?"

"Of course, Max. I'm so glad to see you too."

Then as Max ran over towards the castle, Tamera and Heather approached Timothy. They hugged as well.

"I'm glad to have you back in my arms, sweetie," said Timothy.

"It's great to see you too, Timothy," Tamera replied, blushing.

Heather was weeping. Timothy held her tightly. The heroes then made their way into the castle, going to the throne room.

"I want to thank you all for rescuing me once again," Luna announced. "And thanks to you, Tessa, for helping us as well. For the time being, Coverdale is safe, thanks to you all."

"We're grateful you are all safe as well," Camille pointed out.

Later in the evening, Timothy and Heather walked with Camille, Tamera, Max and Kirbie to the ship, ready to take them back to their home.

"I'm sorry you two got caught up in this," Tamera stated with a look of sadness on her face. "I bet this was not at all something you expected when we met."

"It's quite all right, Tamera," Timothy told her, giving her a hug. "It was a pleasure to meet you. As with you, Kirbie. You're a lot of fun to be around."

Max gave Timothy a red rose and then kissed him on the cheek. "I wish you would stay," she informed him.

"Thank you," Timothy stated. "But we really should be getting back."

"Don't forget about me, okay?" Tamera reminded.

Timothy kissed Tamera softly on the cheek. "I never will, beautiful."

Tamera blushed once more, her heart melting. Her heart was so tied up in wonder as to why Timothy would think she was beautiful despite having her birthmark on her face. Kirbie was nearly heartbroken, thinking that Timothy should have stayed to be with Tamera. Even Heather was puzzled as to why Timothy didn't ask to stay.

"Best wishes to you and God bless," said Camille.

One week later, Tamera was sitting on the ledge of the kitchen window looking out at the falling rain. Overwhelmed with sadness, tears began to fall from her eyes. Kirbie was getting ready to walk into the kitchen when she happened to see Tamera in the kitchen. She saw how sad Tamera was.

"Let me guess," Kirbie stated. "You're thinking about Timothy too, aren't you?"

Tamera smirked. "Guess I can't hide anything from you, Kirbie."

"I've been thinking about him and Heather too. Heather is quite the young woman. I just fell in love with her."

"I just can't seem to get him out of my mind. It just frustrates me that he went home."

Kirbie smiled. "Tamera, you *are* in love with him! I knew it! Why didn't you ask him to stay here with you?"

"I don't know. I just… assumed he wouldn't want that. Besides, his heart is probably with Max. I'm the weakest of the four of us, and Max is so much more beautiful than I am…"

"Because of your skin?"

Tamera just looked to the floor, tears running down her face. Kirbie walked over to her, placing her hands on her shoulders.

"Come on, love! He's the best thing to ever come into your life, and you're just going to let him live without you? Go there and find him! You never know… he may be doing the same thing you are!"

Tamera thought about what Kirbie told her. After Tamera

gave Kirbie a tight hug, she got up and ran out of the room.

At that moment, Tamera walked down the hallway where she was stopped by Max.
"What are you up to, sis?" Max questioned.
"Well, I... I'm..."
"Hey, can you keep a secret?"
Tamera looked up at Max.
Max continued, "I've decided to go find Timothy and bring him back here. Would you like to go with me?"
"Yeah, I would love to."
Tamera was kind of disappointed, hoping she could find him without Max getting in the way. But she kept that to herself, just hoping she would even be able to find Timothy.
Tamera and Max made their way to Chu Gardens in search of Timothy. They were walking up to different people trying to figure out where he may be. Most of the day they tried to find him in the large city, but nobody could help them.
It was heading towards the evening hours, and Max was starting to feel discouraged as they stood by a fountain.
"What am I going to do?" Max wondered in sadness. "Wherever could he be?"
"Maybe we should split up," Tamera told her. "We'll search a little longer, and then at eight, we'll meet back here."
"But what if we don't find him by then?"
"I guess there's always tomorrow."
Max smiled as she headed off in a different direction. Tamera stood still for a moment and got to thinking about where Timothy could be. Then she remembered how she got to meet Timothy, running into him that evening. She decided to find that street where she met with him.

Tamera indeed did find the street, and she waited for over a half hour, looking to see if Timothy would maybe appear to her, but she never saw him. Tears began to fall down her face as she looked to see it was almost eight.

"It's hopeless," she said out loud. "I'll never find him like this."

Tamera went to turn around when she suddenly ran into somebody, and they both fell to the ground, with Tamera falling on top of him.

"Come on, would you..." Timothy first said, but then saw who it was. "Tamera?"

Heather's face lit up. "Tamera! I was worried I wouldn't get to see you again!"

She had tears falling from her face. "I'm sorry. It's just that I've..."

"What's wrong, sweetie?" Timothy asked.

She was nearly speechless. "I... I just wanted..."

At that moment, they heard somebody yell, "Timothy!"

Timothy then saw Max running towards him. She leaped into his arms with such force that they both fell down with Max still having her arms wrapped around him.

"I don't believe it! We found you! I've missed you so much!"

Timothy chuckled. "I've missed you too, Max."

"Timothy, please come back with us! Please say you'll be with us forever!"

"I couldn't think of a better idea. Of course, I'll go back with you."

Max grabbed his hand and went to pull him away.

"Max, hang on a moment, please," Timothy stated. He let go of Max's hand and walked back to Heather, who looked saddened.

Timothy smiled. "I'm not going, though, unless Heather can come with me."

Heather looked over at Timothy, and then to Tamera, who reached out her hand. Heather grabbed her hand, and then they hugged each other.

Max screamed in excitement, hugging Timothy once again.

"Well, we better be getting back!"

Max was pulling Timothy in her direction. Timothy turned while still walking with Max and reached his free hand towards Tamera, who then grabbed his hand. Timothy pulled Tamera to him and he kissed her on the cheek. Tamera blushed. Then he reached out for Heather, who then wrapped her arms around Timothy.

Timothy, Heather, Max and Tamera walked over to his home, where he and Heather simply grabbed a few things and then they headed back to Coverdale. Kirbie, Luna, Camille and Tessa greeted them.

"Welcome back," Luna stated. "I was starting to get worried."

"Mom," Max stated. "Please let Timothy stay with us!"

Tamera then said, "And Heather as well." She wrapped her arms around Heather.

Luna gave a stern look at Tamera and Max. "Am I supposed to ignore that you two sneaked out of the castle to find them?"

Tamera and Max showed worry on their face.

"Well, it's a good thing I was watching over you two again," Tessa stated. She winked at Tamera, and Tamera smiled.

Luna saw how Max was reacting, and then she looked over to Tamera, and Luna noticed there was a happiness in Tamera's eyes that Luna had not seen in a long time. Luna smiled. "Of course, they can stay." she told them. "In fact, I've taken a liking to them myself."

"Yay, I'm so grateful!" Max cried out. She leaped into Timothy's arms again, and everyone began to laugh after they fell to the floor. Kirbie again pulled Max off Timothy.

"Max, knock it off!"

"Come on, let me have what I desire!"

"He doesn't belong to you!"

"You're just jealous because you can't have him!"

"I don't want him like that!"

They went on as Timothy and Tamera smiled. Timothy then hugged Tamera once again.

Timothy, Heather, Tamera, Kirbie and Max walked down the hallway together. They stopped in front of one of the doors.

"This will be your room, Heather," Kirbie said. She opened the door to the room and they were amazed to see how nicely the room was set up. She hugged Tamera.

"You have a good night, Heather," Tamera told them. Heather said good night to everyone, hugging Tamera and Timothy before going into the room. Tamera, Kirbie and Max led Timothy to a different room.

"This will be your room, Timothy," Tamera stated. She opened the door to see his room, which was as large as the girls' rooms.

"This is so amazing," Timothy commented.

Max was so overjoyed as she jumped at Timothy and wrapped her arms around him. "I'm so glad you're here! I've missed you so much!"

"I missed you too. Thank you for all this."

"Don't thank us," Tamera smiled. "Thank Luna. She doesn't do this for just anyone."

Max yawned, stretching her arms in the air. "I'm beat. I'll see you all tomorrow. Good night, everyone."

"Good night, Max," Timothy, Kirbie and Tamera told her. They watched as Max went into her room, shutting the door behind her.

"Well, good night, you two," Tamera simply stated. "I'll see you tomorrow."

"Tamera, wait a second."

Tamera and Kirbie stopped and turned back towards Timothy, who walked over to Tamera and hugged her tightly. Tamera was surprised.

"I really missed you too. I was hoping I would get to see you again."

Tamera wrapped her arms around Timothy. "I'm so glad you're back with us."

Tamera and Timothy held each other's hands and just stared into each other's eyes for a moment. Tamera blushed as she then lowered her head.

"I'm... really tired. I guess I should..."

"Yeah, me too. Good night, sweetheart. Good night, Kirbie."

Kirbie then hugged Timothy.

"Good night, Timothy."

Tamera and Kirbie turned and walked away, going over to her door. Tamera then turned to see Timothy had walked into his room, his door shut.

"I love you, Timothy," she said with her head lowered before going into her room.

Chapter 4

Timothy and Heather's Training

The following morning, Timothy was sleeping peacefully in the bedroom he was given to sleep in. The sun was shining brightly through the window and he happened to place his blanket over his head to block the sunshine from being in his eyes.

Suddenly Timothy felt something fall on top of him, and it startled him. He sat up quickly in his bed and was surprised to see that Max had jumped on top of him, smiling greatly.

"Timothy!" Max said joyfully. "Are you gonna sleep the whole day away?"

Timothy snickered as he sat up and wrapped his arms around Max. "Good morning, Max. How long have you been awake?"

"I haven't been up too long. Did you sleep okay?"

"Yeah, but the alarm was kind of unexpected."

Max blushed. "I'm sorry. I just wanted to see you and…"

At that moment, there was a knock at the door. Kirbie peeked her head around the door. She was stunned to see Max sitting on top of Timothy. This angered her.

"What in the world do you think you're doing, Max?" Kirbie said out loud as she charged at Max. "Get off him!"

"I want to spend time with Timothy!"

"That was rude to wake him up that way! Do I have to get Tessa after you?"

"Why do you have to be like this?"

At that moment, Heather came to the door. "What's going on…" Then Heather saw Max on top of Timothy. "What do you think you're doing?"

"You're against me too?"

Kirbie pulled Max off Timothy, and then he sat up on the bed. Then Tamera walked through the doorway with her precious smile on her face, her cheeks red from blushing.

"Good morning, everyone. Are you all about ready?" Tamera questioned.

"Yeah," Kirbie answered. "Why don't you and Timothy get acquainted?"

Kirbie forced Max to walk with her.

"Come on, Kirbie, let me go!"

"You're coming with me, Max."

"Ready for what?" Timothy wondered curiously.

"Well, Mom, Kirbie, Max and I were talking about you this morning and decided that if you wanted to live with us, you're gonna have to learn to defend yourself. So, we're going to give you lessons, starting as soon as you get dressed. If you're interested, girls, you can join us as well."

"Gee, I don't even get breakfast?"

Tamera chuckled. She kissed Timothy on the cheek, and then hugged Heather. "I'll see you two out back."

Timothy and Heather got cleaned up and dressed and they made their way out of the bedroom, heading for the back when they were stopped by Queen Luna, who had a sword, a staff and a set of nun chucks in her hand.

Timothy bowed as he spoke, "Good morning, my queen."

Luna smiled. "Please, Timothy, just call me Luna. Tamera told me my girls are going to teach you two on how to defend yourselves."

Timothy rubbed the back of his head. "Yeah, I guess so."

"Well, Timothy, I would like you to have this." Luna held the sword out to him. "We call this sword 'Olympia'. It belonged to my husband, Lorius."

Luna showed Timothy a picture of Lorius. He had matching blue eyes and shoulder-length hair, and was wearing a white long-sleeved tunic with blue slacks.

"We lost him during the Riverton War. He was such a kind and compassionate angel, and I miss him so much, but sometimes he got on my nerves. One day he hid all my make-up from me, and when I went to leave our bathroom, I opened up the door, and I suddenly heard him yell 'Makeup!' Then he hit me right in the face with this huge powder puff that was covered in flour."

Timothy, Heather and Luna began to laugh.

"Timothy pranked me one time as well," Heather commented. "For my thirteenth birthday, when I woke up, I saw a huge spider sitting on my bed, and I freaked out at first, but then I found out the spider was just a toy. I was so upset at him, but he made up by buying me a ring." Heather showed Luna her ring. "And he's done so much for me that I couldn't imagine living my life without him."

"That's good to hear, Heather. Timothy said you're pretty good with a bow and arrow, so we got you this." Luna gave her a bow colored white and gold.

"This is nice, but where are the arrows?"

"Tamera and Tessa will show you."

"Thank you, my queen!"

"Yes, thank you, Luna. I'm sorry for your loss."

"I thank you, Timothy. You all better get outside before Max calls for a search party."

Max and Tamera were outside holding on to their weapons. Tessa was with them.

"How do you think he'll do?" Max questioned.

"I think he'll be all right," Tamera stated. "We can't expect him to be perfect if he's never done this before."

"That's true. I can't wait to get started!"

Timothy and Heather made their way outside, where they noticed Tamera and Max waiting for them.

"Wow, Mom gave you Olympia?" Max asked in surprise. "She really must have taken a liking to you."

"You all set to go?" Tamera asked him.

"As ready as I'll ever be," Timothy told her.

"Well, let's get started!" Max said excitedly.

Tamera walked over to Timothy. "Please don't be upset at us. It's not that we don't believe in you. It's just that…"

"No, baby, I totally understand. If something happens, I want to be sure I can help you all the best way I can."

Tamera blushed.

"Are you okay, Tamera?" Heather asked.

"He called me 'baby'!" she said to her, all smiles. Heather laughed as she and Tamera hugged.

Starting off, Tessa and Max showed Timothy the proper way to hold a sword. In the meantime, Tessa taught Heather how to use her bow. When Heather would pull back on the bow, a magical arrow would form. This amazed Heather. Then the women used their weapons in showing Timothy and Heather how they could defend themselves against other weapons.

"This is a nice sword," Timothy noted.

After a couple hours, the three women continuing working

with Timothy in a sword fight against Max, he was able to somewhat keep up with them.

"I think I'm getting the hang of it."

"Oh, you really think so?" said a voice. At that moment, everyone saw Kirbie approaching, her magical swords in her hands. Kirbie began to glow of purple fire.

"Let's see what you got, Timothy," Kirbie challenged.

Timothy then showed his sword before he tried to strike. After Kirbie blocked his every move, she quickly saw an opening and she ducked down, sweeping him off his feet. Before Timothy could think of doing anything else, Kirbie pointed her glowing sword at Timothy's neck.

"I guess I'm not as ready as I thought," Timothy spoke.

Kirbie chuckled as she stopped glowing, let her swords dissipate and then offered her hand. Timothy reached for it, and Kirbie helped Timothy onto his feet. She kissed him on his forehead, and then Kirbie offered her other hand to Tamera. Tamera grabbed her hand, and then Kirbie placed Tamera's hand onto Timothy's.

"Well, we all have done this most of our lives," Kirbie noted, "and you have only done this for one day. It's going to take some time."

"Don't worry," Tamera stated. "We'll keep working with you and Heather, and over time you'll get better, I'm sure of it."

Max broke through and forced herself on Timothy once again. "Stick with me, Timothy, and I'll train you right!"

"Yeah, right," Kirbie commented.

"What's that supposed to mean?"

"If we leave him to you, he'll end up dead!"

"How can you be so heartless?"

"The truth hurts, doesn't it?" Tessa cut in.

Tamera and Timothy laughed as they walked away.
"They really do mean well, Timothy," Tamera told him.
"I know that. I wished they got along a bit better."
"Yeah, I can understand if they get on your nerves."

At a mountain range that sat in the middle of the island, four people walked over towards the opening to a cave as the rain fell on them. They waited until they happened to see Tori walking out of the cave towards them. She was glowing of her black flames.

"The time has come to take what is rightfully ours," Tori proclaimed. "I will avenge Fiera's death, and will destroy all of those on Coverdale Island who oppose us."

Tori then walked over to the four souls that were standing in front of her. First was a man simply known as "Madness." He had black hair and purple eyes, with devil horns, pointed ears, and other demon-like features on his body. He also had a mark on his forehead that glowed a bright purple. His outfit only consisted of black denim jeans. Next, there was Nexia, who had bluish-black hair and piercing ice-blue eyes, who wore a short blue and white dress. She wielded a thin yet long sword that looked like the color of ice. The third person was Dorian, an elf who had white hair with blue highlights, with bright light-blue eyes, dark gray skin that showed light blue highlights, with a light blue and gray tunic with gray pants. Finally, there was Mornecai. The man, who was very large in stature, had reddish hair, mustache and beard, with light-blue eyes. He simply wore just a pair of black shorts. Standing behind them were a multitude of ninjas who were once loyal to Nuriel but had now pledged their loyalty to Tori.

"Tomorrow morning, we will bring Coverdale Island to its knees, starting with Wolford, and going through every village until we reach Coverdale. We will kill Queen Luna and the Coverdale Trifecta, and everyone will bow to me!"

Everyone cheered loudly.

Later that evening at the castle, Tamera walked over to Max's door. She knocked.

"Who is it?" Max asked.

"Max, it's Tamera. Can I talk to you for a moment?"

Tamera waited until she heard Max unlock the door and open it, and she allowed Tamera to walk into her room.

"What's going on, sis?"

"I wanted to ask you about Timothy. I know you…"

"Isn't he amazing? He's so kind and gentle… I can't stop thinking about him."

"I understand that. He really is a wonderful man."

Unbeknownst to the women, Timothy was walking towards the room heading to another room that Luna told him he could stay in. As he was getting ready to walk by Max's room, he heard Max say, "I really enjoy being around him!" He stopped and stood beside the door.

Tamera continued, "You know what really surprises me is he adores me even with the way I look. It's unusual that…"

Max interrupted. "Do you think I should ask him out?"

Tamera was caught off-guard by Max, but tried to maintain her composure. "Well, I mean, I was thinking maybe *I* could…"

Max laughed. "Come on, Tamera. You really think you have a chance with him?"

Tamera was appalled by Max's comment, but ultimately kept her feelings inside. "Yeah, you're probably right. Well, I guess I should get some rest. Good night, Max."

Timothy quickly made his way around the corner so he

wouldn't be spotted. At that moment, Tamera walked out of Max's room. Timothy then saw Tamera walk by him in the hall, and he was stunned to see she was crying, and trying to wipe her tears from her face as she walked to her room. Leaving the door cracked open, Timothy could see Tamera began to cry again. Hearing Tamera cry nearly broke Timothy's heart. Uncertain of what to do, he walked away, his head lowered in sadness.

Later on, Timothy was outside, his heart filled with frustration as he practiced with his sword. He was still trying to figure out what to do about Tamera. At that moment, he saw Camille walk over to him.

"What are you doing out here, Timothy?" Camille asked. "It's two in the morning."

"Hey, Camille," Timothy sighed. "I just can't sleep."

"What's bothering you?"

"I was getting ready to go to bed when I overheard Tamera and Max talking about me. Apparently, Max is still head over heels in love with me."

Camille rolled her eyes. "Why am I not surprised? Max is obsessed with you."

Timothy sat down on a bench, with his head lowered. "But that wasn't what bothered me so bad. When Tamera mentioned maybe being with me, Max acted as if she wouldn't stand a chance. Then when Tamera walked out of Max's room, I saw her crying. It seemed as if her heart had been broken, and it killed me to see her like that."

"So, that's why you're out here," Camille realized. She sat down beside Timothy. "Max can be a loving person, but she can also be cruel. For some reason, she tends to tear down Tamera a lot. It drives me crazy that she does that."

"I see. So, I've been meaning to ask, and I'm sorry if I offend you…"

"Let me guess: her skin and birthmark?"

"Please don't be upset with me. I still think she's beautiful…"

"I know you do, Timothy. I see it in your eyes when you're around her. She was actually born that way. Tamera has struggled with the way she looks, thinking she isn't pretty at all. But Tamera *is* beautiful inside and out; I know it in my heart."

"I agree with you. I've never met anyone as wonderful as she is."

"Look, I know how Max has acted around you, but between you and me, I know for a fact that Tamera really loves you. But if Max is the one you want…"

"I love Tamera, too, Camille."

Camille smirked. "I knew it."

"It's not that I don't love Max. I do, just as I love you, Camille and Luna. But it's different with Tamera. As I've gotten to know Tamera, my love for her has become so much more than just as a friend. She's such a beautiful woman on the inside as well as on the outside, even with the blue skin. When I'm near her, my heart just fills with such joy and love…"

"Tamera is one of the kindest souls I know. She would give everything to a stranger if it meant that they were happy. And I know she would do anything and everything for you."

"She always seemed like she was happy… well, until last night."

"She sometimes smiles as a way to hide the pain she feels. She has struggled with the death of her family in the War of Riverton. Tamera, wanting to help, made her way to the battlefield, and Tamera nearly got herself killed there. A soldier stabbed Tamera in her shoulder, and in the confusion, as her mother, Celestia tried to protect her, she got killed by Behrlin, as well as her father Minoru."

Minoru had purplish-black hair and red eyes and wore a long black leather jacket with a white flannel shirt underneath, and plaid gray pants. Celestia had darker ice-blue hair and eyes, and usually was dressed in an oversized shirt that belonged to her husband over a strapped dress that was very short in length and was cut on each side of the skirt.

"Tamera believes to this day that she is responsible for their deaths. I've known Tamera since I was a baby, and many times I've seen her struggle with it, even cry about it, and Luna told me that she watched Tamera grow up from the time she was a baby, and after her family were killed, some of Tamera's happiness got lost in her pain.

"But now that you have come into her life, Timothy, Mom told me that happiness that she lost has returned. She is so overjoyed when she talks or even thinks about you, and I couldn't tell you the last time I saw her blush before meeting you."

"I had no idea, Camille. I mean, she always seemed like she was so happy. I didn't know how much she was hurting inside."

"She doesn't like to talk about it, and I don't blame her. It pains me as well to think that Behrlin himself killed my father in the war. I miss him so much. But I am so amazed by my mom, who managed to keep Coverdale Island together while raising three girls on her own."

They stood back up together.

"And the reason she was crying may have been that she doesn't feel she has a chance with you against Max. Although Tamera is strong with her powers, Max and I are stronger than she is, and Max is so much more persistent than Tamera. Max is very outgoing and positive of herself, while Tamera is really quite shy."

"What do you think I should do, Camille? I really want to be with Tamera, but I don't want to break Max's heart…"

Suddenly, Timothy felt someone grab him, and quickly he was pinned to the wall.

"Kirbie, what are you doing?" Camille asked.

"Wait, Camille," Timothy stated. He then turned back to Kirbie. "What's wrong, Kirbie?"

"Last night, my beautiful angel was in tears. She cried for hours over you. She's got it in her head that Max is going to steal you away from her. And you're just letting it happen!"

"Please, Kirbie, it's not like that!"

"Then why haven't you asked her out? What are you afraid of?"

Timothy lowered his head, uncertain as to what to say. Kirbie then let him go.

"She loves you so much, Timothy. Since you have come into her life, she has become the Tamera I had always loved."

"Don't you understand, Kirbie? I *do* love her! I would fight for her… protect her…"

Kirbie again grabbed Timothy, this time hugging him. "Don't lie to me. I know it would be Tamera protecting you."

Timothy snickered as he wrapped his arms around her. "You're right."

"I want you in Tamera's life, Timothy. She needs you, and you need to tell her how you feel before she loses all hope. And don't let me find out if you hurt her."

Kirbie simply walked away.

"Well, she pretty much told you what I was going to say."

"I thought she was going to do much worse to me."

"Remember what I say, Timothy, that Kirbie would die for Tamera. And if you show how much you'll fight for Tamera, Kirbie would die for you too. Good night, Timothy."

"Good night, Camille."

As Camille walked back into the castle, Timothy thought long and hard about Kirbie's words. He knew she was right and that he needed to share his feelings with Tamera.

It was the following morning, and Tori and Nexia stood outside of the cave. Tori for a moment watched as the sun rose past the horizon.

"I'm ready to serve you, my lord," Nexia told her.

"Let's gather the troops. We head for Wolford."

Nexia walked away. Tori looked to the sky.

"We're coming, Queen Luna," Tori spoke to herself. "I will destroy everything precious to you, and all of Coverdale Island will be mine."

Chapter 5

Kirbie to the Rescue!

A young wolf girl named Sandra was walking down the street heading for the local market. The young woman, who had white hair with cat ears and a tail, was wearing a yellow sweater vest over a white flannel shirt, with a short pleated blue skirt and tan pantyhose.

As Sandra was walking down one of the streets of Wolford, she suddenly heard a loud commotion, hearing people screaming or crying out. Sandra looked around the fence at the corner of the street to see people running away from Tori and her henchmen, along with a mass gathering of soldiers.

Sandra then heard loud crying coming from behind the fence. She found the door to the fence and went through, looking until she found who was crying. It was a little boy who had black hair, green eyes, and was wearing a hooded blue sweater and denim jeans. He had bandages on his cheek and above his nose.

"Please help me," the young boy stated.

"It's gonna be okay," Sandra assured him. "Where are your parents?"

"I don't know. We were attacked, and they got separated from me."

Sandra reached her hands out to the boy. "What's your name?"

"Noah."

"I'm Sandra."

"You have... wolf ears?"

"Yeah, I'm originally from Wolf Lake Village. I was born this way."

"Cool! I wish I had wolf ears too... or a rabbit or a cat..."

Sandra snickered as she carried Noah. She walked back out on the street to see if they could spot Noah's parents. As they went to walk on, they were suddenly stopped by Madness. The duo became full of fear. Noah was so frightened he turned his head, putting his face into Sandra's shirt and closing his eyes.

Madness proceeded to strike them down with the claws on his right hand, but before he could do so, someone else grabbed his arm. He turned to see Mornecai standing next to him.

"What are you doing?" Madness asked him angrily.

"Don't kill them," Mornecai stated.

Madness grunted. "Why not? What are they worth to you?"

"Actually, I have an idea for them." Then he turned to Sandra. "Come with us."

Tori had seized control of Wolford. The other henchmen and ninjas were already with Tori. At that moment, Mornecai and Madness walked over with Sandra and Noah.

"Well, what do we have here?" Tori asked.

"It's his fault, my lord," Madness pointed out.

"Actually, my lord," Mornecai defended, "I figured we could use them as bait, kind of like an insurance policy in case the Coverdale Trifecta get any ideas."

"Well," Nexia joked, "the big man has a bit of a soft spot."

"Shut up, Nexia," Mornecai demanded.

"Enough!" Tori spoke, and then she smiled. "I agree. Bring them along. Madness, you stay here in Wolford. The rest of us will attack Chu Gardens."

They did so.

Timothy had awakened the following morning, noticing the rain falling outside. He crawled out of his bed, got dressed and walked out of the bedroom. He noticed Tamera, Max, Kirbie, Camille, Heather and Luna talking to each other. Timothy walked over to them.

"Good morning, everyone," he spoke. "What's going on?"

"We just got word that Wolford was attacked," Tamera informed him. "The town is in complete ruin."

"I'm going to fly there with Tessa to investigate," Kirbie mentioned. "You all stay here and protect Coverdale for now, and I'll keep in contact with you."

"Maybe I should go with you," Max commented.

"No, it will be quicker if we go alone."

Luna hugged Kirbie. "Be careful, okay?"

"I will, Luna. You all be safe too."

Kirbie quickly made her way out of the castle, meeting up with Tessa. They got onto Tessa's motorcycle, heading for Wolford.

"Stay with me, Timothy," Max told him. "Who knows what may happen today." Max wrapped her arms around Timothy above his waist. Tamera looked saddened.

"Tamera, are you all right?" Timothy asked.

"Yeah... I just... I'm worried about Kirbie and..." She stopped talking.

Timothy wrapped his arm around her. "If I know Kirbie well enough, she'll be fine."

Tamera blushed. "You're probably right."

Kirbie and Tessa quickly made their way to Wolford. When they arrived, Tessa and Kirbie were heartbroken to see all the destruction surrounding them. Kirbie pulled out her swords as she walked on, cautiously viewing her surroundings.

As Kirbie and Tessa came around a corner, they were noticed by several ninjas. The ninjas charged quickly at them, trying their best to attack, but Kirbie and Tessa were able to easily strike down the ninjas with their weapons.

Kirbie walked on until she heard a voice.

"I'm impressed."

Kirbie turned to see Madness standing a short distance from her.

"Allow me to introduce myself. I am Madness. And you are?"

"I am Kirbie."

"So, this is the guardian of the Jewel of Coverdale. It's a shame somebody so young has to die so soon."

"I don't intend on dying now," Kirbie stated.

Madness chuckled as he pulled out his sword. "Let's see what you got."

Madness charged at Kirbie and their swords clanged together. Both of them wildly swung their swords at each other, with the other blocking their opponent's attack. Then the two separated from each other for a moment.

"Indeed, you are good," Madness told Kirbie. "Looks like I shouldn't be taking you for granted."

Madness charged ever harder. Kirbie blocked his moves. Madness then pushed his sword and himself into Kirbie, pushing Kirbie backwards, but Kirbie jumped back, maintaining her composure. She charged towards Madness and again they continued to fight with their swords.

As Madness went to strike with his sword, Kirbie ducked down and managed to trip Madness up, and he fell to the ground. Madness was getting upset.

"I've had about enough of you," Madness pointed out. His sword began to glow a light purple. "It's time to end this."

He then charged once again, clashing his sword against Kirbie. He saw that Kirbie herself was glowing the color of purple fire.

"I agree, it *is* time to end this."

Madness growled as he went to swing his sword again at Kirbie, but Kirbie ducked, and Kirbie sliced her sword at Madness, striking his legs. Then Kirbie swung her sword upward, slicing off Madness' hand, and his sword fell to the ground. Madness fell to his knees in pain.

Kirbie then grabbed Madness' sword, tossing it from him.

"When Tori hears about this, you all will die."

"Tori? I should have known."

Kirbie then stabbed Madness in the chest. He cried out loudly before falling to the ground after Kirbie pulled her sword out of him.

Several townsfolk came out from hiding and approached her.

"Thank you so much, Kirbie," said a male child.

She kissed the child on his cheek. "You're welcome. Where are they heading?"

"Towards Chu Gardens," a woman answered.

"They must be planning on destroying all of Coverdale Island."

"Be careful," said a young female child.

Kirbie kissed the little girl on the forehead. "I will."

Kirbie and Tessa left, and Kirbie pulled out her phone. By this time, Tori and her gang had already destroyed Chu Gardens.

It was decided that Nexia would stay behind to watch over the village, leaving Mornecai and Dorian, along with many ninjas, to continue at Tori's side. Fiera walked closely with Sandra and Noah. Sandra noticed Noah seemed as if he was getting tired, so Sandra picked Noah up and proceeded to carry him.

"How much further?" Noah whined.

Dorian answered, "Our next stop is in Esterton."

"And we're not stopping until Tori says so," said Dorian. "So, it's going to be a long day for you, kid."

"What are you trying to prove?" Sandra questioned sternly.

Dorian drew his weapon, pointing it at Sandra. "I ought to slit your throat right now, thinking you can raise your voice to me!"

Mornecai forced Dorian's sword downward.

"Don't start with me, big man," Dorian threatened.

"We need them alive, you fool," Mornecai objected.

"When this is over, I'm gonna..."

"Dorian," Tori interrupted, "Knock it off."

Dorian put his sword away, and he backed off as Tori walked to Sandra.

"You really want to know what this is about, girl?" Tori responded. "It's about revenge. Queen Luna and Princess Camille have thwarted my plans for the last time. After we take down the other villages, we will go to Coverdale and destroy everything precious to Camille and Luna, and I will take the island as my own. And once we finish with them, you too will be finished, you and that spoiled little brat you hold in your hands."

Tori turned away from Sandra. "Let's keep moving."

The enemies and their prisoners walked on.

Back at the castle, Luna noticed Tamera watching from a balcony as Timothy, Heather and Max were sitting outside together. Tamera watched as Max began to laugh and she wrapped her arms around Timothy. Then she saw Heather pulling Max off Timothy, and the two began shouting at each other before Timothy stood between them, trying to get them to calm down. Tamera felt a tear run down her face.

"What are you doing?" asked a voice. Tamera turned to see Luna and Camille walking over to her. Tamera blushed.

"Luna, hi. I'm just looking over the lake."

Luna looked to see Timothy and Max.

"Are you spying on Timothy?" Camille questioned.

Tamera said nothing but blushed.

"Why don't you ask him out, baby?" Luna asked. "He seems to be a wonderful man."

Tamera smirked. "To think I have a chance against Max? Come on, Luna."

"How do you know? Have you talked to him about it?"

Tamera sighed. "No. I'm afraid to."

Luna and Camille looked again to see that now Max was helping Timothy again to practice how to use his sword.

"What are you so afraid of?" Camille asked her.

Tamera leaned against the ledge of the balcony. "Max said something about being afraid of being rejected. I guess that's my biggest fear as well."

Luna wrapped her arm around Tamera's shoulders. "You know, Lorius was the same way, he told me. It actually took me asking him to get him to date me."

Tamera chuckled at Luna's comment. "But Timothy may not do that for me."

"Which is why you need to tell him how you feel."

"I'm sorry to sound rude, but that's easy for you to say. I

mean, look at me, and look at Max. She's so much more beautiful…"

"Now, you know that doesn't work on me, baby. I know what you've gone through, and how others have treated you, but no matter what you say, I still think you *are* beautiful. And my opinion's the only one that matters."

Tamera began to laugh from Luna's comment, and she and Luna hugged. "I'm sorry, Luna. It's just… I'm just not as confident in myself as Max is. I want to tell him how I feel, but it scares me to death."

"I just had this talk with Max, too, surprisingly, so I know she hasn't asked him either. So, you better get to it before she does." Luna kissed Tamera's forehead. "I can see in his eyes it's you he wants, baby. And Heather told me she loves you to death. She's also been disappointed that Timothy hasn't asked you out."

Luna and Camille walked away. Tamera sighed as she watched on. Then she heard her phone rang. "Kirbie? What's going on?"

"Tessa and I are on our way to Chu Gardens. It seems Tori is behind the attack at Wolford, and she's brought some friends with her."

"Oh, no. Tori's back?"

"It looks as if she is going to attack every town and then make her way to Coverdale. I want you all to go to Esterton. That would be the next town after Chu Gardens. I'll get there as soon as I can."

"We're on our way."

Tamera hung up her phone. She then ran out to Timothy and Max.

"Max, I need your help."

"What's going on?" Timothy questioned.

"Tori was the one that attacked Wolford. Come with me."

Timothy, Heather, Max and Tamera ran into the castle, where they met up with Luna and Camille.

"I just got a call from Kirbie," Tamera stated. "She wants us to go to Esterton to stop Tori. Seems she's the one leading the attack on Wolford, and she's on her way to Chu Gardens."

"You better get going," Luna informed them.

"Maybe Timothy should go with us," Max suggested.

Camille was surprised to hear Max's suggestion. "Timothy's not ready for this kind of fight," Camille responded.

"Maybe he should stay here at the castle," Luna mentioned.

"He's good enough that he could take down the ninjas while we battle Tori and the others. We're going to need everyone we can get."

"If this is a ploy to keep him by your side, forget it!" Heather spoke sternly, her arms around Timothy.

Tamera followed, "If he goes with us, he'll die out there!"

"Just like your parents did?"

Tamera was nearly heartbroken by Max's words.

"Max, that was uncalled for," Luna scolded.

Tamera walked away, crying. Camille turned to Max, looking visibly upset.

"Why do you have to be like that? What do you get out of doing this to her?"

Max did not answer, her face showing regret for what she had said.

Timothy chased after Tamera.

"Tamera, wait!" he stated as he grabbed her hand, and they stopped. Tamera was still crying. "Please, Tamera, let's just…"

"How could she throw that in my face? She's always tearing me down! Now she's trying to take you away from me…"

"Come on, sweetie. She hasn't taken me from you…"

"If you really love me, you would…"

Timothy couldn't stop himself as he placed his hands on Tamera's shoulders, and at that moment she stopped talking. Then he gave Tamera a kiss on the lips. Tamera was wide-eyed, stunned at Timothy's actions. At that moment, Luna, Camille, Heather and Max saw Timothy kiss her. Max's heart was now broken, but Heather's heart was overjoyed.

"It's about time," Heather said to Camille.

Timothy then hugged Tamera, not wanting to let her go.

Timothy told Tamera, "I *do* love you, Tamera, with all my heart."

"But how? I mean… I'm…"

"What, your skin?"

"Well, yeah… I'm so…"

"Beautiful. Yes, Tamera, you're the most beautiful person I've ever met."

Still hugging each other, Tamera cried even harder.

"I'm so sorry I upset you, baby."

"No, it's… I want to believe you, but… my heart won't…"

"Well, if I have to prove it to you, that's what I'll do. I'll fight for the one I love."

Tamera's heart melted. She continued to cry. Then Luna, Camille, Heather and Max approached.

"You two can discuss this later," Luna stated. "We've got to help Kirbie, Tessa and the survivors."

"I still think we should have Timothy go," Max persisted. "We'll need everyone we can get at this moment."

"I want to help you, Tamera," Timothy told her.

"All right, but don't stray too far from us, okay?"

Timothy wrapped his arms again around Tamera. "I

promise."

"You need to go, everyone," Luna mentioned. "Please be careful."

Heather hugged Timothy and Tamera. "You two better come back to me."

Timothy, Max and Tamera climbed into a ship. Timothy wrapped his arms around Tamera as they sat together on the ship.

"You know I won't be able to fight if you're holding on to me."

"Well, you're not fighting now."

Tamera blushed. Then Tamera noticed Max seemed to be angry.

"Max, are you okay?"

"Don't worry about it, Tamera."

"Oh… okay. Sorry if I upset you."

"You have no idea."

Tamera didn't say another word.

Chapter 6

The Battle at Esterton

As Timothy, Tamera and Max were making their way to Esterton, Kirbie and Tessa arrived at Chu Gardens, and they came up to the same scene as what they saw in Wolford. This time, Nexia was waiting for the heroes. She approached, holding her long, thin sword, with a horde of soldiers behind her.

"I was told you would be coming, Kirbie," Nexia spoke. "So, what I've heard was correct. You really are a beauty. And you must be strong, too, to have defeated Madness."

Kirbie formed her swords. "Well, I'm sure you won't mind if I demonstrate."

As Tessa charged at the horde of soldiers, Kirbie and Nexia charged at each other, clashing their swords. Kirbie was having a bit of a tougher time trying to block Nexia's sword but was still managing to hold her own. Then some soldiers appeared and made their way towards Kirbie. Kirbie again danced through the fight, striking the soldiers down with her swords. She then stood back a little way from Nexia.

"How cowardly of you, Kirbie!" Nexia said in frustration. "Come over here and actually fight me!"

Kirbie smirked before throwing one of her swords at Nexia. Nexia sidestepped the sword, seeing there was a rope on the sword. Before she could react, Kirbie pulled back on the rope, and the sword flew back and stabbed Nexia in her back. Nexia fell to her knees in pain as Kirbie approached her.

"That's really... how you fight?"

"My father taught me two things: love purely, and fight dirty."

Kirbie then stabbed Nexia again. Then when Kirbie pulled the sword out of her chest, Nexia's body then fell to the ground, lifeless. After retrieving her second sword, she walked back towards Tessa, who was taking out the last of the remaining soldiers. Then Tessa and Kirbie left again.

"Hold on, everyone," Kirbie replied. "I'm coming."

Heading towards Esterton, Tessa and Kirbie were stopped by another horde of soldiers just outside of the village. Tessa landed outside of the town.

"You go help the others, Tessa," Kirbie stated. "I'll take care of these clowns."

Kirbie drew her weapons as she made her way towards the soldiers. Tessa flew away, heading into Esterton.

In the meantime, Tori and the others had made it to Esterton, ready to ensure the same results happened there as it had happened elsewhere. However, before they could do any kind of damage, Tori noticed Timothy, Tamera and Max making their way towards them.

"Well, if it isn't the daughters of the late Minoru and Celestia," Tori commented. "And where's the guardian?"

"She's taking care of those you left behind," Tamera answered.

At that moment, they heard the motorcycle approaching, and saw Tessa making her way to them. She got off her motorcycle and quickly made her way over to Tamera, Timothy and Max.

"Good to see you, Tessa," Tamera stated. "Is Kirbie okay?"

"Yeah, she's just taking care of more of Tori's goons."

Everyone drew or formed their weapons. Tori laughed as she began to glow. "It will be fun watching you all die. Kill them!"

All the enemies charged and a battle ensued as Tori stood back near Sandra and Noah. Tamera's and Dorian's weapons collided fiercely. Dorian then threw a light blue ball of magic at Tamera, who moved out of the way. He fired several others, but Tamera used her ice magic to stop the blasts from hitting her.

Max was using her powers of fire to throw balls of flame at several ninjas. A ninja then tried to strike Max with his staff but Max had formed her magical staff and was able to block the staff. She swung her staff hard, striking the ninja in the face and laying him out.

Tessa was trying her might against Mornecai. Mornecai was trying to strike Tessa as much as he could, but Tessa was doing her best to dodge him. Then Tessa was able to strike Mornecai, and he flew backwards. Tessa was then shocked to see Mornecai back on his feet.

"You're indeed a strong one, aren't you?" Tessa commented.

Timothy did his best to help Max dispose of the ninjas with his sword. In the meantime, Tamera watched as Dorian ran wildly at her to strike her with his sword, but he missed as Tamera sidestepped him, and instinctively swung her ax downward, slicing Dorian's back wide open, and he bled heavily of what resembled glowing blue blood as he fell to the ground, and he died where he lay.

Tessa had noticed that Mornecai had suddenly stopped fighting her. He shook his head and Tessa thought he was acting disoriented. "What happened?" he questioned. "Where am I?" He then looked at Tessa. "Who are you, and... are we fighting?"

Tessa lowered her guard. "Uh... no... I mean... What's your name?"

"Mornecai. I'm from Valemort. Why am I here?"

Tessa noticed that Mornecai's eyes were no longer light blue, but were a shade of orange-red. She answered, "Dorian must have had you under his spell. It must have broken when Tamera killed him."

Tamera then began to glow as she walked over towards where Tori was, next to a house with Sandra and Noah, who was crying and Sandra was trying to comfort. At that moment, Tori pulled out her sword and placed it close to Sandra, the blade almost touching her back. Noah ran over to Tamera.

"Lower your weapon, Tamera," Tori warned, "or the wolf girl dies."

"Tori, you coward," Tamera stated. "Let them go and fight me!"

"I'm not going to make it easy on you. Now lower your weapon."

Tamera let her magical ax dissipate in her hands, and she stopped glowing. Without saying anything, Tori pushed Sandra into Tamera. Tamera, seeing Tori look as if she was going to stab Sandra, grabbed her and spun around. Tori ended up stabbing Tamera, who screamed out in pain.

"Tamera!!" Timothy cried out. Everyone was shocked to see what had just happened.

After Tori pulled her sword out of Tamera's body, Tamera fell into Sandra's arms. Sandra began to cry.

"Hang on, Tamera!" Sandra cried out.

Then as Tori went to strike Sandra and Tamera, she saw someone block her sword with theirs. She was amazed to see

Timothy standing in front of her with a determined look on his face. Tori then snickered.

"You think you stand a chance against me, you fool?"

Tori quickly tried to stab Timothy, but her sword was stopped by a sheet of ice. Timothy was stunned, and he looked over to see Tamera holding her right hand out.

"You *do* love me..." Tamera said softly. She squinted in pain as she held her side.

Tori tried to pull the sword from the ice, but couldn't. Suddenly, Timothy wrapped his arms around Tori's waist and proceeded to pick her off the ground as he screamed loudly. Then he and Tori crashed through a large plate-glass window before falling to the ground with glass falling around him and Tori.

Tessa then ran over towards Tamera and Sandra. In the meantime, Timothy had awakened and made his way over to Tessa, with many cuts on his body from the falling glass. Sandra handed Tamera to Timothy.

"Angelic Rain!" Tessa cried out. Suddenly, a large, swirling golden vortex formed around Tessa, Tamera and Timothy. Then after the vortex dissipated, Timothy looked down to see Tamera's eyes had opened back up, and Tamera lifted up her shirt and felt with her hand that her wound had been sealed up.

After kissing Tamera on her forehead, everyone noticed another kind of glow. They turned to see Tori walking out of the house, her body looking as if it were consumed by a black flame once again.

"I'm done with this," Tori stated furiously. "You all will die, and I will have all of Coverdale Island!"

Max walked over to the others with her staff drawn as well. But before Tori could strike them down, she saw out of the corner of her eye a sword coming at her, and she was able to block it with her sword. She then was stunned to see Kirbie walking towards her with her sword formed. Not only was Kirbie's sword glowing of a fiery purple flame, but her body was glowing as well.

"Kirbie," Tori simply said.

"Hello, Tori," Kirbie responded.

The two approached each other, swords in hand.

"You all hold off the others," Kirbie commanded. "I'll deal with Tori."

Kirbie and Tori then began to swing their swords at each other, with each one blocking the other's moves. Tori then tried to slash Kirbie, but Kirbie leaned back.

Kirbie and Tori exchanged swings of their swords again. Tori managed to get a punch in on Kirbie, but then Kirbie quickly stood her ground as she blocked Tori again from stabbing her.

Tori then proceeded to strike Kirbie with blackened balls of flame, but Kirbie used her sword to block them. Then Kirbie fired an orb of purple fire at Tori, who rolled out of the way.

Tessa, Mornecai, Timothy, Max and Tamera were able to strike down the last of the ninjas. Tori, seeing that she was now disadvantaged, cried out in anger.

"Give up, Tori," Kirbie commanded. "It's over for you."

"Never!" Tori cried out. "I will die first."

She tried to charged blatantly at Kirbie, but Kirbie formed a fist in her hand. As Tori tried to strike Kirbie with her sword, Kirbie punched her fist downward onto the sword, causing it to break. Then as Tori's body went past Kirbie, Kirbie formed one of her swords in her hand and proceeded to stab Tori through her back, heart and chest. Tori gasped loudly before looking down to see Kirbie's sword sticking out from her chest. Kirbie then let the sword dissipate, and Tori fell to the ground, dead.

Sandra and Noah ran over to the heroes.

"Are you okay?" Kirbie asked them.

"Yeah, we're fine," Sandra answered her. "Thank you so much for your help."

"Can we go eat now?" Noah suddenly commented.

Tamera, all smiles, picked Noah up. "Sure, sweetheart. I know a great place."

As Tamera went to walk away, still holding onto Noah, a ninja suddenly appeared from behind another building and screamed as he charged at Tamera and Noah. Tamera, out of instinct, squatted down and turned her body to protect Noah. Tamera figured she would have been stabbed again, but felt nothing happen to her. She looked up in shock to see Celina's sword had stabbed through the ninja's stomach. The ninja gasped, and after Celina removed her sword from his body, he fell to the ground, dead.

Everyone was surprised to see what Celina had done.

"Sorry I'm late," Celina told them.

As everyone made their way to the ship, Mornecai walked over to Celina. "Well, well," he said flirtatiously. "What's your name, beautiful?"

"I'm Celina, and you are?"

"They call me Mornecai. What do you say when this is over, we get us a bite to eat… and a chance to know each other?"

Celina smirked. "Sure… if you think you can handle me."

Kirbie leaned over to Timothy. "Well, that was unexpected."

Timothy chuckled in agreement. Tamera sat down by Timothy. Tamera leaned her body against Timothy's as he wrapped his right arm around her. As Kirbie flew the ship upward, Sandra handed Noah to Celina. Noah hugged her.

"Thank you, Celina."

Celina hugged Noah back. "And what's your name, little one?"

"I'm Noah." He then pointed over to Sandra. "That's my new sister, Sandra."

Sandra was stunned, but joyful to hear Noah say she was his sister.

"Will you be my new parents?" Noah asked Celina and Mornecai.

Celina was speechless. She then held Noah tightly as she answered, "I always wanted a little one of my own."

"Look at how precious you are," Mornecai spoke.

As the heroes arrived in front of Luna's castle, Luna, Camille and Heather waited out front. Heather hugged Timothy. "Welcome back. I was so worried."

"It's okay now, Heather."

Heather then hugged Tamera while helping Luna. Timothy then turned to Tessa, hugging her. "Thank you for saving Tamera, Tessa. I don't know what I would do if I didn't have her with me."

"I'm always happy to help you all," Tessa simply told him.

"I thank you for helping us as well, Tessa," Camille stated as she hugged Tessa.

"You're welcome, Camille."

The next morning, Max was sitting outside the castle on a bench, still saddened that Timothy decided to be with Tamera. Feeling overwhelmed by her emotions, Max began to cry.

Then Timothy walked over to Max. Max saw him approach and turned her head from Timothy, feeling ashamed. Timothy sat down beside her.

"I've got nothing to say to you," Max told him.

Timothy sighed. "I'm sorry if I intruded on you." He stood up and went to walk away.

"What did... I do wrong?" Max finally responded as she grabbed Timothy's hand. Timothy sat back down beside her. "How did I fail to win your heart? Couldn't you see how much I loved you?"

Timothy sat back down beside Max. "But I *do* love you, Max."

"No, you don't. You've given your heart to Tamera! What does she have that I don't?"

"Well, she's closer to my age than you..."

Max suddenly got quiet.

"Come on, Max. Listen to yourself. You really think that because I'm dating Tamera that I suddenly hate you?"

Max sighed, and tears began to fall from her eyes.

Timothy placed his hands on Max's cheeks. "The rest of the family is happy for me and Tamera. Why can't you be?"

"I *am* happy for Tamera but... I just wanted you for myself. I mean... you're so kind, so gentle... I've never met anyone like you. Where am I gonna find someone else like that?"

"It's not the end of the world, Max. You'll find someone."

Max began to cry harder. Timothy wrapped his arms around Max. Max hugged him back.

"I'll always love you, Max, just as I do the others."

"I... love you, too."

Luna woke up to the sun shining through the window. After getting out of bed, getting showered up and dressed, Luna made her way down the hallway. She happened to see Tamera walking up to her.

"Good morning, sweetie."

"Good morning, Luna."

Luna placed her hand on Tamera's cheek. "It's been so long since I've seen you this happy."

A tear fell down Tamera's cheek. "I prayed for so long to find someone who would love me despite my flaws. And he finally answered my prayer. I'm so thankful."

"Hey, Tamera!" said a voice. Luna and Tamera looked to see Timothy and Heather waving to her. Tamera looked at Luna, who told her, "Don't let me stop you, sweetie."

Tamera hugged Luna. Then she made her way over to Timothy and Heather. Timothy held Tamera in his arms. Then Heather hugged both of them before they walked together to the dining area. Luna then said out loud, "Thank you so much, my lord, for bringing Timothy into Tamera's life. I'm so grateful to see her smile again."

Timothy's mother and father, Lana and Leonard, walked into their living room together when they heard a cell phone ring. Lana looked to see who was calling.

"It's Timothy," she stated, and she answered, seeing Timothy's face on the phone. "Hello, son, what are you doing?"

"Hi, Mom! How are things going?"

"We're doing well, Timothy. How are things with you?"

Timothy got silent for a moment.

"Timothy… is everything okay?"

"Mom… I want you to meet somebody."

He handed the phone to Tamera.

"Hi there," Tamera said, blushing. "My name's Tamera. I'm… Timothy's girlfriend. It's a pleasure to meet you."

Lana and Leonard were both surprised. While Leonard

looked as if he was happy to see her, Lana's face showed a bit of disapproval. Before Leonard could say anything, Lana spoke out by saying, "I don't believe this. Don't you see that she has different colored skin?"

Timothy was appalled. He wrapped his arms around Tamera. "I hardly see why that should be any problem…"

"And if you would really think that a beautiful angel like Heather would…"

"Hey, Tamera!" was called out. Tamera and Timothy turned to see Heather approach, all smiles. Leonard and Lana could see and hear what was going on.

"I got you something!" Heather stated. She then pulled out a chain necklace that had what resembled an icicle as a diamond on the chain. "I wanted to show my love for you, Tamera. Do you like it?"

Tamera had tears in her eyes. "I love it. Thank you." They hugged.

"I love you so much, Tamera," Heather stated.

"I love you too, Heather."

Heather joyfully said, "I'm gonna make supper." She saw who was on the phone. "Hi, Grandpa! Hi Grandma! I love you!"

Only Leonard said, "Hello, sweetheart. We love you, too."

Then Heather walked to the kitchen.

"I've only got one thing to say," Lana responded angrily, "and that's…"

Leonard took the phone from Lana. "Congratulations, son. Looks like you've found quite a wonderful woman. You have my blessing."

"Thank you, Dad," Timothy replied. "I appreciate that."

"I look forward to the day I finally get to meet you, Tamera, and I really miss talking to Heather. I love you all, and I'll talk to you later."

"I love you too, Dad."

They both hung up the phone.

"Don't tell me you approve of this?" Lana cried out.

"As a matter of fact, I do." Leonard yawned as he stretched his arms. "I think I'll sleep in the guest room tonight so you can think about if you can be in Timothy's future... and mine."

Leonard simply walked out of the room. Lana lowered her head in sadness.

Chapter 7

Kaseya

It was the start of another sun-shining day in the village of Wolford, located on Coverdale Island. Sandra had awakened to the sun shining in her eyes. She sat up and yawned as she stretched her arms in the air, trying to get herself motivated.

The beautiful wolf girl got herself dressed before walking out to the hallway in her home leading to the kitchen. She was surprised to see Mornecai and Noah already sitting at the kitchen table with a look of excitement on Noah's face. He was watching as Celina was preparing breakfast for everyone.

"Good morning, Sandra," Celina told her.

"Good morning, Celina. I didn't know you were a cook. I thought you were just one of Nuriel's most valiant warriors."

"I am, but I also cooked for Nuriel. He would tell me I was a better cook than the chefs he had, which made me wonder why he kept them."

Sandra chuckled as she sat down by Noah. Noah gave Sandra a hug. Then Celina sat plates of food in front of Mornecai and the children. Then she grabbed her plate and she sat down at the table across from the children, and they all began to eat.

"Are you my new parents now?" Noah suddenly asked.

Celina was stunned by the question. Everyone stopped eating.

"I'm sorry," Noah then replied. "It's just... my parents went to heaven. I really like you both, and I don't want you to leave me."

Celina was touched by what Noah told her. She and Mornecai got up and walked over to Noah and proceeded to hug him. Noah wrapped his arms around them.

"I know I'm not your parent, Noah," Celina stated, "but believe me when I tell you I will do my best to watch over you and Sandra."

"As will I," Mornecai stated.

"Thank you so much."

Before Mornecai and Celina were able to sit back down, they heard a ruckus outside, followed by distant screams of horror.

"What's going on?" Celina wondered as she grabbed her sword.

"You two get to the basement, now," Mornecai demanded. Sandra grabbed Noah and led him down to the basement as Mornecai and Celina went outside.

Mornecai and Celina looked to see the town's City Building was being attacked by a multitude of soldiers wearing metal armor over their chests, arms and legs. As they approached the scene, she was stopped by several of the soldiers. Mornecai, Celina and the soldiers began fighting with each other. Celina was able to hold off the soldiers by striking them down with her glowing purple sword, or with her blood attacks that she learned from Nuriel. In the meantime, Mornecai was striking down soldiers with his brute strength.

Mornecai and Celina walked on towards the City Building, where more soldiers saw the heroes coming at them, and they ran towards them to attack. Mornecai and Celina started off well against them, but eventually were becoming overwhelmed by the soldiers. Eventually they were approached by a woman who had long black hair and glowing red eyes, wearing a black bra along with a black jacket that was unzipped, along with black shorts and thigh-high black boots. She had devil horns on her head.

"Not bad," the woman told Mornecai and Celina. One of the other soldiers then stabbed Mornecai in his stomach. She then pulled out his sword from Mornecai's body. Celina cried out in anger. The woman then approached Celina, grabbing her chin and forcing her to look at her. "It's too bad. I could have used someone like you two." She then looked at her soldier. "Get rid of them."

The soldier grabbed Mornecai and Celina and started leading them away. As Mornecai struggled to breathe, the soldier gave him a bottle that contained a golden liquid.

"Drink this," the female soldier instructed. Mornecai did so. She then led them to behind one of the remaining standing homes.

"Please, get out of here."

"Why are you doing this?" Celina wondered.

"I can't explain. Please go."

The soldier saw others coming to them. She walked over to them as a way to deter them so Mornecai and Celina could get away.

"This area's secure now," the soldier spoke. Let's inform Avilla."

As the soldiers walked away, Mornecai, who saw he was now healed, made his way back over to the home with Celina. They were relieved to see the house was still standing. They entered the house and went down to the basement.

"Oh, thank goodness you're okay," Celina told them.

"What's going on?" Sandra asked.

"We're under attack," Mornecai informed them. "We have

to leave at once."

Mornecai, Celina, Sandra and Noah made their way out of the house and left Wolford as quickly as they could.

In the meantime, the three soldiers walked into the City Building and approached the leader of the group. She had very long black hair, with some of the strands being dark red, with bright red eyes, and wore a black bikini top, short black leather jacket and very short shorts.

"Avilla," said the soldier that helped Celina, "the town is ours."

"Excellent," Avilla told her.

Avilla grabbed a phone.

"Yes, Avilla?" said a voice.

"It's done, Mother. Wolford is in our possession."

"Well done. The others have Esterton, Chu Gardens and Valemort taken over as well. Finally, we have our hold over Coverdale Island, and soon we will be able to take over Coverdale. Queen Luna and Princess Camille will bow down to me. I am sending Caberra to negotiate with them."

"Yes, Mother."

Avilla hung up the phone.

The villagers of Coverdale were enjoying another precious day given to them by the lord. Children were joyously playing in the streets as their parents were working on their chores for the day. At that moment, a man and two of his henchmen charged through the village gates. The muscular man had silver hair, with a matching beard and mustache, with brown eyes, and wore a heavy brown jacket and pants. Many of the children seeing these men ran scared to their parents as the men made their way to the castle.

The men rode their horses to the door of the castle, stopped by Max and Camille, who were talking to each other outside.

"By the name of Queen Kaseya, I command you let me speak to Queen Luna," said one of the men.

"And who might you be?" Camille questioned.

"I am Caberra, of Terehote Forest," said the man. Terehote Forest was located between Chu Gardens and Esterton. "I am here to talk to your queen in regard to a truce to all of Coverdale. And you are?"

"I am Princess Camille, daughter of Queen Luna."

"Please, if you want to save your kingdom, I ask to speak to your mother."

Max and Camille looked at each other.

"I'll go get her. Please wait here with Max."

Camille walked out to the courtyard of the castle, where Queen Luna was watching Tamera and Timothy fighting each other as a way for Timothy to get more practice. Heather was practicing shooting arrows with Tessa. Tessa was pleased with how much Heather had improved on her accuracy.

Tamera swung around her large magical blue ax at Timothy, who blocked her with his sword. At one point, Timothy stumbled over his feet, and he fell to the ground. Timothy then tried to regain his composure, but he then saw Tamera now sitting on top of him, not allowing him to move. Then Tamera let her ax dissipate as she leaned forward and kissed Timothy on the lips.

"That's enough, everyone," Luna announced.

The onlookers applauded at their performance. Luna and Kirbie walked over to Timothy and Tamera as Tamera helped Timothy to his feet, and they hugged each other. Then she hugged Heather.

"Guess you got the better of me again, baby," Timothy said

while snickering. Tamera chuckled as well.

"You two are doing much better," Luna told her. "I'm really impressed."

"Thank you, my queen," Timothy told her while bowing his head.

Kirbie kissed Heather on the forehead. "I'm amazed at how far you've come. Well done."

Heather hugged Kirbie. "Thank you, Kirbie. You and Tamera have been such a blessing to me and Timothy. And thank you for all you've done for us, Queen Luna."

Timothy then held Tamera's hand and he kissed her on the cheek. She blushed. At that moment Camille approached, and then she bowed to them.

"Mom," Camille responded, "Lord Caberra of Terehote Forest is here on behalf of Queen Kaseya. He claims to talk of a truce with Coverdale. He's by the castle gate with Max."

Everyone stood up and joined Luna, Tamera and Kirbie as they walked out towards the entrance and stood next to Max.

"Greetings, everyone," said Caberra, bowing. He noticed Luna approaching, with Tamera, Max and Tessa on one side and Timothy, Heather and Camille on the other side behind Queen Luna. The others stood behind them. "Which of you is Queen Luna?"

"I am," Luna answered. "What brings you to Coverdale, Lord Caberra?"

"Just a simple offering to show your allegiance to Queen Kaseya. She is set to conquer all that she sets her eyes on, and now she has her eyes set on Coverdale Island. All the great queen asks of Coverdale is a small offering of whatever you may desire as a token to show your submission to her, and you will not be destroyed."

"Submission, eh?" Luna questioned. She and Caberra looked over the edge of the wall, overlooking the village and the waters surrounding the castle.

"My parents ruled over this land for many years before God called them home. Their legacy lives inside me, and I have given my oath to protect this land no matter what the cost."

"Be careful what you say, Queen Luna," Caberra stated. "You could regret it. Think of those you love. If you don't submit, everyone here will become slaves, or even worse."

Luna turned away from the moment in thought. She then looked over to Kirbie and nodded. Kirbie then approached Luna and drew her swords, pointing them at Caberra's neck as they glowed. The others drew their weapons as well.

"What is this?" Caberra questioned.

Luna showed her anger to Caberra. "How dare you come into my city and threaten me or my people? To think that you could come into my castle and tell me how you have taken over the rest of the island, and yet you think we're just gonna stand by and let you take over Coverdale as well? How dare you even think that we will bow to a tyrant bent on destroying everything we hold dear?"

"This is madness! You're crazy to think you can stop someone like Kaseya!" Caberra cried out. "When she finds out about this, you will all die!"

Luna then looked over to some of the citizens of the community, and then over to Max, then Timothy and Tamera, and the others behind her. She then stared into Kirbie's eyes. Luna lightly nodded her head, closing her eyes for a slight moment. Finally, Luna turned back to Caberra.

"Tell your queen we see this as a declaration of war, and we will stand and fight."

Then Kirbie kicked Caberra in the stomach and he fell to the ground. Then Timothy, Max and Tamera grabbed Caberra and forced him to the castle gate. They threw him to the ground outside of the gate. As Luna turned and walked away, the others followed by grabbing the henchmen and throwing them off the castle grounds as well.

"Looks like we could be at war again," Luna noted. "Everyone be ready."

Angered, Caberra grabbed his phone. Someone answered, "Caberra?"

"Kaseya, Queen Luna refuses to talk of a truce."

Kaseya sighed. "Why am I not surprised?" She snickered. "I guess we'll have to do things the hard way. Return to the village Tanna assigned for you. I'll keep you informed."

"Yes, my daughter." Caberra cut off the call. "Let's get back to Chu Gardens."

Kaseya, who had tanned skin, white hair and fire-colored eyes, and was wearing a black leather top and pants, disconnected the phone call, sighing as she realized she was going to be getting ready to go to war with Coverdale.

At that moment, a younger woman, who was barely fourteen years old, approached Kaseya. She had brown hair and reddish-brown eyes, with dark red wings, and was wearing a long red dress that had black mesh above her chest and over her arms, along with a black cape and black pantyhose. She had bracelets of white and gold on her wrists and ankles, and a white bow with many diamonds decorated in her hair.

"My dear Tanna," Kaseya stated. "What do you have for me?"

"Mother," Tanna reported, "the plan is in motion. Avilla is

in Wolford, Demora is in Chu Gardens, Elora is in Esterton, and Caberra is headed for Valemort."

"You've done well, Tanna. Soon all of Coverdale Island will be ours, and when my time comes, the island will become yours. I know you will make me proud."

"Thank you, Mother. I won't let you down."

Kaseya kissed Tanna on the forehead. "Queen Luna and Princess Camille will be leading their troops against us soon. Be ready."

"Yes, Mother."

That evening, Luna looked out of the window to the throne room. She was discouraged by what was happening on her island, and how so many innocents were suffering. A tear rolled down her cheek. Then she heard a voice say, "My queen?"

Luna wiped the tear from her cheek as she noticed Timothy, Heather, Kirbie and Tamera standing on the red carpet, bowing to her.

"You sent for us, Luna?" asked Timothy.

Luna walked over to everyone, placing her hands on Timothy's shoulders. "I just wanted someone to talk to."

Luna wiped the tears away from her eyes.

"What bothers you, my queen?" Kirbie questioned.

"I know in my heart what needs to be done about Kaseya and her army. I can't bear the thought of having Coverdale overthrown by a tyrant who is out to enslave all of Coverdale Island. And the thought of something happening to Camille…"

"I don't want to see that happen either, Luna, nor anyone here," Tamera noted.

"I know it seems like the odds are stacked against us…"

"Yeah, but who really listens to the odds anyway?" Kirbie

stated.

Luna laughed as she hugged Kirbie and Tamera. Then she hugged Timothy and Heather.

"Please, my queen, let me track down Kaseya and her army," Kirbie asked her. "I can weaken their forces, and if they do defeat us, at least Coverdale will have a better chance at defeating Kaseya."

"Thank you," Luna told them. "I think I will go to bed now. I'll get a hold of Princess Marietta in the morning. Maybe we can get some help from them."

Timothy bowed. "Good night, Luna, and God bless you." He, Camille, Kirbie and Tamera then left the room. Luna left a few minutes later to go to her bedroom.

Chapter 8

The Plan is in Motion

The next morning, Luna talked with Timothy, Heather, Camille, Tessa, Kirbie and Tamera, in favor of Tessa and Kirbie checking out the other cities. At that moment, Luna, Timothy, Heather, Max, Camille and Tamera approached Tessa and Kirbie.

"Come back to me, okay?" Luna stated.

Kirbie hugged her. "We'll do our best. You make sure Coverdale is safe." She then hugged Max.

"Of course, we will," Max mentioned.

Kirbie approached Timothy, kissing him on his forehead. "Take care of Tamera in case I don't come back."

Timothy was disturbed by the comment. "Don't talk like that, Kirbie."

"Promise me you'll be back," Tamera told her.

"I can't make that promise and you know that."

Tamera hugged Kirbie tightly. "I love you, Ice Goddess."

"I love you too, Kirbie." Then she told Heather, "You make sure they behave, okay?"

Heather smirked. "Sure, but who's gonna keep *you* out of trouble?"

Kirbie chuckled as she kissed Heather on her forehead. Then she hugged Heather, not wanting to let her go. Tessa then approached

"We need to get going, Kirbie," Tessa told her.

Kirbie and Tessa then got into a ship as Timothy, Heather, Tamera, Max and Luna watched them take off to head for Valemort.

"I hope we're doing the right thing," Tessa stated.

"No matter what, we have to do this," Kirbie replied to give support. "I don't want our people to suffer any more."

Before reaching the Seiland Pass they noticed smoke coming from a nearby town.

"That's Valemort!" Tessa proclaimed sadly.

"Let's check it out," Kirbie ordered.

Kirbie landed the ship outside of Valemort. They noticed it was in complete ruin, with smoke billowing from many ruined buildings.

"What happened here?" Tessa questioned. "We just got these towns back on their feet after the last attack."

"Let's search for survivors," Kirbie commanded.

Tessa and Kirbie began searching the town. They heard noise from a distance, and Tessa and Kirbie stood guard, until they saw a large white Newfoundland dog surfacing out of the fog. The dog cautiously approached Kirbie and rubbed his head against her leg. Kirbie reached her hand down, and the dog let her pet him.

"It looks like you made a new friend," Tessa commented.

"It would seem. Let's keep looking."

Tessa and Kirbie walked ever further, towards the northern edge of town, with the dog staying close to Kirbie. Kirbie was then horrified to see a wooden cross with a person nailed to it, covered in blood. A wooden sign with "Coverdale" engraved in it was hanging near the top of the cross.

"You should have heeded our warning," said a man who

approached Kirbie. Kirbie recognized who it was.

"Caberra," Kirbie spoke. They saw several soldiers were with him. Caberra was holding a club in his hands.

"What a treat it will be for my daughter to have the Princess of Coverdale in her possession before she takes over all of the island."

Kirbie formed her magical swords in her hands. Tessa showed off her claws.

"Not if we have anything to say about it."

"I'll take the old man if you want the soldiers," Kirbie mentioned.

"And here I thought I was going to get the challenge," Tessa snickered.

Kirbie ran towards Caberra, and their weapons collided. A soldier charged as well at Kirbie, but Kirbie stopped him by throwing one of her swords, which went through his chest. As the sword was removed from his chest, the soldier fell to the ground, dead. In the meantime, Tessa was able to strike down some of the other soldiers with her claws.

Kirbie and Caberra tried to hit each other with their weapons, but neither was having any luck. Then Caberra seemed to get the upper hand for a moment when he punched Kirbie several times, and Kirbie fell to the ground. Caberra swung his club downward at Kirbie's head, but Kirbie moved out of the way. Kirbie then tripped up Caberra with a low spin-kick, and Caberra this time fell to the ground.

Kirbie stood back up and tried to stab Caberra, but he stopped Kirbie with his club. Then Caberra got back up on his feet, and with his brute strength, he forced Kirbie up against a tree. As Caberra continued to push, he suddenly ended up with a shocked look on his face. He looked back to see Tessa behind him. Then he turned his body to Tessa, and Kirbie saw the blood running down his back from being deeply scratched. Kirbie then took the opportunity to stab the man through his chest. The man then fell to the ground dead.

"Are you okay, Tessa?" Kirbie asked.

"I'm fine." She looked to see all the soldiers had been taken down.

"Well, that was fast."

"I told you they probably wouldn't be much of a challenge."

Kirbie's phone rang. She answered it, "Luna? You okay?"

"Kirbie, we got word that Kaseya and her army are headed this way. I made the call and members of Willshire Kingdom are making their way here. I wanted to let you all know."

"You want us to come back to you?"

"No, you continue on saving the cities. We'll do our best here, okay?"

"Okay, Mom. Be careful."

"You too. Bye, sweetie."

Kirbie disconnected the call. "Kaseya's headed for Coverdale. Some of Willshire Kingdom's soldiers are headed there. She wants us to continue on."

"Very well. Our next stop will be Esterton."

At that moment, the dog walked back over to Kirbie, again rubbing its face against Kirbie's leg. She again petted the dog.

Back in Coverdale, Queen Luna was sitting outside the door of the castle, in deep thought about Tessa and Kirbie. She then looked out towards where Max was standing by the gate. Tamera was standing a short distance ahead of her. At that moment, Laura approached Luna, who she could tell was distraught. Laura, one of Queen Luna's soldiers, had long green hair and darker yellow eyes. She was wearing a black top that had red trim, a red skirt that had white ruffles underneath, with black stockings.

"Queen Luna?" Laura spoke. Luna gave Laura a tight hug. "It's a tough situation we have here."

"We have to stop them, Laura. Where's Lisa and the others?"

"They'll be here. We mustn't give up hope."

Tamera was continuing to look out towards the forest ahead of them. Then Tamera noticed what looked like something coming towards her. Her eyes grew wide as she recognized it was arrows flying through the sky. With her magic, Tamera formed a wall of ice in front of them, and many of the arrows that would have struck her bounced off the thick ice. Seeing what happened, Max ran away from the castle gate.

"Mom! The army is here!" Max yelled out.

"No," Laura stated. "The others aren't here yet!"

"Let's get ready," Luna spoke. "Hopefully we can hold them off."

Members of Kaseya's army approached, led by her and Tanna. The massive horde of soldiers stopped not too far from where Queen Luna and her soldiers were standing.

"Is that… Luna?" asked one soldier to Kaseya.

"It's only a small group," said Tanna. "We should defeat them easily."

The soldier laughed soft but sinisterly. Then he yelled out, "Surrender yourselves, warriors of Coverdale."

There was silence at the moment. Then the soldier happened to see something heading at him. Before he could react, an icicle hit him, turning him to dust.

"Come over and get us!" Tamera yelled.

With that, Kaseya gave the order, and the army charged at the group.

Tamera, before they could get to them, waved her hands up, and a huge wall of blue ice popped up on the army, turning many of the soldiers to dust. At that time, the other soldiers attacked. Tamera danced her way through the battle, swinging her ax to take out many soldiers. Max was using her staff and Laura was using her sword as well. However, the sheer number of soldiers was becoming overwhelming, and eventually the soldiers were able to weaken and then overpower Coverdale's army.

The soldiers laughed, while others celebrated the victory. At that moment, Kaseya and Tanna walked up to the heroes.

"At last, Coverdale has fallen," Kaseya bragged. "And from its ashes a new chapter begins with me as its ruler."

"Take them to the dungeon," Tanna demanded.

The soldiers began carrying out Kaseya's orders.

Before reaching Esterton, Kirbie tried contacting Luna again to make sure everything was okay. However, Luna never answered her phone. That made Kirbie worry.

"It's not like Luna to not answer her phone," Kirbie commented. "Something has to be wrong."

"I sure hope Marietta's army got there before Kaseya did."

Kirbie then happened to see something out of the corner of her eye. "Tessa, look!"

Tessa looked out the window to see two people making their way to Esterton.

"That looks like Mornecai and Celina!" Tessa observed.

Mornecai and Celina saw the ship above them as they made their way towards Esterton. The ship then landed a short distance from them.

"Celina? Mornecai?" was yelled out. Mornecai and Celina then realized who was approaching them. Mornecai hugged Tessa as Kirbie kissed Celina on her forehead.

"Where's Sandra and Noah?" Kirbie questioned.

"A bunch of the villagers are hiding in a cave not too far from here. Sandra and Noah are with them. I heard you two were checking out the villages and hoped I would run into you."

"It will be good to have you by our side, Mornecai," Tessa told him.

"Good to see you too, Tessa. What about Coverdale?"

"I've been trying to get a hold of Luna," Kirbie answered, "but she's not answering. We know Kaseya was heading in that direction. I fear the worst has happened."

"We need to continue on," Tessa instructed. "We're almost to Esterton."

Mornecai and Celina joined Tessa and Kirbie as they boarded the ship and made their way to Esterton.

Luna, Tamera, Camille, Max, Laura, Heather and Timothy sat together in the dungeon, uncertain as to what may happen to them. Timothy was holding Heather in his arms to provide comfort as she slept. Two guards were standing by the door.

"She's so beautiful," Tamera commented.

"Yeah, she means so much to me. I don't know what I would do without her."

"So, how did you two get to know each other?"

Timothy got quiet.

"I'm sorry, I..."

"No, it's okay, Tamera," Timothy noted. "It was five years

ago when we first met. As I told you, I worked at a local grocery store in Coverdale. It was just another day as I woke up and got ready to go to work. I walked out of the house, and as I looked over on the side of the porch, I saw Heather lying on the porch covered in a thin blanket, her head resting on a near-flat pillow. She was holding a single white rose in her hand.

"Heather woke up and saw me and was startled to see me, but once she realized I wasn't going to hurt her, she told me that her parents abandoned her."

"My goodness, that's horrible," Tamera stated.

"Her parents were never found. I brought Heather into my home to take care of her, and the store owner, Kelsie, even helped me out, giving me extra food to feed her with. As time went on, I fell in love with her, as if she was my own flesh and blood. I was able to adopt her, and she's been with me since."

"I... can't imagine the pain she was going through," Tamera noted. "But it looks as if you helped raise Heather to be an incredible woman."

"You know, I don't know why God led her to my home over anyone else's, but now I couldn't imagine not having her by my side."

At that moment, Tanna was walking to the cell door, holding a tray with five bowls of soup. She stood in front of the cell door, and the one guard opened the door for Tanna.

Tanna entered the cell, and she walked over to the prisoners, with the guards standing behind her.

"Are you all okay?" Tanna asked.

"Who are you?" Luna questioned.

"I am Tanna."

"Why is this happening?" Tamera asked. "Why is Kaseya doing this?"

Tanna sighed. "Kaseya is my mother. She is…"

Angered, Max knocked the tray out of Tanna's hand. The guards pulled out their weapons, but Timothy stood in front of them.

"Wait, please!" Timothy pleaded.

"Come on, Timothy! Let's take them! We can escape!"

"No, you can't!" Tanna warned. "Kaseya and her army are still here. They stopped you once, and they would have no problem killing you if you try."

"You're lying!" Max replied.

"Max, please calm down," Camille told her. "How could you possibly think we could escape from here now?"

"Why are we still alive?" Luna wondered.

"I convinced my mother to use you as an insurance policy, to try luring Kirbie and the others here. Right now, they are entering Esterton."

"You're a liar!" Max cried out. "How can we even think of trusting you?"

"Max, stop it," Tamera told her sternly.

"The guards are going to tell Kaseya what's going on!"

The guards removed their helmets. Both men had short brown hair and silver-blue eyes, and were wearing blue outfits with gray armor over them.

"This is Minato and Haruto. They are on my side on this. I assigned them to guard you in hopes nothing would happen to you."

"We didn't want this invasion either," Haruto commented.

"But Kaseya is hell-bent on making sure Coverdale is hers," Minato followed.

Tamera and Heather stood with Timothy in front of Tanna.

"Okay, let's say you're telling the truth… and something's

telling me you are," Timothy mentioned. "What's in it for you to betray your own mother?"

"Of course, I wanted Mother to have Coverdale as her own. I just... didn't think it was going to happen like this. What she's doing is wrong."

Max continued to show her frustration. "And you've done nothing to stop it?"

"Don't you understand? Kaseya is quite powerful, and her army is massive. If she would even find out we were against her, she would kill us. And even though you're alive now, I can't guarantee you'll stay alive. I'm trying my best to make sure you don't die. You're just gonna have to trust me."

"Well, I guess we have that to be thankful for." Timothy picked up the bowls and tray, and he gave them back to Tanna. "Look, Willshire's army is heading this way. Do you think they can defeat them?"

"I doubt it. I think they would be better off to help your friends first."

"I'll send them in that direction," Laura informed them.

"Good. I will continue to help as much as I can."

Tanna and the guards walked out of the dungeon. The guards locked the door and stood guard once again as Tanna left the room.

"Max, your temper nearly cost us our lives!" Camille scolded.

"Would you quit degrading me for once in your pathetic life?"

"Please stop, Max," Luna spoke. "Tanna's right: we will die if we try to escape. We couldn't beat Kaseya's army before. If they would have caught us, we would be dead."

"We just have to believe what Tanna is telling us is true,"

Laura commented.

Lisa and the soldiers from Willshire Kingdom arrived on Coverdale Island, at the dock between Coverdale and Valemort. Lisa, who was Laura's sister, had light blue hair and lighter violet eyes, and wore a short deep purple dress with armor covering most of her arms and legs and around her waist that matched the color of her dress.

As everyone made their way off the ship, Lisa happened to get a text on her phone.

"We need your help. Make your way to Esterton," the text stated.

"What is it, Lisa?" a soldier questioned.

"It's from Laura," Lisa responded. "Queen Luna wants us to go to Esterton. Seems they need our help there."

The soldier showed concern. "What about Coverdale?"

"Princess Marietta told us to follow what Laura and Queen Luna said. That means we better head to Esterton."

Lisa rounded up the army and they indeed made their way to Esterton.

In the meantime, Tessa, Kirbie, Mornecai, Celina and the dog made their way into Esterton. The scene looked eerily similar to Valemort. Seeing all the destruction was breaking Kirbie's heart, and tears began to fall from her eyes.

"To think someone would be so merciless…" Kirbie said. "I can't understand it…"

Tessa wrapped her arm around Kirbie. "Yes, it is crazy to think people would prey on the innocent like this."

The dog saw the sadness in Kirbie's face and jumped up on her to lick her in the face. Kirbie began to laugh joyfully.

"It's good to see love still exists in the world though."

At that moment, a warrior for Kaseya walked up to Kirbie, Tessa and Celina. She had many more soldiers with her. She had red hair and golden eyes, and wore a black armored leotard with armor colored black on her lower arms and legs.

"So, this is Kirbie, guardian of the Jewel of Coverdale," the woman greeted. "I've heard much about you. I was amazed to hear how quickly you took down Caberra."

"And who might you be?" Kirbie pondered.

"I am Elora. I am Kaseya's younger sister." What a force you have proven yourself to be, Kirbie. With you at her side, Queen Luna single-handedly grew Coverdale into a glorious community and have one of the strongest armies on all of Coverdale Island. But your ignorance of Kaseya's existence will now be your downfall."

"I see after last night you got to know us pretty well."

Elora snickered. "Even despite that, Kaseya wants me to give you an offer you cannot, and should not, refuse. She will give you the power of not only ruling Coverdale, but all of Coverdale Island. Coverdale will be enriched with treasures beyond your wildest imagination. All this and more she will give to you and keep you free, if you pronounce Kaseya as the god of all of Coverdale Island. What do you say?"

Tessa, Kirbie, Mornecai and Celina were stunned to hear of such an offer.

"Wow," Kirbie said, eyes widened. Then she looked down to the ground. "That is an offer we couldn't refuse… if we were interested."

"Kirbie, think about all that have suffered because you have resisted us. How many more are going to suffer?"

"But you don't understand, Elora," Kirbie stated. "We only

bow to one god, and not to some power-hungry oppressor who is only interested in enslaving everything and everyone for her own gain. And I know my mother would agree."

Elora became angry. "How dare you defy us? When this battle is over, you and everything precious to you will be destroyed. We will show no mercy to anyone. Coverdale will become a distant memory, and the Jewel of Coverdale will become just another body in the waters of Coverdale Island!"

Kirbie came closer to Elora, with her swords in her hands. "When we are done, Coverdale Island will know that my mother stood up against the odds over the deception of a villain for the sake of freedom, and that even someone who considers herself a god will feel fear flowing through her blood."

Elora swung her enormous sword at Kirbie, but Kirbie moved away. Celina, Tessa and Mornecai got prepared to fight.

"She's all yours," Tessa told Kirbie, then turned to Celina, who also had her sword drawn. "Care to join me, Celina?"

"I would love to, Tessa," Celina stated.

The battle began, with Kirbie and Elora fighting against each other while Tessa and Celina battled the soldiers. Elora's eyes began to glow, and she started firing beams of light at Kirbie, but Kirbie was doing her best to block them. Then Kirbie fired back by shooting off orbs of purple fire at Elora.

"You are indeed a gifted one," Elora told her.

Mornecai, Tessa and Celina continued battling the soldiers. Celina started forming a massive ball of blood in her hand. She then slammed her fist on the ground and a large blast of light took out many of the soldiers.

"You never cease to amaze me, beautiful," Mornecai told Celina.

"Same with you, Mornecai," Celina stated.

Tessa smiled as she rolled her eyes.

Kirbie again charged at Elora with her swords. Once again, their weapons collided over and over at a quick pace, with Kirbie starting to be too quick for Elora. Kirbie then swung her sword at Elora and sliced her eyes. Elora began to cry out in pain.

"You will die for this!" Elora screamed out. "May the gods curse you!"

Celina then took her sword and stabbed Elora. Then she pulled her sword from Elora's body and Elora fell to the ground, dead.

"You looked amazing, Kirbie," Celina complimented.

"As did you all," said Kirbie. "Let's continue on."

Kaseya sat on the throne at the castle in Coverdale. She held a gold cup in her hands and started twirling it around in her hands. At that moment, Tanna approached.

"Something wrong, Tanna?" Kaseya questioned.

"I just wanted to let you know, Mother, that Kirbie and her friends have killed Elora, and are now making their way to Chu Gardens."

"Kirbie is indeed strong. I can see why Queen Luna favored her so much. Send a few more troops to Chu Gardens and Wolford. If they won't heed to my demands, they must be killed."

"Yes, Mother, it shall be done."

Chapter 9

Rescuing the Villages

Luna, Tamera, Camille, Timothy, Heather, Laura and Max sat in a cell, awaiting the fate that fell upon them. Tanna again walked over to the cell door. Timothy saw her standing in front of the door and he stood up and made his way to her. The others saw what Timothy was doing and followed him.

"I wanted to let you know that Tessa and Kirbie are still alive," Tanna informed them. "They defeated two of Mother's most loyal servants, Caberra and Elora, but they still have Demora in Chu Gardens and Avilla in Wolford. A purple-haired woman and red-headed man is with them as well."

"That could be Celina and Mornecai," Tamera noted.

"Kaseya has quite a few people working for her," Timothy stated.

"Actually, we're all a family. As I told you, I'm Kaseya's daughter. Caberra was my grandfather on my mother's side; Demora and Elora are Mom's brother and sister, and Avilla is Elora's daughter."

"Talk about a dysfunctional family," Camille remarked.

"They are the epitome of evil, especially my mother, and as I've said before, she will not stop until she gets what she wants."

"So now what?" Laura wondered.

"Kaseya had ordered me to send more troops to Chu Gardens and Wolford. I instead sent them to Esterton. They should meet up with Willshire Kingdom's army. Hopefully they will be successful, and it will decrease Kaseya's army greatly."

"I can't believe you're doing this for us, Tanna," Timothy replied, holding Tanna's hand. "You're signing your life away by doing this."

"I'm just like you, Timothy. I'm so tired of seeing people suffer, and if I have to die so that others can be saved... it will be worth it to me."

"Just be careful, okay?" Tamera told her.

"I'll try my best."

Tanna again walked away.

At Chu Gardens, Demora had gotten word earlier from Tanna that more troops were coming to help stop Tessa and Kirbie. However, Demora had noticed the troops were nowhere in sight. Demora had silver-white hair with glowing red eyes, and wore a gray button jacket with black pants. He had four cuts that had crossed over each other on his left cheek.

"What is taking them so long?" Demora questioned.

Then one of his soldiers approached him. "Demora, Tessa and Kirbie are entering the city. Should we try to wait for the others?"

"If they are here, we have to try taking them out ourselves. Call Tanna and find out where the army's at."

The soldier did so. Tanna answered her phone.

"Yes, what is it?"

"Where is the army at? Demora wants to know."

"They're on their way!"

"Tessa and Kirbie are already here! We can't wait!"

"I'll get back with you. In the meantime, fall back."

"Yes, Tanna."

The call was cut off. Kaseya saw Tanna was on the phone.
"Is everything all right?"
"Looks like something's going on with the army. They're not in Chu Gardens yet. I'll find out what's going on, and I'll get back to you."
"See to it that you do, my child."
Tanna walked out of the room, pretending to talk to someone.

The soldier reported back to Demora. "Sir, Tanna told us to fall back until the army gets here. Where do you want us to go?"
"We can't just fall back!" Demora said in a rage. "We have to stop them now!"
At that moment, Demora could see Tessa, Kirbie and Celina coming into their view. He became even more angered.
"Get ready to attack. That's an order."
"Yes, sir."

Mornecai, Tessa, Kirbie and Celina cautiously made their way to the town along with the dog. They looked around to see anyone suspicious but at the moment couldn't find anyone.
Unbeknownst to them, Demora was hiding on the rooftop of a house. He waited until he saw the trio coming towards him. Then when he felt the time was right, he jumped off the roof with his weapon drawn to try ambushing them. As he tried to stab Camille, the dog instead jumped in front of her and ended up getting stabbed instead. The dog then fell to the ground. Kirbie was distraught as Demora pulled his sword out of the dog, showing no remorse.
"How could you?" Kirbie cried out in anger. She then charged Demora with her sword formed in her hands, and they

began exchanging strikes with their swords. Then soldiers swarmed around Tessa and Celina, who were by the dog.

"Angelic Rain!" Tessa cried out. Suddenly, there was a large golden vortex that swirled over where the dog had lain. Everyone had to take shelter from the vortex.

The vortex finally dissipated. Everyone was stunned to see that where the dog was lying, now appeared a woman who had the ears and tail of the dog. Her light hair went down to just above the back of her knees, and she had the golden eyes the dog had. She was wearing a dress that was white over her chest to her neck and on her sleeves, and the lower part of the dress was blue. She was also wearing black stockings.

The woman approached the soldiers who charged at her. She suddenly reached down from both sides of her waist and drew out two firearms and began shooting laser beams at the soldiers.

"Now I've seen everything," Celina commented to Tessa.

Fighting resumed as Kirbie continued against Demora. Demora then threw balls of red at Kirbie, but she dodged them as she charged at Demora. Demora then tried to strike her with his sword, but missed. Kirbie spun around quickly and threw one of her swords with much force, this time striking Demora in his side.

Demora dropped his sword as he fell to the ground. Demora went to reach for his sword, but somebody had stepped on his arm. He looked to see the woman standing over him. Without saying a word, she pointed a gun at Demora's head and fired the gun, a laser beam going through his head, killing him instantly. Kirbie then looked to see that Tessa and Celina had taken care of the other soldiers. They then walked over to the woman.

"I guess I took too long to fight with you," said the woman. "I was trying to stay in disguise."

"Well, thank you for the help," Camille told her.

"Are you... Kirbie, Queen Luna's guardian?"

"I am, and you are?"

"My name's Mako. I was originally from Wolf Lake Village, but I moved to Valemort a couple years ago."

"It's nice to meet you, Mako," Tessa told her.

"Well, now that Chu Gardens is secure, we should make our way to Wolford," Kirbie pointed out.

"Sounds like a plan to me," Celina stated.

"Would you like to join us, Mako?" Kirbie asked her.

"I'd love to." Mako reached her hand to Kirbie, who grabbed Mako's hand as they walked together and boarded the ship, making their way to Wolford.

Lisa led Willshire's army to Esterton, and as Tanna had hoped, they did manage to run into the members of Kaseya's army that were actually supposed to go to Chu Gardens and Wolford.

"Take 'em down!" Lisa cried out.

Lisa led the charge as the armies collided. Lisa, using her sword, took down many soldiers as the rest of the army fought to strike down the soldiers.

For several minutes the armies fought until Lisa was able to strike the last soldier down.

"Let's keep going," Lisa instructed. "We have to catch up to Kirbie."

They headed towards Chu Gardens.

Tanna had made her way into the throne room, where she approached her mother with discouraging news.

"Mother," Tanna spoke, "Kirbie and her friends are now heading for Wolford. We found out that the recruits were ambushed by another army, and that army is heading for Wolford to join them as well."

Kaseya was irritated. "They indeed are a tough group, aren't they? I didn't figure we would have this kind of trouble."

"What do you want me to do, Mother?"

"Just sit tight, precious. If they defeat Avilla, we will wait until they come to Coverdale, and the army will certainly destroy them."

"Will do, Mother."

Tanna left the room. Kaseya signaled for two guards to come over to her.

"You, keep an eye on Tanna," she said to the first guard. "You, send out five hundred soldiers to Wolford. See to it that they are killed."

"Yes, my queen," the soldiers spoke as they saluted Kaseya. Then the soldiers left the room.

Tanna was making her way outside when she noticed some of the soldiers being deployed. She walked over to one of the soldiers.

"Soldier, what's going on here?"

"We're on our way to Wolford."

"But I didn't give that order. We need everyone we can get here, to protect my mother."

"It was your mother who gave this order."

He walked away from Tanna. Tanna became very concerned.

"It's not like Mom to give orders without also telling me about it. Could it be that she found me out?"

Tanna decided she would need to let Queen Luna know what was going on. Unbeknownst to her, she was being followed by the other soldier.

Tessa, Kirbie, Celina and Mako were making their way to Wolford, but had stopped to get some rest. Kirbie had awakened to see the others still sleeping. She was feeling nerved up, and she got up on her feet and walked to the edge of the forest. She then got to thinking about Kaseya and what she and her army had done. She started to dance by herself.

Unbeknownst to Kirbie, Mako had also awakened, and she saw that Kirbie was dancing in the forest. Kirbie was still feeling a bit of uncertainty. Mako could see she was upset as she walked over to her.

"You dance beautifully, Kirbie. Who taught you that?"

"My best friend, Billie did. She was amazingly gifted at what she could do." Kirbie lowered her head. "I never knew who my parents were. Billie raised me as if I were her own. She actually was only a couple years older than I was, but she was the one who helped me to become who I am. She disappeared after the Riverton War. I haven't seen her since."

"I'm so sorry. I didn't know…"

"It's okay, Mako. I didn't wake you, did I?"

"No, I was already awake when you made your way to the forest."

"I didn't mind either," said a voice. They looked to see Tessa, Mornecai and Celina walking over to them.

"Are you all right, Kirbie?" Mornecai asked her.

"I was just wondering… what if this ends up being all for naught?"

Celina was caught off-guard. "Are you thinking…"

"I mean… what if we make it to Coverdale, and Kaseya ends up defeating us, and Coverdale stays in her hands?"

Tessa was surprised. "Listen to you. You're the most

confident girl in the world. No matter what had faced you, you were always the bravest of us all, not showing a shade of doubt. Why are you doubting yourself now?"

"It's just that... well, we've never faced anyone like Kaseya before. In other battles I can nearly predict what's going to happen. But for some reason, with Kaseya... I just don't know what to expect, and it scares me to think about it."

"Life is funny like that," Celina spoke. "Sometimes I feel the same way you do, but I push on now because of those who have suffered. I'm not afraid of death, and if I die doing what I believe in, it'll be worth it."

Mako wrapped her arm around Kirbie. "I feel the same way you do, Kirbie, but we mustn't give up."

"Of course not. I'm not saying to give up."

"Just like any other fight, sweetie, we just have to believe that we will be victorious, and that we can set things right for Coverdale. I believe we *can* defeat Kaseya, and I'm not going to let anything make me believe any different."

"Perhaps we can help you as well," said a voice. The four heroes turned to see Lisa, along with Willshire Kingdom's army.

Tessa and Lisa hugged. "You're a little late, aren't you?" Tessa responded.

"We're sorry, we got held up on the way here," Lisa told her. "We battled some of Kaseya's troops in Esterton."

Kirbie hugged Lisa tightly. "I'm so glad you're here."

"We're happy to help, Kirbie. Let's get this over with so we can save Luna."

The army then continued their journey to Wolford.

Tanna made her way back to the dungeon to talk to Luna and the others, again taking them bowls of soup. Luna and the others walked over to her as the guards entered the room.

"Tessa and Kirbie are heading to Wolford to battle Avilla. I just got word that Willshire Kingdom's army is heading there as well. Mother sent more troops there to battle them without my knowledge. I'm certain she's figuring out what I am doing, so this may be the last time you hear from me."

Timothy walked over and hugged Tanna. "I thank you so much for your help, Tanna. I'm sorry things have come to this."

"I should be the one who's sorry. My mother has ruined all our lives. I don't think I would want to live with her being in charge. I'm sure once she's secured Coverdale that she'll go after all of the Exodus."

"Our only hope then may be for Tessa and Kirbie to defeat her," Luna mentioned.

"So, this is what you've been doing, you traitor."

Minato and Haruto tackled the soldier. Tanna walked over to him, and without saying a word, pulled out her sword and stabbed the soldier.

"Tanna, you need to get out of here," Tamera suggested.

"Where is there to go? Kaseya will hunt me down and kill me."

"Go find Tessa and Kirbie," Tamera stated. "You said they were headed to Wolford. They can help you."

"I believe I should stay here. And if I die, so be it."

Saying nothing more, Tanna walked out of the dungeon. Minato and Haruto grabbed the soldier's body and disposed of it.

"Do you really think Tessa and Kirbie can beat Kaseya?" Max questioned.

"I sure hope so," Luna answered.

Chapter 10

The Attack on Coverdale

Kirbie, Tessa, Celina, Mako and Willshire's army had reached Wolford, and all were alert and watching all around them, waiting to be attacked.
"It's so quiet here, Celina," said Tessa.
"Too quiet," Celina followed.
"Let's head for the town square," Kirbie instructed.

As the group reached the square, they suddenly saw themselves surrounded by Kaseya's soldiers. Then Avilla approached the group, with sheer anger in her eyes.
"This ends here," Avilla stated. "I will get my revenge and you all will die."
"Revenge?" Kirbie asked, puzzled. "What did we ever do to you?"
"You killed my mother!" Avilla yelled. Tears began to fall from her eyes. "In Esterton, you killed her... you took her away from me. Now your mother will know how it feels when I take you away from her!"
The soldiers swarmed Kirbie and the others as Avilla stood back, thinking the horde of soldiers would destroy Kirbie and the army. Kirbie fought with all her might using her magic swords, Lisa used her sword and fighting skills, Celina killed many with her sword, Mornecai used his strength, and Mako did so with her

laser guns.

After several minutes of fighting, Avilla was beginning to lose confidence as she saw Kaseya's army had not stopped Willshire's soldiers. She decided to join in the battle, pulling out her double-sided sword. She started taking down some of the soldiers from Willshire Kingdom.

But even with Avilla's help, Willshire's soldiers managed to overtake Kaseya's army, with Kirbie taking down the last soldier. Avilla was so overwhelmed with emotion as she fell to her knees, crying loudly.

Kirbie walked over to Avilla, holding her sword. With tears still falling down her cheeks, Avilla looked up at Kirbie.

"What are you waiting for?" Avilla yelled at Kirbie. "Go on and kill me! Because of you, I've got nothing to live for anyway!"

Kirbie was feeling compassion for Avilla. "It doesn't have to be this way." Kirbie let her sword dissipate.

Still angered, Avilla grabbed her sword and lunged at Kirbie, however she stopped and showed a shocked look on her face. Kirbie was startled for a moment as well until she looked over to see Celina standing next to her, with her sword stabbed into Avilla's stomach. She then pulled her sword from Avilla's body, and Avilla fell to the ground, dead.

Kirbie then began to tear up as she hugged Celina.

"I'm sorry," Kirbie stated. "I let my guard down. I won't do it again."

"It's okay now, Kirbie," Celina assured her. "Let's just make our way to Coverdale and save everyone."

"That's the best thing I've heard all day."

The group got back onto the ship and made their way to Coverdale.

Tanna walked once again up to Kaseya. She was worried of what may happen, but figured if she would avoid her mother, that it would bring about suspicion.

"Mother, Avilla has failed us as well," she reported. "Collin and his army are making their way here."

Kaseya stood up from the throne. "I see. So, all of my family have failed me..." She looked over at Tanna. "And they weren't the only ones."

She slapped Tanna across her face. She was stunned as she placed her hand over where Kaseya had slapped her.

"Mother, what are you doing?"

"I know you've been helping them behind my back! How could you do this to your own mother?"

"Mother, please! I'm sorry..."

"Enough! I should kill you where you stand... Guards!"

Two other soldiers came up to Kaseya and Tanna.

"Put her in the dungeon with the others. Then once we destroy Kirbie and her army, she will die with the rest of them."

The soldiers brought Tanna down to Minato and Haruto.

"She is to be put in the dungeon: Kaseya's orders," the soldier told Minato. "She has betrayed us all."

"How dare you, you traitor," Minato spoke. Haruto unlocked the door as Minato grabbed Tanna's arm. Then Minato forcefully tossed Tanna into the dungeon before Haruto then shut the door and locked it. The other soldiers left the room.

Tanna got back on her feet, and Timothy walked over to her, and they hugged once again. Then Luna and the others approached her. Tamera hugged her as well.

"I'm very sorry, Tanna," Minato told her. "I didn't want to give us away."

"It's all right. You were very convincing."

"What's going on?" Laura wondered.

"Mother found out I was helping Kirbie and Willshire's army."

"Did you find out anything else?" Luna asked.

"Yes, Kirbie defeated Avilla, and they are on their way here."

"We're gonna be rescued!" Max said excitedly.

"Don't get your hopes up yet," Tamera stated. "Remember, Kaseya's army is huge. It's gonna be quite a battle for us."

"Sheesh, way to kill the mood, Tamera," Max grumbled.

Kirbie and the rest of the army stood firm as they became surrounded by Kaseya's army in front of the Seiland Pass, outside of Coverdale. Many of Kaseya's goons were standing tall on top of the mountains and hills surrounding them, with arrows pointed to them. Kirbie, Celina, Mornecai, Mako and Lisa stood in front of the troops, all of them holding hands. Kaseya and more of her troops approached the small army. Three soldiers then approached the group.

"You and Queen Luna have done wonders for Coverdale, Kirbie," said the soldier. "You have amazed Queen Kaseya with the fighting skills that you and your warriors possess, even killing her most valiant warriors. And even despite your blasphemies against her, the queen is willing to forgive and forget the past, and look into the future. She is willing to let you and Queen Luna keep hold of Coverdale and rule it as only she has done these past few years, and even more so, will let you be my admiral for all of Coverdale Island, that is if you and Queen Luna are willing to submit to her awesome power and declare her the god of Coverdale Island, and soon, all of Exodus."

Kirbie, holding her swords, thought for a moment about the offer given to her. She then looked back at the soldiers, each of them who had given their very honor of dying for her and all of Coverdale, and the rest of Exodus.

"You should listen to me, Kirbie," Kaseya told her. "Think of those you love."

Kirbie responded, "I *am* thinking about them, and they would support me in saying I will never join you."

Kirbie threw one of her swords. It struck the soldier beside Kaseya before he had a chance to do anything, and he fell to the ground, dead.

"DESTROY THEM!" Kaseya commanded.

The soldiers fired their arrows. The others were able to use their weapons or magic to block the arrows. As Willshire Kingdom's army began cutting down the many soldiers, Kirbie threw one of her swords at Kaseya. Although Kaseya tried to move out of the way, the sword managed to graze the side of her stomach. Kaseya stumbled backwards after getting hit. She looked to see blood pouring from the wound. Fear gripped her face, followed by sheer anger.

Tessa and Celina made their way quickly into the castle, taking down the soldiers that were guarding it. Then they made their way downstairs to the dungeon.

"Tessa, they are in here!" shouted Haruto.

Tessa and Celina charged at the soldiers.

"Stop!" Minato pleaded. "We're on your side!"

"It's true!" Luna told them.

Tessa and Celina calmed themselves as Haruto opened the door. Tessa went into the dungeon and immediately hugged Luna. Then she hugged Tamera, Camille and Timothy.

"I'm so glad you're safe," Luna said, crying.

"Unfortunately, it's not over yet," Celina informed them. "We still have to defeat Kaseya." She then noticed Tanna. "Who's this young girl?"

"I am Tanna. My mother locked me in here when she found out I betrayed her."

"It's the truth," Timothy responded, his arms wrapped around her. "She's done everything in her power to make sure we were safe."

"I thank you for doing so. Let's not waste any more time and get back out on the battlefield."

Everyone made their way out of the castle.

Kaseya saw that the prisoners had escaped the castle and had joined in on the battle. Even Tanna was helping Kirbie.

"It's time I put an end to this," Kaseya noted. She sneaked her way to where Luna was at, Kirbie saw what Kaseya was up to.

"Luna, look out!" Kirbie cried.

As Luna turned in the opposite direction, Kaseya quickly lunged her sword into Luna's chest, stabbing through her heart. Luna got a shocked look on her face before she closed her eyes and took her last breath. Kaseya then pulled her sword out of Luna's body, and her body fell to the ground, lifeless.

"Luna!" Kirbie cried out loudly.

Kirbie, with her swords still in her hands, charged quickly at Kaseya, filled with much anger. Kaseya swung her sword first. Kirbie blocked. Kaseya and Kirbie began colliding their swords at a fast pace, but Kaseya was able to keep up with every move. Kirbie flew back and threw several orbs of purple fire at Kaseya, but Kaseya blocked them by placing a force field over herself.

Kirbie then tried to strike Kaseya with her sword, but the force field absorbed the blow.

Kaseya suddenly punched Kirbie as she began to glow a blood-red flame, and she flew back a distance from Kaseya, sliding back across the ground. Kirbie slowly got back up and approached Kaseya once again. Kaseya once again punched Kirbie with all her might, and Kirbie slammed to the ground with much force.

"Kirbie!" Tamera cried out, seeing what had happened to her. She ran over to try stopping Kaseya as she went to strike her once more, but Tamera blocked it by forming a wall of ice in front of Kirbie. But the force of the punch broke the ice. It still managed to stop the punch from hitting Kirbie. Kaseya suddenly got hit by what resembled a smoke bomb. As she looked to her left, she then got hit by another smoke bomb on the right. Distracted, that gave Tessa the opportunity to run in with great speed and get Kirbie away from Kaseya.

"We're getting pummeled out here!" Tessa called out.

Kirbie had closed her eyes, losing consciousness. She then began to dream, seeing herself surrounded by light. She then saw herself being covered in a shimmering fiery light. "I'll always be with you," a voice simply said as the fiery light absorbed into Kirbie's body.

Kirbie opened her eyes.

Kaseya then saw Tanna coming up to her. "Mother, please stop this!"

"You think I'm ever going to listen to you, traitor?"

Kaseya began to build a red ball of light from her hands. She then shot a stream of light towards Tanna. Tanna thought this would be the end of her life. She then saw she was very much alive. She looked to her left and was amazed. In front of her was

Kirbie, who was glowing a spectacularly bright color of purple fire. She then formed two swords in her hands that were designed like Avilla's, with the smooth blade on the one side of each sword and the jagged blade on the other.

Kaseya jumped at Kirbie with her sword. Kaseya then swung her sword at Kirbie, who blocked it. Kaseya and Kirbie then began to slam their swords against each other's again at a fast face, but Kirbie was getting to where she was going so much faster than Kaseya. The others were amazed to see how graceful Kirbie was, looking again as if she were dancing.

Kirbie then was able to break Kaseya's sword with hers. Kaseya was shocked as she looked up to Kirbie, wide-eyed.

Kirbie tripped Kaseya up, and Kaseya fell to the ground. She then got up to her knees, still not wanting to give up. Kirbie then began to form a fiery ball of light between her hands. Kirbie then threw the large fireball at Kaseya, and her body quickly evaporated.

Kirbie looked around to see that her army had captured the remaining soldiers. Tamera walked over to Kirbie, hugging her tightly.

"I'm so proud of you, Kirbie," Tamera told her.

Tears fell from Kirbie's eyes. "It means so much to me to hear you say that."

They then looked to see Mornecai carrying Luna's body. Everyone gathered around Mornecai, and were crying in the process, mourning their loss.

"Luna..." Tamera said softly. She kissed Luna on her cheek. Then Timothy approached her, placing his hand on her cheek. Tamera hugged Timothy as she wept. Tanna then walked over.

"I'm just so sorry for what my family did to all of you. I

know I'll never be able to repay you for all the destruction they have done."

Timothy and Tamera hugged Tanna. "I forgive you, Tanna. I know it wasn't your fault."

Tanna was shocked to hear Timothy say that. Tanna hugged Timothy back as she began to cry softly.

A week later, Timothy, Heather, Kirbie, Camille, Max and Tamera had made their way out of the castle. They were each holding a bouquet of red, white and blue roses. They then walked over to the cemetery, where many crosses were set up to commemorate those who had lost their lives in the war. Each cross had the soldier's name, date of birth and date of death.

They all first walked over to two gravestones. One stone read, "Minoru, October 14, 1987 — March 7, 2021; Celestia, September 13, 1990 — March 7, 2021: Forever in our hearts."

Then they walked over to a gravestone setting in the middle of the cemetery. A circle of large stones surrounded the gravesite, aside from an opening that Camille walked through to get to the stone. She fell to her knees as she looked at the stone, which said: "King Lorius of Coverdale, 'The Beloved', August 19, 1986- March 7, 2021." Next to it was a newer gravestone that read, "Queen Luna of Coverdale, the Gold Angel, September 29, 1988- September 12, 2026."

Camille laid the roses in front of the grave.

Tamera and Max couldn't help but cry as she and Kirbie placed some roses on Minoru and Celestia's grave. Timothy then hugged Tamera and Kirbie hugged Heather. Then Kirbie kissed Timothy on his forehead.

"Please, don't leave us, Timothy," Tamera told him. "Promise me…"

"I promise, baby, with all my heart."

The following day, friends, family and other citizens of Coverdale gathered for Camille's coronation. In a different room of the castle, Tamera was combing Camille's long blue hair. Tamera could see tears forming in Camille's eyes.

"Are you okay, beautiful?" Tamera asked.

Camille sighed. "I knew that one day I was gonna have to go through this, but I didn't think it was going to be so soon."

Tamera stopped brushing Camille's hair. "I understand. I still haven't accepted what happened to Luna."

Camille stood up and she hugged Tamera, not wanting to let her go as they cried together.

"We're gonna have to get made up again," Tamera stated.

That got Camille to laugh as she wiped the tears from her eyes. At that moment, the door behind them opened to reveal Kirbie.

"They're ready for you, my queen," Kirbie told them.

Tamera and Camille walked out of the room with an arm wrapped around each other.

In the throne room, as the double doors opened, and everyone stood up to see Camille making her way to the throne, where an archbishop stood beside. She stopped in front of the archbishop, who was holding an orb and scepter.

Next to walk down the aisle was Kirbie, who was holding a large necklace that was worn by Luna. Kirbie made her way to Camille, placing the necklace around her neck. Camille could not hold back the tears as she remembered Luna. Kirbie and Camille hugged each other.

"You'll do great, Camille," Kirbie assured her.

"I hope so. Thank you, Kirbie. I love you."

Next was Tamera, who was holding the crown. Tamera walked up to Camille and she placed the crown on her head.

"You look incredible, my queen," Tamera told her.

Camille and Tamera then hugged. "Thank you, Tamera. I love you so much."

"I love you too, Camille."

Tamera stepped away, standing by Kirbie. Camille then turned to the archbishop, who prayed, "Our precious Heavenly Father, I pray for Queen Camille as she begins her new journey as the Queen of Coverdale Island. Lord, I know her heart is heavy, as all our hearts are, with the losses we have endured in our lives. I humbly pray that you help to guide Queen Camille in the path that you would want her to go down, and she continues the legacy that Queen Luna left behind as a loving and caring queen. Blessed be your name, Lord, and may your will be done, in the precious name of Jesus Christ we pray. Amen."

"Amen," the audience called out.

The archbishop then handed the orb and scepter to Camille. She turned to the gathering of people, holding the orb and scepter in front of her.

"Ladies and gentlemen, by the power vested in me by our lord and savior, I present to you Queen Camille of Coverdale!"

"All hail the queen!" everyone called out, repeating three times before breaking out in applause.

Tamera again approached Camille, and once again they hugged. Then Kirbie, Max, Timothy, Heather and Tessa joined in, wishing Camille well in her new journey in life.

Chapter 11

The Invasion

It was a typical day in the World of Exodus. One month had passed since Camille became the new queen of Coverdale. Sitting in his lonely castle, Behrlin was in his throne room with frustration on his face as he thought about what he needed to do to kidnap Princess Marietta and become the ruler of all the Willshire Kingdom. Behrlin had short brown hair and brown eyes, and was dressed in a hooded dark brown tunic with red trim, with matching pants.

Behrlin's most loyal servant, Solara, entered the throne room and cautiously approached the angered king. Solara had white hair and red eyes, and was wearing a white leotard with blue armor that covered her chest and went down to her knees on each side of her body.

"My beloved Behrlin," Solara saluted, "what do you want to do about Princess Marietta and her sisters? Just say the word, and I will put a stop to them."

Behrlin slammed his fist down on the arm of the throne. "Those pesky women have foiled my plans for the last time! Assemble the troops, immediately!"

"Yes, my king."

Solara was saddened to see that Behrlin was still obsessed with Marietta as she walked out of the throne room, leaving the doors open.

"Why won't you notice me, my lord?" she said softly.

As Behrlin stared blankly at the opening, suddenly, he noticed Solara flying into the door frame to the throne room. She then fell to the floor, knocked out.

"Solara!" Behrlin cried out.

The two guards standing by the doors went to check out what was happening, but then they were thrown further down the hallway. Behrlin stood up from his throne to see a blackened wolf and an armored knight walking through the doorway over Solara. The soldier pointed what looked like a gun at Behrlin.

"Who do you think you are, coming in here?" Behrlin shouted.

"I am Cassian," the man simply said.

"How dare you, barging into my castle..." Behrlin spoke.

"This is our castle now, and you are our prisoners," the soldier interrupted.

A soldier fired off one of his weapons, trapping Solara into a black netting. In sheer anger, Behrlin charged at the wolf and soldier, but the soldier simply fired his gun again, trapping Behrlin as well.

As the sun was setting over Willshire Kingdom, Laura and Lisa were spending time together at Marietta's Castle. Queen Marietta had very long violet-colored hair and violet eyes, and wore a sparkling purple dress that had designs of roses and leaves outlined in sparkled white, and had deep purple armor over her chest and shoulders, along with nude pantyhose.

Laura and Lisa were trying to relax after having the battle with Behrlin. Marietta walked onto the balcony where Laura and Lisa were sitting by a table looking out over the kingdom, carrying a tray that had a pitcher of lemonade and three cups.

"I figured you may want some refreshments," Marietta stated. She sat the tray on the table and poured each hero and herself a glass of the lemonade.

"Thank you, my queen," Lisa told her.

"I'm so thankful to you both. Once again, you two rescued me from the clutches of that evil Behrlin. I'm deep in your debt."

"Maybe we should teach you how to fight, and then he may think twice about trying to kidnap you," Laura commented.

The other two laughed at the comment.

Just as the heroes were taking a drink of their lemonade, they suddenly saw a large explosion in the distance. The shock of seeing the explosion caused them to spit out their drinks.

"What was that?" Lisa cried out.

"It looked like it came from Behrlin's castle!" Marietta pointed it out. "Maybe you should check it out."

Laura sighed as she put her glass down. "A hero's work is never done. Let's go."

The two heroes left Marietta's castle.

Laura and Lisa cautiously approached Behrlin's castle with a wonder as to what caused the massive explosion. This journey into the castle was nothing new to them, as they had just come from there. Yet as they reached the castle and watched the sky fill up with clouds that had a deep, nearly black, shade to them, something, to them, just felt totally unusual, but they couldn't figure out what it was.

When they arrived there, they were puzzled with what they saw.

"Laura," Lisa said, shakily. "This isn't Behrlin's castle…"

"What is this?" Laura asked in confusion.

Laura couldn't understand what was going on. The castle

standing in front of them was totally different in style and size from what they had just previously seen.

"Come on," Laura commanded. "Let's go inside."

The heroes leaned against the wall of the front of the castle, on each side of the door. Laura, as quietly as she could, slowly opened the left door. She peeked around the doorway and looked into the darkened room, which appeared to be empty. She nodded to Lisa, signaling that it was clear, and the two women made their way cautiously into the lobby. As they got halfway into the lobby, several of the torches on the walls suddenly formed fire on them, and the women found themselves surrounded by a horde of darkened spirits. These spirits had an unusual dull appearance: There were no pupils or colors of any kind in their eyes, and they looked darker in color than usual, their skin having a solid black tone.

Laura and Lisa couldn't fathom why they appeared that way. Just as they got prepared to fight against the clan, they heard someone approaching. The spirits made way for the armored soldier who attacked Behrlin and Solara earlier.

"For trespassing here," said the soldier, "you will now be our prisoners."

Laura grabbed her sword and proceeded to strike down one of the soldiers, who turned into dust. This confused Laura. As the horde of darkened warriors surrounded the women, another soldier pulled out his weapon. Saying nothing, he fired the weapon twice, hitting each one and trapping them into a black netting. They tried to free themselves, to no avail.

"Take them," the soldier demanded. Some of the army carried the heroes out of the room.

The following morning, Kaiden, a guardian for Princess Nala, woke up to the sun shining brightly into his eyes. He squinted for a moment to get his eyes to adjust before opening them again away from the sunlight. Then he smiled as he crawled out of his bed. He then walked into another room, closing the door behind him.

Moments later, Kaiden, who had bluish white hair and gold eyes, walked out in his regular clothing: a blue tunic, dark brown pants with brown and gold armor. He grabbed his brownish-colored bow, his bag of arrows and his sword before walking out of his home. He breathed deeply the fresh air as he checked out his surroundings.

Kaiden went to head off on his horse in a westerly direction, towards Princess Nala's castle in the village of Littleton, when he heard a loud scream not too far from him. Kaiden stopped, got off his horse, and ran towards the source of the scream to see what was happening. Just before reaching the castle, he became shocked to see the "Maniton," an enormous ship hovering over the castle. Kaiden then looked to see a large army of spirited beings falling out from the ship.

"What is going on?" Kaiden said to himself in confusion. "What is the Maniton doing here in Littleton?"

Kaiden then noticed Princess Nala, who had silver-blue hair and matching eyes, wearing a long blue form-fitting lace gown that had ruffles across the back, hanging down from her waist. Nala was standing against a tree, with a stain of blood on her left shoulder that had soaked into the strap of her blue dress.

Breathing heavier, she got ready to fight some more against an army of warriors that had surrounded her. Not only was she confused about why she and her kingdom were being attacked by the clan, but it was peculiar to her the way these spirits looked to her. Nonetheless, with her sword drawn, Nala was ready to defend herself the best she could.

The spirits began to attack. Nala sliced the first spirit that met her with her sword, and the spirit just exploded into what resembled a medium-gray dust, and then the dust dissipated into thin air. This surprised Nala. Others went to attack, and Nala fought them off the best she could, with the same dusty explosion on the other enemies. Then a spirit jumped towards Nala. She covered her face with her arms. Out from above her an arrow shot through the spirit, and it blew up into dust. Nala uncovered her face and looked up quick enough to see Kaiden falling down from the tree and landing on his feet next to her.

"Are you okay, my princess?" Kaiden asked her.

"So far," she simply told him. "Thank you for your help."

Kaiden revealed his sword, and he and Nala went into their fighting stances.

The evil spirits again charged, and Nala and Kaiden, becoming separated from each other, kicked, punched, and sliced up whoever charged at them until there were none of the spirits remaining.

Kaiden, with his hands at his knees, tried to catch his breath. The battle was a bit exhausting. Suddenly he heard a blast, and then a loud scream from Nala. Just as he turned around, he looked just in time to see Nala now trapped in the black netting.

"Kaiden, help!" Nala cried out.

But before Kaiden could do anything about it, he suddenly got hit by a black beam, and he was trapped in the netting. The wolf and the soldier who was holding his weapon walked up to the two heroes. Then the wolf grabbed Kaiden's master sword.

Unaware of the chaos going on, the citizens of Catterine Village were going through their normal routine. A young cat girl named

Hanna walked out of her home with a laundry basket. She had dark gray long hair and shiny purple eyes, and wore a black and white maid outfit that had orange accents, along with black and white striped stockings. She sat down the basket, getting ready to hang clothes on the clothesline. A little ghost that had cat ears, that she named Catera, hovered near her.

Then Hanna noticed her two friends, Mia and Mimi. Mia had silver-black hair and golden-hazel eyes, and was wearing a black-strapped shirt and medium purple leggings, while Mimi had pink hair and ice-blue eyes, and was wearing a white tank top with pink trim, and black leggings.

Hanna was excited to see her two friends as she hugged them.

"I've missed you girls," Hanna said excitedly. "How have you been?"

"We're good," Mimi answered. "What 'cha up to?"

"As you can see, just some laundry."

"That sounds like fun," Mia said sarcastically.

At that moment, Hanna's father, Joseph, who had gray hair that faded to blue, with red eyes, came out of the house in a panic. He was dressed in a black sweater and pants.

"Girls! Get in here this instant!"

"Dad, what's going on?" Hanna asked in confusion.

"There's trouble on the way! Come on!"

As Joseph and the three girls made their way into the house, they could hear explosions coming from a distance, heading ever closer to where they were.

"Get down in the basement!" Joseph demanded. They did so. Mimi started crying in fear, with Hanna and Mia trying to comfort her.

Joseph made his way back out of the house, and he looked

up to the sky to see the Maniton overhead. This puzzled him.

Out from the ship came down more of the spirits. This made Joseph even more troubled.

"What is this?" he asked himself as he looked around him, seeing the spirits invade the town. Joseph grabbed his staff and began attacking some of the spirits. But before he could do much damage, one of the spirits fired off their weapon and trapped him in the netting. Then the spirits grabbed him and placed him on the ship. Then a black-haired wolf approached one of the soldiers.

"We head for Spirit Land," the wolf ordered. "Get ready."

The soldiers boarded the ship and left to head for Spirit Land.

After hearing silence, Hanna, Mia and Mimi made their way out of the basement. They were in complete shock to find the village left in ruins.

"What are we going to do?" Mimi asked. Hanna and Mia could not answer.

Chapter 12

Spirit Land

At Spirit Land, many of the residents began to panic as they noticed the Maniton approaching. A princess named Olivia was the ruler of Spirit Land, who watched over the village with her angelic guardian, Michael.

Olivia had blonde hair and green eyes, and wore a blue ruffled shirt worn over a white dress, while Michael had white hair and dark-blue eyes and was wearing a dark-blue jacket and pants, with a white buttoned shirt under the jacket. The jacket had brown trim.

Olivia and Michael saw the Maniton approaching the cloud. Michael flew up into the sky in front of the cloud and in front of the Maniton, but before he could react, he was hit by a black beam, and was trapped in the netting. He fell to the ground before being caught by some blackened spirits.

Olivia was horrified with what happened to Michael. Her eyes began to glow, and she shot out a large beam of light from her hands. At that moment, the Maniton fired off a series of deep black beams towards the light. The beams collided with each other, sending off a large blast.

In the meantime, Tamera, Kirbie, Heather and Timothy were making their way back towards Coverdale. Suddenly the quartet saw the large blast that came in the direction of Spirit Land. They looked to see Spirit Land under attack by the Maniton.

"What kind of ship is that?" Timothy asked.

"That's the Maniton!" Tamera mentioned. "What's it doing attacking Spirit Land?"

Kirbie ran towards Spirit Land.

"Kirbie, wait!" Tamera cried out as she ran after Kirbie. Timothy and Heather followed.

Kirbie noticed the Maniton was firing off beams of black towards Spirit Land, but was being held off at the moment by Olivia.

"What's going on?" Kirbie wondered.

Olivia fought with all her might to try protecting Spirit Land, but the power of the beams being fired by the Maniton was just too much for her. The black beams struck Olivia with extreme force, trapping her in netting. She was then taken by other spirits to the Maniton.

Kirbie saw the Maniton fire the black beams at Spirit Land. The cloud that surrounded the village had turned from a pure white to a deep black.

The Maniton then flew inside the cloud. The armored soldier appeared out of the cloud in his cruiser with four shiny crystals known as the "Diamonds of Allure." He then returned to the Maniton and the ship made its way heading for Behrlin's castle.

Then Kirbie heard something that sounded like a gunshot. She saw a darkened beam fly at her. Kirbie moved out of the way of the beam. She ran towards where Tamera, Heather and Timothy were standing, but she saw them get hit by a beam and became trapped in the netting. Tamera formed her magical ice ax in her hands and freed Timothy and Heather of the netting. Kirbie saw more beams coming at them. Tamera pulled Timothy out of the way. She, Heather and Timothy ran into the bushes. Kirbie then joined them. They could see some blackened spirits who had flown down from a smaller ship to see if they could find them.

After not seeing where they had disappeared to, the smaller ship headed back to the Maniton. Then two spirits flying the smaller ship made their way over to their leader. "Master, we can't find the others."

The soldier smiled. "No matter. We have Olivia in our possession. Let's get back to the castle."

Kirbie, Tamera and Timothy watched as the Maniton flew away from Spirit Land.

"They've taken the Diamonds of Allure," Kirbie pointed out.

"What are we going to do, Tamera?" Timothy questioned.

Suddenly Timothy heard what sounded like branches ruffling behind him. Timothy quickly turned to see someone attacking him, and he drew his sword to block the sword the attacker was using. The attacker landed on her feet and the two stared at each other. Timothy then recognized who the attacker was.

"Noelle? Is that you?"

Noelle took a good look at the man looking at her. "Timothy?"

Timothy smiled as he nodded his head positively. Then Noelle's eyes widened and pure joy showed on her face. "Timothy!" Noelle cried out. She hugged Timothy tightly. "My goodness, I haven't seen you in ages!"

Noelle had long bluish-white hair and piercing blue eyes, and was wearing a white leotard with a white mesh skirt, and white pantyhose.

"I've missed you so much, Timothy," she said as she blushed.

"I've missed you too, Noelle. You're just as beautiful as ever! What are you doing with yourself these days?"

"I'm a warrior now. I've come a long way from when I first met you."

"You certainly have." Timothy then looked over to Tamera and Heather. "Come here: I want you to meet my family."

Timothy then led Noelle over to Kirbie, Tamera and Heather.

"This is my beautiful girlfriend, Tamera, my good friends, Heather and Kirbie." Timothy held Tamera's hand. "Everyone, this is Noelle. I met her a few years ago in Coverdale."

"Nice to meet you all."

"Would you know why the Maniton attacked Spirit Land?" Tamera questioned.

"Why would Kelly Rose attack us after all we have done for Ebalon?" Kirbie followed.

Noelle lowered her sword. "Right now, we're not sure what happened. We do know it's not Kelly Rose that's flying the ship. She has been leading her people away from Ebalon to safety in some caves not far from there."

The group looked back at Spirit Land.

"So, now what?" Timothy questioned.

"I'm going to Willshire Kingdom. Maybe we can find out what's happening." Tamera then looked over at Noelle. "Care to join us, Noelle?"

"I would love to, Tamera."

The group of heroes walked on, heading for Willshire Kingdom.

"It's so good to see you again, Timothy," Noelle told him. "I never thought I would see you again. I've missed you so much."

"I've missed you too, Noelle." They hugged.

"I love your outfit," Tamera commented. "I probably wouldn't look too good in that."

"I think you would," Noelle told her.

"Me too," Timothy followed. That made Tamera blush.

At Wolford, Mornecai, Celina and Sandra were heading back for the village with Noah. Suddenly they became surrounded by several spirits. They all became full of fear as the demonic wolf stood in front of them. Celina drew her weapon. Behind her was his armored soldier holding his weapon. The wolf roared greatly.

Before Celina could react, the wolf jumped onto her, pinning her to the ground. Mornecai charged, but was quickly trapped by the netting fired at him.

"I am Lycan, servant of the Darkness," he announced. "Take me to your leader or you will die."

"My… leader?" Celina asked, confused.

Lycan became forceful. "Where is he?"

"Is he talking about Queen Camille?" Noah asked.

"A queen? Where is she?"

Noah was fearful for Celina. "She's in Coverdale!"

"Noah, no!" Celina cried out.

"We take control of this village," Lycan ordered, "and then we head for that castle."

"Yes, my lordship." A spirit made its way over to Celina, Sandra and Noah, firing off a black beam at each of them, trapping them in the netting.

It was another typical day for Lisa at her home that sat outside of Willshire Kingdom. She was getting herself ready for the party she was to attend at Princess Marietta's castle. Suddenly she heard a knock at her door.

Lisa thought maybe her friend, Laura had arrived to take her to the party. She calmly walked to the door and opened it. To her confusion, she didn't see anyone around. She walked outside to observe her surroundings. She figured it may have been somebody playing a joke on her.

Lisa then turned to see Spirit Land was discolored. She became overwhelmed with wonder.

"What's happening with Spirit Land?" Lisa questioned.

Suddenly Lisa heard something that sounded like a loud chirp. As she turned towards where he heard the noise, she saw a black beam coming straight at her. Before she could react, the beam hit her, trapping her in the black netting.

The leader laughed maniacally as two other soldiers then went to grab Lisa. Then out of nowhere shot a magical purple fireball that hit the spirit's weapon. The three looked toward where the fireball came from.

"Kirbie!" Lisa cried out.

The leader noticed Tamera, Kirbie, Timothy, Heather and Noelle positioned in their fighter's stance. Noelle, Kirbie and Timothy pulled out their swords, Heather had her bow, and Tamera formed her ice ax.

"Who are you," Kirbie questioned, "and what do you want with my friends?"

"I am Cassian, servant of the Darkness," he answered. "And who is this little angel?"

Noelle pointed her weapon at him. "I am Noelle. You will pay for what you have done."

Cassian pulled out his sword. "Kill the others!" he told his spirits. "I'll take care of Kirbie."

Cassian went to battle Kirbie as the other spirits went to grab Timothy, Tamera, Heather and Noelle. One spirit leaped towards Noelle, but Noelle simply spun around and stabbed the soldier with her sword. The spirit crashed to the ground and then exploded into dust. Timothy obliterated several others with his sword while Tamera struck others down with her ax and Heather was able to strike soldiers down with her bow and arrows.

Another spirit got into a massive swordfight with Noelle, but couldn't keep up with Noelle's speed. Noelle sliced the spirit in half, and the spirit turned to dust.

Cassian walked over towards Kirbie. He began swinging his sword at Kirbie but she would either block it with her weapons or would move out of the way. Kirbie swung her swords with great force, knocking Cassian's sword out of his hands. Cassian unexpectedly tripped Kirbie up, and she fell, but rolled back, still holding onto her swords. Cassian quickly grabbed his sword. Kirbie stood in her fighting stance as everyone stood beside her. Noelle stuck her tongue out at Cassian.

"You may have got us this time, princess," Cassian commented, "but we now have the Diamonds of Allure, and soon you'll *all* be finished."

The spirits made way to their craft and took off. Tamera walked over to Lisa.

"Are you okay, Lisa?" Tamera asked.

"Yeah," Lisa told her, and they hugged. "Thank you, everyone." She looked over to Noelle. "And thank you too, Noelle."

"You're very welcome, Lisa," Noelle replied.

"Is it true?" Tessa wondered. "Do they have the Diamonds of Allure?"

"Yes, it's true," Tamera answered in a saddened voice. "We're all in very grave danger, Tessa. I was told a wolf named Lycan was the one responsible."

"He also stole my ship and destroyed Ebalon," Noelle informed them.

"What are we to do about this situation?" Heather questioned.

"We are going to talk to Princess Marietta."

"Let's get moving," Noelle warned. "We don't have much time."

With that, the heroes headed to Marietta's castle.

Chapter 13

Ambushed

At Coverdale, outside of Queen Camille's castle, Tessa, Max and Tanna were walking around the courtyard.

"It's certainly beautiful here," Tanna mentioned.

"I have always loved being here," Tessa noted.

Tanna sighed. "I wonder when Timothy is getting back."

Tessa smiled. "You certainly think highly of him, don't you?"

"Well… when my mom was attacking Coverdale, he was the first to believe that I was on Queen Luna's side. He has done his best to watch over my well-being as well."

Tanna blushed. Tessa hugged her.

"You're not the only one who feels that way about Timothy. He also is so loved by Heather. Tamera's lucky to have him, and Kirbie also thinks the world of him. In fact, if I find someone to spend my life with, I hope he's as kind as Timothy is."

"I agree with you, Tessa," Max commented, knowing she still had feelings for him.

In the meantime, several soldiers were guarding the front gate. Suddenly there was a loud explosion. Several guards covered their faces to protect from the debris and dust. Then when they moved their arms to see after the dust settled, they looked to see Lycan and his spirits walking through the opening.

Lycan ignored the soldier's question, telling his spirits, "Destroy everything, and bring me their leader!"

Queen Camille woke up, hearing an explosion outside. She quickly jumped out of bed and looked out her window. She was shocked to see the castle being attacked by the army of strange beings. She could faintly see Max and Tanna and some of her soldiers attacking the clan.

Max and Tanna had pulled their weapons out and started slicing each enemy with it, only to have them explode into dust. Many of the soldiers were becoming trapped in a black netting. Suddenly Max heard a chirp and before she could react, she saw Max trapped in the netting.

"Max!" Tessa cried out.

As Tessa ran over to her, she heard the chirp again, seeing a beam come at her, but she blocked it. Tanna used her sword to slice Max out of the netting.

Camille ran downstairs, trying to make her way to the battleground. Before she could do so, the doors to the castle got blown off their hinges. Just then Lycan and the two spirits walked into the room to see Camille there.

"Where is your leader?" Lycan questioned.

"I am Queen Camille. I am the ruler of Coverdale."

Lycan laughed, full of excitement. "Excellent. Seize her!"

The spirits grabbed Camille and brought her over to Lycan.

"We rule this land now, Queen Camille," Lycan said to her. The he told his guards, "Take her to the ship."

Outside, Tessa tried to keep up with the sheer numbers of spirits coming at them. Then the spirit aimed its gun at Tessa. Max, out of instinct, pushed Tessa into the bushes as the spirit pulled the trigger. Max then became trapped in the netting. Tanna made her way again over to Max, but she then became trapped in the netting.

Some spirits tried to find Tessa but were unable to, as she had no choice but to retreat. They went back to their leader, who had Queen Camille.

"We couldn't find the dragon girl," said a spirit.

"We better get back," Lycan commanded. "She's as good as dead anyway."

They left the area. Unbeknownst to them, Tessa was hiding in one of the trees above. She waited until the spirits went out of sight. She then cautiously made her way back towards the castle.

Tamera, Timothy, Kirbie, Noelle and Heather arrived at Princess Marietta's castle. They walked into the throne room, where Princess Marietta and a number of guards were waiting.

"Your majesty," Kirbie said as she and the others bowed, "We are in grave danger. The Diamonds of Allure have been stolen, and now Lycan has Olivia and Michael for his prisoners."

"And Cassian, who we think is one of his goons, attacked us as well," Noelle noted.

"I am glad you are here," Marietta responded. "Where are Laura and Lisa?"

"We're not sure," Tamera stated. "Nobody has seen them, nor Kaiden and Princess Nala."

"We have to find them fast," Noelle spoke out.

Marietta mentioned, "I was told these men have kidnapped many of the other heroes in the World of Exodus, perhaps along with Laura and Lisa. Last we heard they had taken over Behrlin's castle. You must go to Behrlin's castle at once."

Timothy's phone rang. He recognized the name on the phone. "Tessa?"

"Timothy... we need you..."

Timothy noticed Tessa was breathing heavily. "Tessa, what's wrong?"

"Coverdale's been attacked! They've captured everyone here..."

"Hang on, sweetie. We're on our way."

Timothy hung up. "We need to get to Coverdale. The castle's been attacked."

The heroes left the castle, getting ready to embark on their adventure.

The group arrived at Coverdale, seeing much of the village and castle had been destroyed. Tamera was distraught as she fell to her knees.

"Don't worry," Timothy tried to assure her. "We'll get them back."

"Timothy, is that you?"

They turned to see Tessa approaching them. Tamera and Timothy ran over to her and she gave them a tight hug.

"I was so worried about you," Tamera told her. "Are you okay?"

"Yeah, they nearly got me too, but I managed to escape thanks to Max. They took her, Tanna and Queen Camille."

"We're on our way to Behrlin's castle. Please come with us."

"Absolutely."

Tamera, Timothy, Heather, Kirbie, Noelle and Tessa flew to Behrlin's castle to see if they could find out what was going on there. Kirbie landed the ship a short distance from the castle. As they approached, they were surprised at what they were looking at.

"What is this?" Tessa wondered. "This isn't Behrlin's castle."

"That's just too weird," Tamera spoke.

"Let's get closer," Kirbie told them.

The heroes sneaked closer behind some rocks by the bridge to what used to be Behrlin's castle. At that point Lycan crawled out from the Maniton, followed by several of his spirits. They met up with Cassian. Lycan appeared to be disappointed at Cassian for his failure to retrieve Tamera, Noelle and Tessa at the village. Then he expressed his disappointment to the spirits that went with him.

"We won't be able to stop them," Noelle noted. "We need help."

"I agree," Kirbie stated. "Let's get back to Willshire."

Lycan, Cassian and their spirits arrived at Princess Marietta's castle with their prisoners. Tanna, Max and Camille's body filled with fear as they noticed the darkened scenery of a castle that sat alone on a mountain surrounded by a deep opening that flowed of rushing water.

"Where are we?" Camille asked as they walked down a long hallway.

"Quiet, you," Lycan instructed. They entered into a darkened room, and Lycan walked up ahead of Camille.

"Master," Lycan spoke, "we have brought the ruler of Coverdale, Queen Camille."

The man turned around and revealed himself to everyone by taking off his helmet. The man had deep black hair and eyes with no pupils, wearing a full-body armor suit.

"Excellent," said the man. He walked over to her. "Allow me to introduce myself. I am Abaddon. You've met my right-hand men, Lycan and Cassian. We are fellow servants of the Darkness."

Camille looked puzzled. "The Darkness? What is all this about, that you would take me from my home and wreak havoc on our world?"

"That's none of your concern, queen."

"Master," called out Cassian. "We may have a problem."

Abaddon and Lycan walked over to Cassian and saw in the crystal ball the group heading back to Willshire Kingdom.

"A clear showing of your failure to capture them," Lycan criticized Cassian.

"Who are these cretins?" Abaddon questioned.

Camille saw who they were.

"Tamera," Tanna stated.

"Kirbie," Camille followed.

Abaddon heard Tanna and Camille speak but did not understand what they said. "What was that?" He approached Camille.

Camille became quiet, not wanting to answer.

Abaddon yelled, "Who are they? Tell me their names!"

Camille locked her lips, refusing to speak. She, Max and Tanna then tried to run away.

"After them, you imbeciles!" Lycan demanded.

"No!" Abaddon called out, and he extended his right hand. Suddenly Tanna, Max and Camille's feet came off the ground, with a black force field swarming around them.

"What's happening?" Camille said as she tried to free himself.

Then Tanna, Max and Camille felt themselves being pulled back into the room with the evildoers. Camille then was forced to face Abaddon. As the force field disappeared, Abaddon grabbed Camille around her neck.

"Don't make me hurt you, Queen Camille," Abaddon warned. "I can bring to you pain you have never felt in your life. Now tell me their names!"

Camille gave in. "The blue-haired woman is my sister, Tamera, and the blonde woman is Kirbie." Abaddon then sat Camille down but then continued to hold on to her. "The girl in red is Tanna, the soldier is Timothy and the white-haired girl is Heather. The dragon girl is Tessa, and the angel is called Noelle."

"So, they think they can rain on our parade?" Abaddon gloated. "Well, we'll just see about that."

"Destroy them," Lycan instructed Cassian, "and do not come back until you do!"

With that, Cassian saluted Lycan and left the room with several spirits.

"Take the prisoners to the dungeon," Abaddon said to Lycan.

"Yes, my lord."

The spirits led the prisoners to the cell where the other prisoners were held.

"Enjoy your new home," the spirit said to them.

Camille began to cry, fearful of the situation as Tanna tried to comfort her. Then Camille noticed someone else in the cell had approached her.

"I don't believe it," the man said in shock. "Queen Camille? Max?"

"Behrlin," Camille stated. Fearful that Behrlin was going to hurt them, Max formed her staff in her hands.

"Max, wait!" said a female voice. Max looked around Behrlin to see another angel approaching her. Camille recognized him.

"Michael?" Camille asked.

"Hello, Queen Camille," he greeted, and they hugged. "I am sorry to see you here as well."

Mornecai, Celina, Sandra and Noah walked over to Camille, Max, Tanna and Michael. Camille hugged Celina.

"Are your sisters okay?" Noah questioned.

"I hope so."

Camille saw others approach. They noticed it was Laura, Lisa, Kaiden, Princess Nala and Solara, along with other members of the World of Exodus.

"What is going on?" Camille questioned.

Laura answered, "Abaddon has the Diamonds of Allure in his possession. He's plotting to take over all of Exodus."

"Why is this happening?" Max asked.

"I don't know," Michael answered. "They've been pretty secretive."

"They will have to be pretty remarkable," Kaiden noted. "Abaddon's army has been really powerful so far. They also have Kelly Rose's ship."

Kaiden's words did not bring comfort to anyone.

Behrlin roared in anger. "I don't care who he thinks he is! He will pay for taking over my kingdom!"

"We will have to trust that they can accomplish their mission," Nala responded.

Upon arriving at Willshire Kingdom, Tamera, Kirbie, Tessa, Heather, Noelle and Timothy heard screaming and panic coming from the edge of town. Alarmed, the group hurried themselves towards where the screams were coming from. That's when they saw a dark Behrlin and several spirits terrorizing the townsfolk. Angered, Tessa approached the figure.

"Hold it, Behrlin," Tessa commanded. "What are you doing

here?"

"I'm going to fuel the Darkness by destroying you and your new friends," the fake Behrlin stated. "Now prepare for your doom."

With that, Behrlin shot fire out of his hands. Tessa rolled out of the way. She then charged at Behrlin, trying to strike him with her claws.

Several spirits charged in the other's direction. Timothy fought with Olympia while Heather fought with her bow, Noelle used her sword, and Tamera used her ice ax. They struck the soldiers with the weapons and they exploded into dust.

Behrlin went to strike Tessa, but Tessa jumped, landing on the fake Behrlin and pinning him to the ground. Then Tessa struck the fake Behrlin through the chest, and he exploded into dust.

"You've got some skills, Tessa," Noelle commented to her.

Tessa smiled. "As do you, Noelle. I'm glad you came to help us."

Then Timothy looked down at the dust that covered him. "That's so peculiar. Why are they turning to dust?"

"They are soulless beings," Tessa pointed out.

"I've never seen anything like this," Timothy noted.

"Believe me, my love," Tamera told him. "In the World of Exodus, anything can happen."

"We need to get to Marietta's castle," Noelle claimed.

As Kirbie was walking away, she thought she saw some kind of flash coming from some bushes. But when she looked over in the direction of the flash, she didn't see anything else out of the ordinary. She just shrugged her shoulders as she walked away and caught with the rest of the group.

The group arrived back at Marietta's castle to meet once

more with her.

"Welcome back," Marietta greeted. "I am glad you are back, and thank you for defeating that evil Behrlin. What did you find out?"

Tessa stated, "Lycan and his goons have taken over Behrlin's castle."

"In fact," Kirbie pointed out, "it wasn't even Behrlin's castle. It was a darker and... creepier castle."

"This is so much worse than I expected," Marietta stated. "I was told that Lycan has scattered three of the Diamonds of Allure at different locations. We're not sure where they are, though. It will be up to you to find them."

"Perhaps we can check out Catterine first," Tessa suggested.

"Yes, we must get going," Kirbie stated.

"What are we waiting for?" Heather said enthusiastically.

"No, Heather," Tamera replied, "I would like for you to stay here to continue to protect Coverdale and the Willshire Kingdom, please."

"I'll stay with them too," Tessa responded.

Heather was saddened. "But I want..."

Timothy grabbed Heather to hug her. "I know you do, sweetie, but Tamera's right. I think you'll be an even bigger help here. They're going to need you and your skills." Timothy kissed Heather's forehead. "Besides, somebody's gotta keep you out of trouble."

Heather laughed. "Sure, but who's gonna keep you out of trouble?"

"I'll try my best, I promise," Kirbie told her.

"Timothy, take this with you," Tessa said to him as she put a necklace around him. "My mother called it an 'Angelic Quartz'."

"Yes, you used it during our missions. It has the power to heal."

"Yes, as long as the person is still alive. You remember what I stated to use it?"

"Yes, thank you, Tessa," Timothy replied. He then gave Heather, Tanna and Tessa a tight hug. "I love you all so much."

"I love you, too, Timothy," they told him.

"And Noelle, I know your powers will come to good use as well. You all will be the Revolution; the ones who will bring back the light against the Darkness. Best of luck to you all, and God bless."

After walking out of Marietta's castle, Tamera stopped and looked over the side of the bridge down to the water flowing below her. She then thought about what happened with those she recognized as being her only family. She then pulled out a picture of her, Max, Minoru and Celestia standing together. A tear rolled down her cheek as Tamera looked over to see Timothy standing next to her.

"Is that your parents?" he asked.

"Yeah, that's Minoru and Celestia." Tamera stated. "I wish you could have met them."

Timothy wrapped his arms around Tamera as tears fell down her cheeks.

"We've lost so many already, Timothy," Tamera told him. "So many out there have lost someone they love because of stuff like this." Tamera sighed. "Why can't we all live in peace and love each other?"

"I wish it were that way too, Tamera. Life isn't fair at all, and people are very cruel. But that's why God put people like us together."

"I just… want everyone back with us. I miss them so much. I hope we can get this over with, and we can be back with the ones we love soon."

Timothy placed a hand on Tamera's cheek. "Don't worry. We'll save them."

Tamera hugged him tightly. "I know we will. Thank you, my love."

"Hey!" Kirbie called to them. "Are you lovebirds coming or what?"

Timothy and Tamera walked with Noelle and Kirbie away from the castle. Kirbie noticed that Timothy was holding Tamera and Noelle's hands. She then happened to catch another flash from behind her. Kirbie once again looked around to see where the flash came from.

"Kirbie, is everything okay?" Timothy questioned.

"I thought I saw something," Kirbie told him. "Perhaps my eyes are deceiving me."

Chapter 14

Palentine

At Abaddon's castle, Camille had the same worry as she got to thinking about the events that had unfolded, and if her family and friends were okay. She pulled out a picture of her and the others that was taken when they were together. Tears came to Camille's eyes as her heart became filled with worry.

Tanna woke up to see Camille staring at the picture of her family with Timothy and Heather. She sat down next to Camille.

"Didn't you get any rest last night, my queen?" Tanna asked her quietly.

"A little bit," Camille told her as she wiped the tears off her face. "It's hard to sleep with all this worry in my heart."

"I'm worried as well. That's such a wonderful picture of Timothy, Heather and Tamera."

"I agree. He's been so loyal to Tamera since they have gotten together. I don't know what I would do if something were to happen to them. And these girls… for all she had gone through in her life, she has certainly been a blessing, especially for Timothy."

"I feel the same way about all those that Abaddon has done this to."

"I sure hope we will be rescued," Camille responded.

"I believe they will succeed."

Camille sighed. "I wish I had your faith, Tanna."

Tamera's head still was full of worry about Camille, Tanna and Max as the crew flew on their ship, heading for Palentine, inside the Terragon Forest.

"So, what is the cloud that was attacked?" Timothy wondered.

"That cloud sits above Spirit Land," Tamera answered him.

"And what about Olivia?" Timothy asked. "Where does she fit in this?"

"Olivia is the ruler of Spirit Land, as well as the guardian of the Diamonds of Allure," Kirbie explained.

"Where is she?"

"She was captured by Lycan, along with Michael, her guardian angel," Tamera answered. "I can't even fathom that the Darkness could take the diamonds away from her."

"Once we get all the other diamonds," Noelle followed, "hopefully you will be able to battle Lycan. If you defeat him and get the final star, peace will be restored and wishes will be able to come true again."

Timothy was so mesmerized that he kind of felt overwhelmed by what Tamera and Kirbie told them.

"I can't believe this is actually happening," Timothy mentioned.

Tamera placed her hand on Timothy's. "Believe me, this is as real as it gets," Tamera stated. "I understand how you feel, but we're running out of time, and we need to get going as soon as possible."

"I'll try my hardest not to let you down," Timothy responded.

The group then was in uneasiness as they saw smoke coming not too far away from them.

"It looks like a big fire outside of Palentine," Noelle said out loud.

"We better check it out," Tamera stated.

After Kirbie landed her ship, the group cautiously entered the forest. They looked all around themselves, trying not to be surprised by anything that may attack. They noticed the smoke getting heavier. They all began coughing slightly.

"We won't last for too long in here," Tamera replied.

Just then the group came up to an opening where several trees had been destroyed by a large fire that was spreading to other trees.

"We have to put it out!" Kirbie stated.

Suddenly Kirbie and Noelle tripped on some wires. With that, they both became trapped in a black netting. Before Timothy and Tamera could respond to them, they became surrounded by a small group of spirits. Then out walked Cassian and several more spirits toward the group.

"Well, look at this," Cassian stated. "If it isn't the guardians of the Jewel of Coverdale and their friends. What a treat this will be for Master Lycan."

Timothy and Tamera revealed their swords.

"After them, spirits!" Cassian instructed.

Two spirits jumped at Timothy and Tamera. Timothy rolled out of the way. Tamera fired a magical arrow from her glowing bow, and the spirits ignited away from them.

Two charged behind Tamera and Timothy and attacked. Tamera then was able to free Kirbie and Noelle from the netting.

"Take them now!" Cassian commanded.

But even as the spirits charged ever harder at the four heroes, and after a bit of battling, Tamera had stuck down the final spirit. Cassian, in disbelief, just looked over to Tamera and Kirbie, who had their glowing weapons aimed at him. Cassian, in frustration, ran away as fast as he could. Everyone in the group sighed greatly.

"That was incredible!" Timothy called out. The remark got Tamera to laughing as she hugged Timothy.

"We still need to put this fire out," Kirbie told them.

Suddenly, a young woman approached where there was still a fire at. She had cat ears and a tail, with light blue hair and eyes, and was wearing a strapped black leotard and light-blue tights. Her hair started spraying out water in the direction where the fire was. Then after the fire was put out completely, another woman approached the water girl. Her hair and eyes were a darker shade of blue.

"Well done, Nellie!" The woman announced in a feminine tone. "Go get refreshed, and we'll take care of the forest in a little bit."

"Okay, Mother."

Nellie kissed the woman on the cheek before walking back towards Palentine.

"Hello, Tamera," the woman stated. "I'm glad to see you and Tessa here. This could have been a real mess."

"It's good to see you too, Holli," Tamera told her.

"And look at how beautiful you are, Noelle."

Noelle blushed. "As with you, Holli."

Holli had longer sky-blue hair and matching color eyes, was wearing a white dress with a brown corset, white detached nylon sleeves. She also had a metallic clip on each side of her head that had the shape of an angel wing above a crescent moon, with three long chains streaming down from each clip.

"And who are your friends? I'm glad you helped us out."

"My name's Timothy."

"I'm Princess Holli, guardian of Palentine. I'm so glad to see you all. Cassian flew overhead in their ship not too long ago, so I thought they may be close. Now our own queen is under Lycan's evil spell."

"You mean Star?" Tamera spoke.

"Where is she?" Kirbie wondered.

"She's at the castle, but he hasn't allowed anyone into the castle since yesterday."

"Please," Tamera pleaded, "let us talk to Star."

Holli sighed. "Okay, this way. Let's get you all cleaned up."

Holli led the Revolution into Palentine, where many different villagers were trying to live in peace and harmony. First, they saw Nellie and other water-citizens swimming in a large lake. Then they saw to their left a sun-girl glowing so another citizen, colored red, could see underneath a rock that other citizens had lifted up.

"As you see," Holli stated, "we are normally a very harmonious clan. But since Star turned her heart to Lycan, we are now living in fear every day."

"Where can we find her?" Timothy wondered.

"Uh, actually," Tamera pointed out, "I think she found us."

The woman approached the group, with other smaller black spirits with her. She had white hair with deep black eyes, and was wearing a white, black and red military-styled dress with red tights.

"Queen Star," Holli spoke fearfully.

"Excellent job, Holli!" Star spoke out. "You led our enemies to me. Now I will crush them."

"My queen," Holli pleaded, "this madness has to stop!"

"Never!" Star told her sternly. "Lord Lycan has instructed me to stop these fiends so he can rule over all of the World of

Exodus. If I must destroy you as well, so be it!"

The spirits charged. Before anyone could react, Holli ran towards the spirits.

"Holli!" Tamera yelled.

Before Holli could reach the spirits, Star suddenly jumped on Holli, pointing her large sword on her. Holli was shocked.

"You dare defy my power?" Star bragged.

At that moment, Star was hit in the head, and she fell onto Holli, unconscious. Holli looked to see Kirbie holding her sword.

In the meantime, Tamera, Timothy and Noelle attacked the spirits with their weapons. Timothy struck down the last spirit with his sword.

Star woke back up, but started gasping for air. Then a much larger spirit came out from Star's mouth before she fainted once again. The spirit had a blackened armored look with horns on the helmet and had white eyes that had no pupils.

"Foolish mortals," the spirit said.

"Who are you?" Kirbie asked.

"I am Duska, spirit of the Darkness," the being introduced himself. "I am one of Lycan's most loyal spirits."

Duska twirled its hands, and large trails of black sand formed, flying at the heroes, who moved out of the way. Duska, with its mind, threw more sand at the heroes. Then they all fell to the ground from the sand slamming into them. The speed of the sand hitting them was causing cuts in their skin.

Duska threw more trails of sand again at the Revolution. Tamera and Kirbie put up a wall of ice. The ice stopped the sand from hitting the heroes. Then Duska flew up high into the air while screaming in a rage. As the others got back up on their feet, Duska screamed out, "Now I have no choice but to destroy you all!"

Duska fired a beam of black at the group. Tamera and Kirbie, out of instinct, performed the ice move again. Duska concentrated on penetrating the ice. Then out of the corner of its eye, Duska saw Noelle jumping towards him. Before Duska could react, Noelle sliced Duska with her sword, turning Duska to dust, and the beam dissipated.

At that moment, Holli ran over to Star, who was still lying on the ground. She had awakened, her black eyes now a beautiful shade of red.

"My queen, are you okay?"

"Holli… what's going on? I don't remember anything…"

"You were under a spirit's control, but we defeated it. I prayed it really wasn't you behind all of this."

"I worked too hard to give you good spirits a good home," Star told them. "Why would I ever think of ruining that? I thank you all deeply for what you did for us, and all of Palentine."

"Anytime, Queen Star," said Tamera as she and the others bowed at her presence.

"It's almost nightfall. Would you like to stay and rest?" Holli wondered.

"Why, yes," Kirbie smiled. "Thank you."

The group celebrated more until they heard an unusual laughter, and they turned in the direction the laughter came from. They were surprised to see a woman walking towards them with a very young girl walking beside her. The beautiful woman had reddish-brown hair. One eye was the color of fire, the other the color of ice, and she wore a form-fitting short black strapless dress with glossy tan pantyhose. Suddenly the little girl, who had very long purple hair and blue eyes, and was simply dressed in a white leotard with red trim, and red tights came up to Timothy, hugging him.

"Kids really like you, don't they, Timothy?" Noelle questioned with a smile.

Timothy chuckled. "I guess so."

"Looks like Orion found a new friend." Then the woman said softly, "Forgive me, but Orion's kind of clingy."

"Rain!" Tamera said joyously. Tamera ran over to her and gave her a hug.

"It's good to see you again, my ladies."

Tamera walked over to Timothy, grabbing his hand and leading him over to Rain.

"Timothy," Tamera spoke, "I'd like you to meet Rain and Orion."

"Nice to meet you, Timothy," Rain spoke.

Orion was still holding on to Timothy.

Timothy picked Orion up in his arms. Orion hugged him tightly.

"I'm grateful that you are helping Tamera on this journey, Timothy," Rain mentioned.

"Thank you, and it's nice to meet you both."

Kirbie and Noelle walked over to them. "It's been a long time, Rain."

"Indeed, it has, Kirbie. And it's great to see you, Noelle." Then Rain examined the group. "Wow, what an unlikely group of heroes: A small yet brave dragon girl, a courageous swordsman, a guardian of the Jewel of Coverdale, and a princess bent on revenge. This mission should be really interesting."

"Indeed," Noelle mentioned.

"I just happened to see you guys defeat Duska. That was some great teamwork you showed there."

"Well, thanks..." Timothy spoke.

Rain interrupted, placing her hand on Timothy's shoulder. "But if you really think you are anywhere near ready to battle Lycan or Abaddon, well, think again. As time goes on, you will see enemies that will make Duska or even Behrlin look like a cakewalk."

"So why doesn't Lycan just come and destroy us, if they think we are so easy to beat?" Timothy questioned.

"He doesn't think you are easy to beat, but that's what he has his goons for. If you *are* that easy, they should take care of you. Besides, he has the job of making sure your family and the others don't escape his grasp."

"Well, we won't quit until we get them back," Kirbie responded.

"Don't think I'm telling you to give up, Kirbie," Rain spoke. She kissed Kirbie's forehead. "I know if you do right you will succeed. Just don't let your ego overtake your heart from doing the right thing. You are truly the only ones who can stop the evil from overtaking us." Rain hugged and kissed Tamera on the forehead. "Be strong, take heart, and let God guide you."

Orion kissed Timothy on the cheek, then Timothy gave her to Rain before they left.

"Tomorrow we'll go to Perisia," Tamera stated. "For now, let's get some rest."

The Revolution was led to an inn, where they stayed the night.

That night, Tamera was looking at some news reports on her phone. She walked over to Timothy with a smile on her face.

"Looks like you got a fan, Timothy," Tamera told him as she showed him the news report on the phone. The headline read, "Timothy Leads the Revolution to Victory!"

Timothy read part of the report out loud. "After many of the villagers of Palentine were attacked by some of the evil spirits once again, Timothy used his leadership prowess and led the members of the Revolution to defeat those who had attacked the helpless citizens in the village, and even managed to take down the one who was leading the charge."

Tamera then showed Timothy on her phone the picture that was taken of him battling one of the spirits he fought in Palentine.

Timothy was puzzled by the news report. "But that wasn't me. I was just battling the spirits. It was you three that took down Duska."

"Well, somebody's got their eye on you. That doesn't surprise me."

"Why do you say that?"

"Well, Kirbie told me that on different occasions, she has been seeing what looked like flashes of light coming from various places."

"You mean, like, from a camera?"

"Something like that. And this wasn't the only story."

When Kirbie searched on her phone about Timothy, she showed him four other stories, including a story titled, "Timothy: The Most Wonderful Member of the Revolution." Timothy then saw a picture of himself holding Tamera and Noelle's hand.

"You're quite the ladies' man, aren't you?" Tamera teased.

"This is preposterous!" Timothy stated, somewhat irritated. "I'm not the leader of this group, and you, Tamera and Noelle are the true members of the group. I'm nobody."

Tamera hugged Timothy. "No, you're not. You're doing your best to help us defeat this evil. That's not nothing, and you certainly have our respect for trying."

Timothy blushed. "Thank you, Tamera. I appreciate that."

Tamera then lowered her head. "So, how did you and Noelle meet?"

"I met her five Christmases ago in Coverdale. She was on a mission at the time, but when she left, she had to go back to Angel Cove, so we hadn't seen each other since then."

Timothy looked to see Tamera looking sad.

"Tamera... you're not suggesting that..."

"No, I didn't mean it like that. It's just... please forgive me. I guess I should learn to be more confident about myself."

Timothy wrapped his arms around Tamera. "I give my word to you, Tamera: I love you with all my heart. I'm not going to let anyone take that away."

"I love you too, Timothy. I really appreciate you."

Chapter 15

Catterine Village

The following morning, the members of the Revolution got ready and the group walked out of the inn. They noticed at a distance in the sky there was a deep-black cloud lingering above.

"What is that?" Timothy asked.

"That's Spirit Land," Tamera told him.

"I thought the cloud would be white."

"Normally it is a pure white, purer than any other cloud in the sky," Noelle told him. "But now that Olivia has been taken, it is black, the color of the Darkness."

They continued watching the cloud a little longer, noticing powerful streaks of lightning shooting down to the ground.

"If we don't get the diamonds back," Noelle continued, "we will be destroyed."

The Revolution wasted no time heading off for Perisia.

Cassian and his spirits stood a little distance away from Abaddon and Lycan, who were watching the Revolution getting ready to head for Perisia. Then the vision faded out of the crystal ball.

"B... boss?" Cassian stuttered.

Lycan unexpectedly turned and roared ferociously. Cassian screamed in horror and then fell backwards.

"You idiots!" Lycan then screamed to them. "You were told *not* to come back until they were dead!"

"We thought they were, your wickedness," Cassian pleaded. "We were sure that Duska would take care of them..."

Lycan roared before shouting, "I am tired of your failures!"

"They are indeed a strong group together," Abaddon mentioned. "Timothy's quite the fighter. If he is anything like what Tamera seems to be, he won't quit. And Noelle and Kirbie aren't pushovers by any means."

"What do you think we should do?" Lycan asked.

"We need to separate them," Abaddon suggested. "If they reach Warrington, Symphony can do that trick the best."

"Make sure it gets taken care of," Lycan told Cassian. "Get back out there and get the job done, or else if they don't kill you, I will do it myself!"

Cassian gasped and in fear ran out of the castle.

"Please be safe, everyone," Camille whispered to herself as she and Tanna looked at the picture.

The Revolution traveled in their ship, heading to Perisia. Kirbie was looking down at a forest, where they saw members of the Darkness had a small cat girl with white hair pinned up against a tree. Kirbie then landed the ship near where the enemies stood.

The spirits looked to see the Revolution approaching them. They made their way over to Kirbie and the others, but the Revolution was able to take down the soldiers.

Tamera approached the young cat girl.

"Are you okay, young one?" Tamera wondered.

"Oh, thank you so much!" the girl told her, giving her a hug.

"What's your name?" Kirbie asked.

"I'm Mia."

"Hi, sweetheart. I'm Kirbie and this is my sister, Tamera, her boyfriend, Timothy, and our good friend, Noelle."

"It's nice to meet you all. Will you please walk me home?"
"Sure, sweetie."
Mia grabbed Kirbie's hand, and the Revolution walked with Mia.

In the meantime, Lycan and Abaddon watched as the group traveled on during their adventure.
"And to think, they'll be walking into a big surprise," Lycan chuckled. "The knights will see to it that they will finally be taken down."
"They'd better," Abaddon noted. "We can't tolerate any more failures."
The prisoners overheard what the maniacal men were discussing and became overwhelmed once again with worry. Camille lowered her head in sadness.
"We have to believe they will be able to overcome anything, my queen," Tanna told her in comfort. "We have to have faith that God will deliver them to us and overtake the evil."
"I know, Tanna. It's still upsetting to see them risking their lives for us. I do pray that they come to us safely."

When the Revolution and Mia arrived at the village in the middle of Catterine Village, they were shocked at the sight: the village had been leveled.
"Oh, no," Tamera cried out.
"The Darkness attacked our village several days ago. We've been doing our best to try to pick up the pieces since then."
At that time, a woman ran out to the Revolution, seeing Mia with them. The woman had a mix of black and white hair with one fire-colored eye and one ice-colored ice just like Rain had. She wore a black jacket, a black plaid pleated mini-skirt and

black pantyhose.

The woman tightly held Mia as tears fell from her eyes.

"Oh, thank goodness you're safe, baby," the woman told Mia. "I was so worried about you. Where did you go?"

Then Joseph walked over to the woman. "Calm down, Catherine. Let's be thankful she's safe with us."

Catherine wiped the tears from her eyes. "I'm sorry. It's just... they killed her and Mimi's parents. I don't want to lose them either."

"And you all will be next," said a voice in an evil tone.

Everyone turned to see Cassian standing behind them, with seven dark spirits behind him. To their left, they noticed many of the villagers trapped in a large cage.

"You did this..." Tamera said softly.

"Well, this time I had some real help," Cassian snickered. Surrounding him were the darkened spirits, each having the same features but had different colored eyes: red, purple, blue, green, yellow, orange and white.

"Last time you may have gotten the best of me, but this time you will face my wrath and will submit to Lycan and Abaddon. Spirits, attack!"

The four members of the Revolution stood firm against the seven spiritlings. Kirbie battled with the orange-eyed spirit. The orange-eyed spirit tried to get a jump on Kirbie, but Kirbie stood firm with her swords glowing. Kirbie then tried to capitalize, but the spirit was able to get Kirbie off her feet. Then the spirit threw a black flame at Kirbie, but Kirbie rolled out of the way, just missing her as she felt the flame hit the ground next to her.

Timothy tangled with the green-eyed spirit. After Timothy missed hitting the spirit, the spirit grabbed Timothy by his shirt and forced Timothy down to the ground.

Tamera was being double-teamed by the red and white-eyed spirits. The red-eyed spirit pounded the ground, and the wave knocked Tamera to the ground. That gave the opening for the white-eyed spirit to grab Tamera from behind.

Then Noelle tried battling the yellow and blue-eyed spirits. Noelle was trying to strike down the blue-eyed spirit, but it was too quick for her, and the two spirits attacked Noelle, forcing her to the ground.

"That's it everyone," Cassian said cheerfully. "Take them all!"

Kirbie and the orange-eyed spirit continued exchanging blows. The spirit tried getting a hold of Kirbie, but Kirbie moved out of the way, and the spirit floated past Kirbie. Kirbie was then able to attack the spirit with her swords and the spirit turned to dust.

The green-eyed spirit threw black flames at Timothy, but he dodged all the flames using his sword. He then made his way over to the spirit, who was still trying to hit Timothy with the flames, but was unsuccessful. Then Timothy simply sliced the spirit, turning it to dust.

Cassian saw the change in momentum and became frustrated.

Tamera once again tried taking down the red and white-eyed spirits, but still wasn't having any luck, until she was joined by Kirbie, who focused on the white-eyed spirit, and Tamera focused on the other. After dodging more of the spirit's attacks, Tamera was able to strike down the spirit she faced with her ax as Kirbie struck down her spirit with her swords.

Noelle first was able to get the better of the yellow-eyed spirit before focusing on the one with blue eyes. The spirit thought to have the better of Noelle until she managed to go out of the spirit's line of sight. Then she attacked the spirit from behind, stabbing it with her sword, and it turned to dust. Cassian was livid.

"I can't believe this!" Cassian yelled. "The spirits were supposed to destroy you and I was going to finally win my masters over."

"It's going to take a lot more than that to stop us, Cassian," Kirbie warned.

"Oh, really? Well, maybe I have one more trick up my sleeve."

Then the Revolution noticed a ship much smaller than the Maniton approaching them. A ladder fell down the side of the ship, and Cassian grabbed the ladder. Then the cage the villagers were in started lifting up with the ship.

"So long, suckers!" he yelled.

Before the ladder could come clear off the ground, Timothy grabbed the ladder as well and climbed up to where he was able to cut the rope to the cage, and it crashed to the ground. Joseph, Catherine and Mia ran to the villagers.

Timothy then jumped down to the ground as well, but hurt himself in the process. Many of the villagers were hurt from the fall.

"Gather everyone up!" Kirbie instructed.

Tamera tended to Timothy.

"Baby, are you okay?" she asked.

"Yeah," she answered. "I just cut my leg, that's all."

"Mia!" was yelled out. She, Joseph and Catherine turned to see Mimi, Hanna, and her ghost, Catera, running over to her. They all hugged each other.

"Thank you all so much for saving us," Joseph told the Revolution.

"Please stay with us for tonight," Catherine asked.

"We would love to," Kirbie answered for the group.

The group slept together in a room in one of the remaining homes, with Tamera clinging tightly to Timothy. While still in his sleep, Timothy had a dream. He was walking down a mountainous path that had nothing but deep openings along each side of the path. He felt really cold and was shivering. Timothy drew his sword, thinking the worst was yet to come.

Timothy then came to an intersection where two paths went off from the original path, and there were two gates on each path. The path that went to the right was very wide and had lots of room to walk. The other path was very narrow, and some of the sides of the path were crumbling. When he turned and opened the large gate to walk down the wide path, he heard much evil and maniacal laughing. Then there was a blast of cold wind and rain that hit Timothy, and he felt much colder than before. Startled, he walked back from the path, shutting the gate. Timothy turned to the left and opened the smaller gate. There was no noise, other than the creaking of the gate. He opened that gate, waiting for something bad to happen, but nothing did. Worried, he began to walk down the narrow path.

Timothy watched with every step to make sure he didn't walk off the edge. The fear he felt in his heart was nearly overwhelming, and tears began to fall from his eyes. Yet the further he walked down the narrow path, the more comfortable he felt.

Finally, Timothy came upon a trail where there was now land and green grass and flowers on each side of him. He then noticed the sun shining brightly above him and the clouds gave way to a sparkling blue sky.

A woman walked over to him, giving him a hug. Then the woman pointed for him to walk forward. Timothy did so, holding the woman's hand. As he did, there was a large, nearly blinding glow in front of him, and out of the glow a hand reached out to him. Timothy reached out as well and his hand grabbed the other hand.

"Remember," a voice stated.

Timothy woke up, gasping. He felt tears rolling down his cheeks, but his heart was nearly overjoyed and he couldn't stop smiling. He turned to see a chimp with white hair staring at him, looking grumpy. Tamera woke up from feeling Timothy move. She saw the tears in his eyes.

"Timothy, what's wrong? Are you okay?"

"Well... I had this strange dream."

"What about?" asked Kirbie, who was sitting up.

"I'm sorry if I woke you, Kirbie."

"You didn't. I was just lying here being lazy, I guess."

"So was I," Noelle spoke as she also sat up.

"So, what was the dream about?" Tamera pondered.

"I was walking down this trail. It was so cold and dreary. And then I came up onto two paths, one with a large gate, and the other with a small gate. I first opened the large gate and went to walk down the wide path, but heard this evil laughter, and became overwhelmed by a very cold wind. So, I went down this thin, narrow path with the small gate." He looked into Tamera's blue eyes. "At the end of the path I became engulfed in warmth, and this woman pointed me to this hand that reached out to me from a strange glow. Then I heard a voice say, 'Remember'."

"Well, that's certainly an interesting dream," Kirbie said.

"What did the woman look like?"

"Well, she had really long blue hair… and these beautiful deep blue eyes."

Tamera gasped, hearing the description of the woman, and she began to tear up. Kirbie consoled Tamera.

"What?" Timothy stated. "What did I say that…"

"I think you just saw her mother, Celestia," Kirbie informed him.

"The dream reminds me of a passage in the Bible," Tamera mentioned as she was drying the tears on her face.

"What is that one?" Kirbie pondered.

Tamera explained, "It's from the book of Matthew. It says, 'Wide is the gate and broad is the road that leads to destruction, and many will enter through it. But small is the gate and narrow the road that leads to life, and only a few will find it'." (7:13–14, NIV)

"That's great, but what does that have to do with his dream?" Tessa pondered. "Are we supposed to go down a certain path or something?"

"Well, the only path I want to take is the one that leads to our loved ones being rescued," Timothy replied.

"I hope that is His will for us," Tamera stated.

The Revolution got set to leave Catterine Village to continue on their adventure. Before leaving, the children approached the group.

"I just wanted to thank you all for what you did for me and my family. I'm really grateful," Mia told them.

"You're welcome, Mia," Tamera stated, and she gave Mia a hug. Then she and Kirbie hugged Hanna and Mimi. Just then Kirbie looked up to the sky and was startled.

"Look at that!" Kirbie yelled.

Everyone noticed a large cloud of smoke arising a distance away from them.

"That's over by Solevia!" Tamera informed them.

"We better check it out!" Noelle mentioned.

The Revolution quickly left for Solevia.

"Be careful!" Mia called out to them.

Chapter 16

Solevia

The group traveled as fast as they could until they arrived on the outskirts of Solevia. They were saddened to see that the entire town was left in ruins, worse than what Catterine was.
 "This has to be the work of the Darkness," Kirbie stated.
 "Let's search for survivors," Tamera instructed.
 The group split up: Noelle went north, Timothy and Tamera went to the east, and Kirbie went to the west.

Noelle came up to a building that was left in rubble. She noticed an arm sticking out from the rubble of the building. She ran quickly over to where the arm was sticking out and tried to unbury the person trapped.

Timothy and Tamera cried out "Hello?" and "Is anyone here?" to see if there would be any response, but there was nothing more than the crackling of fire.

Kirbie was also crying out for a response. Suddenly, Kirbie thought she heard something. Kirbie listened in as well until she heard the noise.
 "It sounds like someone's calling for help," she said to herself.
 Kirbie then walked over to a small home that had been badly

damaged.

Noelle finally dug out the person that was buried: a little brown-haired, green-eyed girl that was no more than eight years old. She was wearing just a simple yellow sweater and a sky-blue skirt. Her leg had been badly cut and she was bleeding. Noelle found a large towel and wrapped it around the girl's leg.

"Are you okay?" Noelle asked.

The girl began to cry. "Oh, thank you! I thought I was going to die!"

The girl hugged Noelle. She hugged her back. The little girl then let go of Noelle to dry her tears.

"What's your name, sweetheart?"

"Annie."

"I'm Noelle. What happened here?"

"It was this large… evil looking dragon. The dragon, along with some blackened spirits, destroyed the city."

"Where is everyone?"

"They were carried off into the heavens."

Noelle was stunned. The little girl grabbed Noelle's hand.

"Are we going to die?"

"No. I'll protect you, sweetheart."

Noelle and the girl walked away from the scene.

Kirbie made it over to where the call for help was, behind a large, destroyed building. She looked to see a boy who had brown hair and bright red eyes, who was wearing a blue shirt and green pants, with his leg caught by a heavy piece of concrete.

"Oh, thank goodness," said the boy. "The Revolution's here."

"You know of us?" Kirbie asked.

"Everyone knows about the Revolution, Kirbie."

Just then Timothy and Tamera approached.

"What happened?" asked Tamera.

"We were attacked by Cassian and his army," the boy answered.

"Let's get you out of there," said Timothy.

The Revolution all helped to pick up the concrete, and the boy crawled out. Then the Revolution all dropped the heavy block.

"How's your leg?" asked Kirbie.

The boy tried to stand up on his leg, but the leg that was trapped could not support him and he fell. Tessa and Timothy caught Luke before he hit the ground.

"Angelic Rain!" Timothy called out, and the boy was healed by the vortex.

At that time, Noelle came to them, still walking with the little girl.

"Luke!" said the little girl.

"Annie! You're all right!"

Annie shrugged her shoulders. "More or less."

"I saw a little house that was still standing," Kirbie responded. "You two can take shelter there."

Kirbie led everyone to the house that amazingly survived the attack from Cassian. Tamera laid Annie on the bed as she was sleeping, and Luke wrapped a large stick on his leg to use as a splint.

"My brother, Logan, is probably in deep trouble," Luke mentioned. "He went to find Cassian."

"We better go help him," said Kirbie.

"I will stay behind to make sure nothing happens to Luke

and Annie," Noelle stated. "Be careful."

Tamera, Tessa and Timothy all left to find Logan. They were saddened to see the town in as bad a shape as the other villages beforehand.

"Finding him will be like finding a needle in a haystack in this mess," Timothy replied.

"Let's split up again," Kirbie stated. "I'll search the west if you want to search the east."

Timothy and Tamera nodded and they separated.

Abaddon and Lycan were watching Tamera, Tessa and Timothy as they walked through the ruined city.

"This is our chance," Lycan noted.

"Yes," Abaddon agreed. "Destroy them."

Tamera and Timothy again were calling out to see if anyone would respond to them.

"Hello?" Tamera yelled.

"Hello, Tamera," said a voice.

Tamera and Timothy stopped to see Cassian staring at them.

"Not you again," said Tamera.

Kirbie also looked to see if anyone had survived from the attack on the town. She thought she had seen somebody and went to check on them. That's when Kirbie heard a loud cry come from the sky. She looked up to see a dragon flying overhead. Then she noticed herself being surrounded by the Darkness.

"Just great," Kirbie stated.

Luke, after checking on Annie, walked out from the house. He stood beside Noelle.

"It's almost too quiet," Luke told Noelle.

Just then, a large hammer flew over Luke, slamming through the wall of the house.

"Annie!" Luke yelled.

Annie woke up from the commotion and quickly ran to Luke.

Just then three huge spirits appeared in front of them.

"Take them down, Noelle!" Annie told him.

At that moment, Noelle pulled out her sword. She charged at the three spirits and began attacking them. The spirits were trying to work together to stop Noelle, but their size was a disadvantage to them as Noelle flew quickly around them at different spots. Then one by one, Noelle was able to strike the spirits down.

Tamera and Timothy readied themselves as they stood against Cassian and his spirits. The Darkness ran to them. Tamera and Timothy revealed their swords and they made their attack. Cassian tried to stab Tamera, but Tamera quickly jumped out of the way, spinning and hitting Cassian powerfully with a spin kick. Spirits jumped at Tamera but she moved out of the way. As one spirit charged, Tamera stabbed him and he turned to dust.

Kirbie readied herself as she was surrounded by members of the Darkness.

"Let's dance," Kirbie told them.

The enemies attacked, but Kirbie began using her swords, striking many enemies that approached her while looking as if she were dancing. Kirbie was able to strike several spirits down, turning them to dust.

Cassian continued to fight Timothy. A ball of fire from Cassian flew towards Timothy. Tamera fired an arrow from her bow and it blocked the fire from hitting Timothy. As Timothy got ready to round up the evil leader, he and Tamera suddenly heard a large roar from above them. Timothy saw the large dragon heading towards him.

"The dragon!" Tamera screamed.

Timothy and Tamera got of the way before the dragon could grab them. Cassian then ran from the scene.

"We've got to find the others!" said Tamera to Timothy.

They headed off to find their friends.

In the meantime, Kirbie was still fighting other members of the Darkness. She managed to finally strike down the last of the spirits, turning them all to dust. Kirbie then showed up by Timothy and Tamera.

"Where have you been sis?" Tamera asked, teasing. "You missed all the action."

"Well, I had a bit of action of my own, love," Tessa informed her.

At that time, Noelle, Luke and Annie came up to them.

"Why aren't you still in the house?" Kirbie asked sternly.

"I insisted that Noelle come here to help you fight the dragon," Annie responded.

At that moment, the dragon went to swoop down at the group again. They tried to get out of its way, but the dragon managed to grab Timothy. As Tamera went to give chase, Timothy grabbed Olympia and sliced the dragon's leg with it. The dragon screamed and let go of Timothy. Timothy began to fall, but Tamera formed a slide made of ice and he slid over to where Tamera was standing.

"That was fun. I want to do that again!"

Tamera laughed at Timothy's comment. The dragon turned around and flew back at them. Tamera then fired off an ice arrow at the dragon. The arrow hit the dragon's left eye, and it cried out in pain. The dragon then turned its attention at Kirbie and Noelle, firing a large white beam at them from its mouth. Kirbie and Noelle took cover out of the way of the beam.

Then the dragon landed on the ground. This time it shot out a huge wave of fire from its mouth. Everyone tried to get out of the way, but Kirbie's arm became burnt. The dragon made its way over to attack Kirbie. Before it could, Tamera threw her ax, striking the dragon. The dragon screamed out as it flew at Tamera. It slammed hard into Tamera, who fell to the ground.

"We've got to help them!" Timothy told the others.

"We need a distraction," Noelle told them. "That way we can attack from behind."

"I've got an idea," Luke stated.

The dragon once again approached Tamera. At that time, Luke stood between the dragon and Tamera. The dragon went to fire the beam at Luke. Luke dodged the beam.

"You missed me!" Luke taunted.

Angered, the dragon fired its beam again. Once more Luke dodged it.

In the meantime, Kirbie ran up near the beast.

"Let's see how you do without sight."

Tamera fired another arrow and hit the other eye, blinding it immediately. The dragon cried out in pain from the attack. That's when Noelle took her sword and sliced the head off the dragon's body, and the dragon turned to dust.

"Is everyone all right?" Tamera asked.

Timothy noticed the large burn on Tamera's face and arms. Annie hugged Luke as Tamera hugged Timothy. Then Annie again hugged Noelle.

"You're my hero," Annie told her.

Noelle said nothing, but nodded and rubbed Annie's head. Then at that moment Logan, along with many of the villagers from Solevia appeared, walked over to the heroes. Excited, Annie ran over to Logan, giving him a tight hug. Logan had the exact features and clothing that Luke had, but looked several years older than Luke.

"I thought I had lost you, Logan," Annie told him with tears in her eyes.

"It's okay now, Annie," Logan responded. "I'm here now."

Logan then also walked over to Luke, and they shook hands.

"I don't know how to thank you all for saving us," Luke stated.

"Hey, don't forget that you helped as well," Kirbie mentioned.

"What's going to happen to us?" Annie questioned. "I've lost my parents. I have nowhere to go."

"I'm sure we can help take care of you, Annie," Luke answered.

"That's right," Logan followed. "You don't have anything to worry about."

The Revolution was relieved to hear Logan and Luke's kind words to Annie. After saying their goodbyes, the Revolution left Solevia.

Lycan and Abaddon watched in their crystal ball how Cassian and the dragon had failed his mission of destroying the Revolution.

"This can't keep happening!" Lycan yelled. "What's it going to take to stop them?"

"Whatever it takes, they have to be stopped," Abaddon replied. "Mark my words: The Revolution will soon meet their end."

The Revolution, after their tough battle against the dragon, decided to give themselves a rest over by Stephania Pond. At that time, the other members sat around a fire that Tessa had built for them.

Tamera stepped away for a moment, walking over to the pond. She saw Timothy staring over the pond. Tamera sat down on the ground by the lake. Timothy gasped and turned to see Tamera.

"Tamera, you scared me," Timothy stated.

"I'm sorry," she simply stated.

"You know, Tamera, I've been thinking about everything that's been going on here, and I've seen how tough some of the enemies are that we have faced. I'm certain as the journey goes on, they will only get tougher. What if there comes a time where we can't accomplish the task that has been placed on us?"

Tamera placed one of her hands on Timothy's shoulder. "We mustn't give up hope, Timothy. I believe, even as our foes may get stronger, that God will help us through the battles and will make us stronger as well."

"Tamera's right," said a voice.

Timothy then turned to see who had spoken when he felt someone holding him. He looked to see it was Orion.

"Hi, sweetie," Timothy said to her.

Tamera and Timothy then saw Rain approaching them.

"Hello again, Rain!" Tamera spoke. She hugged Rain.

"Hello, Tamera. Please, forgive me if I'm intruding. How are you, Timothy?"

"I'm fine, thank you. I was just caught off-guard."

Rain laughed. "That's kind of her thing. Once she gets attached to someone, good luck in getting her to let go."

Noelle, Tessa and Kirbie ran over to the pond.

"What's going on?" Kirbie questioned. Then they saw Rain and Orion. Kirbie snickered. "Hello, Rain. Your timing is impeccable."

"What brings you here, Rain?" Noelle wondered.

"I saw you all, with the help of Luke, defeat the dragon. Indeed, I am impressed. But Timothy, you are right: as you go on, the foes are only going to be tougher. It may even get overwhelming. But Tamera is right as well: you mustn't give up hope."

"We'll be ready for them!" Tessa stated.

Rain smiled. "I'm sure you will, Tessa." Then Rain walked over to Timothy and Tamera. She grabbed their hands.

"I believe in you both, as well as Kirbie, Noelle, Tessa, your loved ones, our loved ones, and anyone who fights the battle with you. You are the Revolution, and you will bring peace again to the World of Exodus." Then Rain told Timothy and Tamera, "Stand firm, stand tall, follow the path that God has placed for you, and you indeed will win."

Orion waved to them while smiling. Then Rain and Orion left the area.

"At least she's on our side," Noelle noted.

"Of course, she is," Tamera replied. "I love Rain as much as I do my mom, and she would also do anything for anyone."

Timothy and Tamera noticed Kirbie looking at her phone, nearly in tears from laughter.

"Kirbie, what are you reading?" Timothy asked.

"Well, it looks like you made the news again," Kirbie told him. She showed Tamera and Timothy the headline from the article on her phone: "Why Timothy is Loved by the Ladies."

The article showed pictures of him being embraced by Tamera, Tessa, Noelle, Kirbie and Rain.

"Aren't you just the player?" Tessa teased.

"Yeah," Noelle said as she wrapped her arms tenderly around Timothy. "Look what you've gotten yourself into with all these ladies."

"Come on, that's not who I am! I'm…"

Tamera hugged Timothy. "We know that, Timothy. It's okay. Someone's just trying to get your attention."

"I didn't mean to upset you, Timothy," Kirbie told him. "Look, let's get some rest for now. We've got some long days still ahead of us."

Chapter 17

The Crystal Cave

During the night, the Revolution was sleeping by the fire to keep warm. Timothy had awakened after hearing a noise. Out of the corner of his eye, he saw something flickering from a cave a short distance from where they were sleeping. The curiosity of it made Timothy get up and he headed for the cave.

At that moment, Tamera had awakened and she noticed Timothy was heading towards the light in the cave.

"Timothy," she said, "where are you going?"

Timothy walked into the cave, and he was awestruck as he saw the walls of the cave shimmer brightly.

"It's amazing!" Timothy stated.

He continued to check his surroundings. As Timothy looked up to the ceiling of the cave, his foot ran into a large diamond that moved as if it were a switch. Then a cage fell from the ceiling and trapped Timothy. Then diamonds came up from the ground and surrounded Timothy's legs, causing him not to be able to move. At that moment Timothy looked to see three female figures approaching him. The women's skin all looked as if it were made of diamonds: one was blue in color, one was green, and one was red.

The blue-skinned woman walked over to Timothy. "So, what do we have here?"

"An intruder, eh?" said the red-skinned woman.

Then out of nowhere a beam of ice shot into the cave. The beam destroyed the cage, freed Timothy out of the diamonds, and threw the women off their feet. The women then saw Tamera was standing in front of them, with Tessa, Kirbie and Noelle walking towards Tamera. As the red-skinned woman went to attack again, the blue-skinned woman gasped and shouted, "Ruby, wait!"

Ruby stopped after hearing her friend call out.

"What for, Sapphire?" Ruby questioned.

"It's Tamera," Sapphire responded.

Emerald, the green-skinned woman walked over to Tamera and hugged her.

"I'm terribly sorry," Tamera told Sapphire. "I was just trying to protect my boyfriend. I didn't know it was you."

"So, you all must be the Revolution?" Emerald asked.

"Then you must be the Gem Girls," Tamera followed.

"Why are you in our cave?" Ruby pondered.

"Well," Timothy answered, "I saw a light coming from here, and I just wanted to see what it was."

"This is our home," Sapphire replied. "How would you feel if someone just explored your home without your permission?"

Timothy lowered his head. "I'm sorry, I didn't really think of it that way."

"Excuse me, I'm sorry to bother you," said somebody from behind, and everyone turned their attention in the direction of the voice. "I was hoping you would help me find someone."

The Gem Girls saw a young woman standing behind them. She had dark gray hair and blue eyes, with cat ears and a tail, and was wearing a blue and white maid-styled top and skirt with white stockings. She had many blood-colored scars on her body. The Gem Girls readied their weapons once again.

"Who are you?" asked Ruby.

"My name's Theresa. I'm wondering if you could help me find somebody."

"Everyone's coming in tonight," Ruby noted.

"What do you want from us, Theresa?" Noelle wanted to know.

"Look, I don't know what you think I am, but I assure you I just want your help."

Tamera walked over to the girl, who looked saddened. Theresa placed her left hand on Tamera's right cheek.

"You have a birthmark too?" Theresa said to her.

Tamera lifted up the lower part of her shirt to reveal the large birthmark on her side.

"Do yours just appear out of nowhere?" Theresa asked.

"Actually, I was born with them."

"I'll bet you were teased just as much as I am in Hallaway. What's your name?"

"I'm Tamera, this is my sister, Kirbie, my boyfriend, Timothy and our friends, Noelle and Tessa."

"What's Hallaway?" Timothy asked.

"That's the name of the town not far from here," Kirbie informed him.

"What do you need help with, sweetie?"

"I'm looking for this little girl. Can you help me?"

Theresa showed Tamera a picture of a mouse girl.

"Her name is Lauren. She's a little mouse girl, only about four feet tall. Watch out though. If she's provoked, she can be pretty vicious."

"Why are you interested in her?" Noelle wondered.

"She's my best friend. I've been worried about her with all this trouble going on in Exodus. I hope you can find her and bring her back to me."

Noelle signaled for Tamera to walk over to her, Kirbie, Tessa and Timothy. They stood in a circle.

"I don't trust her," Tessa pointed out. "Something just isn't right about her."

"But if she's right and her friend is in danger," Timothy commented, "we can't ignore that. We should at least try to find her."

"I agree," said Tamera.

"Then I guess we're going to Hallaway," Kirbie responded.

The group turned their attention back to Theresa. "Okay, Theresa, we'll check it out," Tamera told her.

"Great!" Theresa said in joy, hugging Tamera. "I'll wait here while you bring her back. And would one of you stay here and guard me as well?"

"Maybe I should," Noelle told her.

Tamera was uncertain. "But we may need you…"

"I'm sure you'll be all right. I guess I'll keep the Gem Girls company as well."

The Revolution walked out of the cave in search of Lauren. Noelle watched as they walked off, unaware that warriors of the Darkness were hiding in the shadows. A spirit then fired a beam at Noelle, and she became trapped in the black netting. Before the Gem Girls could do anything, the spirit trapped them in a black net as well. A Gem Girl the color of black, along with several spirits around her, walked over to Theresa, who showed fear on her face. She grabbed a phone.

"It's done, Lycan," the Gem Girl spoke. "They fell for my trap. I have Noelle trapped, and the others are headed for Hallaway."

"Good," Lycan said in delight. "Soon we will rule over this world."

As nighttime rolled in, Tamera, Timothy, Tessa and Kirbie arrived at Hallaway in their ship.

"It's too quiet here," Timothy noticed.

Tamera, Timothy, Tessa and Kirbie walked around the town for a while without finding anything peculiar. Then as they got to the northern edge of town, they happened to see a really small woman who looked like the one Theresa described. She had ears and a tail like a mouse, with short silver-gray hair and red eyes, and wore a green and white tunic with black leggings.

They could see the young mouse girl looked as if she were very depressed. The three heroes approached. The girl at first only saw their shadows, and her claws extended out to look like large swords. The three then came into Lauren's view.

"Lauren, is that you?" Tamera asked her.

Lauren's eyes grew wide, shocked that the woman knew who she was. The girl retracted her claws.

"How do you know me?" Lauren asked.

"We met a friend of yours in the Crystal Cave," Timothy informed her.

"Do you mean Theresa?"

"Yes!" Kirbie said joyfully. "She's really worried about you."

Lauren looked down to the ground. "I really don't think that's true."

Tamera squatted down in front of Lauren. "Why would you say that?"

"We had an argument earlier. She thinks I'm too aggressive with her and told me she doesn't want to be my friend any more."

"How can that be?" Kirbie questioned.

"When we play together... I have a tendency to get a little

too joyful, and I end up cutting Theresa with my claws and..." Lauren grew angry as tears fell from her eyes. She then covered her face as she began sobbing. "I hate these things!"

Tamera reached out for Lauren, and they hugged each other.

"So those marks on Theresa... aren't birthmarks?" Tessa stated as she looked at Timothy.

Lauren tried to calm herself down. "No, they're... old scars from me. She tells people they're birthmarks. And because of me, she gets teased about how she looks. But Theresa really is beautiful, so much more than I am."

Tamera held Lauren close. "But you're beautiful, too, Lauren."

Kirbie insisted, "We should take you back to Theresa, sweetie."

Tears fell from Lauren's eyes again. "I'm scared to..."

"Hey, it'll be okay," Tamera assured her. "I'll be there with you."

"And besides," Timothy followed, "if Theresa really *is* your friend, I'm sure she will forgive you for what happened in the past."

"I don't know what to say," Lauren responded. "Thank you all so much."

Tamera, Timothy, Tessa and Kirbie, along with Lauren, went back to the Crystal Cave and met up with Theresa. They could not see Noelle or the Gem Girls in their sights.

"Noelle?" Kirbie called out.

Then Timothy, Tessa and Kirbie became trapped in the netting. Seeing what had happened, Tamera and Lauren hid in one of the darkened corners so they could not be seen. At that time, the darkened Gem Girl approached.

"Now I have the other members of the Revolution," said the Gem Girl.

"You won't get away with this, Onyx!" Sapphire said to the black Gem Girl.

But when the woman turned around, she saw the spirits were gone. This confused her. She then turned back around to see Tamera in front of her, swinging her ax. Onyx had no time to respond before she was struck down by Tamera, and she turned to dust.

Tamera and Lauren got Timothy, Tessa and Kirbie out of the netting. Then they freed Noelle and the Gem Girls.

"Lauren!" Theresa called out.

"Theresa?" Lauren replied. Theresa reached her hands out to hug Lauren, but Lauren was hesitant to do so.

"Lauren, I... I'm really sorry about what I said to you. You're not careless. I know what you do to me is not your fault. I really was worried about you."

"I... I was worried about you too, Theresa. I love you."

"I love you too, Lauren."

Lauren leaped into Theresa's arms, and they hugged each other tightly. Then Theresa walked over to Tamera, who squatted down in front of the two girls.

"I'm... sorry I... lied to you, Tamera," Theresa told her. "I was afraid if I told people that Lauren was doing that to me, that they would take her from me."

Emerald walked over to the girls. "Hey, I have an idea. It sounds as if your claws are controlled by your emotions. What if we could try to help control your emotions, and then you'll be better able to control your claws?"

Lauren was joyful. "Really? You would do that for me?"

"Of course," Emerald answered.

"Besides," Ruby commented, "I wouldn't want to lose those I loved either."

Lauren and Theresa were excited. Lauren jumped into Emerald's arms, and as her hands came across Emerald's back, they could hear her claws scraping across Emerald's back.

Lauren was frightened, but Emerald smiled, "It's okay, Lauren. They didn't hurt me."

Then Theresa walked over to Tamera, giving her a tight hug. Then she told Tamera, Kirbie and Timothy, "Thank you all so much for bringing Lauren back to me. It means so much to see her back with me again."

"It was our pleasure, sweetie," Tamera told her.

Chapter 18

Perisia

After a night of much-needed rest, the group made their journey to Perisia. Tamera, Tessa and Kirbie noticed Timothy was mesmerized by the beauty of the landscape he saw out of the window. Kirbie noticed his thrilled reactions, sensing he was excited about seeing the scenery.

"So, Kirbie," Timothy asked, "where do you think your world came from?"

Tamera noted, "We all have our thoughts about it: some say we were the coincidence of an explosion in space, while others say we were created by a divine hand."

"The hand of God?" Timothy wondered.

"Indeed. That's what I believe."

Kirbie continued, "Whatever it is we believe, it doesn't stop us from seeing our existence is very real, and that there are those who will do what they can to destroy it."

Tessa commented, "That's why there are those like us to do what they can to protect it."

"There are a lot of things we cannot answer," said Tamera, "and I believe we're not supposed to. I leave it in our creator's hands."

As they made their way towards Perisia, suddenly there was a beam that was fired at them. Kirbie quickly turned the ship so that the beam would miss them. Kirbie then returned fire. The beam Kirbie fired struck the right-side motor, causing it to malfunction. Then Kirbie fired off another shot and it destroyed the left wing of the plane. Cassian tried escaping in the plane, but the plane lost altitude until it crash-landed north of Perisia.

"They never quit, do they?" Timothy pondered.

"They're like an irritating rash that won't go away," Tamera answered.

The Revolution, a little later, arrived in Perisia. As they walked through the town, a young girl happened to see Tamera walking with her friends.

"Tamera! Kirbie!" the girl yelled.

Tamera and Kirbie looked to see the little gold-haired girl, who had gray eyes and was wearing a gold and brown dress with white armor across her chest, brown gloves and gold sparkled tights, giving them a tight hug.

"Julietta!" Tamera stated. "How have you been?"

"I'm good! I'm glad you're here. I've really missed you!"

"We've missed you too," Kirbie told her.

Then she hugged Tessa. "I'm so glad to see you too, Tessa!"

"Likewise, sweetheart," said Tessa.

"You should come by and see Mom and Grandpa! They would love to see you all here, and maybe you can help them with the problems they are having."

"What's going on, sweetheart?" Tamera questioned.

"It's been terrible, Tamera. Someone keeps trying to attack our home, doing their best to take our Keramina. We've been able to hold them off a bit, but they still are taking much of our supplies."

Julietta led the Revolution to her home, a large mansion sitting on the edge of Perisia. When they entered the home, Julietta called out, "Mom, guess who's here!"

Then a woman who had golden hair with sky-blue eyes walked over to the Revolution. She was wearing a longer red top with black-mesh sleeves, a pink bow and white-ruffled trim, with a long black skirt.

"Welcome back, everyone," said the woman.

"It's great to see you as well, Judetta."

"And look who you have with you: Noelle. How have you been?"

Noelle blushed, simply smiling.

Tamera turned to Timothy. "Timothy, I would like you to meet Judetta."

Timothy walked over to Judetta.

"Judetta, this is my boyfriend, Timothy."

"I welcome you to Perisia, Timothy."

"Thank you, Judetta."

"Judetta, the new shipment of Keramina is…"

A man walked over to the group. The man had gray hair, mustache and beard, with bright yellow eyes, and wore his military outfit that was mostly brown and white, with a red cape and silver armor. He saw the members of the Revolution.

"Well, if it isn't the Revolution!" He hugged Kirbie and Tamera. Then he turned to Noelle, shaking her hand. "I am grateful that you are helping to defeat this tyrant, Noelle."

"Thank you."

"Timothy," Tamera introduced, "this is Judetta's father, Ligwud. He's the king of Perisia."

"I am also grateful that you are helping the Revolution, Timothy."

"Thank you, Ligwud. I appreciate that."

The room became quiet.

"I'm so sorry, I didn't mean to upset you."

"No, it's all right, Timothy," Judetta told him. "You didn't know. He was another victim of the Riverton War. His name was Joshua."

Suddenly there was a loud explosion outside that shook the walls of the office. As the walls of the mansion shook, Kirbie, Tamera, Tessa, Noelle and Timothy looked out one of the windows and saw there was a large crater in the yard where a cannonball had landed.

"Where did that come from?" Tamera questioned.

"It's Captain Gator," Ligwud responded in frustration. "He wants to kill us and steal our supply of Keramina for Abaddon and his goons."

"What is the Keramina used for?" Timothy wondered.

"It's just like your jewel," Ligwud stated. "It can also heal some wounds. Your jewel, however, is much stronger."

"Please stop him," Julietta pleaded. "He needs to stop terrorizing us."

"It looks like he's out in the river," Noelle pointed out.

"And he's got company... lots of it," Tamera followed.

Timothy was amazed. "Those are big ships. How do we get to them?"

"You can use my ship," Ligwud told them. "It's parked at the docks just a little way from here. I'll help you."

"I'll watch over the mansion," Tessa responded. "Please be careful, everyone."

"We better get going," Tamera told them.

"Please be careful," Julietta told them.

The trio made their way to the dock, leaving Kirbie at the

mansion to protect Ligwud's family.

The Revolution gathered up by Ligwud's large wooden ship.
"Are you ready?" Noelle asked.
"How are we going to stop three large ships?" Timothy pondered.
"We better get it figured out." Tamera pointed to the north. "Here they come."
They watched the three ships come ever closer to them.
Noelle, Tamera and Timothy loaded up in the ship. They readied everything and made their way sailing northward into the Orinoco River, heading right for the captain's fleet. They were surprised to see Captain Gator looked like a cross between a human and an alligator.
On Captain Gator's ship, one of the crewmen, looking through a telescope from the crow's nest, saw Ligwud's ship heading towards them.
"Captain," shouted the crewman. "It's Ligwud's ship! It's charging!"
Gator laughed. "The old fool…"
The crewman looked again through his scope. "The Revolution is with him!"
"Everyone to your stations!" Gator called out.
Out of nowhere Gator, who could stand like a human, saw a beam of light soaring through the air. The light struck the crewman that was in the crow's nest. The crewman exploded into dust. Gator looked to see Tamera was firing arrows from the ship.
"Shoot them down!" Gator demanded.
Two other crewmen began firing beams of black at the crew while two others began shooting cannonballs at Ligwud's ship. Noelle was doing her best to dodge the beams while Ligwud was

trying to steer his ship to dodge the cannonballs.

Tamera fired another arrow at Captain Gator's ship. The arrow hit its target, turning the crewman to dust.

"Let's stop these guys!" Tamera stated. She pointed to Ligwud. "Keep the ship going."

He saluted and said, "Aye aye, Captain!"

"Timothy, help us load the cannons!"

"You got it, baby!"

Timothy helped Tamera and Noelle to load the cannons.

"Ready!" Timothy called out.

"Fire!" Tamera yelled.

More and more cannons were fired at each ship, with both ships taking damage. Then Ligwud was able to steer his ship close to Gator's. Tamera, Noelle and Timothy boarded Gator's ship and proceeded to strike down other spirits.

The captain became enraged as he took to one of the guns, firing at Ligwud's ship. In the meantime, Tamera struck down Gator's crewman. She then struck Gator, and Gator fell to the ground, almost getting knocked out. He slowly went to grab a laser he was carrying, but Tamera stood next to Gator and knocked the laser out of his hand. She then pointed her sword at Gator.

"Lycan and Abaddon will destroy you," Gator said, in pain.

"Not if we can help it," Tamera stated, and then she stabbed Captain Gator, who turned into dust. They then raided the other ships. Timothy and Tamera then used some of the cannons to destroy the other ships.

The sun began to set as the group arrived back at Perisia in Ligwud's ship. As the group pulled the ship up to the docks, they saw in surprise they were being greeted by the citizens of Perisia, who were cheering for what the group had done for them.

The group was all smiles as they walked off the ship and onto the dock, and the citizens swarmed the group with louder applause and screams and were getting hugs from some of the citizens. Finally, Julietta approached the group. Tessa walked over to Julietta and gave her a tight hug.

"Thank you," Julietta told her, then she also showed attention to the others. "You all saved our lives."

"How can we ever repay you?" Ligwud asked.

"You already have, Ligwud," Tamera stated, "for helping us to defeat Captain Gator."

"Will you be back to visit?" Julietta asked Tessa.

"You bet we will," Kirbie told her. They hugged.

"Please come back to see us," Judetta encouraged.

"We will," Tamera told them. "Take care of yourselves."

The Revolution waved to the citizens of Perisia as they walked away.

Kirbie was scrolling through her phone once again.

"Wow, whoever is reporting this stuff sure is fast!" Kirbie noted. She showed Tamera, Timothy and Noelle the report on her phone: "How Timothy Stopped a War."

Tamera read the article: "Timothy has shown to be a true miracle once again, as he led the members of the Revolution to defeat the evil Captain Gator, preventing him from stealing the beloved Keramina, and saving those who live in the prosperous town of Perisia."

"I'm really getting tired of this," Timothy stated. "I mean, if they want to report on this stuff, fine. But stop twisting what happened."

"Yeah, the press can be such a joy," Tamera followed.

Chapter 19

Warrington

The group crossed the bridge of the Orinoco River to continue on their journey as the townsfolk returned to Perisia. In the meantime, they were being watched again by Abaddon.

"Laugh now," Abaddon said in sheer anger. "But when you get to Warrington, you won't know what hit you."

"So, what can we expect in Warrington?" Timothy pondered.

"Probably the same stuff we've been running into," Tamera answered.

Timothy chuckled. "Of course, smarty pants." They laughed as Timothy and Tamera wrapped one of their arms around each other.

"Well, Symphony Lynn is the ruler there," Kirbie informed them, "and I haven't heard the most positive news about her."

"What do you mean?" asked Timothy.

"She's just like a lot of leaders out there, sucking in all the glory for herself, and really not thinking too much about the townsfolk. The town's been going downhill for a while now."

Noelle yawned. "I'm beat. We should get some rest."

"Indeed," Tamera agreed. Everyone said good night to each other.

Lycan watched carefully as the Revolution all fell asleep for the night.

"Come tomorrow," Lycan said out loud, "the Revolution will be no more."

Without another word, Lycan walked away.

It was morning, and the sun broke over the horizon, but there were also lots of clouds in the sky. Timothy awoke, and he looked down to see Tamera had wrapped her arm around him. Then Tamera awoke after feeling Timothy move. She pulled her arm off him and blushed.

"Sorry," she responded.

"It's all right, baby. How are you doing?"

"I'll let you know when I'm awake a little longer."

Timothy chuckled at the comment. Noelle then awoke. At that time, they looked up to the sun shining through some darker gray clouds. They saw the fire had gone out, and the morning was still a bit chilly yet. Tamera then woke Kirbie up.

"It looks like it's going to rain," Timothy pointed out.

"Yeah," Tamera agreed. "We better get to Warrington before it does."

Everyone grabbed their stuff and made their way on their ship.

It wasn't too long before the group arrived at Warrington. Everyone noticed the townsfolk were staring at them.

Timothy approached one of the citizens. "Excuse me, ma'am, we're looking for…"

The woman scoffed and walked away from him. Tamera and Timothy then walked to another lady to ask her about Symphony, but she also walked away without saying a word.

Noelle tried the same thing with some children, but before she could get a word in, one child threw some mud on her, and she fell to the ground. Before she could react to that, the other child then dumped a pail of water over her head. Then they laughed as they ran away.

"It's like everyone's got a terrible attitude," Timothy noted.

Noelle tried to wipe the mud off her face. "I guess I needed a mud bath."

"There's the city hall," Tamera mentioned. "Let's see if we can find anything there."

They all walked into the city hall on the east edge of town, with people still just staring, commenting or laughing at them. They came into the large lobby and looked around.

"Where should we go?" Timothy questioned.

"Well, look who we have here," said a voice. The group turned to see a slender woman with very pale skin, black hair, with two pigtails colored black and red. She was dressed in a black jacket, shirt and skirt that had white ruffles on the end of her sleeves, down the front of the shirt, and on the top and bottom of the skirt, and wore black fishnet pantyhose.

Kirbie knew instantly who it was. "Hello, Symphony."

Symphony chuckled. "Well, if it isn't the Revolution. What a surprise."

"It's no surprise to see you here," Tamera noted.

"I'm finally on top, just where I wanted to be."

"Who suffered for you to get there?"

Symphony laughed. "You're just as feisty as ever, Tamera. This may be a shock, but I'm actually happy to see you. I need you to help me with a little problem I've come across, if you don't mind."

Tamera rolled her eyes. "Typical of you to ask for something that benefits only you, Symphony."

Symphony chuckled. "Ooh, and I see you've been hanging around Kirbie too long, Tamera. It actually has to do with my daughter, Melody."

Tamera and Kirbie looked puzzled. "Since when have you had a daughter?" Kirbie questioned.

Symphony pulled out a picture of a beautiful little girl with deep brown hair and green eyes. "I adopted her just a couple months ago. She's my pride and joy. I think she was kidnapped by the Darkness. I was told she's still in Warrington, but not sure where. Nobody's been able to find her."

They all looked at the picture.

"How do we know this isn't a trick?" Noelle asked.

Symphony chuckled. "Relax, Noelle. We both want the Darkness out of the way in the name of peace. Why don't you help me find my daughter? I know you're the best at what you do."

They all looked at each other to see what each wanted to do, and everyone nodded their heads in approval. "Okay, Symphony," Tamera stated for the group, "we'll see if we can find your daughter."

"Thank you," Symphony said with a smile. "You must hurry. I don't think there's much time."

With that, the Revolution walked out of the room, heading for the outdoors. Then Symphony grabbed a phone and said, "The plan is in motion."

"Excellent," said Lycan. "Cassian is on his way."

The Revolution stood out in front of city hall and checked their surroundings.

"How will we ever find Melody here?" Timothy wondered.

"It's a good-sized town," Tamera followed.

"Be lucky it's not Riverton," Kirbie pointed out. "It makes Warrington look like a dwarf."

"The best we can do is split up," Noelle figured. "Timothy,

why don't you and Tamera take the west side? Kirbie, you check out the northeast, and I'll go southeast."

"Be careful, you two," said Timothy.

"You, too," Kirbie spoke before the group separated.

Timothy and Tamera walked down a lonely street, each keeping their guard up. They were uneasy at how quiet it was.

"Where did everyone go?" Timothy asked.

"I don't know," Tamera told him. "Let's keep looking."

They held each other's hand as they walked onward.

Meanwhile, Kirbie was experiencing the same thing.

"This town was swarming with people," Kirbie stated to herself. "How did they all just disappear?"

Kirbie was just as puzzled as she walked on.

Noelle checked out the southern part of the town. She happened to come up to an arena that sounded as if it were full of people. Thinking she may be able to find Melody there, she decided to check it out.

Timothy and Tamera came across an intersection. As Timothy looked to the left, he glanced what she thought was a little child who had run in behind a house.

"Tamera, I think I saw her."

Timothy chased after the girl, and Tamera followed behind. They ran around several homes, trees, and bushes until Timothy and Tamera stopped suddenly in their tracks. The two stood face-to-face with two beings that were formed with sand.

Kirbie walked down through a commercial district. She

happened to see what looked like somebody walking into one of the markets. Kirbie walked into the store and looked to see where the person had gone. Just then she noticed the back door opened slightly. Thinking the person had gone to the back, she decided to do so. When he did, she was shocked to see she was now facing a huge figure that was made of stone.

Noelle walked out towards the center of the arena floor. The audience booed at her. When Noelle looked around, she noticed that the townsfolk began turning into members of the Darkness.

"Oh, great," Noelle said to herself as she pulled out her sword.

Lycan again got a hold of Symphony, with Abaddon listening.

"Symphony, how's it going?" Lycan asked her.

"You're in for quite a surprise, master," she responded.

Lycan was thrilled. "Excellent. Keep in touch."

Camille's worries grew, uncertain if the Revolution could hold out this battle. Tanna comforted Camille, trying to assure them the Revolution would succeed.

Timothy and Tamera both used their weapons on one of the sand men. The sword went right through the body, not affecting it. Tamera then used her ax, but the ax passed right through the figure.

The one sand man punched Timothy in the face. Not only did he fall from the punch, but the sand had also torn up his face.

"How do we stop them?" Timothy asked as Tamera tended to him. Then she thought about her magic. Her eyes grew wide.

"I feel so stupid," she spoke to herself. She used her ice on the sand creatures, and they solidified.

"It looks like Symphony tricked us," Timothy stated. "We better find the others."

Kirbie had to dive out of the way of the stone man's enormous fist. The when Kirbie struck the figure's arm with her fire magic, the stone man's arm fell off. Tessa then punched the stone man's leg with much force, causing the stone man to lose its balance, and it fell over. The stone man fell apart.

"Oh man," the stone man stated.

Tessa walked over to the talking stone head. "Sorry." She then kissed the stone's head before she ran away.

"I can't believe I was rocked."

Noelle took her stance as she got ready to fight. The members of the Darkness charged at her. She started off fighting off as many as she could, but then the odds became quickly overwhelming. In no time, the clan had Noelle off her feet.

Then out of nowhere, Noelle's sword glowed and a sharp beam blasted outward, destroying many of the spirits, turning them quickly into dust. Noelle continued to fight, and then Timothy and Tamera joined in the battle with Noelle, fighting as hard as they could until every one of the Darkness was defeated.

"I'm glad you're okay," Timothy told Noelle as they hugged each other.

"Have you seen Kirbie?" Tamera asked in worry.

"Not yet," Noelle replied. "We were hoping she was here."

"We think Symphony tricked us," Timothy informed Noelle. "We were attacked as well by two sand men."

"We better find Kirbie fast, and then get some answers from Symphony."

The group left the arena.

Timothy, Tamera and Noelle ran as quick as they could towards city hall. Looking onward, he was relieved to see Kirbie heading towards city hall as well. They approached to see Symphony standing in front of the building.

Back at Abaddon's castle, Lycan and Abaddon watched as they saw Symphony standing against the Revolution. Behind Symphony approached her army out of city hall. In front of her approached the Darkness, led by Cassian.

"This is it," Lycan smiled while watching the battle with Abaddon. "We'll finally see the end of the Revolution."

"Symphony," Tamera called out. "This has to stop. Lycan is using you, and when this is all said and done, he will destroy you, too."

"No!" Symphony yelled. "Nobody is taking my town away!"

Her hands reached up to the air. A swirling wind shot out from around Symphony. The Revolution was thrown backwards, as well as Cassian and the Darkness.

"Symphony," Tamera yelled. "Fight with us! Help us defeat Abaddon and Lycan!"

"NO!" she yelled. "You will *all* die!"

At that moment, a person stood between them, wearing a hooded black cape.

"Who do you think you are?" Symphony wondered.

"Please don't do this, Symphony," the woman pleaded. "They are after the same cause. They can help you defeat Abaddon and his clan."

"No!" Symphony told her. "It's *my* time to rule!"

Symphony created her windstorm once again. Kirbie and Tamera put up a wall of ice. The wall blocked the heavy gust of wind.

Abaddon and Lycan were shocked at what had just happened. Lycan grabbed his phone.

"Kill the witch!" Lycan commanded to Cassian. Then Cassian gave the order to his spirits. The Darkness charged valiantly against Symphony's army and the Revolution. Tamera battled against Cassian. Timothy and Noelle took on Symphony's army. The mysterious woman fought off the Darkness. That left Kirbie to handle Symphony. Kirbie formed her swords and prepared to fight, glowing purple.

"You don't stand a chance, cat girl," Symphony chuckled.

"We'll see about that, Symphony."

Symphony pulled out her second sword as well. The two began to battle fiercely, wildly swinging their swords at each other.

Tamera threw ice at Cassian. Cassian moved out of the way. Cassian grabbed Tamera, but Tamera quickly flipped Cassian over her shoulder. Cassian got back up, did his best to attack, but Tamera tripped Cassian up. Feeling he couldn't win this fight, Cassian ran off again like a coward.

Timothy attacked Symphony's army with all his might using Olympia. Noelle used her sword to help Timothy destroy the clan. In the meantime, the hooded woman kept the Darkness at bay using her lightning attack.

Symphony blocked several attempts by Kirbie to attack. She then pushed Kirbie as hard as she could. Then Symphony used her windstorm spell and Kirbie slammed against a wall. Kirbie charged in after her. Symphony tried sword fighting against Kirbie some more, but Kirbie was able to get the upper hand on her. Eventually she was able to knock one of the swords out of Symphony's hand. Symphony tried again to attack, but Kirbie was able to knock the other sword away. Then Kirbie pinned Symphony against the wall, with her swords up against her neck.

At that moment, the woman with the hood over her head walked over to them. Kirbie then proceeded to stab Symphony in the stomach with one of her swords, and Symphony's body turned to dust.

The woman approached Kirbie ever closer. "Kirbie? Kirbie, is that you?"

Kirbie was puzzled. "How do you know me?"

The woman then pulled the hood off her head. She revealed herself to be a cat girl who had white hair and one blue eye and one brown eye. She was dressed in a dark blue sleeveless top and a dark blue plaid miniskirt with black stockings. Kirbie was stunned.

"Billie?" Kirbie said softly as tears began to fall from her eyes. The two hugged each other tightly. "I thought you were dead. You disappeared after the war…"

"I'm so sorry, Kirbie. After what happened I… I couldn't bear to stay around. The pain was just too much for me to bear. Please don't be angry with me."

"I could… never be angry with you, Billie. It's because of you that I am who I am."

"I couldn't be prouder of you, Kirbie."

Suddenly, something began to glow above where Kirbie and Billie stood. After a bright flash, Kirbie and Billie looked to see a star appear. It floated over to where Kirbie stood.

The others saw the star hovering over Kirbie. When she went to reach for it, the star suddenly turned black, and it faded into dust. Everyone was puzzled.

"What happened?" Timothy questioned.

"I'm not sure," Kirbie answered. "Everyone, this is Billie."

"It's great to meet you all, and I thank you so much for saving us."

At that time the citizens of the village started coming out from their homes. They were thrilled to see the Revolution standing tall, and they cheered for them.

"Thank you for your help, Billie," Tamera stated.

"So that picture of Melody that Symphony showed us..." Timothy mentioned.

"I'm really not sure who that was."

"Please come with us," Kirbie asked.

Billie smiled as she shook her head. "I have to protect the people of Warrington. God be with you on your journey. I will pray for your safe return."

"But... I don't want to leave you."

"Don't worry, sweetie. Once this is over, I promise I'll come back to you."

Kirbie kissed Billie on the forehead. Then Billie began to cry. "I remember when you always did that when we were together."

"So, what's next?" Timothy questioned.

"We head for Riverton," Tamera informed them.

After Billie said goodbye to the Revolution, they got back on the ship and headed off.

Fuming, Abaddon slammed his fist on the table. Camille and the others watched as Abaddon cried out in rage.

"Abaddon..." called out a voice. Abaddon walked to the screen and saluted the person that called for him. Nobody was able to see on the screen whom the person was that called out to Abaddon.

"Why are they still alive?" asked the person in a deep, dark voice.

"We were set back by Symphony, who betrayed us, master," Abaddon explained. "But rest assured the Revolution will not make it out of Riverton alive."

"Hear me when I say this: If you fail me, there will be dire consequences. Is that understood, Abaddon?"

Abaddon saluted again. "Yes, master. We will not fail you."

The screen went black. Everyone was now in disbelief, that it was somebody else leading the charge of this invasion, and not Abaddon like they first thought. They sat down with the others and they prayed together for the safety of the Revolution.

Chapter 20

The Pristine Mountains

Evening had rolled around after the Revolution left Warrington to continue on their journey. After a tough battle against Symphony and the Darkness, the group arrived at Corona Jungle, a small area that rested northwest of Warrington and southeast of Riverton. The Revolution took shelter at a cottage that was made mostly of sticks and clay.

During the night, Tamera had a dream. Timothy was walking cautiously through a narrow street in a large city. He looked around while holding Olympia. Suddenly there was a darkened arrow that hit him in the shoulder. Timothy fell to one knee. He became stunned after seeing the magical arrow disappear that a large wound was in his shoulder.

Before Timothy could react, he saw himself surrounded by members of the Darkness. Timothy stood back up, still holding his sword. He began fighting against the Darkness, destroying them and watching them turn to dust. Out of nowhere, Timothy got hit by another dark arrow in the back of his other shoulder. This time he fell to the ground on his stomach.

As Timothy rolled to his side, looking back, his eyes filled with uncertainty and fear. There he saw what looked like an evil Tamera approaching him with a sword in her hand. The eyes that were normally a pure, beautiful green on Tamera were a glowing bright red, almost the color of blood. The evil Tamera pointed her ax at Timothy.

"Tamera?" Timothy asked in fear.

Still holding her ax, she pulled her arm back.

"Not any more," she spoke before swinging the ax forward.

At that point, Tamera woke up, gasping loudly. Timothy woke up hearing Tamera gasping.

"Tamera?" Timothy said softly.

Tamera pulled her body away from Timothy, still acting as if he were in a panic. "No! Get away!" Tamera yelled.

Timothy was shocked. He could see the fear in Tamera's face. Her yell woke Noelle and Kirbie, and they looked at Tamera and Timothy, wondering what was going on.

"Baby, what's wrong?" Timothy asked in concern. "Are you okay?"

Tamera looked over at Timothy. Then she looked at his hands and saw there was no blood on them. She looked over to Timothy's shoulder as well and realized there was no wound there.

Breathing heavily, Tamera looked over at Timothy. Timothy placed his left hand on Tamera's right cheek.

"Tamera?"

As Tamera tried to calm herself down, she became so overwhelmed with emotion that tears rolled from her eyes as she hugged Timothy, refusing to let him go. She tried to tell Timothy what happened in the dream but was too upset to say.

"What happened, baby?" Timothy questioned as she hugged him.

Kirbie and Noelle watched on.

"My love must have had a nightmare," Kirbie stated.

"Look how terrified she is," Noelle reacted.

Once Tamera was able to regain her composure, the Revolution readied themselves for their journey to Riverton. At that time, a young, blue-haired girl, named Alana, approached the group. Alana had sky-blue colored shoulder-length hair tied back in a ponytail, with violet eyes. She was wearing a simple tank top and leggings, both colored black.

"Good morning, everyone!" said the beauty.

"Hi, Alana," Kirbie stated. They hugged.

"I heard some commotion coming from your cottage, and I just wanted to make sure you all were okay."

"Yeah, we're fine," Tamera told her. She held tightly to Timothy's hand, then leaned against him, smiling.

"Timothy," Kirbie introduced, "this is Princess Alana, the ruler of Corona Jungle. Alana, this is Timothy. He is helping us on our journey."

"Nice to meet you," said Alana as she shook hands with Timothy. "Please, join me at my home, and I will serve you breakfast."

While walking over to Alana's home, Kirbie was looking once more at her phone.

"Timothy, check this out," Kirbie told him.

Kirbie showed Timothy what was on her phone: a page with the headline on the top: "Timothy's Fan Club: Leader of the Revolution." Then there were pictures of Timothy fighting against some of the spirits in previous battles. Kirbie then showed some of the comments. One said, "Timothy's the greatest!" Another said, "He's my hero through and through! Thank you, Timothy!" And yet another stated, "The Revolution is nothing without Timothy."

"Wow," Tamera stated. "Now you have a whole fan club?"

"The more you show this to me, Kirbie, the more irritated I get."

"That wasn't my intention, Timothy."

"Yeah, I think it's great you're getting the attention," Noelle followed.

"But it's at your expense. How could they give me all this recognition but not to you, Tamera and Noelle? We're a team on this!"

Kirbie lowered her head. Timothy then calmed down as he hugged Kirbie.

"I'm really sorry, Kirbie. I know this isn't your fault."

"No, you don't have to apologize. I guess I didn't think of it that way."

Arriving at Alana's home, she set down a tray of fruits, vegetables and grains on a table, and the members helped themselves.

"So, you're on your way to Riverton?" Alana wondered.

"Yes," Tamera answered.

"What's it like?" Timothy questioned.

"Riverton is the largest city in the World of Exodus," Alana educated him. "It is the backbone of our needs. Everything like the food and water we're serving, we could get from Riverton. That is, until Prince Kain disappeared recently."

Timothy was stunned. "Disappeared? How?"

"Nobody really knows," Kirbie commented. "What's really strange is that nobody really seemed too concerned about it."

"What was Prince Kain like?" asked Timothy.

Tamera answered, "He was first the ruler of Corona, but three years ago, he became the ruler of Riverton. The town became a wonderful place, and Prince Kain even launched a powerful commerce to the rest of Exodus. Now that he has been lost to us, that commerce program is faltering, and the town is going sour quickly. They've not been able to find anyone who wants the role."

"What about you, Alana?" Kirbie asked. "You do wonders for Corona. I bet you'd be a great princess for Riverton."

"Thank you, Kirbie," Alana smiled. "But my life is here with these people. Besides, that's such a large responsibility. I like the simplicity of Corona Jungle."

"Well, it sounds like we really need to get to Riverton," Noelle mentioned.

"I agree," Tamera voiced her opinion. "We'll have to go through the Pristine Lake and Mountains, and then pass through Cecaria before reaching Riverton."

The group gathered their things.

"Be careful," Alana told the heroes. "I'm not sure what is going on there, or why Prince Kain disappeared, but something is definitely wrong there, and you need to be on your guard every waking moment."

"Thank you, Alana, for everything," Tamera spoke. "We'll do our best to find him."

After saying goodbye, the Revolution made their way out of Corona Jungle.

Back at Abaddon's castle, Abaddon watched, through his crystal ball, the group making their way towards the Pristine Mountains. A door opened. Abaddon watched as Lycan walked into the room. He held up a magic wand.

"That's Solara's wand," Behrlin pointed out.

"Which one shall be the victim, your grace?" Lycan

questioned.

"Go after Tamera," Abaddon answered. "She is the gentlest one in the Revolution. If we take her out of the equation, the others will surely fail because they won't want to hurt her."

"If they make it to Riverton," Lycan commented, "I'll assure you, they won't know what hit them."

The evil ones all began laughing maniacally.

"I feel so helpless," Camille stated, and became so full of anger that she began to cry. The others hugged to comfort her.

"I'm sure she'll be all right," Tanna tried to assure her. "They've come this far. They'll find a way through it."

As they made their way to the Pristine Mountains, the Revolution admired the scenery that surrounded them. They noticed the area started becoming more and more filled with hills and valleys. A little bit further, the group finally made their way to the beginning of the Pristine Mountains.

"Wow," Timothy said, mesmerized. "This is amazing. Look at the size of those mountains!

"Once we get through the Pristine Mountains and the lake," Kirbie mentioned, "we will travel on to Cecaria."

"There's a lake in the mountains?" Timothy asked in surprise.

"Yes," Tamera replied. "It's in the middle of the mountain range."

Everyone cautiously walked down a small trail that curved through the mountainside. Noelle and Kirbie felt uncertainty as they were traveling down the narrow trail. They kept their eyes opened at every moment. At that point, Tamera noticed Timothy was deep in thought.

"Is something bothering you, Timothy?" she asked.

"I can't get out of my mind as to what happened this morning, Tamera," Timothy stated. "When I came up to you, you acted as if I were your worst enemy."

Tamera sighed. "I know, and I'm really sorry. I thought I was still stuck in the nightmare I was having."

Everyone stopped walking.

"Can I ask what happened?" Timothy asked.

Tamera lowered her head in sadness. "I dreamed that you were fighting against the Darkness. Then you got hit by these two black arrows. Then I saw myself approaching you while you were on your knees in pain. I had these... evil red eyes and..."

Tears started rolling down Tamera cheeks again, and she wiped the tears away.

"I tried to kill you..."

Kirbie and Noelle were amazed.

"But Timothy, I wouldn't..."

Timothy interrupted, hugging Tamera. "I know that, baby. It was just a nightmare."

"I'm really sorry I acted that way. You've been so wonderful to me, and I just don't want to lose you."

"And you won't, my love," Timothy assured her. He then reached in his pocket. "This is probably inappropriate, but..." Tamera saw that he was holding a jewelry box. "Tamera, my love, will you marry me and be mine forever?"

Tamera was speechless. Her eyes were wide open, as was her mouth, which she had covered with her hands, seeing she was in pure shock. Then she smiled greatly as tears of joy now fell from her eyes.

"Yes, yes, yes!" Tamera kept crying out as she jumped into Timothy's arms. Kirbie was so thrilled that she couldn't help but hug the two as well while they were still on the ground. Even

Noelle had a smile on her face.

"Congratulations, you two," Kirbie told them.

"When this is all over," Timothy told Tamera, "I will be honored to have you as my wife." He placed the ring on Tamera's finger.

"And I'll be honored to have you as my husband."

They all got back on their feet, and Timothy held Tamera's hand as he and Tamera walked away from Kirbie and Noelle, still talking about their future wedding. Kirbie and Noelle watched as she walked on. Noelle then said to Kirbie, "As the leader of my own army, I have seen the worst in people. I've seen people turn on others in a heartbeat. But the thought of Tamera being evil... that doesn't sound possible."

Kirbie sighed. "I know, but you and I both know that in the World of Exodus, anything can happen. Besides, in the Bible, Satan has angels working for him. Regardless of what happens, we have to keep our focus on rescuing our friends."

"Absolutely."

Kirbie and Noelle caught up with Tamera and Timothy.

"How far is it through the mountains?" Timothy asked in worry.

"Don't fret," Kirbie assured him. "We're almost to Pristine Lake."

Tamera looked above her to the sky and noticed a large hawk and several others still a good size but smaller than the one leading the flock. She didn't think anything of it until she noticed the hawks had suddenly changed direction, swooping down towards the group, with their claws extended out.

"Look out!" Tamera yelled.

Kirbie, Noelle and Timothy looked to see the hawks heading towards them, and they readied themselves for battle. Tamera revealed her ax. Kirbie, Timothy and Noelle prepared to fight as the hawks swarmed at them.

Tamera ran towards the hawk as it swooped down at her. As Tamera closed on the hawk, she swung her ax at the hawk, but missed as the hawk dodged in another direction. In the meantime, the others tried to hold off the other hawks, but the other hawks had the upper hand due to their quick and agile flying abilities.

The lead hawk charged at Tamera with its claws drawn, but Tamera moved out of the way. As the hawk went to pass by, Tamera swung her ax, cutting part of the hawk's wing. The hawk howled in pain and began descending towards the ground. The other hawks heard their leader cry out and charged in flight after their leader. Tamera also ran after the hawk, the other hawks helped him ease his way to the ground.

Kirbie, Timothy and Tessa approached the hawks, ready to attack, until Tamera thought she recognized the injured hawk.

"Hawkore?" Tamera spoke. "Is that you?"

The other hawks prepared to attack, but the leader yelled, "Stop!"

Surprised, the hawks turned to their leader. The lead hawk approached Tamera cautiously.

"Tamera?" the hawk simply spoke.

"I remember you," said Tamera. "You fought with my family in the Riverton War."

"That was a few years back."

"Why did you attack us?" Kirbie demanded to know.

"We thought you were members of the Darkness. We were told Noelle's ship has been used in some of their attacks. Please forgive us."

"Well, if you don't mind," Noelle exclaimed, "we'll be on our way now."

"Indeed. And if you'll excuse us, we have our own problem to take care of."

The hawks got ready to fly away. Tamera became filled with concern for them. "Wait!" Tamera cried out, and the hawks stopped from leaving. Tamera approached Hawkore. "What problem?"

"There's a large piranha swimming in Pristine Lake. It has killed several of our hawks who have tried to get food, and now they are afraid to get food from there so we have had to make long journeys in order just to get food. We've actually thought about living elsewhere, but this has been our home for generations."

Timothy and Kirbie stood beside Tamera. "Well, we're headed in that direction anyway," Tamera said. "We should be able to help you with your problem, if it's okay with you," she told them.

"This could be very dangerous."

The others came up to Hawkore.

"It's probably no more dangerous than what we've already been through," Kirbie stated. "We would be happy to help you."

"Let's go to the lake," Tamera advised.

The group continued on their way along the long, narrow, curvy trail until they finally reached the lake in the middle of the mountain range. The group approached the lake, noticing the lake was calm.

Suddenly the water began rippling violently. Tamera grabbed Timothy, pulling him away from the edge of the lake. Then the large piranha surfaced out of the lake. The green and purple piranha showed off its large teeth, leaving the group mesmerized.

"Awe, come on!" the piranha cried in a feminine voice. "I'm hungry, and you all would make a great appetizer."

"Oh, yeah?" Tamera said, flustered. "Feed on this!"

She shot ice into the mouth of the piranha, and it cried out in pain. Noelle shot a beam of light from her sword, but the piranha quickly descended into the lake.

"Come on, everyone!" Tamera told them.

"Be careful!" Hawkore responded.

They all dove into the lake. They swam down towards the bottom of the lake until they saw an opening. They then swam quickly into the opening and found a place that had no water in it. They all crawled out and breathed for air.

"I don't see it," Tamera stated and the others looked around.

Unexpectedly, Timothy felt something grab his foot. He cried out and grabbed Tamera's hand before they both got pulled down into the water. The others cried out and then dove down after him.

"Hang on, Timothy!" Tamera cried out.

Tamera made her way to the piranha and stabbed it in the eye with her sword. It cried out, letting go of Timothy. Timothy then began to lose consciousness as Tamera led him up back to the surface. Kirbie saw them and she and Noelle also headed for the surface so they could get more air. The piranha gave chase as quickly as it could in sheer anger.

Kirbie and Noelle surfaced. Tamera then popped out of the water, holding onto Timothy. Kirbie and Noelle helped them out of the water before the piranha jumped out of the water to grab him. Before the piranha could reach him, Kirbie threw one of her purple fireballs at the piranha, and the piranha cried out again in pain.

Timothy awoke as Tamera placed him on the ground, and

Noelle flew back towards the piranha. Tamera helped Timothy on his feet. Kirbie worked to freeze the piranha in its place. At that moment, Noelle jumped and sliced the piranha with her sword, killing the piranha.

Tamera ran over to Timothy, hugging him tightly. "Are you okay, my love?" Tamera asked.

"I'm fine, baby. Kirbie was right: it would be you protecting me."

"Are you... mad about that?"

"Not at all. I'm always grateful for you."

Tamera blushed.

Hawkore and his army landed in front of the Revolution.

"I don't know how to thank you all," Hawkore told them. "Now we will be able to take care of ourselves and our families."

"You're welcome," Tamera replied. "And listen, about what happened earlier..."

"Don't worry about it," Hawkore assured her. "I've had worse battle wounds, and I'll rebound from this. Besides, it was an honor to battle you. If you ever need anything, you let us know. We've got your backs."

"Thank you, Hawkore," said Kirbie. "Take care of yourselves."

The group all shook hands or claws with Hawkore and his army. Then the group headed on their way out of the mountain range.

Chapter 21

The Children of Cecaria

As the sun fell into the horizon, the Revolution arrived in Cecaria, a small village that sat a few miles away from the Pristine Mountains. As they walked into the town, they noticed something just didn't feel right about it. They checked their surroundings and felt things were again too quiet.

"Where are the children?" Kirbie wondered.

The group looked around to see there wasn't a single light on in the houses, with no noises of anyone's presence.

"It seems like the town's been deserted," Timothy mentioned.

Suddenly children from all different directions swarmed in around the group. Tears were flowing from their eyes; many were crying out loud. To everyone's surprise, they all swarmed around Tamera and Kirbie, pleading for them to help them.

"What's going on?" Tamera asked the crying children.

"Our families have been taken," said a young girl with fright in her voice.

"Please help them," said another.

Then Rain, Alana, and Orion approached them. "The Darkness has been coming over here from Riverton," said Rain. "I fear something very wrong is going on there too."

"We try as hard as we can to hold them off," Alana spoke, "but they keep sending more and more of their clan. We don't know how much longer we can keep the children safe."

The group of children stayed so close to Tamera that she had trouble walking. They all continued together as they made their way through the silent town. As they stood in the middle of the town, Tamera threw her arm out, and everyone stopped in their tracks.

"What is it, Tamera?" asked Kirbie.

"Can you hear that?"

They stood in silence until they managed to hear a slight commotion. Tamera formed her sword as she walked to the south, and Timothy quietly followed with Olympia, ready to strike. Kirbie and Noelle stayed behind guarding Rain, Alana, Orion and the children. The further Timothy and Tamera walked, the more they heard the commotion until they noticed that there were lights on and conversation going on at the inn. They approached cautiously before opening the door and walking in.

When the group's presence was made known, the music went silent; everyone stopped what they were doing and looked over in their direction.

The group was disturbed by the sight they saw: many of Lycan's dark spirits, all again with their black skin.

"The Darkness," Tamera whispered.

The clan just stared at the heroes. Timothy just snickered.

"Hi, everyone," Tamera stated. "Anything good going on?"

The sprits stared menacingly.

"Sorry, we didn't mean to interrupt," Timothy spoke. "We'll be on our way now."

Tamera and Timothy backed their way out of the inn, hoping they could just make their escape, but the spirits screamed as they charged at them. They ran out into the street as they fought fiercely with the spirits. Just like others before them, whenever the spirits got hit, they would just explode into dust.

Timothy, Kirbie, Noelle and the children became surrounded by several spirits. Kirbie grabbed Timothy's hands. She forcefully swung Timothy in a circle. He began to flutter-kick the spirits, and they all exploded into dust. Noelle used her sword as well to subdue many of the clan.

Rain got separated from the group as she got cornered by several spirits. Rain slammed her fist into the ground and hit the spirits with a concussive blast of light, destroying the spirits that surrounded her.

Alana was also swarmed by the spirits. A piercing white wave shot out from all around Alana, and when the wave hit the spirits, they began to shake violently until they exploded to dust.

Tamera battled against members of the Darkness until after a few more moments of fighting, Tamera struck down the last spirit, and the battle was over.

"Very impressive," said a strange voice. The group heard the voice and stood firm in their fighting stances. "But let's see how well you can do against me."

The heroes became disturbed as they noticed more of the Darkness behind the mysterious human who had dark brown hair and light-yellow eyes, and was wearing a hooded tunic and pants colored black, with dark gray armor over his tunic. They also had Hawkore and his friends in their possession.

"Who are you, exactly?" Tamera questioned.

"I am Soneyo, the new conqueror of Cecaria."

"Conqueror?" Timothy asked, puzzled.

"Of course, and with the help of the Darkness, I will destroy all of you, and continue to spread the reign of Abaddon and Lycan through all of Exodus!"

Tamera raised her sword. "Not if we can help it."

Soneyo laughed maniacally and yelled, "Kill them all!"

With that, the Darkness began to attack Kirbie, Noelle and Timothy while Tamera set her sights on Soneyo. Alana sheltered the children in a building before Rain joined in the battle. As the members of the Darkness were being diminished, Soneyo ran away, laughing. Kirbie, Timothy and Tamera saw him leaving and they gave chase as Rain and Noelle stayed behind to guard the children.

Soneyo and the Revolution ended up together inside a dark cave. Soneyo stopped, turned around, and widely opened his mouth. Tamera and Kirbie became concerned. Suddenly a purplish mist spewed out of Soneyo's mouth. The mist absorbed into the group's skin, turning their skin color to a light purple.

"What is this?" Kirbie questioned as she and the others looked at their own skin. Suddenly everyone began to feel a little sickly, except for Tamera. Then an onset of pain began to swarm in each member's body. They all cried out in pain, falling down to their knees, and then their backs, unable to overcome the painful sensation.

Soneyo couldn't help but laugh at what he had done. He was certain he had neared the guardians to their defeat.

Then Soneyo was surprised to see himself struck by an arrow from Tamera. As he realized what had happened, he then saw Tamera jump at him, swinging her ax and striking Soneyo across his chest. He fell to the ground, dead.

Then a glow came up over where Soneyo stood, and another star revealed itself over Tamera. Once more Tamera reached for it, and again the star faded to black before turning into dust that blew away in the wind.

"What is going on with these diamonds?" Timothy asked, puzzled.

"Decoys," Tamera said softly.

"What was that, love?" Kirbie stated.

"They're decoys," Tamera mentioned. "We think we're getting the diamonds, but I bet that Abaddon actually has them."

"Well, what are we waiting for?" Noelle spoke. "Let's keep going!"

The group emerged out of the cave, admiring the now star-filled night as they made their way back to Cecaria. Upon entering, they were greeted by a gathering of children who hugged them (especially Tamera) and by the adults who cheered joyfully for them. Tessa freed Hawkore and his soldiers. Then they were approached by the princess of the town.

"Thank you all so much for what you've done for us," the princess told them. "We don't know what we would have done without you all."

"You're welcome," Tessa simply said.

"I am ready for some rest," Timothy stated, and the others agreed.

"Please stay at the inn," said the princess, "and you can continue your journey in the morning."

Later that evening, Kirbie and Noelle noticed Timothy and Tamera sitting on a bench, talking to each other as they looked up to the sky. They got to thinking about their families and friends, hoping they were okay. Then two young girls walked over to Timothy and Tamera, one of them holding a basket of fruit.

"Hi!" said the one girl joyously. "Here's some food for you and your friends!"

"Thank you," Timothy responded, smiling as she grabbed an

apple. "What's your name?"

"I'm Serenity," answered the girl that held the fruit bowl.

"And I'm Destiny!" the other girl followed.

Serenity had golden-brown hair and golden eyes, while Destiny had darker brown hair and hazel eyes. They both wore plaid sleeveless vests and skirts, with buttoned long-sleeved shirts and red bows tied in front of the vests, and tan pantyhose.

"I'm Timothy."

Then a tune started to play. More of the children came out in front of Timothy and Tamera and began to dance.

"Ooh, I love this song!" Serenity said joyfully.

"Tamera, will you dance with us?" asked Destiny.

"Sure," Tamera said without hesitance. The girls helped Tamera off the bench and they went to dance together. Timothy, Kirbie and Noelle watched as Tamera danced with the children.

After about three minutes, the music stopped, and the children laughed and cheered as they tackled the Revolution, hugging them with as much love as they could. They couldn't stop laughing as their hearts were exploding with joy. The people around that watched them applauded and whistled at them.

"Okay, children," said Alana. "Let's get to bed. The Revolution's got a big day tomorrow."

The children sighed sadly, but then said good night to Tamera, Timothy, Noelle and Kirbie as they walked away. A tear flowed from Tamera's eye as she smiled while watching the children.

"Watching you dance with the children reminded me of when I would hang out with my family," Tamera told Timothy, holding his hand. "I really miss them."

"So do I," Timothy replied.

In the meantime, someone was continuing to watch Timothy

and the others. She had herself ready to take more pictures of Timothy when she sensed someone beside her. She looked up and got spooked.

"I finally found you," Kirbie told her.

The girl went to run away, but Kirbie grabbed her before she could run away.

"Well, let's get some rest," Tamera said, yawning. "We have a big day tomorrow."

The Revolution walked into the inn. They saw Kirbie already in the inn, holding onto a young woman who had pink hair and purple eyes, who wore a white and dark-blue top with a burgundy tie, and a dark-blue skirt that matched the blue on her top, with tan pantyhose. She was holding on to a camera.

"Hey, Timothy, I found your secret admirer," Kirbie told him. Madison was blushing deeply as Timothy approached her. She felt as if she had butterflies in her stomach.

"What's your name, sweetie?" Timothy asked her.

"I'm... Madison..." she answered shyly.

"It's nice to meet you. So, are you the reporter that's telling all these stories about me?"

"Including this latest one." Kirbie showed Timothy the headline to Madison's latest story: "Timothy: The Hero of Cecaria."

"Are you mad?" Madison asked in worry.

"Well, it's just that... we're a team. I know they have told me how much they need me, but I know I wouldn't be where I am without them as well. I just don't think it's fair to them that I'm getting all the recognition."

Madison lowered her head. "I'm really sorry. I never meant to upset you. I know you and Tamera are dating, but... I've... fallen... in love with you..." Madison blushed even more. "This was my way of thanking you for what you are doing for us." Then she turned to Kirbie, Tamera and Noelle. "And don't get me wrong: I really appreciate what you all are doing as well. It's so incredibly brave that you are battling against the Darkness."

Kirbie kissed Madison on her forehead. "We thank you for that, Madison. And I'm sorry if I scared you so bad earlier."

"So, does this mean I can't report on you any more?"

"I'm not going to tell you to not do your job, sweetie. All I ask is that you also acknowledge the other members of the Revolution. Just promise me that, okay?"

"And make sure not to get yourself in any kind of danger," Tamera responded.

"I promise."

Timothy kissed Madison on the cheek. "Good. In the meantime, let's get some rest. It's gonna be a long day tomorrow."

"Um… can I… stay with you all?" Madison asked. "I mean… I don't want to intrude…"

Timothy looked over to Kirbie, Tamera and Noelle.

"It's okay with me," Noelle answered.

Tamera smiled as she nodded positively. Timothy reached his hand out to Madison. She blushed once more as she grabbed Timothy's hand, and then grabbed Tamera's hand.

"So, how long have you two been dating?"

"For a little while," Tamera answered. She showed Madison the ring Timothy gave her. "We're engaged now."

"That's wonderful!"

The next morning, while everyone was sleeping, members of the Darkness, led by Cassian, sneaked into Cecaria while storm clouds blanketed the sky. Cassian signaled for the clan to stop, and they all hid behind a bunch of bushes. He looked around to see the guards that were watching the town. Then he held up his wand. Suddenly a big black blast shot out from around him. The guards were put to sleep.

The Revolution was awakened by screams they heard outside. They all rushed to the door and went outside. They saw the town being invaded by the Darkness.

"Are you kidding me?" Timothy spoke.

"Well, there's no rest for the wicked," Tamera responded.

Tessa snickered in agreement. They joined in as a big battle ensued.

Cassian went to leave town with Serenity and Destiny in his grasp. Suddenly a big flash appeared in front of him. Cassian was shocked to see a ghost in his way.

Rain threatened, "Let them go!"

"Not a chance," Cassian stated.

Cassian tried to slice Rain with his sword, but Rain jumped back.

"Get her!" Cassian yelled to the Darkness.

The Darkness charged at Rain as Cassian made sure the children stayed by his side. Rain's hands began to glow. Then she was able to shoot blue balls of lightning from her hands, hitting the spirits and turning them to dust. But during the fight, a spirit of the Darkness sneaked up behind her. Before Rain could react, the spirit hit Rain in her head and she fell to the ground unconscious.

The Revolution saw what happened to Rain, and saw her, Serenity and Destiny being carried off by a spirit, with Cassian by his side.

"Tamera!" Serenity and Destiny cried out.

"Serenity! Destiny!" Tamera called back. Tamera and

Timothy went to chase after them as Noelle and Tessa stayed behind to protect the other townsfolk. Just as they went to pass a corner of the cottage, a spirit appeared around the other side of the cottage and trapped Timothy in the netting. The spirit then went to hit Tamera, but she fired an arrow at the spirit, turning the spirit into dust.

Tamera tended to Timothy, freeing him out of the netting and helping him to his feet. Then they noticed Cassian and the Darkness disappearing into the forest.

"Serenity and Destiny were..." Tamera spoke, worried.

"So was Rain," Timothy mentioned. "Don't worry, we'll get them back."

In the meantime, Abaddon and Lycan again watched through their crystal ball. After seeing the Revolution leaving Cecaria, the ball fogged up, and then cleared up again, revealing Cassian's face.

"My lords," Cassian greeted, "The plan is in motion. Soon the Revolution will enter Riverton. Once there, I will destroy them, and you will have free reign over this world!"

"Excellent, Cassian!" Lycan stated happily. "You've done something right for a change!"

"Yes, my lord and king, I will not fail you this time."

Cassian's face faded out of the ball.

"Finally," Abaddon said in relief.

Just then, a voice said out loud, "Yes, finally you are prevailing."

Abaddon and Lycan turned their attention to a screen.

"Yes, master," Abaddon assured him. "The Revolution is still on the hunt, but they will in no way leave Riverton alive, and you will rule all of this putrid world."

"Victory will soon be ours!" Lycan followed.

"Good. Mark my words, the end will be near and I *will* rule."

The transmission ended. The prisoners heard the strange voice and became more at unease.

"Who is that?" Camille questioned.

"I'm not sure," Laura told her. "I've never heard that voice before."

"What could he possibly be thinking, being so cruel like this?"

"We have to keep our faith that Tamera and the others will save us," Tanna commented, hugging Camille.

In the meantime, they could not stop thinking about what this mysterious person had in store for the Revolution, and if he could actually be stopped.

The Revolution got ready to leave Cecaria the next morning. After saying goodbye to the others, Madison walked up to Timothy.

"Looks like I'll have a lot to cover again," Madison mentioned.

"Madison, perhaps you should stay in Cecaria," Timothy asked of her. "If Tamera and Kirbie are right about Riverton, that's the last place I want you to be, okay, sweetie?"

Madison pouted a moment, but then said, "Okay. Just come back to me... all of you."

"We'll try our best, Madison," Kirbie told her.

Chapter 22

Arriving at Riverton

The Revolution arrived on the outskirts of the large city of Riverton. Timothy looked along the southern edge of the city.

"Wow, this city *is* huge," Timothy noted.

"There's a lot that goes on here, good and evil," Kirbie told them.

"Yes," Tamera agreed. "We better keep a sharp eye."

"Where do you think they would have taken Rain and the children?" Noelle questioned.

"We'll tear this city down trying to find them," Tamera spoke.

Everyone walked into the eastern part of the city. They looked around to see many of the citizens just doing their normal everyday things.

"Well, so far, nothing seems out of line," Kirbie stated.

Just then they heard a trumpet sounding, and then a band of people with gray hats that had spots of different colors on each hat marched towards them.

"Great," Noelle spoke, rolling her eyes. "A welcoming committee."

"This is a bit strange," Tamera noted.

As the parade of folks reached the heroes in two lines, they then separated from each other to the side, and a single character that had short dark purple hair and silver eyes, who was wearing a fancy black military-styled suit, approached.

"Welcome to Riverton, members of the Revolution," greeted the stranger. "My name is Corpace, and I am the newly appointed king of Riverton."

Tessa gave a look of uncertainty. "That's odd: Alana told us they hadn't replaced Prince Kain."

Corpace and the others laughed. "Alana, the princess of Corona Jungle? Oh, she makes me laugh sometimes. No, child, I have decided to step up and run Riverton until they find our dear Prince Kain. What a sad tragedy."

"Do you know anything about it?" Kirbie questioned.

"We're also looking for a ghost and two little girls that were kidnapped out of Cecaria this morning by Cassian and the Darkness," Tamera enlightened. "Have you heard about them?"

"You mean they kidnapped Rain?" Corpace questioned.

"Yes," said Noelle.

"I'm afraid I don't know about them or about Prince Kain's whereabouts. I just got back from the Willshire Kingdom but a few moments ago, before being notified that you were all on your way here."

The Revolution seemed uncertain about that answer but said nothing.

Corpace continued, "Please join me at my home, everyone. I need your help, and we can talk about things there."

The group walked to Corpace's mansion. Looking in the lobby, they were mesmerized to see all the gold plating that was on the building.

"I bet they spared no expense to build this," Timothy stated.

Corpace overheard him. "Yes, this mansion is the heart of Riverton."

They started off walking down a long hallway.

"So, what plans do you have for Riverton, now that you are king?" Kirbie asked Corpace. "You have some pretty big shoes to fill, I'm told."

"I want to leave a powerful legacy for the city, just like Prince Kain did. He did amazing things for us, as I am sure you heard. I want to do the same thing."

"That's very admirable of you," Tamera spoke.

Corpace bowed. "Thank you, my dear."

Corpace opened up a set of double doors and the group walked into a large living area. The Revolution was amazed at the beauty of the room.

"Now, if we could get down to business," Corpace instructed, "I have a mission I need you to accomplish for me. There's a lot of havoc out there right now, and I need to have order restored so I can get Riverton back to where it needs to be."

"So, what would you like us to do for you?" Tamera wondered.

"The Darkness has been terrorizing our fair city, just as you say they did to you all in Cecaria. On the northern part of town, the residents are being terrorized by a group of spirits that each has a special ability. They must be defeated so that my citizens can know peace once again. Will you help us?"

"Don't worry, King Corpace," Kirbie assured him. "We'll take care of them and be back in time for dinner."

Corpace was pleased. "Excellent. Here's a map of the city, showing where you need to go. And take this device so we can keep in contact. Good luck to you all."

With that, the group made their way to the district.

The group arrived at their destination. They looked around but couldn't see anything too peculiar.

"I hope this isn't like what happened in Warrington," Noelle responded.

Just then the group noticed the citizens stopping what they were doing, and they all ran into their houses in fear.

"I've got this feeling something's going to find us," Kirbie spoke. Everyone pulled out their weapons, ready to fight.

"I think it did," said Tamera.

Just then something sped towards them at a blazing speed. Before the group could react, the object slammed into the group, knocking them all off their feet. Everyone looked to see what happened as they got back on their feet. Just then the object headed back in their direction. They again got hit by the object, and were again slammed to the ground.

"What's happening?" Timothy cried out.

Kirbie looked to her left and saw a large hammer sitting beside her. She grabbed the heavy hammer as she saw the object speeding towards them once more. Kirbie, with all her might swung the hammer downward and sideways, and the hammer managed to collide with the object. Kirbie then was thrown backwards by the sheer force of the hammer also flying backwards. The object went off its course and crashed hard into one of the homes. The owner of the home, a female, ran away screaming. The Revolution saw the object, which resembled a fiery fox.

At that time, another spirit fox appeared in front of Timothy. He swung his sword at the spirit, who quickly moved out of the way of the sword. Then the fox slammed down its feet, and a blast of wind shot from its feet, knocking Timothy off balance. Then Timothy went to get up, but the spirit pushed Timothy back on the ground with its foot. Then, just as the spirit fox went to attack Timothy, Noelle struck the spirit with her sword, turning it into dust.

In the meantime, two more spirit foxes, that also had the ability to fly, attacked Tamera. Tamera used her magical ax and fought against the spirits with all of her might.

As Kirbie tended to Timothy, a spirit fox shot black flames out of its mouth. Tamera stood in front of them and created a wall of ice and it deflected the fire.

Then Kirbie saw the fox tried to speed away from her, and then charge back at her at great speed. Kirbie simply threw a ball of purple fire in its direction, and it struck the fox, turning it to dust. Then Timothy distracted the one spirit fox to come at him when Kirbie used the heavy hammer again to hit the fox, turning it to dust.

At that time, Tamera's phone rang. "Hello?"

"Hello, warriors," Corpace greeted. "I trust the job is done."

"Yes, Corpace," Tamera answered confidently. "We have defeated the spirits."

"Excellent. I have another situation I would like you to take care of."

"We'll show them what we're made of, sir," Timothy stated.

"I like your confidence, young man. I have been told that Lycan has unleashed some large spirits and they are wreaking havoc in the Commercial District downtown. Please check it out and see what's going on."

"Don't worry," Kirbie assured him. "We won't let you down."

"Good luck, warriors." The transmission ended.

"We better get going," Noelle insisted.

"Maybe we'll find Rain and the children there," Tamera hoped.

The Revolution went on their way.

At that time Lycan called in on Corpace.

"What's taking you so long?" Lycan told him.

Corpace then turned back into Cassian. "Don't worry, your wickedness. My plan is going the way I want it to. I will put the Revolution into ruin, and you all will be rulers just the way you want it."

Lycan, Abaddon and Cassian all laughed together at what they thought was good news to them.

The Revolution looked around as they rolled into the Commercial District. Again, the town seemed peaceful as money and goods were being passed around.

"This is getting old," Timothy mentioned.

"Am I the only one that thinks we are being led on a wild goose chase?" Noelle quizzed, feeling uneasy about the whole situation.

"It wouldn't surprise me if he was," Kirbie replied.

Just as they walked through the district, they noticed two large spirits with light brown spiked shells getting disgruntled with one of the sales clerks. One of the spirits pushed a table down as the other grabbed the clerk, expressing anger to him.

"Hey, let him go!" Timothy cried out.

The spirits looked over their shoulders and were stunned.

"The Revolution!" one of the spirits spoke in surprise. The one then let go of the clerk and they both grabbed their large hammers and shields. The townsfolk ran from the scene.

Tamera formed her ax as Timothy took out Olympia once again. Kirbie and Noelle stood firm, ready to fight. The spirits then attacked the group. Noelle and Kirbie fought one as Tamera and Timothy fought the other. Timothy swung his sword, but the spirit used its shield to block the sword, and then used his hammer against Timothy. Then he pushed Tamera away with great force using his shield. Kirbie and Noelle were also having trouble with the other one. Their attacks were being blocked by the Hammer Brother's enormous shield.

"We need to stop them now!" Tamera called out.

But their spirits were dampened further as two more spirits appeared, the same size as the first two.

"Oh, that's just great!" Noelle cried out.

The other two spirits joined in the fight. Timothy kept swinging his sword quickly as he could against one of the brothers as Kirbie tried to battle against the other. The spirit pushed Timothy off his feet. It then tried to smash Timothy with his hammer, but Timothy rolled out of the way before the hammer could connect. Kirbie had better luck as she tripped up the spirit she was fighting.

Tamera used her ax to fight against her spirit, and finally got the upper hand when she sliced off the spirit's left arm, causing its shield to fall. Then Tamera sliced it deeply in the chest, and the spirit exploded into dust.

Noelle made her made out of her spirit's view. The spirit then could not find where Noelle was. Suddenly the spirit felt Noelle's sword stab through its chest, and the spirit blew up into dust.

Kirbie grabbed the hammer away from her enemy after striking its arm. Then she jumped up and tried to strike the spirit, but the spirit swung downward with the injured hand, hitting Kirbie and knocking her unconscious. She then was grabbed by the spirit and it ran away.

At that time, Tamera, Noelle and Timothy all ran to each other.

"Is everyone okay?" Noelle questioned.

"Yeah, but where's Kirbie?" Timothy spoke.

Everyone looked around, calling for Kirbie, but there was no response.

"The spirit she was fighting must have taken her," Tamera commented.

"Well, we need to keep moving," Noelle responded. "You two head back towards Corpace's mansion to try finding her. I'll check around in the meantime to see if I can spot her."

Timothy and Tamera walked down one of the long stretches of road trying to head back to Corpace's mansion. Along the way, they came upon a large auditorium. Timothy began to view a poster that had a picture of Prince Kain. Below the picture was a message that said, "Shine the Light." Timothy then began to read the smaller message below that.

Tamera walked a bit further, admiring the beauty of the auditorium. Just then, she heard what sounded like a little girl crying in the distance.

"Serenity? Destiny?" Tamera called out.

Again, she heard the crying. Tamera went to investigate. She got a glimpse of a girl running into a room.

"Serenity, wait!" Tamera shouted.

Timothy finished reading the poster and when he looked around, he noticed that Tamera was nowhere around.

"Tamera?" Timothy called out as he started searching for her. "Baby, where are you?" He continued looking.

Tamera entered the same room the girl ran into. The room was very dark.

"Serenity?" Tamera yelled again.

Suddenly a light came on and she saw Serenity holding a wand that had a triangle, square and circle twirling around the lighted end. Tears were flowing from her eyes.

"Will you help me?" asked Serenity.

"Of course, I will," Tamera replied. "Where's Rain and Destiny?"

Tamera approached Serenity, reaching out her hand to her. Suddenly Serenity pointed the wand at Tamera. A darkened beam struck Tamera in the chest. Tamera fell to the ground. Her blue pupils turned into a deep red.

"Just what I wanted to see," said Cassian, who the little girl turned into. Cassian laughed maniacally, knowing Tamera was now under his control. Two spirits appeared out of the dark and helped Tamera up, and the group all left the stadium.

Kirbie woke up slowly, and still in pain. She saw Serenity standing over her.

"Are you okay, Kirbie?" asked Serenity.

Kirbie sat up slowly.

"Easy, kiddo," Prince Kain told her. Kain had black hair with a mustache and beard, with brown eyes, and wore a thick brown jacket and matching pants. Rain was standing with them.

Kirbie squinted in pain. "Where are we?"

"I'm not certain," Kain replied. "I believe we're at Corpace's mansion. What happened to you?"

"We were all battling a group of spirits, and mine got the best of me. He hit me really hard with his hammer."

"Are the others okay?" Rain wondered.

"I'm not sure. We were all having trouble. What I'm wondering is how I ended up here."

"I don't know, but I *do* know we need to get out of here. I can only imagine the chaos that could be waiting for them."

Kirbie saw Serenity and Destiny sitting on each side of Kain, and then was stunned to see another familiar face sitting by Destiny.

"Madison!" Kirbie cried out. "What are you doing here? Timothy asked for you to stay in Cecaria with Alana!"

"I know! I'm sorry, I... I just didn't want him to leave me... I was worried about him... and you and Tamera as well. I was getting some pictures as well and..."

"You disobeyed Timothy just so you could do your job?!"

"Please, Kirbie, don't be mad at her," Serenity begged. "She has done wonders in making sure we have been doing well."

"Yeah, and she's given us a lot of comfort," Destiny also defended.

Kirbie calmed down as she came over to Madison and hugged her. "I'm sorry, Madison. I have a tendency to lose my temper at times. But it's because I worry about those I love."

Madison was stunned. "You actually... love me?"

"Well, you do get on my nerves but... I've taking a liking to you. And if I know Timothy well enough, I'm certain he really loves you too."

Tears fell from Madison's eyes. "That means a lot to me. I've never had anyone who really loved me. I've always been alone since I lost my parents in the Riverton War, and my stepparents didn't seem to care for me at all. I was just... there, you know?"

"Tamera and I lost our parents in the war as well. I guess we were fortunate that Queen Camille took care of us. She was and still is a wonderful woman."

"How I wish I could have had that when I was growing up."

Noelle searched around frantically trying to find Tamera and Timothy. She became more and more worried about them.

"Maybe I shouldn't have left them alone," Noelle said to herself.

As she continued to run around, she called for them. There was no response. As Noelle continued to look around, she finally happened to notice Timothy over by the auditorium. She quickly ran over to Timothy.

"Where's Tamera?" Noelle asked.

"I can't find her," Timothy told her in worry.

"What do you mean? What happened?"

"I don't know. It's like she just... disappeared."

Noelle was flustered. "Great. First Kirbie was taken, and now Tamera's nowhere to be found. I shouldn't have left you two alone."

"It's my fault. I should have kept a more open eye out for her."

"Well, there's no time for bickering. We need to stay together and do what we can to help our friends." They held hands as they continued searching for Tamera and Kirbie.

Abaddon and Lycan continued to watch on from Abaddon's castle.

"This is awesome!" Lycan yelled. He then walked over to the cage the prisoners were in. "Who would have thought that Tamera would become our newest ally?"

Camille punched Lycan in the face, and he fell to the ground. Lycan, in sheer anger, jumped back up and tried to grab Camille, who had been shielded by Laura, Lisa and Tanna. Camille broke free and punched Lycan again. Lycan then grabbed Camille.

"Enough!" Abaddon yelled. "Leave her be, Lycan."

Lycan stopped trying to attack and walked back over to Abaddon. Then Abaddon walked to the cage.

"Your sister has proven to be quite the warrior, Queen Camille," Abaddon taunted. "Now you will see her strength being used against the Revolution."

Camille's frustration grew. "You monster!"

Abaddon just laughed as he walked away from the cage. Luna broke down in tears once again, feeling completely helpless as she fell into Tanna's arms.

"Continue with the plan," Abaddon ordered. "Destroy them." He walked out of the room as Lycan continued watching through the crystal ball.

Chapter 23

Dark Tamera

Noelle and Timothy began walking towards Corpace's mansion. Just as they went to cross into an intersection, Noelle felt something bite her in the leg. She looked down to see a large cobra biting into her leg. Noelle used her sword and sliced the large cobra's head off. Then they noticed themselves being surrounded by a massive group of cobras. Timothy and Noelle readied to battle them. The cobras tried to attack, but Noelle and Timothy used their swords to kill the cobras. During the fight, Noelle started feeling dizzy.

"Noelle?" Timothy said.

"Timothy, I'm..." Noelle passed out. Timothy felt helpless as he used Olympia and tried to fend off the cobras best as he could but was becoming overwhelmed. Timothy then noticed somebody approaching them from the west. He couldn't see who it was at first, until he started seeing her face. The person now was dressed in a black dress and had deep red hair, but had the familiar blue skin. Using the bow in her hand she pointed an arrow towards Timothy.

"Tamera?" Timothy spoke out loud.

Then suddenly, a flash appeared from behind the cobras to the left of Timothy. A woman stood firm next to Timothy, wearing a gray dress, black sleeves that were not attached to her skirt, black skirt and boots, all having gold trim, along with a gold tie. She had golden hair and eyes. Then a golden swirling beam shot out from the woman's hands, hitting the cobras and destroying them instantly. Timothy then looked to see if the person he thought was Tamera was still around, but nobody was there. The woman then tended to Timothy and Noelle. She pulled out a syringe and gave Noelle some medicine.

"Thank you, whoever you are," Timothy told the woman.

"I am Lena," said the woman. She saw the person Timothy was holding on to.

"Is this... Princess Noelle?" she asked.

"Yes, it is."

At that moment, Noelle began to wake up.

"Timothy?" she stated.

"Are you all right, Noelle?"

"I'll live." She then saw Lena and was surprised. "Well, hello, Lena."

"Hello, Noelle. Please, come into my home."

Timothy helped Noelle on her feet and they followed Lena into her home. Timothy looked around and saw a picture that had Lena with Ligwud, Joshua, Judetta and Julietta.

"That's Ligwud and his family!" Timothy noted.

"Joshua and Judetta are my parents," Lena informed Timothy, "and Julietta is my sweet little sister. She brings me the Keramina Juice to sell in Riverton." Lena chuckled. "That picture was taken before the Riverton War."

"That makes sense. You do have a wonderful family. Ligwud helped us to defeat Captain Gator."

"Yes, I heard, and I'm grateful for what you did. I gave you some of the Keramina Juice, Noelle. It helps against poison attacks."

Lena continued working.

"So, who was the woman that attacked you and Noelle?"

Timothy stated in uncertainty, "The person looked just like Tamera."

Lena snickered. "You mean the Ice Goddess?"

"Yes, she disappeared and we've been searching for her and her sister, Kirbie."

"No, it couldn't have been Tamera. She's too gentle to be an evil being. I'm sure it was somebody else."

Timothy sighed. "I'm not saying it was her, but the resemblance was almost uncanny. She even had a birthmark on her face just like Tamera does. She took off before I could find out." He lowered his head in thought.

"I absolutely love Tamera and Kirbie. I really miss her parents, too. I heard about Max. I'm really sorry about what happened."

"Thank you, Lena. That broke my heart." Timothy then turned to Noelle. "If you feel strong enough, we better get back to the mission so we can save our friends."

Noelle managed to stand up and support herself. "I think I'll be fine."

"It was nice to meet you, Lena, and thanks again for your help."

"Any friend of my family is a friend of mine, Timothy. Good luck to you all, and God be with you on your journey."

The pair walked out of the house and continued on. Noelle noticed Timothy seemed disturbed.

"Are you all right, Timothy?" Noelle asked in concern. "If you're worried about me, I'm fine, really."

Timothy smirked. "I know, and I'm glad to see that, but something else is bothering me. While you were poisoned, before Lena appeared, someone else stood off in the distance. I saw the person aim a weapon at me."

"Well, at least Lena got to us when she did."

"Yeah, but what's disturbing is that the person looked so much like Tamera."

Noelle gave a confused look. "Tamera?"

"Yeah. I mean the person had a different color hair, but she looked so much like Tamera in the face, even having the birthmark."

Noelle snickered. "Come on, you don't think that Tamera would hurt us, do you?"

"No, of course not, Noelle, and I don't think it was actually her... but I just can't get over how much it looked like her. Then again, I guess it could be possible. You all keep saying anything can happen here, and the longer the journey goes the more I believe it."

"Well, no matter what, we have to continue on."

"I know. Let's get back to Corpace's mansion."

The duo again walked on.

Kirbie and the others patiently sat in the cell they were being held in, hoping their friends could help in rescuing them.

"So, Corpace is the one behind all this?" Kirbie questioned.

"Yes, he imprisoned me because I found out that Corpace is actually Lycan's right hand man, Cassian."

That shocked Kirbie even more. "That means the others are in big danger."

Rain followed, with tears in her eyes. "And what's worse is that I've learned that Cassian has taken control over Tamera..."

"Tamera?" Kirbie spoke.

"Yes, he has placed a spell on her. She is now doing Abaddon's bidding."

That bothered Serenity. "You mean Tamera… is evil?"

Tears flowed from her eyes. Madison hugged her for comfort.

"Listen, Serenity," Madison told her. "It was not Tamera's choice to be evil. I'm sure deep down she still loves you as much as she had before. Right now, we have to stick together so that we can help her, okay?"

Serenity nodded, and she and Destiny hugged Kirbie.

"Is Timothy okay?" Madison questioned.

"From what I know he is still with Noelle," Kirbie answered.

"They will save her," Serenity said confidently. "They're the best out there."

"How are we gonna get out of here?" Destiny wondered.

"Hey, quiet in there!" yelled one of the spirits.

Everyone sat down together, pondering how to escape the prison.

Noelle and Timothy continued heading towards Corpace's mansion. About four blocks away from the mansion, they suddenly heard something like rumbling.

"Did you feel that, Timothy?" Noelle asked.

Noelle and Timothy cautiously checked their surroundings. Suddenly they felt the rumbling underneath their feet.

"I felt that one," Timothy reacted.

As they looked down, they saw the ground cracking underneath them. Before they could react, the ground opened up. Timothy fell into the opening, but Noelle grabbed him and they flew upward. As they came back on a solid foundation of ground, they noticed three large demons that were glowing with fire crawling out of the opening. Noelle and Timothy pulled out their swords.

"What a way to heat things up," Timothy stated.

Then Noelle and Timothy began to battle with the demons. They first tried using their swords but it had no effect. Noelle then stood in front of Timothy as he fired his beams of light, but they also had no effect.

Noelle and Timothy got cornered by two of the demons against a building wall while the third one approached from behind. Noelle grabbed Timothy's hand and they flew upward to prevent from being trapped too much longer and landed behind the three demons. Then the demons turned around and began throwing fire at Noelle and Timothy, who dodged the fireballs.

Noelle and Timothy fought with all their might against the demons, but were being overpowered. They mostly just tried dodging the demons' attacks, but were starting to get exhausted. They figured they needed to come up with a solution or they would soon meet their fate.

As Timothy made his way away from the demon he was fighting, he looked down the one road and saw the dark-haired woman standing in the distance.

"Tamera?" Timothy said to herself.

The mysterious being once again aimed her arrow at Timothy. Timothy couldn't understand what was going on, and just stared at her. This time the woman fired a black arrow from her bow, but Noelle fired off a beam of light, absorbing the beam of darkness. The woman then just walked away.

"Wake up, Timothy!" Noelle cried out. "I need you!"

Timothy came back to his senses as he helped Noelle once again. Timothy looked to his left and saw a water pipe. He used Olympia to slice the pipe open, and water shot out of the pipe, hitting the demons. The fire was put out on the demons, revealing just their bare skin. Angry, they charged again at Noelle and

Timothy, but this time Noelle and Timothy was able to destroy them, and they turned to dust. Noelle breathed a sigh of relief.

"This is getting rough," Noelle stated. In the meantime, Timothy felt even more disturbed as he seemed more confident that it was Tamera that tried to attack him.

"That had to be Tamera," Timothy said, feeling certain of his words.

"I still refuse to believe it," Noelle said to Timothy. "Tamera loves you too much to ever turn against you. It has to be somebody else that they made look like Tamera. They're just trying to psych us out."

They continued on.

In the meantime, Abaddon and Lycan watched on as Noelle stayed in the distance, trying to keep eye on Timothy. The waiting was making Lycan antsy.

"What's she waiting on?" Lycan questioned, getting frustrated. "I would have them finished up by now!"

"Hush!" Abaddon told him. "If she fails, you'll get your chance."

"She won't fail," Lycan felt inside. "The Revolution cares about her too much to ever hurt her. You heard what Noelle said."

Camille heard the words that the men spoke of.

"So, she *is* evil now…" Camille stated.

"Don't give up hope, Mom," Tanna responded. "The Revolution will find a way to bring her back."

"I hope so." Camille sighed. "I miss them all so terribly."

The two spirits were still on guard in front of the cell that Kirbie, Prince Kain, Serenity and Destiny were being held in. After hearing a loud bang, the spirits looked into the cell to see Kain using a rock to bang against the cell bars that covered over a window.

"Hey, you, stop that!" said one of the guards.

Kain ignored the guard and kept banging the rock on the bars. Frustrated, the guards opened up the cell door and walked in. They noticed the other prisoners were nowhere to be found.

"What do you think you're doing, old man, and where are the other prisoners?" asked the other guard.

Unexpectedly, two arrows came out from one of the darkened corners. The arrows struck the two spirits, who were turned to dust. Kirbie dropped down and landed feet first on the floor.

"Let's go, everyone!" Kirbie instructed.

The group then ran out of the cell. Several spirits tried to stop them, but Rain, Kirbie and Prince Kain were able to fight their way through them. Eventually they were able to make their way out of the castle.

Everyone continued to run as fast as they could, with Kain carrying Serenity and Kirbie carrying Destiny until they went to run around a corner, and Kirbie slammed into somebody, and they all fell to the ground.

"Timothy!" Kirbie cried out. She grabbed him and then slammed him against the wall of the house.

"Hi, Kirbie," Timothy stated. "I know you're mad, but it wasn't my fault."

Then Kirbie brought Timothy back down to where his feet were touching the ground, and she then held Timothy tightly. "I know, Timothy. I'm really glad you're safe, though."

Then Timothy saw Madison.

"Madison, is that you? Why are you in Riverton?"

"I'm sorry, Timothy. I was captured while working on one of my stories."

"She watched over Serenity and Destiny," Kirbie defended. "She's been a blessing."

"Please don't be mad," Madison pleaded. "I'm really sorry I didn't listen to you."

Timothy hugged her. "I'm glad you're safe too, Madison." Then he hugged Serenity and Destiny. "It's great to see you two as well."

"Have you seen Tamera?" Kain wondered.

"We may have," Timothy answered. "We've been seeing this woman with blackened hair, who looks so much like her."

"Yes," Rain told him. "She was put under Cassian's spell."

Timothy sighed sadly. "So, it was her."

"What do you mean?" asked Kirbie.

"She tried a couple times to put an arrow through me."

"And Cassian is posing as Corpace," Kain informed them.

Just then they noticed somebody approaching them. The Revolution looked over and saw the Darkness in a large number surrounding the group. They were almost blown away to see the one that was guiding them was none other than Tamera, forming her bow in front of them. What was even more disturbing was her blood-red eyes.

"Our worst nightmare has come true," Kirbie explained.

Without hesitation Tamera fired off an arrow from her bow. The group quickly moved out of the way. Rain and Kain sheltered Madison and the children. Tamera then fired another arrow, this time at Timothy, who had broken away from the rest of the group.

"Tamera, stop it!" Serenity cried out.

"Don't worry," Kain assured her. "They will help her."

Then the Darkness charged in against the Revolution. Noelle and Kirbie worked together to stand against them. In the meantime, Tamera was still firing darkened arrows at Timothy as she walked closer to where the battles were taking place. Timothy was afraid to attack Tamera in fear of badly injuring her.

"How do we stop Tamera?" Noelle pondered.

"We just have to stand our ground," Kirbie answered. "Don't you dare hurt her!"

"I wasn't going to. I'll do everything in my power to help her."

Noelle and Kirbie continued to fight off the Darkness. In the meantime, Timothy was backing away from Tamera when he lost his footing, but was able to stay standing. That opened the door for Tamera to shoot an arrow at Timothy. The arrow pierced his shoulder, and he fell down in pain.

"No! Timothy!" Madison cried out. In a sheer rage, Kirbie and Noelle tried fighting off the Darkness even harder.

Timothy watched as the arrow disappeared and blood came out from the wound.

"Baby, it's me!" Timothy cried out. "Why are you doing this?"

Then as he went to get back on his feet, another arrow pierced him in the other shoulder. Timothy fell down to his knees again.

As Timothy looked up, he saw Tamera approach him. Tears were flowing from Timothy's eyes as he stared right at the point of her now black ax.

"Baby…" Timothy spoke. "Please."

At that moment, Serenity broke away from Madison.

"Serenity!" Madison and Destiny cried out. Madison ran after her.

Without a care, Serenity ran over to Tamera and pushed her with all her might. Tamera fell down to the ground. Serenity charged at Tamera, and Tamera went to stab Serenity, but stabbed Madison instead when she jumped in front of Destiny. Madison fell to the ground, holding her arm, and Serenity used her hands to apply pressure to the wound.

Noelle then charged at Tamera, but Tamera grabbed her arm and flipped her over her shoulder. Kain grabbed Serenity to get her away. Noelle got back up and they started exchanging and blocking moves. Kirbie, holding a syringe, sneaked up behind her and grabbed Tamera, but Tamera quickly twisted her body, whipping Kirbie around. Kirbie's legs flew upward and hit Noelle in the face, knocking her down. Kirbie, however, continued to hold on to Tamera. She dropped herself backwards, landing on Kirbie. Kirbie had the wind knocked out of her.

Noelle again got to her feet, as Tamera turned her attention to Noelle. She fired an arrow in her direction.

"NO!!" Timothy cried out as he pushed Noelle out of the way. The arrow penetrated deep into Timothy's already injured shoulder. He fell to the ground. Seeing the syringe in front of him, he grabbed it. Kirbie saw him do so.

"Timothy!" Kirbie yelled. Tamera approached Timothy with her red eyes glowing as he made his way over to Madison. Tamera walked over close to Timothy, aiming her bow.

At that moment, Kirbie pushed Tamera with all her might, and Tamera fell down to her side. Timothy, with what strength he had left jumped onto Tamera, stabbing the syringe into her arm and administering the Keramina Juice. Tamera flipped Timothy off her, but as she went to stand up, she began to cry out in pain. She fell to her knees, still crying out.

"What if it kills her?" Noelle cried out in concern.

"It's too late!" Kirbie stated.

Suddenly, Tamera screamed loudly, and there was a large blast that shot off out of Tamera's body.

Everyone looked over to where Timothy was now holding Tamera's body. Timothy had his eyes closed as he was breathing heavily, tears falling from his eyes. Then he felt a hand resting on his cheek, and he opened his eyes quickly. Timothy then looked to see Tamera looking at him, smiling greatly with tears falling from her eyes that were back to the beautiful pink everyone knew. Her hair was also red instead of black.

Timothy became so overjoyed he teared up more as he and Tamera hugged each other tightly.

"Thank you so much, Timothy," Tamera told him. "Mom was right. I did need you to watch over me."

Serenity and Destiny ran cheerfully over to the two and hugged them as well.

Prince Kain, Rain, and Kirbie laughed in joy as they all ran over to Tamera, Madison and Timothy and they all hugged each other.

"Welcome back, Tamera," Rain stated joyfully.

"It's good to be back with you all again," Tamera told her.

"Now, let's go get the scum that did this to you," Timothy responded.

Kain, Madison, Serenity, and Destiny stayed behind as the Revolution headed for Corpace's mansion.

Chapter 24

Confronting Cassian

The Revolution cautiously made their way to the front of the mansion. It was another eerie silence.

"Tamera! Kirbie!" They heard somebody cry out. Everyone looked over to see a woman running towards them. She had pink hair and blue eyes, dressed in an off-blue jacket and skirt, with black stockings, and was carrying a mail bag. She was running from some other spirits. Tamera fired ice at the spirits to deter them away from the woman.

Kirbie then noticed one of the spirit foxes speeding her way. She threw one of her swords at the fox and it blew up into dust.

Two more fox spirits went at each side of the woman and went to dodge her. Timothy tackled the woman in an effort to get the foxes to slam into each other, and they did so, turning into dust.

"Are you all right?"

"I am, thank you. I'm Melanie."

"I'm Timothy. It's nice to meet you."

As Tamera watched on, she suddenly felt as if someone was behind her. She turned around to see the fox spirit getting ready to shoot fire at her. Suddenly the spirit's face got smashed with a hammer. Tamera then looked up to see Kirbie holding the hammer. With a big smile on her face, she shrugged her shoulders. Kirbie snickered.

Timothy and Melanie approached Tamera, Noelle and Kirbie.

"Everyone," Melanie spoke, "I have urgent news for you. Coverdale and the Willshire Kingdom were raided again by Abaddon's army. Both castles have been destroyed, and Lycan has kidnapped Princess Marietta and the others."

"Oh, no," Timothy sighed. "Heather..."

"Tanna..." Tamera said in worry. The others were in shock as well.

"We have to save them," Kirbie stated.

"First, we need to stop Corpace before Riverton meets the same fate," Noelle exclaimed. "I can't wait to get my hands on him."

"And you're going to get your chance," said Corpace, who appeared with more members of the Darkness. Then a big flash of light shined around him. The Revolution all had to close their eyes until the bright flash dissipated, and Tamera and Tessa were shocked to see Corpace's true form.

"Cassian!" Noelle yelled.

"The time has come to destroy the Revolution, so that Lycan and King Abaddon shall rule over everything!"

With that, the horde known as the Darkness charged after the Revolution. The group fought against them with all their might. The Revolution continued until every member of the Darkness had been destroyed.

"Well done, Revolution!" Cassian smirked. "But let's see how you do against these guys!"

Out from behind Cassian appeared false images of Laura, Lisa, and Behrlin.

"I told you I would get my revenge!" Behrlin stated.

Cassian's wand glowed at the tip. Then Cassian fired the

wand once at each of his allies. The three each trembled for a moment, and then each one grew, doubling their normal size.

"This isn't good," Timothy responded.

"The bigger they are, the harder they fall," Tamera responded.

Behrlin fired a beam from his hands. The Revolution all moved out of the way of the beam. Then as Timothy tried to stand up, Laura went to slam her sword down on him, but Tamera grabbed Timothy before he could be crushed.

Lisa caught Kirbie off-guard as she swung her foot and kicked Kirbie. Kirbie flew quite a way back, slamming into the wall, and then falling to the ground. She was knocked unconscious.

"Timothy," Tamera shouted. "Check on Kirbie!"

Laura then cast a wind spell. Tamera was thrown back into the wall as well, and she fell to the ground, but managed somehow to stay conscious. Slowly she got back on her feet.

Noelle threw a beam of light at Lisa, hitting her foot with it. She cried out in pain. Behrlin saw what happened and tried to body-slam Noelle, but Noelle moved out of the way before getting crushed. Instead, he knocked Lisa over.

"You idiot!" Lisa cried.

Laura went over to help them up.

Timothy ran over to Kirbie, who was just regaining consciousness.

"Are you okay, Kirbie?" Timothy asked.

"Yeah, thank you," Kirbie told him. She got back on her feet.

"Let's get them," Timothy replied.

"Come on," Cassian said impatiently. "Get rid of them already!"

The giants got back on their feet. Noelle threw more beams

of light and Tamera fired her arrows into Laura and Lisa's legs. Timothy took out Behrlin's feet with Olympia. Laura and Lisa became heavily confused. Behrlin fell down against the mansion, damaging it greatly.

"You imbeciles!" Cassian cried out.

With all three down, Tamera used her ax, Timothy his sword, and Noelle used her sword to strike down the three evil beings, turning them to dust.

Cassian saw what happened and he growled greatly.

"All right," Cassian muttered. "If they can't do it, I'll beat you myself!"

He waved his wand to the sky, and icicles began to fall over the Revolution. They tried to take shelter, but one caught Timothy, cutting his arm deeply.

Then from his wand, Cassian fired meteors towards them. Kirbie and Tamera put up a block of ice and blocked the meteors from hitting them.

Cassian wasn't fazed. He fired a beam to the ground, and the ground broke open. A stream of lava shot from the ground and went towards where the Revolution was hiding. Everyone got out of the way, but Tamera got hit by a little bit of lava, instantly burning her face. She held her hand over the burn, feeling the pain.

"How do we stop him?" Timothy asked.

"We just have to keep fighting him with what we got," said Tamera.

Tamera noticed that Cassian fired a beam of darkness towards the group. They moved out of the way. Nearly at an instant, Tamera fired a beam of ice. The ice hit Cassian's arm. He dropped the wand.

"Now's our chance!" Tamera told them.

As Cassian went to grab the wand, Kirbie fired off a purple fireball to hit Cassian in the shoulder, and he fell to the ground. At that time, Timothy swiftly ran in and grabbed the wand before Cassian could. Cassian lunged at Timothy, but then suddenly had a shocked look on his face as Tamera pierced her ax through Cassian's chest. Cassian then exploded into dust.

Timothy looked at Cassian's wand.

"Who wants to hold this treasure?" Timothy questioned.

"I think *you* should, Timothy," Noelle suggested, and the others agreed.

Timothy smiled as he grabbed the wand. The end of the wand, which was a deep black color when Cassian had it, and had turned purple in Kirbie's possession, was a shade of baby blue.

Then a glow and a flash occurred, and everyone looked to see a star appear to them. Tamera once more reached for it, and just like the other two, it turned black and faded into dust.

"What about the children?" Kirbie asked in concern.

From behind them they heard a loud cheering. They turned to see a large crowd of people approaching them, cheering, laughing, and crying joyously, led by Prince Kain. Then out of the crowd, the Children of Cecaria, led by Rain, Madison, Serenity and Destiny, swarmed around Tamera. Tamera fell backwards as the children all tried to hug her, and everyone laughed. Then the kids ran to the other members as Serenity and Destiny stayed by Tamera.

"Thank you so much, Tamera!" Serenity stated.

"We may not have been here if it weren't for the Revolution!" Destiny followed.

Tamera hugged Rain. "I'm glad you're okay."

"I was so worried about you too, sweetie."

Madison ran over to Timothy, giving him a hug. "Thank goodness you're all okay."

"It's great to see you too, Madison."

Then Prince Kain approached. "I thank you all dearly for what you've done for us. We are all indebted to you."

"You would have done the same for us, my prince," Tamera responded. "It's an honor to help you and your family here in Riverton."

Then Alana walked into town and saw the damage. "I leave you all alone for a little bit and look at what happens!"

Everyone laughed.

"Alana!" the children cried happily, and they swarmed around her.

"Are you all ready to go home?" Alana asked them.

"Yeah!" they yelled out loud.

Alana smiled as she, with the children, walked over to Tamera. Alana helped Tamera back on her feet.

"You all have been such a blessing," Alana told Tamera and the others. "These children mean the world to me, and I can't imagine being without them." Alana hugged Tamera. "Thank you so much."

"You're welcome, Alana," Tamera told her. Alana hugged the others as well.

"Will we get to see you again, Tamera?" Serenity wondered.

Tamera bent down to look into Serenity's eyes. "Don't you worry, sweetie. I'll be by your side again before you know it."

"We'll never forget you," Timothy followed.

"And if you get into trouble, just let us know, and we'll be right there for you!" Kirbie stated.

Serenity and Destiny hugged Noelle, Kirbie and Tamera tightly as Madison again hugged Timothy. Then they all said their goodbyes as Alana led the Children of Cecaria back to their home.

Abaddon and Lycan watched what had happened, and then the vision faded off from the crystal ball. Lycan roared in extreme anger, and he started destroying tables and chairs.

"That's it!" Lycan then yelled. "I will destroy them myself!"

"No!" Abaddon told him. "We *cannot* lose our focus here! If we do, they will surely destroy us!"

Lycan retaliated. "They are getting too strong! We have to act now!"

Just then the mysterious figure came up on the screen.

"You are failing me, you foolish mortals!"

Lycan spoke first. "Master, it was Cassian that failed you…"

"If one of yours fails me, then you all have failed me!"

Abaddon became hesitant. "But master…"

"Enough! If you fail me again, I will destroy all of you! Lycan is right: you must lead your army against them. You must stop them before they reach the castle!"

Abaddon bowed his head. "Yes, my lord."

With that, the image disappeared from the screen. The prisoners listened in on the conversation.

"Who is that person?" Camille wondered.

"Well, I'll tell you," Olivia spoke. "Abaddon's not afraid of anyone, but for him to stutter like that…"

Kaiden followed, "He has to be powerful."

Camille looked to her left and became startled as Lycan approached the cage.

"Mark my words," he warned. "Once we release Abaddon's army on the World of Exodus, *nobody* will stand in our way!"

Camille's body filled with fear as Lycan stared at her. Then he walked away.

"Ready the troops for battle!" Lycan yelled.

After leaving Riverton, The Revolution stopped to get some rest for the evening. Tamera was sitting alone by the fire, and she had taken off her engagement ring that Timothy had given to her and was staring at it.

"Tamera?" said a voice. She looked up to see Timothy looking down at her. "Kirbie said you wanted to talk to me?"

"Yeah, please sit with me."

Timothy sat down next to Tamera. "What's on your mind, baby?"

"I've been thinking about what happened to me in Riverton: when I was turned evil by Cassian. After going through what we all have been through, it made me question if having a relationship is even possible, with the heartache I caused you."

"Tamera, that wasn't your fault," Timothy tried to assure her. "And besides, I chose to go on this journey with you. I want to be with you. I would die for you, sweetie."

"I'm sorry, but I can't have that. I lost my parents, my sister... I lose everyone that's important to me. I don't want to lose you too."

Timothy was a bit disturbed. "Wait a minute. So, it's okay for you to die for me, but I can't do the same for you? That's not how this is supposed to work!"

"That's not it! Don't you understand what..." Tamera stopped speaking as she felt tears falling from her eyes. She then handed the ring back to Timothy.

"I'm really sorry."

Tamera then ran away from Timothy, still crying. Kirbie saw Tamera running away. Kirbie then approached Timothy. He looked saddened.

"Kirbie, I didn't mean to make her cry," he pleaded. "I was just..."

Kirbie placed her right index finger on Timothy's lips. "I already know what's going on." She then sat by Timothy. "She talked to me about it a little bit ago. I begged her not to break up with you, but she was convinced that if you stayed with her, you would be killed."

"But every day, we run into that risk. Heck, I could simply trip and die because I hit my head on something."

"Believe me, Timothy, you don't have to explain that to me. Tamera has always struggled when it comes to losing someone, and I know her love for you is so strong, but like I said before, she fears for losing you too if you two get too close."

"I know she still loves me... maybe I should just give her some time to think about it. I mean... I don't want to do anything to push her away."

"Well, don't worry, Timothy. No matter what, I will continue to watch over you as well, because I still believe you are the best thing to ever happen to Tamera, and I won't ever let anyone take that away."

Kirbie and Timothy hugged. "I appreciate that. Thank you so much."

Kirbie walked back over towards the fire as Timothy got up and walked out into the forest. Timothy just couldn't get Tamera out of his mind, and was wondering what he could do for her. At that moment, Kirbie walked over to him. She could see tears start to fall from his eyes. She went over and hugged him.

"Please don't give up on her, Timothy."

"I wouldn't think of it, Kirbie."

Chapter 25

Hollifax Village

The following morning, The Revolution got out of their ship and approached a large mountain that sat alone, along with a village that sat a short distance from the north side of the mountain.

"That's Hollifax Peak," Noelle told Timothy, "Nestled right in the middle of the Calanine mountain range."

"This world never ceases to amaze me," Timothy told them.

"There's also a village near Hollifax Peak," Tamera told him. "We'll be stopping there on the way to get some more rest."

Tamera was acting more and more like the Tamera of old to Timothy, seeming more joyful than she was before. That was something Timothy was happy to see.

The clan walked on. Kirbie happened to catch a strange noise coming from a cave that led into the mountain.

"Shh," she spoke. "Do you hear that?"

The rest of them listened in, and heard the chattering coming from the cave.

"What is that?" Tamera said as the chattering got louder.

Then out of the cave appeared a horde of gruesome-looking spiders that had extra-long fangs.

"We're gonna need more than a swatter to exterminate these pests," Noelle noted.

The group got ready to fight. One of the spiders turned around and fired its webbing. Timothy got tied up in it. Before anyone else could do anything, the other spiders did the same thing. All of the Revolution became trapped in webbing. Then the spiders approached closer to their foes. Tamera managed to form her ax and cut up the webbing, freeing herself. Then Tamera freed the others. Tamera shot off arrows to hit the spiders with. Kirbie and Timothy charged at the spiders and struck them down, turning them into dust.

"Well, that was fun," Tamera said sarcastically.

Suddenly, Tamera, Kirbie and Noelle became engulfed in a gray smoke around them.

"Tamera!" Timothy yelled.

Then the smoke cleared, Tamera saw herself wearing a tight one-piece short black dress with a sky-blue body stocking covering her arms and legs. Her hair was sparkling. She then saw Kirbie and Noelle in the same outfit.

"Well, this is an interesting look," Tamera questioned, in total shock.

Then Tamera looked over and saw a beautiful young girl walking towards her. The girl had light blonde hair with cinnamon eyes and was wearing a red and gold top, a gold belt that had a large purple buckle, with a purple skirt that had gold trim around the bottom of the skirt.

"Tamera, it's you!" said the young girl.

"Kendra!" Tamera yelled. She ran over and gave her a tight hug.

Kendra then did the same to Kirbie, and she was wearing the same outfit as Tamera.

"Wait a minute," Kirbie cut in. "Kendra, what are you doing?"

"I like you and Tamera," she replied. "You'll protect me from evil."

"Did you do this?" Tamera asked joyfully. "I mean the outfit's nice, but…"

"You all have the body for it."

"Well, she's right about that," Timothy commented. Tamera blushed.

"Honestly, Kendra, what is this about?" asked Kirbie.

"I want you all to stay with me! We've been attacked by these ugly spiders."

"Like the ones that attacked us earlier," Tamera pointed out.

"And there's a much larger one that lives in that cave. Will you stop him for me?"

"Of course, we will, sweetie!" Tamera told her positively.

"I'll change you back to your other outfits. Shala-kala-boom!"

Tamera, Noelle and Kirbie were again were covered in a smoke cloud. When the smoke cleared, this time Tamera and Kirbie were dressed in silver tied shirts that didn't cover their stomachs, along with short-pleated silver mini-skirts.

"Wow, you must have good taste!" Noelle told her.

Kendra shrugged her shoulders. "I'm sorry. Sometimes my magic doesn't cooperate."

"Well, I guess we should defeat the spider," Kirbie stated.

Tamera picked up Kendra. "It's okay, sweetie. We'll be back soon."

The others agreed, and the Revolution made their way to the cave. On their way, Timothy noticed Tamera feeling uneasy.

"Are you okay, Tamera?" Timothy asked her. "Are you worried about this fight?"

"It's not that… I'm just worried about Camille and the others."

"Camille's been on my mind too. I really miss her."

"And then there's this outfit. I mean, do you like it?"

"Yes, it does look good on you all," Timothy noted. Tamera blushed. Kirbie kissed Timothy on his forehead, and then Noelle hugged him, also blushing.

As the Revolution went further into the cave, they heard a loud cry. They stopped in their tracks. Suddenly they were all sprayed with webbing and again became tied up. Then the large spider, along with several smaller ones, approached.

"Just what I always wanted: to be a spider's lunch," Kirbie sighed.

Kirbie, Noelle, Tamera and Timothy revealed their weapons. They freed themselves from the webbing just in time. They then used their weapons to strike down the smaller spiders.

"We've got to take him down!" Tamera spoke.

The spider then crawled back into the darkened cave.

"Where did he go?" Tamera asked as they went deeper into the cave. They walked cautiously forward into the darkness. Then Kirbie felt some stones fall on her from above.

"Move it!" she cried out.

Everyone tried getting out of the way as suddenly the large spider fell from the ceiling and crashed to the ground. Noelle and Kirbie cut down some of the spider's legs, causing it to be unable to move. Then Tamera fired an icicle into the spider's eye. Timothy struck the spider powerfully with a glowing Olympia. The spider cried out deeply before falling to its death, turning to dust.

"I don't ever want to see a spider like that again," Timothy responded.

"Shala-kala-boom!" was yelled. Tamera, Noelle and Kirbie were once again engulfed in a smoke cloud. This time when the smoke cleared, they were dressed in tight gold short dresses and white pantyhose. Their natural hair was sparkly again.

"This is beautiful!" Tamera claimed.

"Wow, I love it!" Noelle followed.

Then Kendra appeared to the group.

"Thank you so much, everyone. You've been so kind to me. Hey! Would you like to join me at the party in Hollifax Village?"

"We'd love to," Kirbie answered.

"Great! Please, follow me!"

Kirbie decided it would be good for the group to maybe relax and get their mind off what they had just endured. She was hoping this would also help to bring Tamera back to Timothy. The others followed closely.

The Revolution arrived at Hollifax Village, located not far from the peak named the same. The citizens of the town greeted Kendra and the Revolution with many cheers. Tamera looked to see many of the citizens were either colored like fire, or colored like a light blue ice.

Kendra walked over to a woman who was swimming in the pool.

"Princess Sonata! Look who's here!" Kendra said cheerfully.

Everyone looked to see the beautiful, taller woman with very long purplish-gray hair and eyes of blue, simply wearing a two-piece dark blue bikini, climbing out of the pool they had set up, and she approached them.

"Welcome, Tamera... Noelle," Sonata ecstatically said. "It's great to see you!"

"Hello, Sonata!" they both said.

"It's great to see you as well, Kirbie!"

"As with you, Sonata."

"And who's the stud?"

"This is... my good friend, Timothy," Tamera introduced.

"Welcome to Hollifax, Timothy."

"Thank you, Princess Sonata. It's a pleasure to meet you and Kendra."

"Shala-kala-boom!" Kendra yelled once again as she waved her wand. Tamera and Kirbie were now dressed in lacy white tops, mini-skirts and tights, but she left their hair sparkly.

"Why am I not getting this right?" Kendra pondered.

"Kendra, it's okay," Tamera told her. "This is amazing!"

"It almost reminds me of a wedding dress," Kirbie commented.

"Marry me, Kirbie!" Noelle teased.

They both laughed as they hugged each other.

Sonata put on a white see-through cover-up.

"Forgive me for Kendra's behavior," Sonata said. "Her heart truly is in the right place. I'm glad to hear you defeated those nasty spiders for her."

"It's okay, Sonata," said Tamera. "Thank you."

Suddenly there was a strong rumbling coming from Hollifax Peak. Then the power in the city shut off.

"What's happening?" Timothy wondered.

"It's Hottle, the lava spirit! Something's wrong with her!"

The citizens began to run and scream in a panic as the peak suddenly erupted. After seeing the thick smoke, the lava, a purplish color, began to flow outward. The river of lava also flowed now in the same color.

"The lava's purple!" Kirbie stated.

"Is that normal sometimes?" Timothy wondered.

"No, it's not," Sonata answered. "There must be something

wrong with Hottle. We use the lava to power our city, but the purple lava is disrupting this."

"We better check it out," said Tamera.

"I'll take you there!"

"Great!" She held out her hand to Sonata. Sonata grabbed Tamera's hand. Tamera also held Timothy's hand.

Sonata led the Revolution to an opening leading into Hollifax Peak.

"Please hurry," Sonata told them, "or we will soon be engulfed in the lava."

"Please be careful and save Hottle for me," Kendra asked.

Sonata then headed back to the town as the Revolution entered the volcano. Timothy was wiping the sweat off his forehead, feeling the intense heat coming from the erupting volcano.

Finally, the group came into the opening, and they were shocked to see an enormous horde of small blue ice-colored spirits focusing their power onto Hottle, a lava spirit, who was crying out in pain.

"There's so many of them," Timothy noted.

"We have to stop them," Tamera replied.

The Revolution appeared to the icy spirits. They turned their attention to the Revolution. They suddenly rushed towards each other, and they formed into one gigantic icy spirit, much larger than Hottle was. The large spirit then shot a bolt of icy lightning at Hottle, who again screamed out in pain, and a large mass of purple lava shot from Hottle out of the volcano.

"We have to do something!" Timothy cried out.

Tamera charged at the spirit and struck it with her glowing

ax, but to her surprise, it had no effect. The spirit then fired an icy lightning bolt at the Revolution. The Revolution took cover away from the bolt.

At that time Timothy got a radical idea. He ran over to Hottle, who was nearly lifeless.

"Angelic Rain!" Timothy yelled. The swirling vortex of gold covered over him and Hottle. When the vortex dissipated, Timothy was happy to see that Hottle had returned to her normal lava color.

"Fire Beam," Hottle stated telepathically. Then Hottle began glowing brightly. Hottle shot out a large beam of fire at the spirit, who cried out until it evaporated into a huge plume of dust.

The Revolution opened their eyes to see only Hottle remaining in the middle of the volcano. The river of lava that was once purple was now back to its normal red. Then the power had been restored to the city, and the town celebrated.

"Thank you for saving me," Hottle spoke telepathically to the Revolution. "Now Hollifax Village is safe once again. God be with you on your journey to saving the others."

"Thank you as well," Kirbie responded.

Then the Revolution returned to Hollifax Village. They were greeted by the thankful residents.

"We are so grateful for you all," Sonata told them. She hugged Tamera. "Hollifax Village is now back to its glory thanks to you."

"It's very late," Noelle said. "Do you have an inn for us to stay in?"

"Yes, please stay for free as a token of thanks for what you have done."

The sun was beginning to set over the World of Exodus as Kirbie and Noelle, who were quickly in flight in a ship they borrowed from the Princess of Hollifax, raced for the Willshire Kingdom.

"How will we ever defeat Abaddon," Kirbie questioned, "if his army is with him? The army is huge!"

"I don't know," Noelle simply answered, "but I'm not giving up without a fight."

They continued their trip until they were able to reach the ruins of the Willshire Kingdom. After landing the ship, they hid behind some large bushes and spied over the remains.

Kirbie and Noelle then cautiously walked in the direction of the castle. They expected to get ambushed at any moment, so they revealed their swords, but to their surprise, they were able to reach the castle without incident.

"The place is deserted," Kirbie mentioned.

Kirbie and Noelle approached Princess Marietta's castle. As they made their way through the lobby, Noelle heard somebody groaning. She looked to see somebody buried in a pile of rubble. She quickly tried to unbury the person. When Noelle did so, she found Heather, unconscious but still breathing. Noelle noticed the side of her outfit looked as if it may have been saturated. She placed her hand on her jacket and then lifted her hand up to see it was now covered in Heather's blood. As Noelle stayed by Heather, Kirbie ran into the doctor's quarters and saw a bottle of Keramina Juice along with syringes sitting on a shelf, surprised the bottle wasn't busted. Kirbie then ran back to Heather and gave her a dose of the Keramina Juice. Then Noelle held Heather in her arms.

"Heather, can you hear me, sweetie?"

Heather opened her eyes.

"Princess Noelle? Is that you?"

"It is, beautiful. Are you all right?"

"I think so," Heather answered. "Thank you for freeing me. I was kind of having this crushing weight on me..." She went to stand up, but then she flinched, feeling a sharp pain in her side. She fell down to her knees.

"Easy, sweetie. You're still hurt."

Heather clutched her side and saw the blood on her hand. She pulled apart her outfit in that area and saw what used to be an open wound that was now closed up, but still there.

"I gave you some of the Keramina Juice," Kirbie informed her. She gave Heather the bottle and syringes. "You'll need more to get the wound to heal completely."

Heather hugged Kirbie. "Thank you so much, Kirbie. I owe you one. How are Timothy and Tamera doing?"

"They're fine," Noelle informed her. "They sent us here to check on you. Timothy really misses you as much as Tamera does."

"I miss them too. I hope we can get this over with so we can be together again."

"What happened here?"

"Lycan's army attacked us. We tried to fight them off, but they just totally decimated us. They took the chancellor and many others as prisoners and then headed back to his castle on the Maniton."

"He's using my ship to his advantage," said Noelle.

"But we never saw their leader, unless he stayed in the ship," Heather informed them. "It doesn't surprise me he wasn't fighting on the front lines."

"That's what his goons are for," said Kirbie. "Where are the other citizens?"

"Lisa and Tessa took many of the survivors to Lorelei Pond. They are hiding in a cave not far from there. Look, you better get going. We all need you to stop them."

"What about you, sweetie? Are you sure you'll be okay by yourself?"

"I'll be fine. I'm going to Lorelei Pond. I know Timothy and Tamera would want me there." Heather and Noelle held each other tightly. "You better go. Please tell Tamera and Timothy that I love them and I'm okay."

"I will, beautiful," Noelle promised.

"Give everyone our love," Kirbie asked.

"Indeed," Heather stated.

With that, Heather proceeded to head for Lorelei Pond, and Noelle and Kirbie headed off to get back with the rest of the Revolution. Heather blew a kiss to them.

Chapter 26

Wolf Lake Village

Tamera was sitting next to a fire in the early morning as she watched Timothy peacefully sleeping. She was feeling overwhelmed with feelings for Timothy, and she decided to take a walk in the forest.

Tears began to fall from Tamera's eyes from thinking about Timothy, and as she wiped the tears from her eyes, she suddenly felt someone wrap their arms around her legs. She was startled as she looked down, but then calmed down when she saw it was Orion. Tamera smiled as she picked up Orion and hugged her tightly.

"What's wrong, sweetie?" said a voice. Tamera then looked to see Rain approaching her.

"Hi, Rain," Tamera said softly as she and Orion hugged her. "I broke up with Timothy last night, and I'm still kind of torn up about it."

"You did?" Rain was stunned to hear the news. "But why? I thought you adored him."

"I did! I mean... I do... but I..." She cried ever harder.

Rain placed her hands on Tamera's cheek. "Calm down, sweetheart. Did Timothy do something to you?"

"The only thing he did was love me with all his heart. It was my fault we split up. I thought if we would stay together, that he would end up dead, so I figured it to be better if we weren't together."

Rain lowered her head in thought for a quick moment, then told her right out, "That doesn't make sense, Tamera. He's got a better chance of living with you by his side. Now he's by himself in battling the Darkness."

"Not exactly. Kirbie and Noelle are with him."

"You know what I mean. You need to go back to him."

"But what if he doesn't want me any more?"

"I didn't say to jump back in his arms, sweetie. I'm just saying to stand by him in defeating the Darkness. No matter what, he needs you, and so do Kirbie and Noelle. And you need them if you stand a chance at saving the others. You understand me?"

"I do... I do." Tamera and Rain hugged again. Orion continued to hold on to Tamera as well. "Thank you so much. And thank you, Orion. I love you both so much."

Orion kissed Tamera. Then Tamera gave Orion to Rain as she turned around to make her way back to Hollifax.

While Tamera was walking back to the campfire, Timothy, still asleep, dreamed that he and Tamera were in an area covered in pure darkness. With their swords drawn, he and Tamera stayed on their guard as they checked their surroundings. Then, out of the dark, the Darkness appeared and surrounded Timothy and Tamera. The clan charged at them, but amazingly they were able to hold them off.

After they finished, Timothy looked to Tamera's hair, and it looked discolored. Tamera grabbed some of her hair and gently brought it into her eyesight, and was amazed to see it was of a different shade of blue.

Just then Tamera and Timothy heard an evil laugh. They

looked up and gasped as a darkened figure stood in front of them. Suddenly large wings flashed in front of them. Tamera then was grabbed by a large chain.

"Tamera!" Timothy yelled.

Tamera began to glow brightly, as if she was engulfed in a white fire. "Come and get me!" she yelled.

A big flash of light followed.

Timothy had awakened back at Hollifax, stretching his arms as he sat up. He checked his surroundings to see the sun shining through the windows.

"Good morning, Timothy," Tamera stated.

"Good morning, Tamera. Where are Kirbie and Noelle?"

"I wanted them to check out the Willshire Kingdom to see if they could find Tessa, Heather and Tanna. I've been so worried about Heather, as well as the others."

"I have been too. Did you get any rest?"

"Don't worry, Timothy. I'm fine. We'll be heading out as soon as she gets back."

After getting ready, the two made their way out of the inn.

"Good morning, Timothy," Kirbie greeted.

"You didn't stay up all night, did you, Kirbie?"

"No, we actually haven't been up long," Noelle answered.

"Hello, sis," Tamera stated. "What did you find out?"

"Melanie was right, love," Kirbie said. "All of the Willshire Kingdom has been destroyed by Lycan's army. I found Heather nearly buried under the castle, but she's fine, and she was heading for Lorelei Pond. They have a shelter there, she told us, and Tessa and Lisa were already there. Heather wanted me to tell you both she loves and misses you."

Timothy breathed a sigh of relief. "Thank you, Lord." Then he asked, "So, what do we do? How do we defeat them?"

"The best way we can," Tamera answered. "In the meantime, we head for Ebalon."

"Shala-kala-boom!" was yelled. Tamera and Kirbie again were covered in smoke. When it cleared, Tamera and Kirbie looked to see they were wearing their normal outfits. Sonata and Kendra approached them.

"I finally got it right!" Kendra said excitedly.

"Good morning," Sonata told them. "I knew you were getting ready to head to Ebalon, so I wanted just again to say thank you and wish you a safe journey."

"Thank you, Sonata," said Noelle as they hugged.

"Will you come back to see me again?" Kendra asked.

Tamera picked Kendra up and they hugged each other. "Of course, I will, sweetie," Tamera told her. "Please take care of yourself."

The group made their way to Ebalon.

"Let's split up to see if we can find anyone," Tamera noted. "Timothy and I will take the west side if you and Noelle want to take the east side, Kirbie."

"Sounds like a plan, love," Kirbie responded.

"Be careful," Noelle followed.

The members went off in different directions. As Kirbie was searching around, she saw some movements around one of the destroyed buildings. She decided to investigate. Suddenly she saw a white-haired girl with ice-blue eyes, who was wearing a white form-fitting tank top and very short black leather shorts with tan pantyhose.

"Kelly Rose?" asked Noelle.

Kelly recognized her. "Princess Noelle?"

The two hugged each other.

"Why are you here, sugar?" Noelle asked her.

"We were told about what happened here. I'm just searching for survivors. The ones I have found, I moved them all to safety. They're in a cave not too far from Lorelei Pond. So, what are you doing back here?"

"We're on our way to Abaddon's castle."

At that moment, Timothy and Tamera gathered where Noelle and Kirbie were.

"Kirbie, are you okay?" Timothy wondered.

Then Tamera and Timothy saw Kelly.

"Kelly, is that you?" Tamera asked, approaching him.

Kelly recognized Tamera. "It's good to see you again. Who's this with you?"

"This is Timothy. He's a dear friend of mine."

"Nice to meet you, Timothy. I'm Kelly Rose."

"Same to you, Kelly."

"I was heading back to Lorelei Pond to make sure everyone's all right."

"We're heading to Abaddon's castle to battle Lycan and his goons."

"Kirbie told me, Tamera. Please be careful."

"We will."

Kelly left for Lorelei Pond as the Revolution headed in a different direction.

The Revolution continued on their journey, heading for Abaddon's castle, but before making it there, they came across Wolf Lake Village. The group noticed the children playing around in the streets. They were like what they had seen at

Catterine Village, but instead were wolves.

"I wish I could still be free like a child," Kirbie stated.

"You and me both," Timothy agreed.

They then saw a woman approach a group of kids playing together in a large sandbox. The woman had purplish-gray hair and ears and a tail like a fox.

"All right, kids, it's time for supper!" the woman yelled.

The kids all got out of the sandbox. Timothy and Tamera noticed some of the children were the ones she saw in Cecaria.

Serenity and Destiny were with the group of children. They happened to glance to their left and saw their favorite heroine.

"Tamera!" they both cried out. The Children of Cecaria ran to Tamera and again tackled her joyfully.

"I'm going to get you some pillows," Timothy teased.

Then the other children came over as well.

"Everyone, this is Tamera and the Revolution!" Serenity introduced.

"It's good to meet you all!" Tamera told them.

"Show us what you can do!" said one of the children of Wolf Lake.

Tamera formed her sword and it began to glow. Then Tamera formed her bow and shot one of her arrows into the air. It erupted like a firework.

"That was wonderful!" said the girl.

The woman then noticed the Revolution approaching them. The woman then walked over to them, giving Tamera, Noelle and Kirbie a hug.

"It's good to see you again," she told Kirbie and Noelle.

"Same here, Avalon."

Avalon was dressed in a light purple coat she wore over a black sweater along with black slacks. She had purplish-gray hair, that came down to her waist, along with violet eyes.

She then noticed Timothy. "And is this Tamera's boyfriend?"

Tamera blushed, hearing the comment. "This is my kind-hearted friend, Timothy."

Avalon hugged Tamera tightly. "I thought I was your someone special."

"Of course, you are, Avalon. It's just…"

Avalon laughed. "It's okay, Tamera. I'm just teasing you."

Avalon and Timothy hugged. "It's nice to meet you. It looks like Tamera has found someone truly special."

"I think of her the same way. She's very special to me."

Tamera once again blushed.

Then Alana and several other children of Wolf Lake approached, along with three other women.

"It's good to see you all again," Alana greeted.

"Is this the Revolution?" asked one child.

"They are amazing!"

"We're so glad you're here!"

Avalon smiled. "Timothy, let me introduce you to some of our citizens. This is my little sister, Amelia."

Amelia had a brighter shade of long purple hair, that reached down to her thighs, with golden eyes. She was clothed in a darker purple long-sleeved buttoned sweater over a pink tank top with denim shorts and black tights that had cutouts in the front and back of the upper part of her thighs.

"It's so good to see you!" Amelia mentioned as she also hugged Timothy. "I'm really glad you and Tamera are together!"

Tamera was having trouble with Avalon and Amelia saying she and Timothy were together, but tried to keep a positive outlook on things.

"And these are some of the children who are really special to me: Heart and Danni."

Heart had white hair with purple eyes and wore a strapped purple dress with dark purple mesh sleeves and pantyhose that matched the color and pattern of her sleeves, while Danni had dark gray hair and blue-gray eyes and had on an oversized white sweater over a black tank top with black leggings.

"These children are very special to me," Avalon noted.

"Are they yours?" Timothy asked Avalon.

"No, I don't have children of my own," Avalon responded. "They're Amelia's."

"And I love them with all my heart," Amelia stated.

"Are you headed for Abaddon's castle?" asked Heart.

"Yes," Kirbie stated. "We're going to rescue our friends and families."

"You're all so brave in doing this for everyone," Danni complimented.

"Thank you, Danni," Tamera responded.

"Amelia, you have your hands full watching all these kids," Timothy noted.

"Yes indeed," Amelia mentioned. "But I love each and every one of them."

When they walked towards the center of town, Tamera happened to catch a glimpse at a young girl who was watching them. The young girl saw that Tamera looked at her. Terrified, the young girl hid herself from Tamera's view.

Timothy noticed Tamera looking elsewhere. "Is something wrong, Tamera?"

"No, I just thought I saw someone."

"Please stay with us and get something to eat," Alana told them.

"We would love to," Noelle stated.

The group sat down to eat. Before beginning, Alana happened to notice someone wasn't with them.

"Has anyone seen Natalie?" Alana asked.

"We haven't seen her for a while," Destiny finally stated.

"Maybe we should look for her," Avalon responded.

Serenity happened to see her in the distance. "She's over there."

They saw a young girl with wolf ears sitting at a different table by herself. The girl, who had ears and a tail like a wolf, had brownish skin, longer dark brown hair and purple eyes, and wore a pink dress over a white shirt, with pink tights.

Tamera noticed her entire right paw was covered in dried blood.

"Oh, sweetie, you're injured," Tamera stated, noticing the blood on her hand.

"Are you okay, Natalie?" Timothy wondered.

"Who are you two?" Natalie said softly.

"I'm Tamera, and this is my friend, Timothy."

"Your skin... is blue?"

Tamera lowered her head. "Yeah, it is."

Natalie unexpectedly gave Tamera a hug while blushing. "I really like it. You look so different... so beautiful..."

Tamera wrapped her arms around Natalie.

"I'm surprised," Avalon spoke. "She normally isn't that affectionate. She's always so quiet and shy."

Natalie noticed everyone staring at her. Feeling embarrassed, she blushed again before running quickly away.

"Natalie!" Tamera called out, and she chased after her. Timothy followed as Kirbie stayed behind.

Timothy and Tamera searched for the girl frantically. Then as they walked up to an old building that was sitting in the forest, they heard some noise coming from inside. Tamera looked into the building from a busted window and saw Natalie sitting on the floor, her arms and head resting on her knees.

"Natalie, are you okay?" she asked.

"I'm sorry... it's just that... I'm very shy, and... I couldn't handle everyone staring at me like that..." Tears began to fall from her eyes.

"I understand," Tamera told her. "I'm sorry if we upset you."

Natalie leaped into Tamera's arms. Timothy then approached them. Natalie then hugged Timothy after he fell to his knees. Timothy wrapped his arms around Natalie to give her comfort.

Suddenly, Timothy, Tamera and Natalie heard screams coming from a distance. They came out and they met up with Noelle and Kirbie. The townsfolk were in extreme shock as they stared at the Teladine River.

Kirbie walked over to the water that was colored red. She dipped her hand into the river. When she brought her hand out of the river, she was stunned.

"It looks like... blood!" Kirbie cried out.

Screams got louder from the townsfolk after hearing what Kirbie stated.

"Where's the river come from?" Tamera questioned.

"Outside of Death Mountain," Alana told him.

"Death Mountain," Timothy spoke. "How comforting."

"We have to find out what's going on," Kirbie demanded.

"Do you have to go?" Natalie asked Tamera, holding her hand. Tamera squatted down, facing Natalie.

"I do, sweetie. I have to find out what's happening to the

river. But don't worry. I'll be back shortly, okay?"

"Okay," Natalie said softly as she hugged Tamera, not wanting to let her go. Alana walked over to Natalie. "Honey, she needs to go."

Natalie let Tamera go. Timothy then told her, "I promise we'll be back."

"I'll hold you to that," Natalie said smiling, but with tears in her eyes.

The Revolution made their way to Death Mountain.

"I didn't want them to leave," Natalie said with her head lowered.

"I know, Natalie," Avalon stated. "Don't worry. They'll be back to see you."

The trio arrived near Death Mountain. They followed the trail of the blood-filled Teladine River.

"What could be causing this?" Timothy wondered.

"Perhaps we'll find out over at that mill," Noelle pointed out.

They noticed the water flowing into Teladine Mill looked normal, but the water coming out was colored like blood.

"Let's check it out," Tamera ordered.

The Revolution slowly walked through the mill. As they walked back outside to the back of the mill, and they saw a sorcerer, filled with a maniacal laughter, shooting bolts of red light into the gears of the mill.

"Why is he doing this?" Timothy questioned.

Then almost as if they appeared from thin air, members of the Darkness swarmed around the Revolution. They pulled out their weapons and began attacking to turn the menacing foes into dust.

Then the sorcerer approached the Revolution. He had gray

hair and black eyes, with wolf ears and a tail, and was wearing a dark brown leather vest and pants.

"Well, if it isn't the Revolution," said the sorcerer.

"Who are you?" Tamera questioned.

The sorcerer uncovered his face, smiling devilishly.

"Arawolf," Kirbie smirked. "I should have known."

"Indeed, it's been a long time, Kirbie." Then he turned his attention to Timothy and Tamera.

"And this is Noelle, Tamera, and Timothy, an outcast, on a mission to save their precious families and friends. Such a shame that all you have done to this point is nothing but a waste."

"It's you who is just wasting your time," Tamera spoke, pointing her ax at Arawolf. But Arawolf, like lightning, moved as Tamera fired ice at him. Then he extended out his hands, and Noelle, Kirbie and Timothy became trapped in a tar-like wrapping colored red. They began getting squeezed.

"Now you have a choice, Ice Goddess," Arawolf told her. "Surrender yourself to me, or your friends will die. What's it going to be?"

"No, don't do it, Tamera!" Kirbie told her.

"Don't worry about us!" Timothy pleaded. "Save the others!"

Tamera stared directly at Timothy. Timothy looked back at Tamera, knowing she had something in mind to do. Tamera's ax disappeared and she fell to her knees as if to surrender herself. Arawolf approached Tamera, laughing softly.

"What do you have to say for yourself, Tamera?" Arawolf asked.

Tamera just looked up at Arawolf in sadness. Then she simply said, "Just this."

Tamera quickly formed her bow and fired off an arrow again

and pierced Arawolf with it. As the glow of the attack dissipated, suddenly Arawolf, now in the form of a wolf, jumped on Tamera, pinning her down. Tamera screamed in fear.

Suddenly, a wolf, the color of brown, jumped at Arawolf, knocking him off Tamera. Tamera then got up and stood behind the wolf.

Arawolf growled. "Well, if it isn't little Natalie. I'm surprised to see you here."

Timothy was stunned. "Natalie?"

"Arawolf, this has to stop. The villagers don't deserve this!"

Arawolf laughed. "You're actually going to defend those sorry excuses for human beings: the very people who have done nothing but treat you like dirt?"

"That doesn't give us the right to do this!" She looked over to Tamera. "Besides, they're not all bad."

Arawolf snickered. "You mean them?"

"I… have fallen in love with her… and Timothy."

"Enough! You're just talking nonsense!"

Arawolf smacked Natalie hard with his claw, slicing her face. Natalie fell to the ground unconscious. Then Arawolf jumped at Tamera, but before he could strike her, she stabbed her magical ax through his chest. Arawolf suddenly turned into dust.

Noelle, Timothy and Kirbie were freed of the traps. Timothy ran over to Natalie, who had turned back to her human form. As Timothy lifted Natalie up, she woke up and looked into his eyes.

"Timothy?" she said softly.

"Are you okay, sweetie?"

"I… I think so. Where's Arawolf?"

"I took care of him," Tamera mentioned. "He won't hurt you again."

"That was brave of you to do that, Natalie," Timothy told

her. "Thanks for saving us."

Natalie wrapped her arms around Timothy, crying. "What's wrong, sweetie? Did I say…"

"That was… the kindest thing anyone ever said to me."

Timothy and Natalie hugged each other tightly.

"Natalie! Natalie, where are you?" cried out a voice.

"Amelia?" Natalie spoke. "Amelia! We're over here!"

Amelia had tears in her eyes when she came over to Natalie, hugging her tightly.

"Don't do that to me, sweetie," Amelia scolded. "I was so worried about you!"

"I'm sorry, Amelia," Natalie responded.

"Amelia, Natalie saved my life," Tamera informed her. "She stopped Arawolf from striking me down."

"And Tamera stopped Arawolf as well! She saved us!"

Amelia hugged Natalie even tighter. She then noticed the cuts on Natalie's face.

"I'm proud of you, Natalie. That was a wonderful thing you did for Tamera."

Natalie smiled. "Thanks, Amelia."

Then Amelia hugged Timothy. "Thank you for watching over her, all of you."

"Let's get back to Wolf Lake," Noelle stated.

Timothy walked over to Tamera. "She really does love you."

"I'm not the only one, Timothy," Tamera smiled.

The Revolution arrived back at Wolf Lake to applause and cheers. They noticed the Teladine River had turned back to its normal color. Some of the children jumped into the river and played in it.

"You did it!" Alana told the Revolution. She hugged

Tamera.

"Thank you all so much," Natalie told the Revolution. "I love you."

"We love you, too, Natalie."

Natalie hugged Tamera. "Thank you for saving us."

"It's time to get to Abaddon's castle," Noelle claimed.

Timothy kissed Natalie on her forehead. "I promise I'll come back for you."

"I'll be waiting."

Avalon hugged Timothy, and then kissed his forehead. "You better take good care of Tamera, you hear me."

Timothy snickered. "I promise, with all my heart."

Avalon grabbed Tamera's hands and placed them on Timothy's hands. Then Timothy and Tamera hugged each other tightly.

Everyone said goodbye to each other. Then Alana, Serenity, and Destiny made their way to Cecaria as the Revolution headed for Abaddon's castle.

Chapter 27

The Legend of Oculus

The stars were shining above the heroes as they walked along their way towards Abaddon's castle. But Kirbie was feeling drained out from being awake early in the day, and her eyes started getting really heavy. Tamera happened to see Kirbie struggling to stay awake.

"Are you okay, sis?" Tamera asked her.

"I'm great, love," she responded. "I just feel really tired."

"I think we're all drained from that last battle," Timothy mentioned.

They looked ahead to see a sign: "Oculus' Tower. Vacancy available."

"Let's get some rest here," Tamera instructed. "We can stay here for the night."

Noelle finally realized where she was at and her eyes got wide.

"We can't stay here," Noelle informed them.

"Why not?" Timothy wondered.

"Because of the legend of Oculus. Legend has it that this place is haunted by a big eyeball named Oculus. He haunts those who sleep in this hotel. Once you enter, they say you never leave."

"Well, that's comforting," Timothy thought out loud.

"I've heard that, too," Tamera stated, "but that's just a myth. Many people have stayed in this hotel without a problem."

"Perhaps we should have stayed in Wolf Lake instead of moving ahead," Noelle told everyone.

"Nonetheless, we're here," Kirbie said. "Let's get a room and crash for the night."

The group cautiously walked into the hotel. At the front desk was a young woman who was finishing up some paperwork. The woman, who had brown hair and eyes, was wearing a yellow jacket over a blue sleeveless sweater and white long-sleeved shirt that had a red bow on the neckline, and a red plaid dress.

"Hi, welcome to Oculus' Tower!" the woman said joyfully. "I'm Ashlie! What can I do for you this evening?"

"Hi, sweetheart," Kirbie spoke. "We would like to rent a couple of your rooms."

"That's great! For how long?"

"Just for the night."

"How many?"

"Four."

"That will be one hundred coins. Oh! And please take these complimentary eyeballs!"

Noelle was thrown off-guard. "Eyeballs?"

"Yeah! They're marshmallow gummies!" Ashlie took one out of the package and showed it to the Revolution.

"Is it too late to go back to Wolf Lake?" Kirbie questioned.

Ashlie laughed. "Oh, I bet you've heard about the Legend of Oculus! Don't worry. That's just a legend, that's all."

"How long have you worked here, sweetie?" Timothy wondered.

"Three years! It's a pretty easy job, and I like meeting new people like you!"

Tamera sighed. "Let's just pay her and get some sleep."

Kirbie and Tamera each gave Ashlie sixty coins, also

covering for a tip for Ashlie. Ashlie put the money in her register and then opened up a small cabinet, grabbing two keys out of it.

"Okay, the keys are for room 204 and 205, upstairs on the right side."

"Thank you," Kirbie told her, and the group walked away.

"Have a wonderful night!" Ashlie told them.

Kirbie and Tamera slept in Room 204 and Timothy in 205. During the night, Timothy was resting peacefully in the bed in his room. Suddenly, Timothy awoke when he heard some commotion in the lower floor below. Curious as to what was going on, Timothy put his regular clothing back on, grabbed his sword and walked out of the room.

As Timothy made it downstairs, he looked to see the lobby had been ransacked. He looked around elsewhere but didn't see anything. Then out of the corner of his eye, he saw two girls hiding behind the counter. He walked over to them, recognizing both.

"Madison?" Timothy spoke. He saw she was comforting Ashlie. "You both all right?"

Ashlie cried loudly. "It was terrible! These ugly black beings came in and started tearing the place apart!"

"Shh, calm down," Madison told her. "They'll hear us."

Indeed, they did, as many spirits surrounded Timothy, Ashlie and Madison. Timothy prepared his sword, and Ashlie would not let go of Madison.

"I'm really scared," Ashlie spoke.

"Don't worry. We'll get through this," Timothy assured her.

The spirits charged at Timothy, and he was trying his best to strike them down with his sword, yet because of the number of spirits, Timothy was getting a bit overwhelmed. Then one of the spirits trapped Timothy, Ashlie and Madison in netting. But before the spirits could grab the trio, they began getting attacked by Tamera, Noelle and Kirbie. Try as they may, the spirits were not able to get the better of the three women, and it was Kirbie who struck down the last spirit with her swords.

Noelle, Kirbie and Tamera then freed Timothy, Ashlie and Madison from the netting. Before Madison could do anything else, Ashlie again jumped into Madison's arms.

"Oh, thank goodness it's over!" Ashlie cried out. "Please stay with me! I don't want to go through this again!"

Madison hugged Ashlie before hugging Timothy. Then Madison saw Tamera and Kirbie. Tamera had a look of uncertainty on her face. Madison suddenly let go of Timothy.

"I'm so sorry," Madison told Tamera. "I'm not trying to steal your boyfriend. It's just…"

"It's okay, Madison," Tamera assured her, blushing. "We're just good friends."

Kirbie was irritated at Tamera for continuing to avoid Timothy, but at the time said nothing.

"Let's get back to sleep," Kirbie replied.

"Let me sleep with you!" Ashlie said to Madison, who was shocked at her words. Madison blushed deeply. "I don't mean that! I just… don't want to be alone…"

"You can sleep with us, sweetie, if that's all right," Noelle told her.

"But the beds are only big enough for two people…" Ashlie told her.

Timothy looked at Kirbie and Tamera.

"Well, Tamera, why don't you sleep in Timothy's room?" Kirbie suggested.

Tamera blushed. "I really don't think that's a good idea. I'm not his any more…"

Kirbie had finally had enough. "Why are you doing this to him? Can't you see how much he loves you?"

"I know he does, but his heart's with Noelle..."

Noelle stepped in. "We're just friends! I don't want him like that..." She turned her head slightly as she blushed. "I mean, I..."

"You see? You love him too! He's better off with you! He'll die if he stays with me!"

"You don't know that!" Kirbie stated.

"I *do* know that! Mom did, Dad did... even Luna did! You're just too stupid to realize that..."

Tamera realized what she said, and she looked at Kirbie to see the stunned look on her face. Tamera ran away from the group, tears falling from her eyes.

"Tamera, wait, please!" Timothy called out.

Kirbie fell to her knees, crying as well. Noelle comforted her.

Tamera ran outside away from the hotel, stopping at a place where a stump was left from a tree that had been cut down. Tamera had her face covered as she began to sob loudly. Then Tamera felt somebody wrapping their arms around her waist. Tamera moved her hands and opened her eyes to see Timothy on his knees beside her.

Tamera was surprised. "Timothy?" She could see Timothy also was teary-eyed.

"I'm so sorry, Tamera. I never knew you were in so much pain."

Tamera continued to cry as she looked down at him.

"I love you so much, and it kills me to see you so sad. Please let me share this burden with you. You shouldn't have to bear this alone."

Tamera was objective. "No, Timothy, that's not fair to you!"

Timothy placed his hands on Tamera's cheeks, wiping away her tears. "Please, Tamera, I want to do this. I would do anything to see you smile again."

Tamera was so overwhelmed by Timothy's words. She suddenly jumped into Timothy's arms, crying ever harder.

"I don't deserve to be with someone like you, Timothy."

"Yes, you do, Tamera. I love you, and I would do anything for you."

Tamera continued to cry as she and Timothy held tightly on to each other. At that moment, Kirbie, Noelle, Ashlie and Madison walked over to her.

"Is love really this complicated?" Madison wondered.

Noelle smiled. "You have no idea, sweetie, but it's definitely worth fighting for."

Tamera then walked over to Kirbie. Tears continued to fall down her cheeks. "Kirbie…" She cried ever harder. "I'm sorry… I know… you're not stupid… this is… all my fault…"

Kirbie at first said nothing, but just wrapped her arms around Tamera. "I still love you, Tamera. I just wish… you would trust in what I say."

Tamera continued to cry as she wouldn't let go of Kirbie. Then Noelle walked over to Tamera. She reached out her hand, and Tamera grabbed it. Then Noelle reached for Timothy's hand, and when he grabbed Noelle's, Noelle then placed Timothy and Tamera's hands together.

"No matter what," Noelle stated. "Whether as friends, or more than friends, you two need each other. Promise me that you two will stay by each other's side."

"I promise," Timothy replied.

Tamera tried wiping the tears from her face. "I promise,

too." Then Tamera and Timothy hugged each other, not wanting to let go.

"That's what I want to hear," Noelle responded.

Tamera did indeed sleep in the same room as Timothy as Madison and Ashlie slept in Kirbie and Noelle's room. Then morning arose as the clouds dominated the sky, and rain was falling over the area. Tamera woke up to the pitter-patter of rain hitting against the windows. Then Timothy woke up hearing Tamera crawl out of the bed. The two gathered their things and as they opened the door to walk out of the bedroom, they saw Kirbie walking out of her room yawning and stretching, trying to get herself more awake. Madison then followed.

"Looks like it's time to go," Tamera commented.

The group was getting ready when Tamera heard a knock on the door. She walked over to the door to answer. She didn't see anybody. As she stepped out, suddenly she was sliced across her left eye. Tamera fell to her knees, crying out in pain as she held her hands over her bleeding eye.

"Tamera!" Timothy cried out. He, Noelle and Kirbie drew their weapons. Ashlie hid behind her desk in fear, with Madison trying to comfort her. As Tamera tried to stand back up, a spirit then stabbed his sword into Tamera's stomach.

"NO!" Timothy screamed out. Kirbie charged hard at Lycan and the other spirit when they suddenly became trapped by netting. As they got prepared to trap Timothy as well, Timothy took off his necklace and threw it at Tamera.

"Angelic Rain!" Timothy yelled. The golden vortex appeared. Unsure of what was happening, the soldiers retreated with their prisoners.

"It's over," Lycan stated. "The Ice Goddess is dead, and the others have been captured."

"Excellent. Head back to the castle," Abaddon ordered.

With that, everyone grabbed the trapped members of the Revolution and went on their way, heading for their destination. Tamera, seeing the men had left, drank the potion.

Abaddon watched in the crystal ball as Lycan approached the castle. Abaddon was filled with joy, feeling that victory was in his grasp.

"So," Abaddon spoke, "It's finally over."

"I can't believe it!" Lycan responded. "They actually stopped them."

Then Lycan and his spirits brought in Timothy, Noelle and Kirbie. They were placed in the cell with the other prisoners.

"Timothy!" Camille cried out. They hugged. "I've been so worried about you."

"I'm so glad you're okay," Timothy told her.

"Where's Tamera?" Olivia asked.

"If I heard right," Laura replied, "she is gone."

Camille was stunned. "No, it can't be!" She began to cry.

Just then the strange voice spoke out again. "This is our time," the voice told Abaddon.

"Come," Abaddon told Lycan. "It's time to take over this world. We will unleash the army." Then he told the spirits, "Send the prisoners to Hellito."

Abaddon and Lycan left the room, and a spirit walked over to a panel, flipping on a button. Suddenly everyone in the cage disappeared.

The prisoners appeared on a lonely cliff, including the ones held in the dungeon. As they checked their surroundings, a bright flash appeared in front of them. A humanoid figure colored black, with white lines running all through its body, appeared in front of them. The figure opened its eyes, revealing them to glow the color of fire.

Timothy turned to the prisoners and saw their faces in complete shock.

"Who is that?" he wondered.

"Welcome," said the floating figure. "I am Darcia."

Everyone was left speechless.

"Fire Light," was spoken by Darcia. Her eyes began to glow, and a huge orange wave flowed from her eyes, hitting the prisoners. When the wave disappeared, it was revealed that the prisoners were all turned into statues.

Chapter 28

Preparing for the War

"Tamera?" said a soft voice. "Can you hear me?"

Tamera opened her eyes to see Heather, Tanna and Madison looking down at her, with tears flowing down Heather's cheeks. Tamera sat up, and Heather wrapped her arms around her. "Oh, thank you, God." Heather stated. "I thought we lost you, Tamera."

"Heather?" Tamera was puzzled. "What happened? Where am I?"

"You're at Lorelei Pond."

"How did I get here?"

"Madison and I found you at the hotel, unconscious, so we brought you here."

"Where's Ashlie?"

"She stayed back at the hotel."

Tamera lifted up her shirt to see the stab wound on her stomach had healed.

"You were stabbed again?" Tanna wondered.

"Yeah, but... I don't understand..."

"We found this lying next to you," said Heather.

Heather gave her a necklace, and Tamera's eyes grew wide as she recognized it. "It's the necklace that Tessa gave to Timothy. He must have used it on me. He really does love me."

"Wait a minute," Tanna stated. "How did you ever get the

idea that he didn't? You are all he ever talks about!"

"Is she awake, my child?" another voice stated. Tanna nodded. Tamera turned to see an older man standing next to Tanna and Madison. "How are you feeling, Tamera?"

"I'm fine, thank you." Then she recognized the man. "Aren't you... Prince Kain?"

"I see you recognize me. Welcome to Lorelei Pond."

"Where are the others?" Camille wondered.

"They were captured by Lycan and his men."

"Oh, no," Tanna gasped.

"It couldn't come at a worse time," Kain pointed out. "I was just told that Abaddon's army is on the move. They'll be here within the hour."

"What are we going to do?"

Tamera got on her feet, forming her ax. "We have to face them."

Madison was shocked. "Are you kidding? That's suicide!"

"What choice do we have?" Tamera cried out. "They are certainly going to kill us. If I am going to die, I'm going to die fighting."

She began to walk in the direction of Abaddon's castle.

"Tamera, wait!" Heather cried out. Tamera turned to see Heather come up to her. She blushed. "I... I know it may be a losing effort but... I want to go with you. You shouldn't have to go alone. And if it means getting Timothy back..."

"No, I can't risk losing you. It's better if you stay here with Tanna."

Heather hugged Tamera back. "I love you, Tamera. Please be careful."

"Excuse me, Tamera," Kain interrupted. "But if you are going to do this, you better get moving. The army's making its rounds. I wish you the best of luck."

"Please bring Timothy back to me!" Madison cried. "I miss him already!"

"You're not the only one," Tamera said as she blushed.

Tamera walked away. Heather was disturbed.

"She needs me, Kain," she said, with tears in her eyes.

Kain walked up to her and said, "Do what you think is right, child."

Heather smiled, grabbed her bow, and ran after Tamera.

Tamera continued walking on her own towards the outskirts of Abaddon's castle, with worry in her heart still plaguing her as rain began to fall around her. She bowed her head.

"My Heavenly Father, we're about to face the biggest challenge we've ever faced. I just pray that you will stand beside me and Tamera as we embark on this journey to save those who have been overwhelmed by this evil. Be with them all forever and always, in the name of Jesus Christ I pray, amen." After praying, she got back on her feet and walked onward.

The massive army, led by Lycan, approached outside of Abaddon's castle. Lycan stopped in his tracks, seeing somebody approaching them, and he signaled for his army to stop. The enormous horde of spirits looked ahead of them. There they saw Tamera appearing over a small hill, and while standing on top of the hill, just stared ahead, her hair blowing in the wind.

"I thought Tamera was dead," a soldier said out loud.

Lycan noticed that it was only Tamera standing in front of him. He laughed as he saw the two lonely warriors ready for battle. In the meantime, Tamera continued to look on, seeing the overwhelming number of enemies she standing against. She formed her ax. Then she looked over and saw Heather standing by her.

"I thought I told you to stay with the others," Tamera spoke calmly.

"You did, but I wouldn't be able to face Timothy if I told him I let you face a horde of soldiers by yourself. Plus, you haven't seen what Kain has taught me."

Tamera smirked as she and Heather stood firm.

"They're not leaving!" said a spirit.

"Give them a minute to let it sink in," Lycan told him.

Tamera and Heather walked a short distance forward.

Another spirit was in shock. "They're actually going to do this!"

"Destroy them now!" Lycan screamed, and the army charged.

Tamera and Heather prepared themselves as the army reached them. Then with all their might, they began to strike down the army. Tamera used her ax to take down many of the spirits, turning them to dust, as Heather used her bow. Tamera, in doing her fighting, looked almost as if she were dancing while swinging her ax. Tamera would slice many up with her ax or shoot some with her ice magic.

Heather's bow began to glow, and as she swung her arms and bow out, a large shockwave formed, destroying many of the soldiers.

Then Tamera formed a ball of glowing ice in her hands. She then threw the ball and struck down several more spirits. Tamera also shot out more ice from her hands.

"Come on, finish them off already!" Lycan commanded angrily.

Tamera and Heather continued to fight valiantly against the

spirits. Tamera stretched out her arms, and her hands began to glow. An icy blast shot from her hands, absorbing many of the spirits.

Lycan was getting frustrated. "It's only two women!" he yelled. "Get in there and destroy them!"

The army charged ever harder against Tamera and Heather. As Tamera got prepared to attack again, she got struck in the back by a spirit. She fell to her hands and knees, almost knocked senseless.

"Tamera!" Heather cried out as she ran over to Tamera. "Are you okay?"

Several spirits surrounded Tamera and Heather.

"Wait!" Lycan stated before the spirits could strike them down. He approached Tamera, who was breathing heavily while still in Heather's arms. Tamera and Heather looked up at Lycan, thinking this would be the end of not just their mission, but also their lives.

"Very impressive," Lycan snickered. "I thought you died at the hotel. This time, I'm gonna make sure you both die."

Tamera and Heather looked up after hearing the roar of an engine and saw the Maniton approaching them. Abaddon was driving the ship.

"Finally, it will end here," Abaddon spoke calmly.

Lycan went to swing his claws at Tamera and Tanna when his paw got hit by a small arrow. Lycan was shocked as he looked over to see Kain a short distance from him, standing atop a larger hill.

"Kain?" said Tamera.

"Just as I figured, you were in a pickle," he answered. "So, I thought that I would bring you some reinforcements."

At that time another large ship, named the "Gold Atlas"

appeared over the hill, along with many other different warriors from the World of Exodus who had walked up beside Kain, all ready to fight beside Tamera and Heather.

"Spirits, attack!" Lycan commanded.

Abaddon's army charged again. The Gem Girls first swarmed into the crowd of enemies, slashing them quickly with their swords. When it got a little too crowded, the trio held back their swords, and they began to glow. Then they slammed the swords down to the ground, and an explosion of fire ensued, wiping out many of the spirits.

Tanna pulled out her large gun and began striking down many spirits. When she became surrounded by spirits, she twirled with fire formed in both hands, and she turned into a fire tornado, burning up all the spirits that surrounded her.

Celina was taking down many with her sword. One soldier tried to sneak up on Celina, but before the soldier could, he was punched with much force by Mornecai. The soldier slammed against a tree and turned to dust.

"Thanks again, big guy," Celina told him.

"Anything for you, beautiful," Mornecai responded.

Celina rolled her eyes as she smiled.

Lauren popped up over a hill, slicing up many of the spirits with her twin blades. She would also use various kicks and punches to turn the spirits into dust.

Kendra and Sonata were approached by several spirits. First, Kendra whipped out a black frying pan and began striking several with it. Then when a spirit tried to strike Kendra with its sword, Sonata spun around, kicking the spirit with her foot. Her shoe had sharp blades all around it. Then Kendra pulled out her wand.

"Shala-kala-boom!" she yelled. The spirits became covered in smoke. When the smoke cleared, they all were wearing gold dresses. The spirits were confused.

"I've got to get some new spells."

Sonata chuckled. Then her hands glowed a light blue. She then fell to her knees, slamming the ground. A huge blast swarmed out from Sonata, turning the spirits to dust.

"You're awesome, Sonata," Kendra commented.

"Thanks, sweetheart," Sonata chuckled.

Hawkore and his friends were also taking care of things by striking spirits with their claws.

Ligwud, Judetta and Lisa joined Tanna and continued fighting as well with their swords.

Tamera took down even more spirits with her sword or icicles as Heather continued fighting with her bow. Tamera was impressed with Heather's skills.

"That's how you do it, sweetie," Tamera told her, sneaking a kiss onto Heather's cheek. Heather blushed.

Abaddon got angry at what he was seeing in the battle.

"Let's even things up a bit," Abaddon told them. Abaddon pressed a button, and the Maniton started firing lasers at the war below and the Gold Atlas in front of them.

With that, the Gold Atlas began firing back at the Maniton. The two ships continued to fire at each other, but the Maniton was getting the advantage. In an effort to save the ship, the Gold Atlas had no choice but to retreat.

"We've got to get on the Maniton!" Tamera stated.

"Go ahead, Tamera!" Heather told her. "We can handle it from here!"

Tamera waved down Hawkore, who flew down to her.

"Can you fly me up to the Maniton?"

"Sure thing, Tamera. Hop on."

Tamera crawled onto Hawkore's back and Hawkore flew up

into the sky. He was able to avoid the ship's efforts to shoot him down. He then flew up to a door on the ship.

"I'll stay as close as I can. Be careful."

"You too, and thank you, Hawkore."

Tamera sneaked onto the ship.

Ligwud was approached by a horde of Abaddon's spirits. Ligwud raised up his hands, and an enormous green ball formed in front of him. He then thrust his arms forward, and a large green stream shot out in front of him, turning more spirits to dust.

At that time, Kain made his way through the army until he confronted Lycan.

"Finally, I will kill you off, Kain," Lycan spoke.

Lycan blew fire at Kain, but he rolled out of the way. Kain threw a lightning bolt from his rod, but Lycan quickly dodged it. He then threw a magical star at Lycan as well, but the star missed as Lycan rolled. Then several spirits charged at Kain.

"Here's a little trick Tamera taught me," Kain claimed, aiming his rod at the spirits. A bright red beam in the shape of a heart shot out at the spirits. The beam turned Lycan and the spirits into dust.

Abaddon was watching the battle progressing. Abaddon was getting angry at the results. Suddenly there was a large blast, and the door blew off its hinges. Abaddon saw Tamera enter the room.

"Tamera!" Abaddon called out. "How did you get in here?"

"So, you're the henchmen behind this?" Tamera asked.

"No... I'm the follower of someone much greater than I am. And even if we fail, none of you will have a chance against her."

Abaddon pulled out his sword and swung it at Tamera, but Tamera blocked it with her ax. They began fighting against each other. Abaddon began to get the upper hand on Tamera, slicing her left hand. When Abaddon went to strike her down, Tamera suddenly punched Abaddon. Abaddon suddenly gasped, and had a look of shock on his face. Tamera looked to see that her hand, which was glowing an icy color, had penetrated Abaddon's metal suit and pierced his chest. He then faded off into dust.

The ship began to descend to the ground. Tamera was able to escape out of the ship with the help of Hawkore. The ship then crashed to the ground and a large explosion ensued.

Tamera and Hawkore landed back on the ground by her friends and family. Heather ran over and hugged Tamera tightly.

"I'm so glad you're safe, Tamera," Heather stated.

Suddenly a warp appeared behind Tamera and Heather. They were pulled into the warp before anyone could react.

"No, Heather!" Celina cried out.

"Tamera!" Sonata yelled.

Celina looked at Kain. "Where could they have gone?"

"I'm not sure," Kain answered. "But we have to find them."

Tamera and Heather got up and looked around to see they were sitting on a cliff. They saw several statues around them. Tamera and Heather noticed the statues looked like those from the World of Exodus. Tamera hugged the statue of Camille.

"My little angel," she said sadly.

"They're... statues?" Heather spoke, completely puzzled.

Tamera then noticed a statue of Timothy. She walked up to the statue, with more tears flowing from her eyes, and hugged it. Heather did the same.

"I've missed you so much," Tamera whispered tearfully.

"Timothy?" Heather stated sadly.

"Just where exactly are we?" Tamera asked as she and Heather checked their surroundings.

Chapter 29

The Final Battle

Tamera and Heather were still confused at where they were located. Suddenly, there was a yellow flash of light that came from the edge of the cliff. Tamera and Heather looked up to see Darcia appear in front of them.

"Welcome to Hellito," Darcia simply said.

Tamera turned to the being, angered. "Who are you?"

"I am Darcia. I have heard much about you, Ice Goddess. You may have been victorious to this point, but now it's time for you to die. Fire Light."

The bright orange flash again shot out from Darcia, covering over Tamera and Heather. When the light dissipated and Tamera opened her eyes, she noticed a glow of blue light surrounding her. She turned to see Heather was now a statue like the others.

"Heather!" Tamera yelled out in sadness.

"Amazing. My spell didn't faze you. Never mind. I have other ways to destroy you. Fire Wall."

A bright flash of fire swarmed at Tamera. Within moments, Tamera noticed her body had turned white, but was then turning back to her original color.

Before Darcia could make her next move, Tamera angrily fired several beams of ice at Darcia, but she absorbed the beams of ice. She laughed maniacally.

"Your puny attacks will not work on me, Ice Goddess,"

Darcia stated. "I still have the Diamonds of Allure. Now watch what I can do. Dark Cannon."

A cannon appeared in front of Darcia, and a large ray of black light fired off, hitting Tamera. She fell down to the ground violently. Tamera stood back up and tried to shake off the effects. She looked back up to Darcia.

"Fire Smash."

Darcia turned into a large spear and sliced across the cliff, hitting Tamera and slamming her into a large rock. Tamera fought with all her might to get back on her feet.

"Dark Blades."

Darcia changed into two large blades of blackness. The blades then grabbed Tamera, picked her up high into the air, and then slammed her down aggressively onto the top of the cliff. Tamera then barely had enough strength as she turned herself over and got up on her knees.

Darcia suddenly began to scream loudly. Tamera cried out in pain, coughing up blood.

"Chain of Darkness."

A long fiery chain appeared in Darcia's hand. As Tamera fought to stand back up, Darcia whipped the chain and wrapped it around Tamera. With the chain, she picked Tamera up. Tamera screamed in pain loudly as the chain began to squeeze her. Darcia then whipped the chain around, pulling Tamera off the ground and with a quick speed then slammed her forcefully into the cliff.

Tamera was almost lifeless, on her hands and knees. Darcia hovered over to her. She again wrapped her chain around Tamera and picked her up, forcing Tamera to look at her.

'Why do you even do this for Exodus, my dear?" Darcia wondered. "I know your story: how people taunted and teased you because of your blue skin. I know they don't really appreciate you. So, I'm willing to spare your life, and theirs, if you just join with me, and we together will rule over all of Exodus."

"You're... wrong, Darcia," Tamera responded. "I am loved... by my friends, my family, and by the kindest man I have ever met. And I know how this story goes: you claim we will rule together, but in the end... you'll be ruling and I'll just be another one of your slaves of the Darkness."

Darcia became angry. "You stupid girl. To think that you would risk your friends' lives like this."

"Because they feel as I do... they would rather die than be your servant."

Darcia then flipped the chain backwards, and Tamera was thrown backwards. Tamera fell into the abyss behind Darcia. She fell many feet down until she landed on a cliff, where she was impaled by a rock just above her heart. Tamera gasped as all she could do was look directly up, unable to move. Suddenly Tamera closed her eyes.

Tamera was dreaming that she was walking with nothing but a pure white fog around her. She noticed she was mostly without color, other than what looked like a faint blue cast over her.

"Hello?" Tamera cried out. She did not hear a response. She walked a little further forward. Then she happened to see someone approaching her.

"Hello, beautiful," said the person. Tamera recognized the person, and she smiled as tears fell from her eyes. They hugged each other.

"I've missed you so much, Mom," Tamera told her.

"I've missed you too."

"So, does this mean that I'm... dead?"

"Well, most people don't survive a fall like that."

Tamera chuckled. "No, I guess not." Then Tamera showed sadness. "But that means… I won't get to see Timothy or Heather again…"

"Actually, that's not quite true."

Tamera was wide-eyed. "What do you mean?"

"The Lord has decided it's not time for you to come home yet. He wants you back on Exodus, to take care of the evil that has plagued everyone."

Tamera couldn't believe what Celestia was saying. "I'm…"

"Oh, and I'm supposed to give you this." Celestia held out her hands, and they began to glow. When the glow dissipated, Tamera could see a golden sapphire in her hand. Tamera was amazed even more.

"That looks like… the Golden Sapphire!"

"Yes," Celestia replied, "and with this, you will be able to defeat Darcia."

Tamera and Celestia hugged again. "I wish you and Dad could come back with me."

"So do I, but I'll always be watching over you, Tamera. I love you so much."

Tamera began to cry again. "I love you too, Mom."

Celestia kissed Tamera on her cheek. She then placed the Golden Sapphire on Tamera's chest. Then a bright gold flash consumed them.

Darcia turned her attention to the statues. Darcia tried to strike the statues with her chain, but then she felt her chain being grabbed.

"What the…" Darcia wondered.

She turned around, and her eyes grew wide as a large

whirlwind formed. The wind, like a hand, grabbed Darcia and threw her against the cliff. Darcia then looked up as she saw the whirlwind come onto the edge of the cliff. Then the whirlwind began to dissipate, and to her shock, she saw Tamera, whose whole body was sparkling brightly. Her red hair and green eyes were now gold and sparkling as well. Her lips were a shade of gold, although her skin remained unchanged. She also had angel wings that were gold and sparkly, and was wearing a very short white lace dress that had a gold underlay with sparkling white pantyhose and gold shoes.

Darcia could see Tamera facing her with her eyes closed as Tamera was hovering in front of her. Then Tamera suddenly opened her eyes that were now colored gold.

"But how?" asked Darcia.

Darcia was shocked as she looked over to Tamera, seeing a golden jewel in her chest just above the low neckline of her dress.

"Is that… the Golden Sapphire?" Darcia cried out.

Darcia proceeded to scream loudly as she had before, but Tamera wrapped her angel wings around her as she glowed the color of gold, and the deafening sound had no effect on Tamera.

"Never mind," Darcia said. "I'll destroy you again. Dark Cannon!"

The cannon once again appeared and fired off a beam. Tamera waved her hands while spinning her body, and the beam swooped around Tamera's body and hit Darcia. This angered Darcia more as she was slow to get up.

"Fire Smash!" Darcia cried.

Darcia again tried to use the vicious fire spear. This time Tamera, using Sonata's move, fell to her knees and slammed her fists to the ground to deter the spear, the more powerful shockwave of golden fire knocking Darcia back from Tamera.

Darcia got back on her feet, almost winded.

"Dark Blades!" Darcia screamed.

The two blades went to grab Tamera once more. Tamera held out her arms, and the blades shattered into pieces after hitting Tamera's fists.

Darcia had finally had enough. As her strength was dwindling, she got desperate to use what worked for her before.

"Chain of Darkness!"

She whipped the chain and grabbed Tamera around her arms and chest. Tamera, though, closed her eyes and as Darcia picked Tamera up off the cliff, she broke free of the chain's grip. Tamera eased herself back on the cliff.

Darcia got extremely aggravated.

"Flaming Blast!"

A glow of black light shot out towards Tamera. She was able to stop the light with her right hand. Then Tamera said in a calm tone, "Angelic Wave."

Tamera levitated into the air with her angel wings fully opened. Her body and wings began to glow brightly. As Darcia fired off the black light again, a powerful golden beam of fire shot out from Tamera's whole body, absorbing the black glow, and the beam slammed into Darcia. Darcia went up in flames the color of the beam. She screamed loudly before a gigantic explosion followed, leaving the whole area engulfed in a blinding light.

At that moment, everyone was freed out of being a statue. Heather and Timothy hugged each other. Tanna then ran over to Timothy and Heather and hugged them.

"I've missed you so much, Timothy."

"I've missed you too, Tanna."

Then they hugged Camille, Max, Celina, Sandra, Noah, Noelle and Tessa. When Timothy and Heather checked out their surroundings, they saw somebody lying on the ground, still with the sparkling gold features. Timothy and the others ran to her. They were surprised when they saw who the person was.

"Is this... Tamera?" Heather questioned.

Timothy sat on the ground and picked up Tamera's body, resting her against him. "My goodness, she's even more beautiful!" Timothy commented. They all noticed the jewel in her chest.

"Is that the... Golden Sapphire?" Camille pondered.

"I guess it *does* exist," Tessa commented.

"Tamera?" Timothy cried out. "Can you hear me?"

Suddenly Tamera opened up her eyes.

"Timothy?" Tamera said softly.

Timothy was tearfully overjoyed and could not stop himself from giving the heroic angel a hug. Heather placed her hands on Tamera's shoulders.

"You did it, baby," Timothy told her.

"You haven't called me that for a long time. I've missed it so much."

Timothy helped Tamera back on her feet. "I love the new look," he told her. "You're absolutely beautiful."

Tamera placed her hand over her cheek, where part of her birthmark covered.

"Yes, it's still there, baby, but it's okay."

Tamera blushed as she kissed Timothy on his lips. "I know it is, my love."

"Where did you find the Golden Sapphire?" Max asked.

"I didn't find it... it was given to me... by Celestia..."

Timothy was surprised. "Your mother?"

"I saw her in a dream..." Tears rolled from her eyes. "She helped me to save you..."

Timothy hugged Tamera again, and wouldn't let go. "She's still watching over you."

"Yes, she is."

Noelle made her way over to Tamera and hugged her. "You're the most amazing person I've ever met, Tamera. I feel like I have a sister of my own now."

Tamera blushed. "Thank you, Noelle. I love you."

They hugged. "I love you, too, Tamera."

"Let's go home, everyone," Olivia told her as she opened up a warp back to the World of Exodus.

Tamera and the others joined Kirbie, Kain and the other heroes. Kirbie walked up to the golden angel with her eyes wide.

"Tamera... is that you?" Kirbie asked joyfully.

Tamera smiled as she nodded.

"Wow... I knew you were always beautiful, but..."

Tamera hugged Kirbie tightly. "Thank you, Kirbie. I love you so much... I can't imagine my life without you."

Tears fell from Kirbie and Tamera's eyes. "I love you, too, my love," Kirbie replied.

Kain then stated, "You certainly are a valiant warrior, Tamera. I'm grateful for what you have done."

"Thanks, Kain, for helping us as well. And thank you, Heather."

"Thank you as well, Timothy," Camille told him. "I'm so glad to have met you."

Madison then ran over to Timothy, Tamera, Noelle and Kirbie, hugging them.

"You're all so amazing," Madison told them.

"All hail our heroes, the Revolution!" Kain yelled. Everyone cheered for Timothy, Tamera, Tessa and Kirbie.

Camille hugged Heather, Tamera and the members of the Revolution.

"Well, done, Golden Angel," Camille told Tamera with a smile.

"I am so glad to have you all in my life," Tamera told them. "I don't think I could have done this if it weren't for all of you believing in me."

A tear fell down Tamera's cheek.

"Because of all everyone here did," Tessa commented, "the World of Exodus has been saved. Thank you, indeed."

"We are truly indebted to you all," Marietta replied.

"You're welcome," Tamera said softly. Everyone group hugged.

"Now let's go home and celebrate!" Tessa said.

During the journey home, Kirbie was overjoyed to see Timothy, Tamera and Heather growing ever closer as a family. Finally, the gathering of heroes reached Coverdale, where some of the town had been rebuilt, and they were getting ready to rebuild Queen Camille's castle. When they walked up to the castle, Tamera, Noelle, Kirbie and Timothy were amazed to see many of the people that they had met during their journey were there, and the townsfolk began applauding and whistling for the heroes. The Children of Cecaria were there as well, along with Alana, Avalon, Hanna, Mia, Sara, Heart, Danni and Natalie. Natalie joyfully ran over to Timothy as Serenity and Destiny ran over to Tamera, Madison and Tessa.

"I'm so glad you came back, Timothy," Natalie replied.

"I wouldn't break my promise, sweetie," Timothy stated. "I

talked to Alana, and... well, how would you like to be a part of our family?"

Natalie's eyes grew wide as she looked at Timothy, Tamera and Heather.

"You really mean it?" Natalie asked.

Timothy looked over to Tamera, who was all smiles. Then he looked at Heather, who was smiling as she said, "I always wanted a little sister."

Tears fell from Natalie's eyes as she ran to Timothy, and they hugged each other tightly.

Everyone sat together around a large campfire that evening, sharing in a feast of celebration. At that moment, Heather stood up and began hitting her glass with a fork to get it to ring. Everyone turned their focus to Heather, seeing she was holding four white roses.

"Everyone, I would like to propose a toast to the members of the Revolution." First, she walked over to Noelle and Kirbie.

"First, to Noelle and Kirbie, I want to say thank you for helping everyone to be safe. I'm really grateful for everything you've done for all of Exodus."

Everyone applauded as she hugged Noelle and Kirbie and gave them each a rose.

"Next, to my best friend, Timothy. You are one of the kindest and gentlest souls I have ever met. I know I've told you how much I love you for all you have done for me, and for so many others as well. I thank you as well."

Heather and Timothy hugged, and she gave him a rose. More applause ensued.

"And last, but certainly not least, to our golden angel, Tamera. Just when we thought all hope was lost, you fought valiantly for us, and you alone were able to defeat Darcia and the Darkness... with a little help, of course."

Heather pointed at the Golden Sapphire. Others laughed.

"Nonetheless, as happy as I am for the others, there's nobody we all are prouder of and more thankful for than you, Tamera."

Tamera and Heather hugged as Tamera received her rose, and everyone gave Tamera a standing ovation. Tamera was joyfully overwhelmed with the reception. Timothy hugged Tamera tightly once again as everyone applauded.

"I'm so proud to have you in my life, baby," Timothy told her. "You really are an incredible angel."

Tamera blushed. "Thank you, Timothy."

Then they turned to Noelle, Kirbie, Heather and Natalie, reaching their arms out to them, and they walked over to them and they all hugged each other.

"I'll never forget what you two did for me," Tamera stated. "Thank you for making me realize how important Timothy really is to me."

"You're welcome, Tamera," said Noelle.

"I love you both, now and forever," Kirbie told her.

"And thank you for helping my sister, Timothy," Camille responded. "I'm so glad you're a part of her life."

Timothy and Camille hugged each other tightly. Then Rain and Orion appeared. Orion came over to Tamera and she pulled out a bouquet of red roses and handed one to her. Then she gave a rose to Timothy, Kirbie, Noelle, Heather, Camille, Natalie and Tessa, along with many of the children.

Then Tamera walked over to Timothy, blushing.

"Is the offer... still on the table? Can I still... marry you?"

Timothy reached into his pocket and pulled out the jewelry box and opened it to reveal Tamera's engagement ring.

"There's still nobody I would want to spend my life with than you, baby."

Timothy then put the ring back on Tamera's finger. Tears of joy fell from Tamera's eyes as she hugged Timothy and wouldn't let go.

"I thank you, Revolution," Rain announced, "for saving the World of Exodus. God truly blessed us by bringing you all into our lives."

Everyone applauded.

"Ready to go home, Timothy?" Tamera wondered.

"Absolutely," Timothy smiled. "I think we could use some downtime."

Tamera smiled and kissed Timothy.

Timothy and Tamera were getting ready to call it a night. As Timothy was already sitting in the bed, Tamera walked in, looking at her phone. She seemed a bit disturbed.

"Are you all right, baby?"

"Check out this article Madison wrote."

Tamera gave Timothy the phone. He saw the article title, "Rise of the Golden Angel." Then he began to read the article, "After a long struggle in all of the World of Exodus, the Revolution were able to defeat the Darkness, thanks to Tamera, who has now become the Golden Angel. With her newly found gift, she was able to stop the leader of the Darkness, a spirit known as Darcia in the world of Hellito."

"You're upset about this?" Timothy asked Tamera. "She did what I asked: she acknowledged the right person."

"But she hardly acknowledged the others."

"You were the only one that defeated Darcia. This deserves your recognition."

"You're just being biased."

"Of course I am, and Heather, Noelle and Kirbie would feel the same way!"

Tamera blushed before she and Timothy kissed, saying good night and falling asleep.

Chapter 30

The Wedding

Natalie had just awoken at the new home that she, Tamera and Timothy were staying in. As she walked out to the kitchen, Tamera, Heather, Camille and Kirbie walked into the house. Natalie first saw Tamera and was excited.

"Is that your wedding dress?" Natalie asked.

"Do you like it?" Tamera wondered.

"It's incredible! You look so beautiful."

Tamera hugged Natalie. "I'm glad you approve of it."

"Can you get Timothy?" Kirbie spoke. "We want him to see it."

"Absolutely! Wait here."

Heather and Natalie walked over to Timothy's bedroom and knocked on his door. Timothy then opened the door, still wearing his pajamas to see Heather and Natalie standing at the door.

"Good morning, ladies. Is everything okay?"

"Get dressed, Timothy," Heather told him. "We want to show you something."

"All right, I'll be out in a moment."

A couple minutes later, Timothy walked out of his room, and Heather and Natalie led him into the living room, where Tamera, Kirbie and Camille were waiting for him.

"Timothy! What do you think?" Kirbie called out.

Timothy looked to see Tamera wearing her wedding dress. The dress had a lacy top with mesh sleeves and neckline. The front of the skirt was very short in length in the front, a bit longer in the back. She also wore sparkling white pantyhose, high-heeled shoes and a veil.

"My goodness, you're incredibly beautiful," Timothy told her.

Tamera blushed greatly. "Thank you, Timothy. I can't wait to see you in your tuxedo."

"I can't believe the wedding's only a week away," Camille commented.

"Oh, my goodness, there's still so much to do! How will we get things planned out so quick? Who's going to..."

Kirbie laughed as she hugged Tamera. "Calm down, my love. I've already talked to Camille and Tessa. They've got everything planned out."

"And many others are willing to help to make this the best day of your life," Timothy told her, his heart bursting with joy.

Tears rolled down Tamera's eyes, but she was smiling as she again jumped into Timothy's arms. "I don't know what I would do without you and the others. You're all so amazing."

"We all love you so much, baby."

The following week, guests from all over the World of Exodus arrived at Queen Camille's castle in Coverdale. In one of the other rooms, Heather, Noelle, Natalie and Kirbie were with Tamera getting her ready for the big moment. Kirbie was combing Tamera's golden hair.

"Are you ready for this, love?" Kirbie asked her.

Tamera sighed. "As ready as I'll ever be, sis."

Heather wasn't comfortable with that answer. "Don't tell me

you're having doubts."

"You know, for the longest time, during our mission, all I could do was have doubts, or come up with stupid excuses for not being with Timothy. And now that I'm sitting here, thinking about all that we have gone through in the past, and how much I want Timothy to be with me all the days of my life… I've never felt more confident. I want to do this."

Kirbie put her arms around Tamera. "Now that's what I want to hear."

There was a knock on the door, and then it opened.

"Hey, we're getting ready to start," Timothy spoke. "Where's my best man?"

"Timothy!" Noelle cried out. "It's bad luck to see the bride before the wedding!"

"Oh, come on, I don't believe that!"

"We'll be ready, my love," Tamera told him.

"See you soon, baby."

Timothy closed the door. Then as Tamera stood up to face Kirbie, Kirbie placed the veil on Tamera's hair. Tamera noticed Kirbie had tears falling from her eyes.

"What's wrong, Kirbie?"

"Nothing. It's just… I can't believe how beautiful you really are."

Tamera started tearing up as well, and the sisters hugged each other.

"Thank you for everything, Kirbie," Tamera replied. "Don't ever leave me."

"Are you kidding? I'm going to protect you and your family so much that you'll probably get tired of me."

Tamera, Heather, Noelle, Natalie and Kirbie laughed.

"I'll never grow tired of you, Kirbie," Tamera replied.

Then Queen Camille entered the room. "Are you ready, ladies?"

"You bet," Tamera answered.

Timothy stood on the right side of Queen Camille with his best man, Heather, along with his groomsmen, Noelle, Madison, Tanna and Natalie.

"I can't believe you picked me as your best man," Heather said softly to Timothy, blushing. Then they looked at the women beside them, all wearing sparkling blue dresses.

"You know we're all women, right?" Madison asked.

"Yeah, where's your dress?" Tanna teased.

Noelle rolled her eyes. "Well, that certainly would be different."

"You would look great!" Natalie commented.

Timothy snickered as the women all walked to him. "Of course, but there's nobody I would want beside me and Tamera for our wedding than you five. Every one of you has a special place in my heart."

Heather blushed. "You don't how much that means to me."

They all hugged.

Tamera had chosen Kirbie as her matron of honor, with Rain, Tessa and Max as her bridesmaids. Each woman walked down the aisle holding a bouquet of different roses: Kirbie's was red, Rain's was silver, Tessa's was blue, and Max's was yellow.

Next were Theresa and Lauren walking down the aisle in gold dresses as the ringbearers.

Finally, Tamera walked down the aisle wearing her beautiful wedding dress, with her veil over her face. She was holding a bouquet of white roses. Tamera then stood and turned, facing Timothy, who was all smiles. Timothy lifted up the veil, and saw

Tamera had tears on her cheeks.

"Are you okay, baby?"

"I... couldn't be happier, Timothy. This is the best moment of my life."

Timothy grabbed Tamera's hands. "Same here."

Camille opened up a Bible before saying, "Dearly beloved, we are gathered here in the sight of our dear Lord and savior, and in front of these witnesses, to join Timothy and Tamera in the grounds of holy matrimony. Who gives this woman to be joined in marriage with this man? Oh, yeah, I do."

Everyone laughed as Camille and Tamera hugged.

"Tamera has asked to do a reading from the word of God."

Camille handed Tamera the Bible.

"I would like to read from 1st Corinthians, Chapter 13: If I speak in the tongues of men or of angels, but do not have love, I am only a resounding gong or a clanging cymbal. If I have the gift of prophecy and can fathom all mysteries and all knowledge, and if I have a faith that can move mountains, but do not have love, I am nothing. If I give all I possess to the poor and give over my body to hardship that I may boast, but do not have love, I gain nothing.

"Love is patient, love is kind. It does not envy, it does not boast, it is not proud. It does not dishonor others, it is not self-seeking, it is not easily angered, it keeps no record of wrongs. Love does not delight in evil but rejoices with the truth. It always protects, always trusts, always hopes, always perseveres. Love never fails.

"And now these three remain: faith, hope and love. But the greatest of these is love." Tamera gave Camille the Bible back.

Tamera then turned to Timothy. "Timothy, when we met in Coverdale, I have to admit it was love at first sight. I knew there was something about you that I never found in anyone else. And as we got to know each other during our times together, I knew I was right: you were indeed something special. No matter what had happened, even when we were apart, against each other, and even with all the struggles I was battling in my life, you never lost your love for me.

"I read those Bible verses because it reminds me of the love you possess for me; that you truly do understand what love is."

Lauren gave Tamera Timothy's ring, and Tamera placed the ring on Timothy's finger.

"I promise, Timothy, to give you all of my heart, to love and cherish you all the days of my life, so help me God."

Then Timothy said to Tamera, "I remember the first day we met as well, Tamera, when you literally knocked me off my feet." Others laughed at the comment. He continued, "When I first saw you, as you know, I was physically attracted to you from the start. I had never seen someone so beautiful in my life.

"Then as we grew together, I got to know the person behind the beautiful face, and I found the most important beauty in your heart; how kind, gentle and loving you really were. I couldn't imagine now living my life without you." He was given Tamera's ring by Theresa. Then he put that ring on Tamera's ring finger. "I promise, Tamera, to give you all my heart, to love and cherish you all the days of my life, so help me God."

Camille then asked, "Do you, Timothy, take Tamera to be your wife, to have and to hold, in sickness and in health, for richer or poorer, till death do you part?"

Timothy smiled greatly as he answered, "I do."

"And do you, Tamera, take Timothy to be your husband, to have and to hold, in sickness and in health, for richer or poorer, till death do you part?"

Tamera smiled as well, a tear running down her cheek. "I do."

"Then by the power vested in me…"

Tamera interrupted by first putting her hand on Camille's cheek. "I'm sorry, sis, but I have something to say really quick."

Others gasped, thinking something upsetting may be happening.

Timothy smiled. "I was hoping we were going to do this."

Timothy pulled out more rings from his jacket pocket. Tamera and Timothy then held out their hands that had their wedding rings on.

"We are wearing these rings to symbolize our love for each other, to become as one, but we decided to make rings for three special girls that have become part of our family. It means so much to us to have them in our lives, and we felt this was the best time to recognize them. I'll let Timothy take it from here."

Timothy announced, "Madison, Natalie, Tanna?"

The three girls walked over to Timothy and they gave each other a hug. They then extended their hands out to Timothy.

"Natalie, I can't tell you enough how truly loved you are by me, Tamera and Tessa. You are one of the kindest and most gentle souls we have ever met, and you've shown how amazing you are to not just us, but through everyone you meet. Words can't describe our love for you."

"Thanks, Timothy. I love you."

"I love you too, sweetie."

Timothy continued, "I know we weren't in the best of terms when we first met, Madison, but as time went on, you just happened to grow on me, and I found love and respect for you when you stepped up and took care of so many others and showed how kind and loving you were to them, including Tamera, when she nearly died at Oculus' Tower. You have a charm about you unmatched by anyone, and Tamera and I truly love you."

Madison hugged him tightly. "Thank you so much, Timothy."

"Tanna, I truly thank you for saving us from your mother in Coverdale. You also took care of us while we were imprisoned there. We have so much appreciation for what you did for us, and this may not have been possible if it weren't for you. We have a never-ending love for you as well." Timothy put the ring on Tanna's finger.

"Thank you, Timothy," Tanna told him as they hugged.

"What about Noelle?" Heather questioned.

Noelle showed a ring already on her right hand. "We already took care of that, sweetie."

"Timothy, look!" Tamera pointed out. "There's a fourth ring in your hand."

Timothy looked at the ring. "Oh, yeah, there is. That means we have someone else we would like to recognize."

Heather was curious as to who the other ring was for. Though she figured it wasn't, she was thinking about how wonderful it would be if the ring was for her. Her thinking caused her to blush, and she looked to the floor. Suddenly she heard Timothy say, "Heather?"

Heather looked up to Timothy, wide-eyed as he held out his hand to her.

"You okay, sweetie?"

"Yeah... I'm okay, Timothy."

Then Heather grabbed Timothy's hand, and he had her stand in front of him and Tamera.

"Heather, six years ago my world was changed when God brought you into my life. I was so puzzled as to why out of all the people God could have picked to help you, he decided to choose me. Yet even to this day, I am so glad that he did that. These last seven years I've watched you grow into an even more beautiful and precious woman, and even through the pain you have endured, you never stopped smiling."

Timothy placed the ring on her finger. "I'll never stop loving you, Heather, and with this ring, Tamera and I proclaim our love to you."

She looked over to Tamera, who was smiling. Tears could not stop falling from Heather's face, whose cheeks were also red, feeling embarrassed from all the attention. She cried as she hugged Timothy.

"I'm so sorry, Heather. I didn't mean to make you cry."

"It's okay… I'm just… so happy to have you and Tamera in my life."

"I love you, and I always will."

"I love you, too, Timothy."

Heather did not want to let go of Timothy.

"Hey, save some of that for me, would you?" Tamera stated, and everyone laughed at the comment. Heather hugged Tamera as well, again not wanting to let go. Then everyone went back to their places.

"Okay, Mother. We're ready."

"That was a wonderful moment, Tamera," Camille commented. "I'm so proud of you and Timothy. Anyway, by the power vested in me in front of God, these witnesses, and the city of Coverdale, I now pronounce you man and wife. You may kiss the bride."

Overly excited, Tamera jumped into Timothy's arms and they kissed. Everyone laughed joyously.

Camille announced, "Ladies and gentlemen, I present the

happy couple, Timothy and Tamera!"

Everyone gave the newlyweds a standing ovation. Timothy and Tamera then hugged Tanna, and then the children all ran to Timothy and Tamera, giving them hugs.

At the following reception, Timothy and Tamera were dancing slowly together as soft music was playing. In the meantime, Heather and Natalie walked over to Sonata.

"Um... could you play... another slow song so we could dance with Timothy and Tamera?"

"You got it, sweet stuff," said Sonata as she winked at the two females.

Serenity, Destiny, Sara, Hanna, Mia, Heart, Danni, Noah and Sandra joined Sonata.

Timothy and Tamera stopped dancing as the music finished up. Everyone applauded. Then Heather and Natalie walked over to Timothy and Tamera.

"Timothy... is it okay if we dance with you and Tamera... I mean, I don't..."

Tamera smiled. "I would love to dance with you." Timothy and Tamera both extended a hand to Heather and Natalie. They reached out for both hands and Timothy and Tamera brought Heather and Natalie to them.

Heather stood in front of Timothy, with their arms wrapped around each other, and then Tamera wrapped her arm around Natalie as they slowly danced together. Many others then began to dance as Sonata sang while holding Kendra's hand.

At that time, Kirbie, Tessa, Madison and Tanna joined in the dance. Kirbie danced behind Tamera, wrapping her arms around Tamera. Tanna wrapped her arms around Tessa as Natalie did so to Madison, kissing her on the cheek as well. Other couples danced with each other as well.

The next morning, Kirbie made her way over to visit with Timothy, Heather, Natalie and Tamera. She happened to notice Timothy sitting on the porch outside the house.

"Hey, Timothy."

"Hi, Kirbie. Have a seat."

"Thank you." She sat down next to Timothy. "Is everything okay?"

"Yeah, the others are still sleeping. Thank you so much for agreeing to have Heather and Natalie stay at the castle while we're on our honeymoon. We really appreciate it."

"Hey, it's no problem. You two deserve it. It's been a wild ride, hasn't it?"

Timothy chuckled. "It sure has, but I wouldn't change a thing. Tamera is so wonderful to me. And you already know how much Heather and Natalie mean to me. They've been a big help as well."

"That's good. There have been times I've thought about settling down and having a family, but I'm so much on the move, doing what I can to help Willshire, Coverdale and Riverton. Having a boyfriend would throw a big wrench in my life. Plus, I'm not sure if they would like that I would be stronger than them."

Timothy snickered. "You know, there are days I wonder about how my life would have gone if, on that lonely Sunday evening, I wouldn't have run into Tamera. What a coincidence."

"No, I don't believe it was coincidence," Kirbie proclaimed before kissing Timothy's forehead. "I believe you were destined to be together."

"And I'm so thankful God gave her to me, as well as

everyone I've met: you, Luna, Camille, Kirbie... everyone I've met on Exodus... I couldn't ask for better."

All of a sudden, Timothy got tackled once again by Heather and Natalie. Seeing that made Kirbie laugh.

"Come on, Timothy!" Natalie stated with much joy. "Come to the castle with us!"

"I told Natalie I was going to visit Camille before we left," Tamera smiled.

"Care to join us, Kirbie?"

"Certainly."

Everyone got ready to leave. Timothy grabbed Tamera's hand. She turned to Timothy, and he kissed her passionately.

"I love you so much, my golden angel," Timothy told her. "And I'll love you all the days of my life, no matter what."

Tamera hugged Timothy, tears of joy falling down your cheeks. "Now and forever, I'll always love you, Timothy."

Timothy and Tamera then hugged Kirbie, Heather and Natalie.

The End